OTHER BOOKS BY DANIEL PETERS

Border Crossings

The Luck of Huemac: A Novel About the Aztecs

Tikal: A Novel About the Maya

The Incas

RISING FROM THE RUINS

RISING FROM THE RUINS

Daniel Peters

Random House New York

 Published in the United States by Random House, Inc., New York, and simultaneously in Canada by Random House of Canada Limited, Toronto.

Library of Congress Cataloging-in-Publication Data
Peters, Daniel.
Rising from the ruins / Daniel Peters.
p. cm.
ISBN 0-679-43306-6
I. Title.
PS3566.E7548R57 1995 813'.54—dc20 94-28918

Manufactured in the United States of America on acid-free paper
2 4 6 8 9 7 5 3
First Edition

This one is for you, Bro'

Acknowledgments

The author wishes to express his deep gratitude:

To my sources. In creating the fictional Mayan site of Baktun, I have drawn upon the research and scholarship of many dedicated Mayanists, more than I can name here. I am especially indebted to the contributors to the following: *Tikal Reports,* William R. Coe, gen. ed.; *Palenque Roundtable,* Merle Greene Robertson, gen. ed.; *Excavations at Seibal,* Gordon R. Willey, gen. ed.; *The Classic Maya Collapse,* T. Patrick Culbert, gen. ed.; *A Forest of Kings,* by Linda Schele and David Freidel; *Bearing Witness,* by Gertrude Blom; and *Guatemala: Eternal Spring, Eternal Tyranny,* by Jean Marie Simon. Many of these sources were made available to me by the University of Arizona Library.

To my kindly informants, William Haviland, Dave Gregory, Deni Seymour, and Pat Culbert. You did your best to educate this amateur and must not be held responsible for the accuracy of my archaeological fabrications.

To my gentle yet unerringly perceptive readers, Linda Alster, Tony Backes, Dennis Evans, Susan Lescher, Barry Munitz, and Blackburn Peters. Your encouragement and advice helped me get it right.

To my editor for going the distance yet again.

And to Annette, my venerable child bride and one-woman revitalization movement, who crossed all the borders with me, to places both real and imaginary, and never let me lose my way. The best part of the whole journey is that we're taking it together.

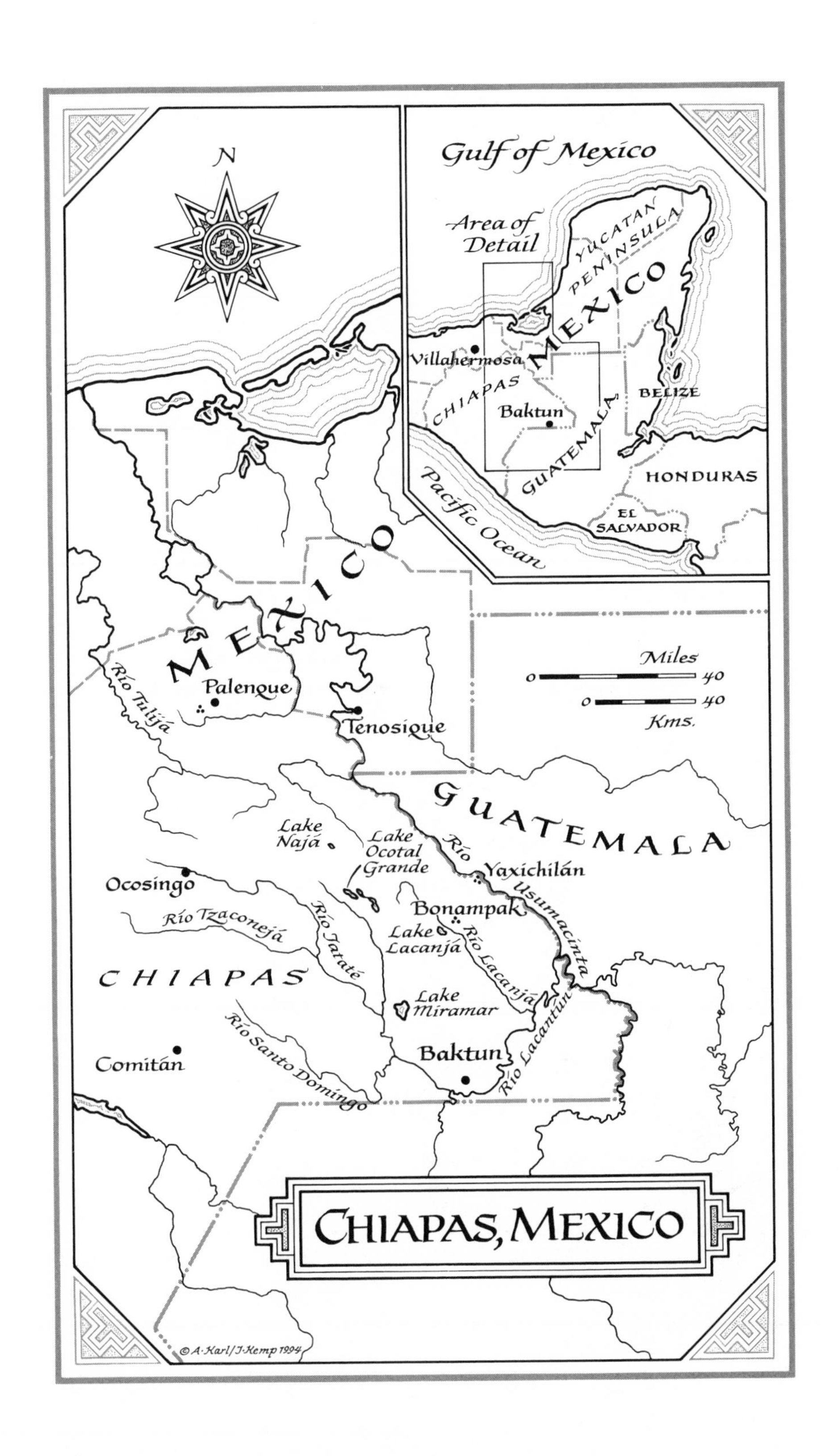
N
Gulf of Mexico
Area of Detail
YUCATAN PENINSULA
MEXICO
Villahermosa
CHIAPAS
Baktun
GUATEMALA
BELIZE
HONDURAS
EL SALVADOR
Pacific Ocean
MEXICO
Miles
0 40
0 40
Kms.
Río Tulijá
Palenque
Tenosique
GUATEMALA
Lake Naja
Lake Ocotal Grande
Río Usumacinta
Yaxichilán
Ocosingo
Río Tzaconejá
Río Jataté
Bonampak
Lake Lacanjá
Río Lacanjá
CHIAPAS
Lake Miramar
Río Santo Domingo
Comitán
Baktun
Río Lacantún
CHIAPAS, MEXICO
© A. Karl/J. Kemp 1994

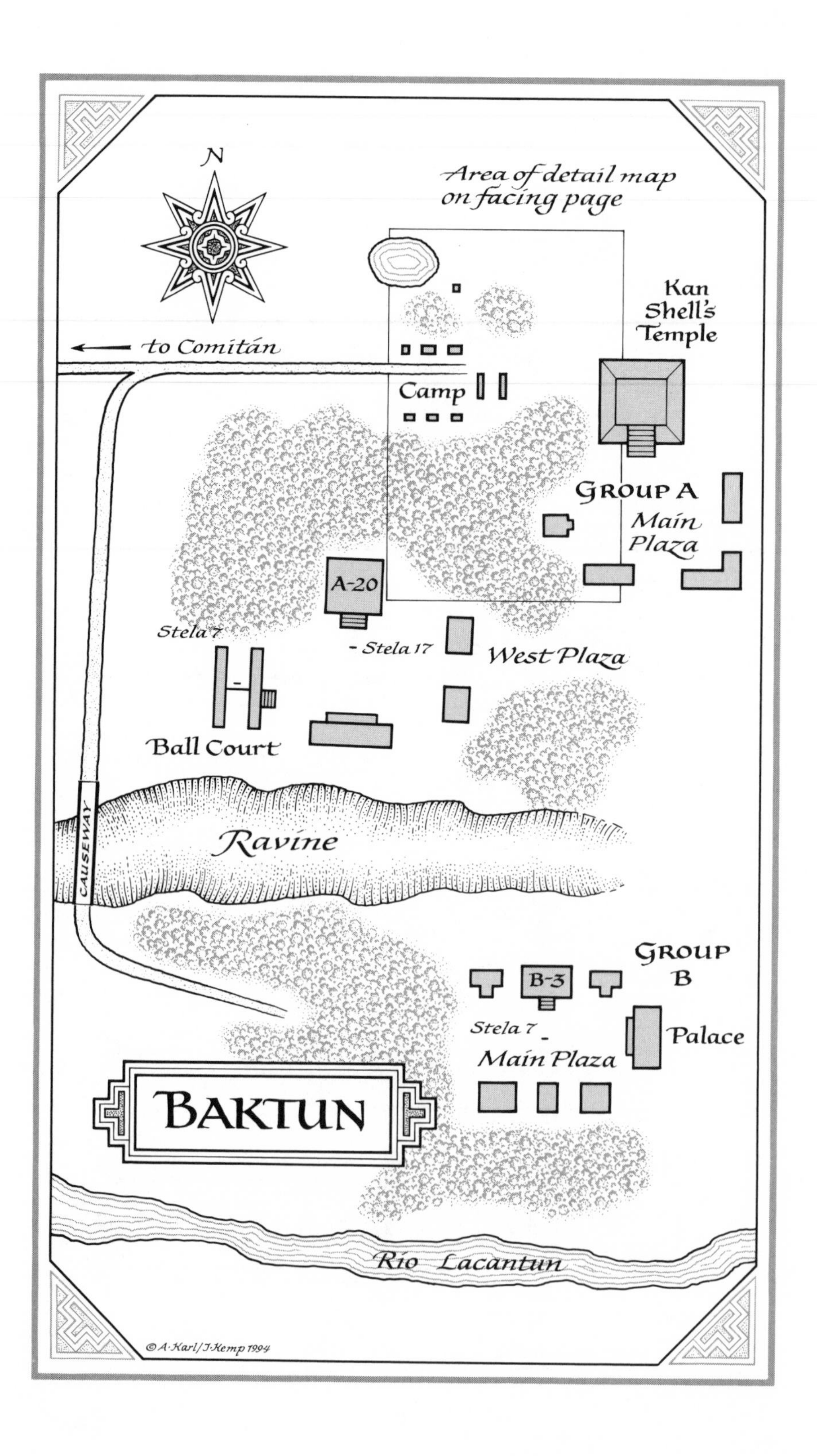
N
Area of detail map
on facing page
Kan
Shell's
Temple
to Comitán
Camp
GROUP A
Main
Plaza
A-20
Stela 7
- Stela 17
West Plaza
Ball Court
CAUSEWAY
Ravine
GROUP
B
B-3
Stela 7
Palace
Main Plaza
BAKTUN
Río Lacantun
©A·Karl/J·Kemp 1994

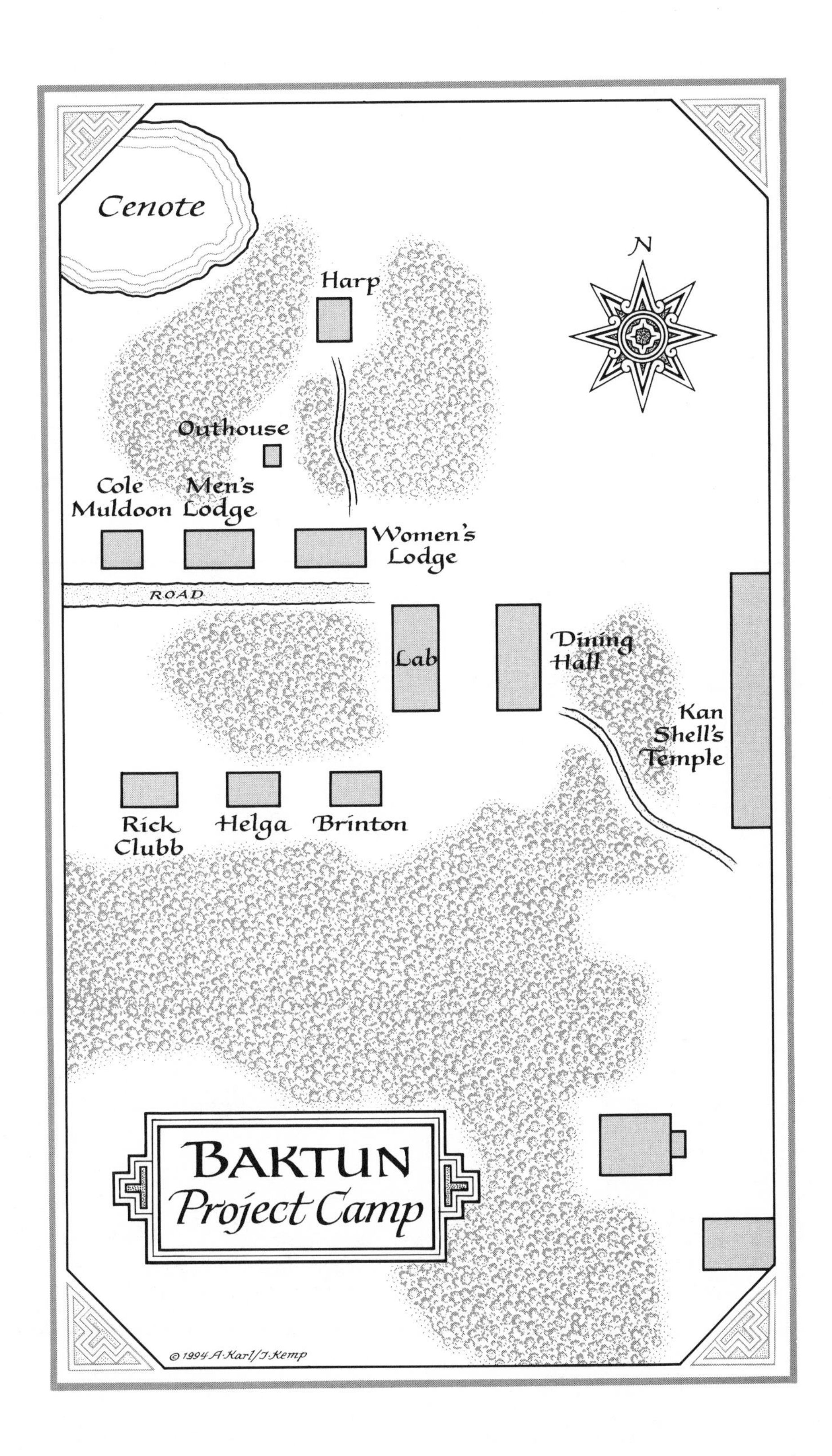
Cenote
N
Harp
Outhouse
Cole
Muldoon
Men's
Lodge
Women's
Lodge
ROAD
Lab
Dining
Hall
Kan
Shell's
Temple
Rick
Clubb
Helga
Brinton
BAKTUN
Project Camp
© 1994 A·Karl/J·Kemp

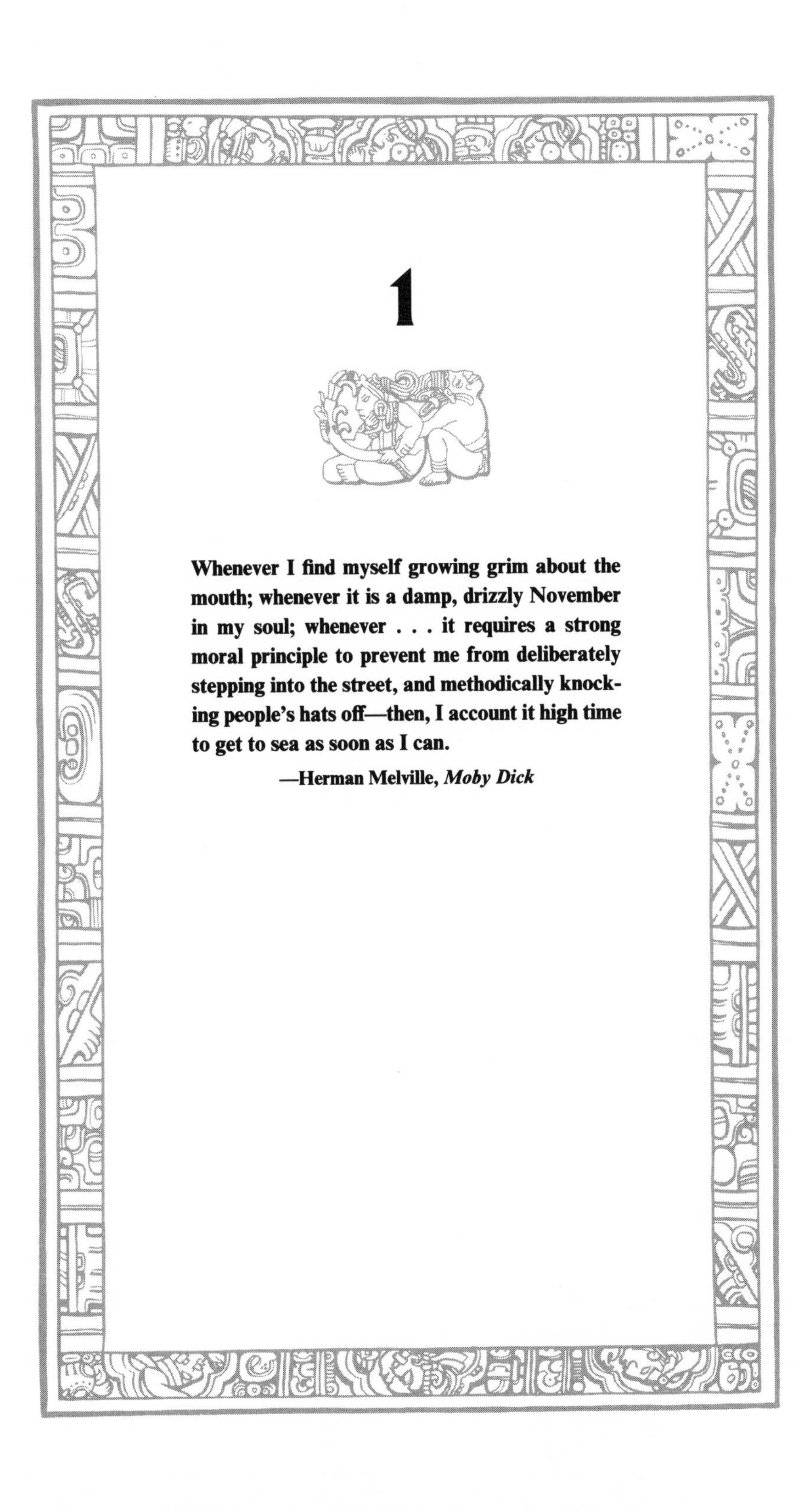

1

Whenever I find myself growing grim about the mouth; whenever it is a damp, drizzly November in my soul; whenever . . . it requires a strong moral principle to prevent me from deliberately stepping into the street, and methodically knocking people's hats off—then, I account it high time to get to sea as soon as I can.

—Herman Melville, *Moby Dick*

IT WAS the big elf he wanted.

He'd decided that beforehand, even though it would've been safer to snatch one of the smaller ones closer to the street. He could've taken a toadstool as well, in that case. But he'd learned not to alter his objectives in the middle of a foray, so he climbed the winding flagstone path that led up through terraced beds of ivy to the front door. A glow of light from inside the house revealed his prize: a foot and a half tall, lime green, with a stocking cap, a corrugated beard, and a blank-eyed grin that appeared more demented than jolly.

Gotcha, he thought as he lifted it up, and was surprised by how much it weighed. Then a plug in the bottom popped free and gravel came pouring out in a thunderous torrent, spilling all over his feet. Before he could move there was a sudden explosion of light, and doors crashing open, and a German shepherd came rushing out barking and snarling. His heart jumped into his throat and he tucked the elf under his arm and bolted through the ivy, seeing the hedge just in time and hurtling it like a halfback. That stymied the dog and he just kept going, heading in the wrong direction but running for all he was worth.

The first squad car appeared only moments later, it seemed, blue lights whirling but no siren at two in the morning. He had a one-block lead and made it over the hill and down another block before going to ground among the shrubs at the corner of the park. He hid himself behind a thick clump of vegetation and pulled the hood of his sweatshirt up over his head, averting his eyes as the blue-and-white slowly cruised past, shining a spotlight over the foliage. When it was gone, he started out across New Belvedere Boulevard, which had a deep concrete culvert as a divider. He'd just made it to the bridge when another set of headlights swung down onto the boulevard, coming his way, and he went down into the culvert without waiting to see if it was more cops.

It was. Crouching behind an abutment, feeling like Jean Valjean, he saw a spotlight sweep the culvert and heard the crackle of the radio as the car circled over the bridge and went down the other side of the boulevard. It occurred to him that this much force wasn't an accident; they'd been waiting for him to make another run. He briefly contemplated ditching the elf but decided it didn't make much difference at this point. He just had to get his ass home without being seen.

So the elf was still under his arm as he scrambled up out of the culvert and took off up the street. He stayed in the shadows where the trees blocked out the streetlights, grateful now for the late Maryland fall and the oaks that didn't drop their leaves until midwinter. There was a cut-through in the middle of the block that would take him over to his street, and he was almost to it, flagging badly, when the lights again appeared behind him. He made the turn onto the narrow walkway that ran between the hedges and chain-link fences of the adjacent backyards and doubled over, gasping for breath. Then he realized how exposed he was and pushed himself into a run, praying that the damned black mutt who lived ahead on the left didn't come roaring out and throw himself against the fence like he always did in the daytime. He was suddenly aware that dogs were barking all over the neighborhood, but at least the feared mutt didn't appear, and then he was flinging himself around the end of the last hedge, hitting the ground with a jolt and rolling with the elf wrapped in a tight embrace, glancing back just as the spotlight came stabbing down the walkway. Or had it caught him?

Staggering to his feet, he started toward the sidewalk, thinking only six more houses and he was home free, when another backward glance revealed a car coming down this street. Damn! No sidewalk now, hell-bent across the front yards, dodging sprinklers and bicycles and the ubiquitous azaleas, but no fences, thank god. Didn't dare look back or he'd surely fall . . . almost there but dying . . . hearing the rush of tires on asphalt. Then he was passing the carport, resisting the impulse to hide behind the cars and heading for the front door, glad he hadn't left any lights on for himself . . .

Then sound and light and the time it would take to get through the door coalesced into an instinct to take cover, and he dropped onto the middle landing that led up to the door, flattening himself behind a low brick retaining wall and the tangle of fancy foliage Usher had planted to increase the value of his property. The beam of light went right over him, hovering on the screen door. The car seemed not to be moving past, and he tucked his chin into his shoulder, his breathing loud as a shout and beyond calming. He had a vivid insight into how you died of fright: Your heart simply beat itself to a pulp against your breastbone. They had him now for sure, lying on his own front stoop with the elf pinned under him like a recovered fumble. There would be no way to explain this to anyone.

The spotlight swung away but the car continued to idle while voices reverberated on the radio. Were they calling their friends in for the capture? It went on so long his breathing had almost returned to normal, except for a persistent low shudder of dread. He envisioned Caroline in her robe, blinking in the blue lights as she watched them pat him down and then arrest him for elf theft. Officially petty larceny or maybe malicious mischief. Unless they searched the house and upped the charge. Grand mal larceny.

But then the big engine grumbled and the cops rolled on, and he went limp with relief. Yet he had enough cunning to stay still and listen, in case they'd had the cunning to leave someone behind on foot. Hearing nothing, he gradually raised his head, peering through one of the spindly azaleas that hadn't bloomed last spring and was now engulfed in weeds. Nothing moving, but he waited some more before duckwalking to the door, scanning the street through another nonbloomer. It took the last of his courage to reach up for the doorknob, and the last of his strength to pry open the door and crawl inside without a sound. Safe.

He lay on the floor for a moment, sweat soaking through his clothes, the elf lying blank-eyed beside him. No, not safe, he decided upon reflection. *Spared.*

THIS HAD BEGUN about a month ago, on a day too warm and hazy for September, when he'd realized for the first time that it was in fact September. And he was about to spend his second autumn in New Belvedere, in this house, with no book in progress and no teaching job to distract him. Despite his agreement with Caroline, he had felt compelled to make a pitch for what they were missing. So, on that warm September day, he adopted a casual pose in the entrance to the kitchen while Caroline sat at the dining room table, sorting through a week's accumulation of mail.

"Remember in Vermont, this time of year, how the strawberry creeper and the tall grass start to turn red, and then the leaves change and then peak, luminous and flaming, so that the evergreens on the hills are surrounded by patches of gold and scarlet and magenta? The air is so crisp and clear that every object has a distinct outline, even at a distance, yet it's still warm enough to smell the grass. The Canada geese start going by overhead in huge, straggling vees, honking like they're in a hurry . . . "

"Harp, you're speaking in prose," Caroline pointed out. "You cribbed all of that from one of your notebooks."

He had, in fact, but he hadn't seen any reason not to be precise in his nostalgic yearnings.

"Remember walking over to the Alexanders' pond, picking apples on the way up the hill? And the orchard on Lee Hook Road would start selling their golden delicious cider . . . pure ambrosia."

"I'll start on Canada if you keep this up," Caroline warned.

"O Canada," Harp warbled, "home of the pinhead and the pinecone, the cretin and the moose. I rescued you from those frozen wastes."

"And took me to the backwoods to tend goats and grow dope."

"The happiest years of our lives, admit it. You loved it there."

"Of course I loved it!" Caroline said in exasperation. "It just wasn't rich in jobs for sociologists. C'mon, Harp, cut it out. You *promised* that it was going to be my turn now . . . "

"Yeah, I know, this is rotten of me. It's just . . . I look out the window here, and do I witness the beauties of fall? No, I see the chain-link fences of my many and close neighbors, and their houses that are just like this one, and their kids and dogs and three vehicles per household." As he spoke, a lawnmower started up somewhere near at hand, and Harp rolled his eyes. "And the pariah shall be cast out into the land of the Tinkerers and the Mowerites, and he shall be lost there forever . . . "

Caroline laughed. "It's only for one more year, Harp. The Ushers will be back next June and then we'll *have* to move. In the meantime, why don't you write another novel? The more money we have, the greater our options."

Harp grunted and straightened up in the doorway. "Why don't I go to the mall instead, and see what's left on the racks at Woolco? They're going out of business, you know. Too high-toned for the neighborhood."

"Just go, Harp. I have a class at one and this's the first chance I've had to look at the mail in a week."

He made the Demon Queller face at her, but she didn't glance up from her sorting. Journals in one pile, personal correspondence in another, professional correspondence in a third. Harp had written letters to a number of old friends in recent months, and only two had responded, one with a postcard. Uncertain what was on his face, he headed out alone for the New Belvedere Mall.

Just for the hell of it, he went to the carport and made a stab at starting Trusty Rusty, his thirteen-year-old VW Beetle. The car had been a wedding gift from his in-laws when he'd married Caroline's older sister Janet in 1970. When he and Janet split about two years later she'd let him keep it, and it'd brought him back to the States a few years after that. Until very recently it'd taken him everywhere, in all kinds of weather. But now he got the same dead clunk he'd been getting for three weeks, which made him curse and slam his hand against the steering wheel. The last repair job, just last spring, had cost him over four hundred dollars, and he couldn't justify sinking more money into it right now.

He slammed the door, too, and went down the street on foot. It was not yet eleven but already so warm and muggy that he stripped off his sweatshirt and tied it around his waist. Even so, by the end of the block he was feeling breathless and spaced out, and he didn't know what was going on until he reached the boulevard and came out from under the shelter of the trees, so that he could see the sky and feel the wind. The *grey* wind. It blew down out of a sky that was bright but a solid, featureless grey, like a clouded mirror, and it seemed to envelop him completely, swallowing up all words and thoughts and leaving him aswirl with vagrant impulses and inchoate yearnings. It stirred the frizzy clumps of hair on both sides of his head while simultaneously stirring up a sickly excitement in the pit of his stomach.

His father had tried very hard to make a golfer out of him when he was young, an effort that might've succeeded were it not for the prevalence of grey winds during the spring golf season. Harp had been two over par through twelve holes in the Junior Varsity Tournament when he'd yielded to a bold impulse blown euphorically on the wind. Why not simply hit it through the crotch of the big oak in front of him, rather than chipping out into the fairway? It had seemed thrillingly plausible, right up to the moment the clubhead came through the ball—and was shown to be utterly absurd when the ball came ricocheting back an instant later. He never came that close to par again and soon abandoned the game for basketball, where he didn't have to take all the shots himself.

He came out of his reverie two blocks down the boulevard, heading away from the mall, and he didn't try to correct his course. Why pretend he had a destination when his feet knew better? He walked until he began to see houses that didn't all look alike, which told him he was approaching the boundary of what he knew as New Belvedere. The various neighborhoods outside were also part of the township, but they were afterthoughts as far as Harp was concerned, departures from the master plan. The real New Belvedere was distinguished by its lack of variety and gave the appearance of having been conceived by a single, extremely limited mind. There were perhaps four or five versions of the same two-story, red-brick Cape Cod, repeating endlessly for block after block, wedged together on narrow slices of land, the backyards securely fenced and the front lawns trimmed within an inch of their lives.

Turning inward, Harp let the wind blow him toward the heart of the tract, where there were no deviations from the plan. He knew he was rubbing salt in the wound, arousing further dismal comparisons with the places he'd walked in Vermont and Vancouver, but he couldn't help himself. This didn't get to Caroline the way it got to him. She'd been born too far above it, and all her training—professional and otherwise—had made her inordinately lucid and dispassionate about matters of class. On their first walking tour through the neighborhood she'd pointed out all the positive features that might be weighed in the balance against the aesthetic deficit, and then ended by saying, "For a certain class of people, what you own isn't as important as *that* you own." She hadn't seemed to be sneering, either.

That had also been the only walk she'd taken with him, Harp recalled with some bitterness. Even as a sociological phenomenon, it hadn't been worth a second look. To him it was Darkest Suburbia, a man-made wilderness that churned up a primal, middle-class anxiety in him, claustrophobia alternating with a sense of being terribly exposed, the desire to flee tempered by the nagging fear of belonging nowhere. He wanted to sneer and rage and apologize all at once, and it made him walk with a wooden self-consciousness, afraid of acting like a suspicious character. Not that anyone seemed to be watching; the only other pedestrian abroad at the moment was the mailman, who was pushing his bag ahead of him on an aluminum contraption that looked vaguely like a golf cart.

"How you doin'?" the mailman said as they passed. He was wearing shorts and had the calves of a mountain climber.

"Good," Harp lied, though the cheerfulness of the greeting steadied him. Whatever he was feeling, he was obviously not being perceived as a pariah. He lifted his chin and began to gaze boldly at the houses he was passing, as if there were something he was entitled to see.

That's when he began to see them. Peeking out at him from the shrubbery of about every third house. Some were half-hidden among the azaleas and dogwood, while others stood in loose groups out on the lawn. There were numerous deer of different kinds: bucks, does, and fawns in family threesomes, single Bambis, miniature stags with twelve-point racks of antlers. There were also rabbits and squirrels and curly-tailed skunks, and white ducks trailing strings of ducklings. Harp was scanning the yards avidly now, skipping past those adorned only with vegetation. The first flamingo he saw was inexplicably colored green and was a double, two birds rump to rump on a common stake. Just around the block was a yard that rose in terraces from the sidewalk, the usual grass replaced with ivy and succulents and artfully placed stones. Flanking the winding path to the house were frogs, elves, and shiny spotted toadstools.

"Oh, wow," Harp murmured approvingly, glancing around so he'd remember where this was. His eyes were drawn to a corner lot across the street, and he followed them right up onto the lawn, to the edge of a circular flower bed ringed with pink geraniums that were still blooming. On the left, inside the circle, a sleepy peon rested his sombrero-clad head on his upraised knees, while his burro stood in the traces of the cart behind him. On the right stood a bronze-colored trio of buck, doe, and fawn, the archetypal family hierarchy.

The centerpiece, however, stumped him completely. It was a plaster birdbath with a double seahorse base, and sitting in the dry circular basin was a fat orange parrot with a bill as large as the rest of its body. Was that someone's idea of a joke? Or had the parrot lost its original perch and simply been given temporary lodging in the bath? It spooked him to think such a bizarre combination might be deliberate.

He heard the creak of a screen door and looked up to see a grey-haired woman in a housedress and fuzzy slippers frowning at him from the stoop. She had the door propped open in front of her like a shield, and Harp smiled what he hoped was a reassuring smile.

"Whatta you doing there?" she demanded.

"I was just admiring your, ah . . . your *lawn animals,*" he said with an even broader smile, pleased with the term.

"My what?"

"Your lawn animals. I was wondering if the parrot got there by mistake."

"They came like that. Now g'wan, git outta here before I call the cops."

"Just asking," he said, holding up his palms as he began to back away. "Do you take them inside in the winter?"

"You nuts? Git!"

"I'm going," he promised, and hustled away before she could get a better look at him. But something besides his curiosity had been piqued, and he went off muttering to himself: "But I'll be back."

AFTER THE elf escapade, however, Harp was lying very low. He stopped wearing his Mid-Atlantic sweatshirt outside the house and didn't go anywhere on foot. Unless he was going somewhere with Caroline or her car was available, he seldom went outside at all, except to sit on the back deck and try to read while his neighbors tinkered and mowed. He didn't know how much of this he could stand, but he was resigned to spending at least the rest of October within the stout, red-brick walls of the House of Usher.

On the surface, the house didn't appear to live up to its name. There was nothing particularly gloomy or sinister about it, certainly nothing that would've stirred the imagination of a Poe. These Ushers (he was Dr. Eugene Usher, an associate professor of geology at Mid-Atlantic; his wife, Joan, worked for the county government and took care of their year-old son) were solid middle-class folks who'd displayed none of the morbid quirks of the aristocracy the one time Harp had met them. They'd radiated such pride in their home and possessions, such concern that it be cared for properly in their absence, that it'd seemed rude to examine the place too closely. Besides, it was the first rental they'd seen that was both affordable and within commuting distance of campus, and they were only planning to stay in it for a year.

When they'd moved in two months later, they weren't sure they'd come back to the same house. Had it truly been this tacky, and they so desperate, that they hadn't noticed? The living room, with its fireplace they'd been told not to use, sported two different sections of carpet, one deep orange and the other olive green, and arranged upon them were a tufted turquoise sofa, an armchair in a faded floral chintz, and a black Naugahyde recliner that didn't recline. None of these provided a comfortable seat, and the end tables beside them were either too high or too low, so that the lamps upon them were always shining their light in someone's eyes.

This room effectively set the tone for the rest of the house, which was home to a veritable herd of white elephants. Each item seemed carefully chosen not to go with any other, and all had the quaint, well-worn look of castoffs from another era.

"Do you think human beings did this?" Harp had asked as they went from room to room, shaking their heads in disbelief.

"Maybe they have a relative in the junk business," Caroline suggested. "Or a charge account at the flea market."

"You'd think they'd have at least a couple nice things, something they bought new. These aren't poor people . . . "

"They may be middle class now, but I'd bet whoever holds the purse strings in the family comes from somewhere farther down the socioeconomic scale."

"Like from the crypt?" Harp had proposed, which inspired him to check out the basement, just in case the Ushers had pulled a bait and switch and hidden their best down there. The basement was in fact crammed with additional furniture, but it was all in even worse shape than the stuff upstairs, much of it actually broken. These people obviously didn't like to let anything go once they'd made it part of the collection. Harp and Caroline had spent days adding to the subterranean stock from the overload above, after which Caroline had pronounced the house "spare, but ugly."

The kitchen was the only room to have escaped the furniture glut, for the simple reason there was no space left to fill. It opened into the dining room and the downstairs hall and was perhaps six by eight, a grudging concession on the New Belvedere master blueprint. You couldn't open the refrigerator and the oven at the same time, and there was no counter space at all near the stove, which added juggling to the cook's necessary skills and had left indelible stains on the worn linoleum underfoot. The two light fixtures were both high overhead and would carry only sixty watts each, and the Ushers had further enhanced the cozy ambience by papering the walls in a semigloss pattern of red bricks and grey mortar.

Harp had become the primary cook during the year Caroline was writing her dissertation, and he'd succeeded well enough to be relaxed about it. But the few real meals he'd attempted here had been tense, enervating adventures, and he'd given up in disgust before he figured out how to make the kitchen work. Caroline wasn't home for dinner half the time anyway, and she hadn't seemed to notice the difference when he quit. For his part, he was sick to death of tuna salad, frozen entrees, and take-out dinners, but whenever he got a hankering for something home-cooked, one glance at the kitchen was enough to numb the yearning and convince him to eat whatever was easiest.

On this night, faced with another solo meal, he had a strong urge to hike over to New Belvedere Road, the town's main commercial drag, a six-lane thoroughfare lined with gas stations, drive-in banks, and every fast-food franchise known to man. He could get a Big Boy Deluxe, or some of Popeyes fried chicken, or the breaded mystery fish at Long John Silver's. But his newfound prudence told him he shouldn't risk being seen on the street after dark. So he settled for a salad with bottled dressing, a single-serving lasagna, and two cans of Schlitz, one of which he finished while watching the local news.

II

The phone rang while he was putting his main course on the table, but he didn't bother to cover it, intending to make short work of what he assumed was a junk call. Someone was always trying to sell him vinyl siding or a subscription to the *Post* or tickets to the Ice Capades, and they always called at dinnertime if they hadn't awakened him before breakfast.

"House of Usher," he snapped into the phone, and heard a familiar chuckle through the long-distance fuzz.

"Harpo?"

Harp was speechless for a moment, the voice of his old friend making his surroundings seem strange all over again. "Brother Rick," he managed. "How you doing?"

"*Doctor* Brother Rick to you. I just got done defending my thesis, and I wanted to call before I got too fucked-up to dial. That sound you hear in the background is Archie firing up the margarita machine."

"Jesus, congratulations. How long's it been? Twelve years?"

Rick laughed, a rich, easy whoop. "One of the examiners told me he'd voted a pass just to keep this from becoming the first katun-length Ph.D. in the department's history. That's about twenty years by the Mayan Long Count, and he was only half kidding."

"I was afraid of something like this, when you didn't answer any of my letters. Either that, or you were still digging in the jungle."

"We are, and we will be for as long as we can get funding and permission. But Brinton Taylor—you remember him, don't you? My mentor from the Field School and the project director? Brinton got on my case and made me write up the preliminary data on the plaza I excavated last season. And the department decided to accept it just to get me outta their hair." Rick chuckled and then was silent for a moment. "Speaking of your letters, Harp, how're *you* doing? The last one sounded pretty down."

"Down? How so? I recall being in a rare upbeat mood."

There was a strangling sound, followed by the rustling of paper. "Here . . . I got it out to read it again. Let's see, your Slogan of the Week is 'I feel much better now that I've given up hope.' "

"Yeah, I saw that on a T-shirt on campus."

"Yeah. And here's how you begin: 'My cat is dead in Vermont, my car is dead in the driveway, my book is buried in the remainder bins, and the sixties have been dead for longer than I care to remember.' "

"All true," Harp acknowledged. "Did I ever tell you about Rufus, the barn cat that used to take walks with me? Some damn kid shot him. And I'd like to shoot my fucking car, which conked out on me again."

Rick paused in a way that seemed significant. "I assumed it was true, Harp. It's the way you strung it all together that made me wonder. That 'dead, dead, dead.' "

"But then I say something about still being alive, right?"

"Nope. You say that the madness is still alive in some hearts, despite the ascendancy of President Bonzo and his band of moral eunuchs." Rick started laughing in spite of himself. "And then you tell me about throwing oranges in the Safeway. Did you really do that?"

Harp had almost forgotten that little incident, which had occurred prior to the elf theft. "Well, it wasn't premeditated or anything. A little temporary insanity. I grabbed one off the top and half the pile came bouncing down on my feet. So I tossed a couple."

"To the other side of the store?"

"I didn't actually see them land," Harp admitted. "But I was two aisles away before anybody came back to check."

"And nobody saw you do it?"

"Just the other vegetables. I have a certain kind of luck these days . . . my most outrageous crimes go unseen."

"As opposed to last year," Rick suggested. "When they all got reported."

Harp found himself shrugging and grimacing into the phone. "It was just that one little bluenose who ratted on me. That's all it took, of course, since the head of the program had other reasons to believe the worst of me."

"We've talked about this, though, haven't we? How when the cultural context changes, outrageousness comes to be seen as aberrant behavior?"

"Yeah, well, I figured I had the right to establish my own context in the classroom. If they can't take a joke, fuck 'em."

"Or fuck you, as the case may be," Rick laughed. "I dunno, Harp, I think you need to get out of Maryland before you start seeing your face on the post office wall."

Harp blew air past the mouthpiece. "Can't. Caroline's got a chance for a tenure-track position at Mid-Atlantic. And it's her turn to go for it."

"Well, look, that's the other reason I called: We're going into the field again in January. You in the middle of a book right now? You didn't say anything in your letter."

"That's cause I'm not. I've started about four different things, but nothing's stuck."

"So why not take some time off and come down to Rana Verde? If you can pay your airfare and give us some grunt labor, we can feed you and give you a place to string up a hammock."

"Feed me to what? Isn't this the 'steenking jungle' I've been hearing about for so long?"

"You're remembering my letters from the first couple seasons. The place's plush now. We call it the Baktun Hilton."

"I bet. You've probably got hot- and cold-running microbes."

"Big black scorpions, too, and fer-de-lance," Rick said proudly. "But it's a fascinating site. There'd be lots to write about."

"I actually considered the Maya as a subject," Harp confessed. "But there was so much stuff in the library, so many tribes and periods. I could never figure out where to start."

"Most Mayanists don't know where to stop. Even if you don't get a novel out of it, you'd be doing something useful and having a helluva lot more fun than you're gonna have in the 'burbs. You could write it up for the travel section of the paper or something. What do you say?"

"I'm tempted, but I'll have to think about it. I'm not making any money this year."

"It's tax-deductible if you write about it," Rick pointed out.

"Yeah, there's that. I'll let you know."

"Do that. It's been too long for us, and I think you could really use a change of scene."

"Either that, or sedation," Harp allowed. "I'll let you get to your margaritas, Doc. Give my regards to Winnie."

"Sure. Best to Caroline. Catch you later."

Harp hung up and turned back to his lasagna, which was now colder than his beer and looked like a stack of bloody waffles. He imagined sitting in the cactus garden in Rick's yard, licking salt off the rim of his glass and watching the Tucson sunset. He'd forgotten to ask how warm it was there, though it was always warm. And not soggy warm, like it was here. The steenking jungle, huh? He took the lasagna back to the Ushers' kitchen for reheating, thinking any place was beginning to look better than this.

WHEN CAROLINE came back into the living room with a fresh glass of punch and stopped to scan the faces in the crowd, the first person she spotted was Roger Hammet. Impeccably groomed as always and sleek in a blue blazer and sand-colored slacks that hung just so, lapping at the tops of his Italian loafers. Dark, sardonic features and eyes that always seemed shrewdly amused. She distrusted his slickness instinctively yet had to admit to a certain animal attraction—her eyes always found him this easily in a crowd. He'd also just been appointed to head the search committee for the position Caroline was after, which complicated the attraction and made the distrust something to be kept well concealed.

It took her another moment to realize that the person Hammet was talking to was Harp. He was not half so sleek in the lighter of his two sport coats, with his hair frizzing out from the sides of his head like the original Harpo, but he still looked surprisingly authoritative, like a professional in his own right. Which he was, Caroline reflected, though it'd been a long time since she'd heard him talk about his writing. It seemed equally long since she'd seen him in anything other than jeans and his grey Mid-Atlantic sweatshirt, skulking around the house like someone who'd given up hope of proper employment. *My husband has been going to seed,* she thought suddenly, recognizing the terminology as her mother's but still finding it apt.

She saw Hammet ask him a question and then turn away at an interruption, giving Harp a chance to pull the face he called the Demon Queller. It was actually the face of the quelled demon in a Japanese netsuke by that name, the face of a being incorrigibly and unrepentently committed to the cause of trouble. It was the face Harp pulled whenever he was royally annoyed and ready to strike back.

"Uh-oh," Caroline murmured to herself, and began to work her way toward the place where they were standing. Hammet had turned back and Harp was going on to him about something, his bushy head bobbing for emphasis and his face dangerously deadpan.

" . . . honorary chairman of the First Annual New Belvedere Parade of Lawn Animals," she heard Harp say as she came up beside them. "We're hoping to get Phil Donohue and Cathy Lee Crosby as our grand marshals."

"Lawn animals?" Hammet queried, acknowledging Caroline's presence with an amused nod. "Do you mean pink flamingos and the like?"

"A classic, unjustly maligned as evidence of working-class vulgarity, when actually it's a symbol of their yearning for a tropical paradise, for Eden. I'm a collector, you know."

"Of lawn animals?"

"I'm collecting data for a monograph on twentieth-century suburban iconography."

"And where do you collect your data?" Hammet asked, breezily playing along now, certain that his leg was being pulled.

"Mostly in the New Belvedere region. Darkest suburbia, land of the Mowerites and the Tinkerers. I conduct most of my excavations at night."

Caroline decided that it was time to step in.

"I should've warned you, Roger. Harp has a wicked sense of humor."

"So I've been learning," Hammet said dryly, giving her a smile that seemed tolerant yet held an edge of mockery.

"I'm only wicked when I'm being humored," Harp said, still deadpan, not giving the joke away even now. He suddenly looked down at his empty glass, then up at her. Then at Hammet. "I was kidding, of course. There is no such place as New Belvedere. I made that part up. Excuse me, would anyone like more wine?"

Caroline watched him go, telling herself forcefully that she shouldn't apologize for him. Not to this man. But it was hard.

LATER, as they walked in from the carport, she remembered the incident and confronted him with it.

"What was all that lawn animal stuff all about? You know that Roger Hammet is one of the powers in the department. In the profession, for that matter. I've told you that, haven't I?"

"Many times. That's why I thought he might be worth chatting up. Then the fucker asked me how I liked being a househusband."

"He *didn't.*"

"He sure did. Instead of asking him how he liked being a shithead, I thought I'd impress him with my scholarly pursuits."

The fact that he didn't laugh made her pause in the doorway, blocking his entrance. He had the sport coat slung over one shoulder and was regarding her with the sour defiance of someone who didn't expect to be taken seriously, no matter what he said. Caroline felt her heart plummet sharply, and there was a shiver in her voice.

"Harp, what've you been up to?"

He took her down to the basement to show her. He led her past the extra sets of dishes, silverware, and cookware they'd removed from the Ushers' kitchen cabinets, past the spare chairs and tables and the broken lawn furniture, past all the less-identifiable junk the Ushers had accumulated in lifetimes no longer than their own. He'd cleared a space between the furnace and the rack of metal shelves that held row upon row of jars and buckets and aerosol cans of old paint, insecticide, and motor oil.

Clustered in the middle of the space, like refugees from the surrounding clutter, were: an adorably bug-eyed Bambi with spindly legs and an upright tail; one of the classic pink flamingos; a slumbering peon, the brim of his sombrero resting on a serape-wrapped arm; a rather sinister version of one of the Seven Dwarfs in lime green; and a small orange parrot with a ridiculously oversized beak. Caroline suffered another inner lurch as she realized that Harp had stolen them from lawns in the neighborhood, just as he'd bragged to Hammet.

"The peon, of course, should have a burro and cart with him, but they were too big to carry away on foot. Likewise, for the motif to be complete, the parrot should be sitting in a birdbath with a double seahorse base. When asked to explain this combination, one of my informants said succinctly: 'They came like that.' "

It was the same mock-earnest voice he'd used on Hammet, but he dropped it abruptly when he saw the way she was staring at him.

"No reason to get upset, Carrie," he said lamely. "They were all easy, except for the last one," gesturing to the dwarf. "The cops chased me right up to the front door but somehow never saw me."

"The cops," Caroline repeated, and drew a breath to steady herself. "You risked going to jail for these?"

"Well . . . I guess that's probably what the cops had in mind."

"What'd *you* have in mind? What *possessed* you?"

He shrugged, eyes narrowing as some of his earlier defiance returned. "Demons," he muttered. "A grey wind . . . "

"That's not good enough, Harp. I'm sorry that you lost the teaching job, and that you miss Vermont so much. But you can't just go to pieces."

"What's to stop me?" he asked, his voice so lacking in defiance that Caroline was brought up short just as her outrage was beginning to acquire some momentum. It was a question, not a taunt.

"C'mon, Harp, you don't know how to go to pieces," she scoffed, though gently. "I've seen you bounce back so many times, from situations much worse than this. You survived living in Vancouver and being married to my sister, just to name two. And all those years before you had a book accepted. You're the most resilient person I know."

"The better to bounce off these walls," he said, casting a sour glance into the shadows. "We haven't been living here, Carrie, we've been camping out. That was okay for a year, but it's gotten *old* for me. I don't have another life to go to."

"I didn't know you had this one," Caroline said ruefully, gesturing toward his silent companions. "Did you really sneak out in the middle of the night, when I was asleep?"

He patted the flamingo on the head and shrugged with a kind of disbelief. "I really did. It was a rush, but I was scared shitless most of the time, too."

"You used to get that rush from your writing," Caroline pointed out, trying not to sound accusing. Harp exhaled sharply and looked at the floor, his arms swinging loosely at his sides.

"Yeah," he said thickly, the only word he could manage, and Caroline went to him and put her hands on his arms to hold him still.

"Harp, would a change of scene help? A couple of weeks in Vermont to see everybody again and visit our land? We could afford that."

"That would hurt too much," he said, shaking his head. "And you might not get me back."

"Forget it, then. I don't want to risk that. What about your family, or your friend Rick?"

Harp grunted in recognition. "Brother Rick invited me down to his dig in Mexico. He thought I needed a change of scene too."

"How much would it cost?"

"Airfare and a lotta sweat, probably. He suggested I write a travel piece for the newspaper to cover costs."

"*Do* it, Harp," Caroline urged. "It might get you going on another book, and it'd definitely keep you off our neighbors' lawns and out of jail."

"I must admit," Harp said with a crooked smile, "that when the time came, I wasn't ready to get busted for elf theft. But who's gonna be the househusband in my absence? Who maintains the camp?"

"Who milked the goats when you were gone in Vermont?" Caroline shot back. "It won't hurt me to have something mindless to do once in a while." She put her arms around his shoulders and pressed herself against him. "I can't let you go to pieces, Harp. You were always the stable one in this relationship."

He snorted but held on to her. "Role reversal," he murmured, and squeezed as if he feared it might be too true.

2

Mesoamerican studies often impress readers as a Sahara of guesses, where travelers crazed with a thirst for certainty suffer various mirages.

—George Kubler

THE READING LIST Rick had sent hadn't really helped. Its length and numerous categories merely emphasized the problem of where to begin with the Maya.

"At the beginning," Rick would've said, being an extremely systematic thinker. But Harp had only a couple of months to educate himself, and he had the mind of a triple jumper, quick to skip past the preliminaries and get to the broad associative leap. He needed that first good piece of the puzzle, the one that gave the intuition some shapes to work with. He needed the germ of a plot and enough characters to give it flesh.

Along with the reading list, Rick had sent a packet of materials on the site itself, which was officially known as Baktun. These included several chapters from Rick's thesis (on the excavation of the West Plaza), some preliminary site reports, Brinton Taylor's Summary of the first four seasons of work, and a batch of offprints of articles from archaeological journals. Harp went for the Summary first, but it quickly proved to be a disappointment, an assemblage of pieces without any explanatory connective tissue. Taylor simply detailed the sections of the site that had been surveyed and excavated, the various projects being pursued by the senior staff members, and the areas to be investigated during the upcoming season. He seemed to assume that his audience already knew the basic nature of the site and would understand what all the pieces were pointing toward, which left Harp feeling like the guy sitting alone in the back of the auditorium, afraid to raise his hand and ask the first stupid question.

He was most of the way through the packet before he found what he was looking for. His handle. It came in the form of an article that had originally appeared in *World Archaeology* under the title "Defying the Collapse: The Persistence of the Classic Tradition at Baktun, Chiapas." The author was an Oliver T. Clubb, whose scholarly affiliation was with Dumbarton Oaks, the museum of pre-Columbian art in Georgetown that was still on Harp's list of places to visit in D.C. Taking that small coincidence as a propitious sign, Harp dove in.

And here, at last, was a *story.* Harp learned that Baktun was a site on the southwestern periphery of the lowland Maya territory, and that it had probably been settled by emigrants from the central Petén sites of Tikal and Uaxactún, sometime during the Middle Classic Period. Like the neighboring sites along the Usumacinta and Pasión rivers, Baktun had experienced its greatest expansion and its cultural and artistic florescence during the Late Classic, from approximately A.D. 700 to 800. During that time, the Baktunis were under the rule of a dynasty founded by a man whose glyphic name meant Lord of Shells and whose power probably came from control of trade between the lowlands and the Pacific Coast, the source of shells and other valuable marine items. Lord of Shells was succeeded by four and possibly five generations of Shell rulers before the sequence was broken during the upheavals of the Terminal Late Classic, when most of the lowland sites stopped erecting monuments to their rulers.

All right, Harp thought, gazing raptly at the line drawings of Lord of Shells and his descendants, portraits lifted from the monuments in exquisite detail by means of night photography. Not only a story, but *pictures,* too! Here was the lord himself, long-nosed and loose-lipped, so that he seemed to sneer as he handed some kind of staff or scepter to his son, Kan Shell. The latter was portrayed at three quarters his father's size, his sloping forehead slightly bowed and his eyelid drooping in apparent deference. But on the facing page, Kan Shell stood alone in a lordly pose, wearing a towering feathered headdress that filled the entire frame above and behind him. The drooping eyelid was arched in a glare that clearly said he no longer deferred to anyone.

But the history of the Shell dynasty, exciting as it was to Harp, was only the lead-in to Oliver Clubb's main argument. Which was, essentially, that while the rest of the major lowland sites were breaking down internally and submitting to foreign influences from without during the Terminal Classic, Baktun had stubbornly kept faith with Classic beliefs and practices. The Baktunis had stopped erecting dated monuments along with everybody else, but construction had continued on a modest scale in the West Plaza, employing traditional building techniques and architectural forms. Even more persuasive, according to Clubb, was the ceramic evidence. At the other places, both the quality and quantity of polychrome pottery had declined drastically during the Late Classic, eventually giving way to an imported fine paste pottery that wasn't painted and that featured distinctly non-Classic images and symbols. At Baktun, on the other hand, the local polychrome tradition remained in force throughout the Terminal Classic, showing some stylistic decadence but no lack of vitality. And no significant amounts of fine paste pottery had been discovered in any of the likely ceremonial areas of the site; the foreigners who had made deep cultural inroads elsewhere had apparently been held at bay here.

Clubb went on with a more tentative and admittedly speculative discussion of what he called "the decadence beneath the defiance," trying to make sense of the tomb looting and the resetting of monuments that occurred in the last fifty years or so before the site's Postclassic abandonment. Even here he found evidence for his hypothesis in the form of a possible "revitalization movement" centered on the monuments of the long-dead Lord of Shells. Harp began to feel that the author was perhaps being too clever for his own good, but he could easily forgive a little overreaching. He liked the notion of one place holding out against history, clinging to its values when everybody else was selling out or going under. It appealed to both his defiant nature and his more covert yearning for a tradition worth defending.

With the centerpiece of the puzzle in place, he began to perceive the pieces of knowledge he needed to pick up next. More about the other, so-called major sites like Tikal, Copán, and Yaxchilán. A clearer sense of what constituted Classic Mayan traits and what was meant by foreign or "Mexicanized" iconography. Some basic knowledge about pottery making and architecture and trade items. Harp realized that he didn't have a clue as to what shells were used for or why they would be a source of wealth and power. He made up several ranked lists for himself, scouring Clubb's notes and bibliography for hints of where to look first.

It was after 1 A.M. when he finished, physically depleted but with his mind still buzzing. Caroline was fast asleep, but with the time difference, it wasn't too late to call Brother Rick. He crept downstairs to the kitchen phone, briefly troubled by the awareness that this was precisely the time of night at which he used to go prospecting for lawn animals.

"Finished so soon?" Rick inquired. "Want me to send some more?"

"I think this'll hold me for a while yet. What can you tell me about Oliver Clubb?"

"He's our ceramics specialist, a collections man Brinton coaxed out into the field. Also a prime asshole, but he knows everything about Mayan ceramics. Is that where you started, with his article?"

"You bet. It's the first thing that gave me any sense of what was going on at Baktun back then. I think it's terrific."

Rick was pointedly silent for a moment. "Yeah, I guess I can see where you might think that. Some of us refer to it as Ollie's Folly."

"Oh. What's wrong with it?"

"You want a list?" Rick asked sarcastically, then laughed. "No, it's not really that bad. He did some solid work on establishing the royal geneaology, with lots of help from Helga Kauffmann. It's after that he goes haywire. But you should test it for yourself. All the data you'll need is there, I think, in my stuff and Muldoon's, and Ulysses Cole's. I take it you haven't read any of that yet?"

"It looked pretty technical," Harp muttered.

"It *is* technical. We like to pretend this is a science. But Clubb's using the same set of data, so all you have to do is match up what he says against what we say. Once you can poke some holes in his theory, you'll know you've learned some archaeology."

"Or earned my debunking merit badge," Harp groused. "Is that all you're gonna tell me?"

Rick laughed wickedly. "I'm a doctor now, I can charge for consultations. I will pose one general query, though. How many holes do you have to dig before you know what's *not* there?"

Harp turned this riddle over in his mind, imagining a cutaway model of the site with numerous holes like well shafts drilled down through the temples and plazas on the surface. A little more imagination conjured up some underground chambers the shafts hadn't hit, burials and caches filled with untapped information. "You mean . . . you might still find a tomb filled with foreign stuff that would blow Clubb's persistence theory out of the water?"

"I doubt it would be that dramatic," Rick laughed, "but it wouldn't have to be. You have to understand that we have whole sections of the site that we've barely sampled, including some we know were important. And of the stuff we *have* dug up, a lot of it still hasn't been analyzed. Furthermore, a good share of what *has* been analyzed remains problematic, which means we're not sure what it means. In other words, it's a little early in the game to be making a strong case for Classic purity."

Harp grunted. "It's late here, but I'll keep that in mind."

"Didn't mean to dampen your enthusiasm, man," Rick said, though he laughed again. "But if you really want to understand this stuff, you're gonna have to get technical."

"You make that sound as appealing as getting my shots."

"A little intellectual rigor won't kill you, and believe me, it hurts a lot less than a gamma globulin."

"Immunity from imagination," Harp grumbled. "Okay, I'll read your shit, and it'd better be good. Just tell me one more thing before I let you go."

"What's 'at?"

"Why do you call it Rana Verde instead of Baktun? The *Green Frog*?"

"Sounds like a good Mexican bar, doesn't it? Actually, it's the name Brinton Taylor gave the site in his mind before he was even sure it existed. That was back in the forties, on one of his first trips to Mexico. He was in Comitán, and this pot hunter offered to sell him a basalt frog that still had traces of the original green paint on it. The guy said it came from a Mayan city on the Rio Lacantún, a place only the Indians knew about. So Brinton bought the thing and gave it to the museum in Mexico City, and forgot about it for about thirty years. Then, about fifteen years ago, a geologist for Pemex, the national oil company, told him about the site they'd found in the rain forest east of Comitán, on the Rio Lacantún, and Brinton made sure he was the first archaeologist to get a look at it. The rest, as they say, is prehistory."

"Great story," Harp said appreciatively. "Have you ever found out if the frog actually came from there?"

"Nope. It fits stylistically, but it'd fit a lot of other places, too. That's why we hate looters so much. Even if something ends up in a museum someday, the best we can say about it is 'provenance unknown.' "

"Whatever that means," Harp agreed. "I don't wanna know tonight. Lemme be intrigued a while longer, before I have to get rigorous."

"Hey, whatever works for you. *Adiós* . . . "

Harp hung up and looked around the nonfunctional kitchen. Non-Classic, he decided as he headed off to bed, and definitely Terminal.

CAROLINE KNEW the way to his daytime lair by now, so she simply bypassed all the clean, well-lit places he might've chosen and took the elevator down to B-2, the second underground level. She came out in the midst of the stacks, the ceiling low overhead while shelves thick with books rose up to meet it on both sides of the narrow aisles. Bare bulbs leaked a weak yellow light through the protective mesh that encased them, providing just enough illumination to make the atmosphere seem truly subterranean. He claimed he liked the quiet down here, though Caroline saw it as a more symbolic acting out: No place to go but up.

It was five-fifteen and there was no one else in sight, which aroused a habitual wariness and made her take a two-handed grip on her briefcase as she wound her way back to the deep shelves that held folios and oversize books. Hearing only the clicking of her own heels, she went quickly around the corner and stopped short, exhaling sharply when she saw that his customary place was unoccupied.

Then she realized he was sitting a short distance away, back against the stacks. His eyes were closed and his hands lay on his thighs, his shoulders slumped in a posture so familiar she didn't recognize it immediately. Then she remembered him saying that he'd started meditating again. They'd both taken it up in Vermont and had been faithful practitioners until a few years ago, around the time she'd begun writing her thesis and Harp had been finishing *Ghost Dance.* She couldn't remember exactly why they'd quit, except that they'd become too busy to spare the forty minutes a day.

He'd straightened up slightly, showing his awareness of her presence, so she went over and kissed him on his bald pate, deliberately rubbing her breasts across his face in the process.

"Favor your mantra," she taunted, and though he opened one eye in a kind of leer, he nonetheless returned to his alpha state without making a grab for her. Caroline deposited her briefcase on the floor and sat down on the chair near the desk, switching on the Tensor lamp he brought in with him each day. The strong beam of light seemed reassuring, and she stretched out her legs and examined the disorderly stacks of books and journals that covered the surface of the desk and filled all three shelves above it. There were huge old volumes—true tomes—from the Peabody Museum and the Bureau of Ethnology and the Carnegie Institute with nothing on their spines to indicate what was inside; equally large but much thinner coffee-table volumes on Mayan art and pottery and textiles, with appropriately glossy covers; several books on deciphering the hieroglyphs and lots of back issues of *American Antiquity;* and recent collections of essays with titles like *The Terminal Classic Symposium* and *Mayan Archaeology and Ethnobotany.*

"Nothing like a little variety," Caroline murmured dryly. As a scholar, Harp wasn't exactly methodical or meticulous. He tended to pursue whatever turned him on wherever it might lead him, filling in the gaps (or not) as he went along and not making too stark a distinction between fact and speculation. His common, wise-guy advice to her, whenever she was struggling with an intractable set of data, was "if you don't know, make it up."

She gingerly pushed his notebook and glasses to one side to see what he was working on at the moment, and the first things to come to hand were a couple of typewritten lists. One was obviously the reading list Brother Rick had sent him, two and a half pages, single spaced, a minidoctorate in Mayan studies. Caroline laughed out loud at the heading of the first section, which was entitled "Seminal Sources (Early Spurts)." From there, it was easy to see the progression Rick had laid out for him, though the distribution of check marks in the left-hand margin showed that Harp had already gone all over the place. The section labeled "Glyphs and the Calendar" seemed to have the lowest number of checks.

"If it's hard to learn, leave it be," Caroline scoffed. So much for all his complaints about "rigor mortis" setting in. The other sheet was a list of the supplies he needed to take with him, the documents he had to obtain, and the innoculations he'd have to endure. Here the check marks formed a nearly solid column along the left, proving that he could take care of business when he wanted to. *No place to go but up.*

Underneath the lists was a blue volume entitled *The Art, Iconography & Dynastic History of Palenque, Part III,* from which an inner foldout was protruding. She opened the book and spread the sheet fully, then just stared in wonder. It was a black-and-white line drawing of some kind of tryptich, three panels in which a total of four human figures all faced inward toward a central altar that held a crosslike standard that was fairly dripping with decorative embellishments and was topped by a bird that looked like a chicken out of some nightmarish cartoon. The figures on the outer panels were likewise festooned with feathered headdresses and backdresses and ornate girdles, one holding a scepter and the other smoking a long funnel-shaped cigar. Or was he blowing something out of a pipe?

"I don't know how to look at this," she said to herself, and jumped when Harp laughed and put a hand on her shoulder.

"Favor your mantra yourself."

"That was mean of me, I admit. What am I looking at?"

He leaned over her and checked the flyleaf. "Tablet of the Cross and Sanctuary Jambs."

"So it *is* a cross. Not a Christian . . . ?"

"Hardly, circa six hundred A.D. Though there have been those who wanted to believe that the Maya were one of the Lost Tribes of Israel."

Caroline stared at it some more. "It's beautiful . . . completely naturalistic and utterly fantastic at the same time."

"Pure Classic," Harp said with satisfaction.

"What does it represent?"

"Some kind of ceremony to help the Sun get through the Underworld. You knew that was where the Sun went at night, right?"

Caroline could feel him smirking behind her. "Of course, doesn't everybody? Is this man smoking something or blowing it out?"

"Probably smoking. They cultivated tobacco and apparently used it in their ceremonies. Along with penis perforators and hallucinogenic enemas."

"C'mon, Harp, none of your scurrilous fabrications. My mind is already boggled."

"I did *not* make those up," he insisted, laughing. "Supposedly, they used stingray spines for wienie stickers."

"And what did they use for enema bags?"

He paused for one beat. "I expect they bought them at the drugstore, like everybody else."

Caroline growled but then had to laugh, and he put both hands on her shoulders to steady himself, renewing his protest even while convulsed with laughter.

"It's true . . . I just couldn't resist . . . "

"You're having too much fun with this, Harp."

"Yeah," was all he could manage, but he began to knead her shoulders, which felt so good that she instantly forgave his teasing. She groaned with pleasure and sank back against his probing fingers.

"How'd your presentation go?" he asked.

"Just fine," she murmured, though she could feel the tension from it loosening under his hands. "Everyone in the class had read my articles, so I could actually talk about what I'm doing *now,* and where I'm going with the book. A couple of Roger's little wise-ass protégés had to demonstrate their skepticism about the validity of a feminist approach, but they shut up once I demonstrated how little they'd read of the important literature. I came away with a couple of ideas I can use, and I think Roger was impressed."

"Good." His hands had begun to wander down over her collarbone, his fingers digging gently into the soft fabric of her dress. It was his favorite, a grey jersey that matched her eyes and was part cashmere, so that it clung without gathering. It clung very attractively, as Harp had often told her, and as Roger Hammet had clearly noticed during her talk. A pang of guilt brought a flush to her neck and cheeks just as Harp's long fingers swept down to cup her breasts, adding a jolt of real lust to her confusion. She blinked wildly and finally pointed at the drawing in front of her.

"What's the bird on top of the cross? Looks like some kind of bizarre chicken."

He bent down and kissed the curve of her neck, and she felt her nipples harden against his palms. "Muan bird," he said.

"Is there such a thing?" she asked weakly.

"Nope. Mythological beast. Make a great lawn animal . . . "

She was flushed all over now, and it had nothing to do with guilt. So she closed the book and switched off the Tensor lamp, leaving only the milky glow of the fluorescent fixture built in under the bottom shelf. Harp helped her stand up, nudging the chair out of the way with his knee so that she could turn and come into his arms. She found herself in a long, open-mouthed kiss quite unlike the fond pecks they'd become accustomed to exchanging, his hands traveling down her sides and back and over her buttocks, stroking and pulling her against him. *My god,* she thought, *necking in the stacks.* But the fear of being discovered in flagrante barely registered, and she let herself sit back on the edge of the desk, her dress riding up her thighs as he pressed forward between her legs.

"You're so beautiful," he whispered, staring at her with a wonder and gratitude that made her feel luminous. She put her hands around the back of his neck and kissed him passionately, loving him for that look. She felt a hand slide up under her dress, and then he was there. God, was he there. She broke from the kiss, feeling delirious.

"No place to go but up," she heard herself say, and Harp let out a whoop of laughter that startled them both. He removed his hand and hugged her as he lifted her off the desk and set her on her feet. Clichéd though it was, she felt distinctly weak in the knees.

"Let's go home and go to bed," he suggested, stuffing his notebooks and the lamp into his shoulder bag.

"Do the Maya always have this effect upon you?" Caroline asked, and he laughed and picked up her briefcase and started them moving.

"Whenever I can get the penis perforators out of my mind . . . "

CHRISTMAS EVE, and Harp slept inordinately late, even for him. Yesterday he'd taken the Metro into the District and gone to the HMO to get the rest of his shots. He'd been afraid he'd have to ride back with a mild case of yellow fever–polio-tetanus-typhoid coming on, but as it turned out, only the gamma globulin taken in the arm had hurt right away. The others had kicked in about twelve hours later, making him feel achy and feverish and weird in a dozen less definable ways. Caroline had stayed up with him through the worst of it, feeding him brandy and chicken soup from the deli while they watched *Conan the Barbarian* on the Ushers' snowy black-and-white set.

He finally got up around noon, just in time to see Caroline off to the Christmas party her feminist study group was having, no husbands or significant others invited. That was fine with Harp, who had a sore arm and a sore butt and a bit of a hangover, in addition to his perennial lack of Christmas spirit. The holiday mood was especially elusive in this climate, which had thus far provided some chilly nights and a few icy rains, but nothing resembling what he knew as winter.

On this Eve, in fact, it was a balmy seventy-two degrees, and when he heard the neighbor on the right start up a lawn mower, he had to go out onto the back deck to see it for himself. Sure enough, there was Mrs. Garfield with her trusty Toro, mowing a landing strip for Santa across her backyard. Steering with only one hand, she waved to him and wished him a Merry Christmas, a greeting he returned when she came buzzing back in his direction.

Only in New Belvedere, he thought, though his bout of heightened immunity had left him too depleted to be properly snide. And it was oddly cheering to be wished a Merry Christmas, even if he had no interest in having one. It occurred to him that maybe he should defer to local custom for once, instead of sneering reflexively. He saw no point in cutting Usher's grass, but there was something on which he could tinker.

He went back into the house and found the box that held his motley collection of tools (most left behind by visiting repairmen), and took it out to the carport, where Trusty Rusty sat alone and silent. The VW repair manual was still lying on the passenger seat, open to the troubleshooting section, and an enterprising spider had spun an elongated web between the steering wheel and the rearview mirror. Harp didn't disturb either one, telling himself as he lifted the rear hood that he was only here to tinker. So he poked and jiggled at random, knocking clots of dirt and rust off of the engine but finding nothing visibly awry. It was not a whole lot different from what he'd done when he was *seriously* trying to find the problem, except that he'd expected to have some effect then, and his curses had been a heartfelt expression of his frustration. Now he cussed for the hell of it, without conviction, and he didn't bother to slam the car door behind him when he tried the ignition and got the now-familiar dead clunk.

"No one's ever accused you of being mechanically inclined," he murmured as he went back to tinker some more. He began to wonder, as he stared into the greasy complications of the engine, if tinkering wasn't something like fishing: It didn't really matter if you caught something every time out. Maybe all the guys in the neighborhood who were constantly working on their motorcycles and RVs and ATVs and primer-coated jalopies were really practicing a form of physical meditation. If they actually *did* know how to fix it, so much the better, but it wasn't necessarily required.

His musings, which he would later decide were a lingering effect of brandy and yellow fever, were interrupted by the appearance of Willard Cousins, his neighbor on the left. Willard and his wife, Judy, had been the interim caretakers for the Ushers, so they were the neighbors Harp and Caroline had gotten to know best. They were raising four kids in a house considerably less spacious than the Ushers', yet in the year and a half they'd been neighbors, Harp had yet to hear either one of them scream. The times he'd been in their living room, they'd all been camped in front of the TV, sprawled out on the couches and the floor and each other, watching whatever was on the screen with placid inattention. Visual tinkering.

Willard was a wiry little guy with a scraggly mustache and a friendly squint, a civilian employee of the Air Force who had introduced himself the first time by saying, in a single breath, "I'm in communications that's all I can tell you." He greeted Harp with an amiable nod, waving a hand at the car.

"Engine trouble?"

"Won't start. Hasn't for almost three months."

Willard took that in as if it made some sense, even as Harp cringed inwardly at the utter inanity of such an admission. He expected the next question to be "And what do you expect will happen today?"

"I useta have one'a these," Willard said instead, running a hand along a rear fender. "Had a big peace symbol on the hood when I bought it, and I just left it there. The Prince George's cops were always stopping me for no reason. What year's this?"

"Seventy."

"Body's in good shape."

"I had it redone about three years ago, before it rusted out completely. I was convinced it would run forever."

"These're nice machines. Real simple. It just quit on you? Won't crank at all?"

"Not a bit."

So Willard bent over the engine and began to tinker, and damned if he didn't seem to be poking about as aimlessly as Harp had. Tugged on the same wires around the condenser or the distributor or whatever it was called. Harp had known the name when he'd troubleshot it, but that hadn't effected a cure. Willard bent closer, separating the different-colored wires between his fingers and tracing each back to its connection. Harp had done that, too, praying that it was something as simple as a loose wire. *Real simple.* But then Willard began to disconnect the wires one by one, something Harp hadn't thought to do, fearing he'd only make more trouble for himself. Willard grunted softly.

"I think I maybe found it. You got a pliers? There, that vise grips'll do . . . "

Harp handed it to him. "I thought I checked those, and they were all connected."

"Yeah, that's how it looks, all right. But on this one here the wire's broke where it's supposed to hook on to the contact. It's connected on the outside but not inside where it counts. Go try it now . . . "

Harp wanted to believe him but was certain that it couldn't be *that* simple.

Still, he slid in under the wheel, depressed the clutch and put it in gear, and gave it a perfunctory crank. And went into shock when it started up with a rattling roar. He put it back into neutral, checked the hand brake, and got out, too stunned to speak. Willard beckoned him over and pointed out a green-coated wire, speaking loudly enough to be heard over the idling engine.

"I just crimped that back together, so you oughta get a new one at the VW place soon as you get a chance. Should hold you for a while, though."

"Man, I can't tell you how much I appreciate this," Harp said fervently. "You've really made my day."

Willard grinned and dropped the hood back into place. "Merry Christmas, huh? Bet you're dyin' to take it for a spin."

"You know it."

"The in-laws'll be arriving soon," Willard said, jerking his head in the direction of his own house. "Stop over for some eggnog later."

"Will do," Harp promised, and pumped his hand before getting back behind the wheel. He saw that the spider and his web would have to go, and reached under the seat for a rag to wipe them away. Then he reconsidered and took the time to coax the spider onto the cover of the repair manual, which he then set down on the ground outside the car.

"Sorry, but this ain't no mobile home," he said, as he shut the door, wiped away the web, and wiggled the gearshift down into reverse. "*On,* Rusty," he intoned, and backed down the driveway.

WHEN CAROLINE turned into the driveway around nine, her headlights caught Harp in the process of stowing something on the backseat of the Volkswagen. She pulled her Toyota up on the right, switched off the lights and engine, and rolled her window all the way down. He straightened up and grinned at her over the roof of the VW.

"Hi there."

"I'm sorry I'm so late. I didn't know it was going to include dinner, but Jeanette had cooked a turkey and everything. I tried to call you but got no answer."

"I was out," he explained, grinning more widely, "riding around. Willard got Rusty going for me."

"Bless his heart!" Caroline said, smiling back at him as she got out.

"What's in the bag?"

"Turkey and dressing, and a piece of pecan pie. For you."

"This's my day," he said, giving her an enthusiastic kiss as he relieved her of the bag.

"You've certainly gotten over your yellow fever. Are you high?"

"Sure," he agreed easily. "I was next door drinking eggnog with Willard until just a little while ago."

"What are you doing now?" she asked, answering her own question by bending to glance through Rusty's rear window. There was a flamingo lying across the seat and a peon hunched over on the floor. She looked back at Harp, seeing that he was wearing his Mid-Atlantic sweatshirt.

"Harp . . ."

"Unfinished business. I've found a proper home for them."

"Where?"

"You wanna come along and see?"

"You want to make an accomplice of me?"

"I could use a driver. Don't worry, I won't get caught."

"How do you know? Is this a regression, Harp? Just when I thought it was safe to let you out in the neighborhood . . . "

"I'll trust *my* instincts today," he told her. "I've been given a great gift, and I have to think there was a reason."

"*Why* do you *have* to think that?"

"Because that's the way it works. You wanna come?"

Caroline stared at the keys he was dangling in front of his grinning face. "If you get me busted for elf theft, I'll never forgive you," she vowed, but snatched the keys out of his hand. He kissed her and held up the bag of food.

"I'll stick this in the fridge and be back with the rest of the captives."

"*Captives,*" Caroline echoed in exasperation, but he'd already bounded off toward the house, leaving her to wonder which of them was crazier.

WHEN HE HAD her circle the block and make a second pass of the Methodist church on New Belvedere Boulevard, she finally understood what he'd meant by a proper home.

"You *can't* be serious, Harp," she burst out. "The crèche? That's adding desecration to elf theft. Look at all the cars!"

"Yeah, it's perfect . . . there must be a service going on. When you swing back again, pull right up into the driveway next to it and douse the lights."

She argued with him all the way around the block and back again, but all he did was laugh and tell her not to defuse the magic with doubt. Then they were coming up on the church again and the street was miraculously empty of moving traffic, and she found herself making the left-hand turn as instructed, taking them right up to the floodlit crèche. Harp at least took the precaution of looking carefully in all directions, but then he was slipping out the door with the orange parrot in his hands. He hustled around in front of the car and darted into the crèche, which was about half of lifesize.

Caroline sat with her heart revving in time with the idling engine, hearing organ music coming from behind the glowing stained-glass windows of the church. Then Harp was back, giggling with excitement as he reached into the backseat and brought out Bambi and the flamingo, angling them past the seat back and the doorframe.

"Hurry!" she hissed, glancing over her shoulder as a car went past on the boulevard. He waited until it was gone before again darting into the crèche.

He returned two more times, for the peon and then the elf, and by the last trip, he was laughing so hard he could barely speak.

"Come see," he burbled, and Caroline realized that as much as she wanted to get away from here, she couldn't leave without seeing what he'd done. She started giggling herself as she let another car pass on the boulevard, then set the hand brake and slipped out the door. She went as far as one of the flood-lights, crouching down behind it to peer into the straw-roofed manger. Harp momentarily obscured her view as he retreated out of the light, gesturing grandly like a ringmaster.

"Ta-*dah*!" he cackled.

For a moment, all she could see was the traditional arrangement of infant and parents, wise men and shepherds, the usual collection of farm animals. Then the mask of familiarity slipped, and she noticed bug-eyed Bambi peer-ing out from among the plaster sheep, and the orange parrot poised like a giant tick on the back of a cow. The peon was snoozing between Mary and Joseph, and the elf, grinning dementedly, seemed to be goosing one of the wise men. The flamingo was planted at a dangerous angle over the cradle, as if about to take a peck at the Baby Jesus.

They were both hooting helplessly as they scrambled back into the car, and Caroline had to put both hands on the wheel to steady herself. Somehow, she got the brake off and the lights on and zigzagged down the driveway to the street, which was again empty. She straightened the car out and tore off down the boulevard while Harp pounded on the dashboard in triumph.

"Wayta go, Care-oh-line! We did it!"

"That was insane!"

"Yeah, but whatta rush! Better even than stealing them."

"I'm too old for this. My heart can't take it anymore."

"Tell me you don't wish you'd brought the camera."

She couldn't, in all honesty, and seeing it again in her mind made her sput-ter with laughter. "It would've made a great Christmas card," she admitted.

"*The Lawn Animals' Christmas!*" Harp said exultantly. "Wanna get the camera and go back?"

"Not on your life. This business is *finished,* right?"

"Right," he agreed. "Though I promised Willard I'd bring him back a bot-tle of mescal."

"Is that the stuff with the worm in it?"

"That's exactly the way he asked for it," Harp said, and settled back in his seat with a contented sigh. "Oughta be real good in next year's eggnog . . ."

3

JANUARY 3, 1984. The day of departure finally arrived, grey and seasonably cold, with a possibility of sleet later in the day. Harp had volunteered to use the Metro, which could take him right to Washington National with only one transfer, but he'd gratefully accepted Caroline's offer to drive him instead. He was traveling as light as possible, but he was more than a little encumbered with Caroline's portable electronic typewriter, a rucksack filled with ribbons, batteries, and other writing supplies, a duffel bag stuffed with clothes, and an airline shoulder bag for his books.

Even after meditating, he was giddy with anticipation, itching to be off. But Caroline had awakened in such a touchy mood that he had to tiptoe around her in his new waterproof boots. They'd been bickering since New Year's Day, when Harp had intercepted a call from her parents and had inadvertently let slip that he was leaving the country just as Caroline had a three-week break coming up. That'd left her defenseless against their urgings that she come to Vancouver for a visit, something she'd happily avoided for the past four years. Now she was stuck, and he wouldn't even be along to share the misery.

Harp hadn't gotten anywhere with apologies, and he'd only made it worse by suggesting that such a visit might be good for her. He was probably the last person who could've persuaded her of that, since there'd never been any love lost between him and his in-laws, who'd hated having him as a son-in-law both times it happened. Caroline had rejected the suggestion as "rank hypocrisy" and then turned it back on him by wondering aloud about the necessity of his trip. Was he over his elf theft or not? If he was, why didn't he just stay home and write the novel, and save the airfare? If he wasn't, then maybe they needed to talk some more about what had caused it. They hadn't really talked about it at all, she'd pointed out, and now that they finally had a chance for some time together, he was going away.

They'd gone round and round on that, pointlessly, since he was packing while they argued and she didn't try to stop that. He'd fended her off without losing his temper, but the effort had cost him, and it hadn't lessened his desire to get away.

After loading his stuff into the trunk of the Corolla, he tossed his new, wide-brimmed panama in on top and quickly got into the car, shivering inside his light canvas raincoat.

"Will you remember to take Rusty out occasionally?" he asked meekly.

"I'll remember. *You* take good care of my typewriter. It was a gift from my parents for finishing my doctorate."

Harp knew that, and he'd already promised three times that he'd guard the typewriter with his life. But he didn't want any more arguments, so he kept his mouth shut and nodded in agreement. As she backed into the street and headed for the Beltway, the box of tapes wedged in between the bucket seats caught his attention.

"Tapes," he said, reaching first for the glove compartment. "Rick said somebody'd be sure to bring a boom box, and that tapes were always good for barter or bribes."

"Take yours, then," Caroline said curtly. He ignored that and pulled out a handful of self-recorded cassettes, reading the labels aloud.

"Steely Dan, Billy Joel, Santana, Zappa and Captain Beefheart, Joni Mitchell . . . "

"Leave me Joni."

"You got her," he said, putting the tape back into the glove compartment and dropping the others into the pocket of his raincoat. He read on: "Let's see . . . The Byrds and Cream on one, Live Dead, Jimmy Buffett, Derek and the Dominos?"

"Just Jimmy Buffett. He's good company in a traffic jam."

Harp complied and turned to the store-bought tapes in their protective plastic boxes. He passed over the classical stuff without comment and saw no point in trying for Linda Ronstadt or Holly Near or any of Caroline's favorite Beatles and Moody Blues tapes, even though some of them were in fact his.

They squabbled over Springsteen's *Born to Run,* Harp arguing that it should be his because of the song "Jungleland." Likewise Santana, because of its Latin beat. He lost on the former, but not the latter. Harp was almost to the end of the box. George Winston would also be soothing in a traffic jam and would probably seem effete in the jungle. Judy Collins was another of Caroline's favorites. The last tape brought him up short.

"Keith Jarrett. *The Koln Concert.*"

Caroline took her eyes off the road for a moment but didn't say anything. He knew that in her mind, she was back in the house in Vermont, a fire rumbling in the woodstove while the wind blew snow against the windows, the two of them sitting on the sofa and sipping tax-free cognac from New Hampshire, listening to Jarrett pull notes from his piano and set them spinning in the air.

"You take it," Caroline said abruptly. "I'll buy another one."

"You're sure . . . ?"

"I want you to have *something* that'll make you think of me."

"You know I love you, Carrie. I'm not doing this to get away from you."

"I know," she said ruefully, and reached over to give his knee a blind squeeze. "Just bring yourself back, Harp. Your whole self . . . "

HARP HAD to change planes in Miami, and when he got aboard the flight to Villahermosa, he found another passenger already ensconced in the window seat to which he'd been assigned. The man had the tray table down and was paging through a ring binder filled with charts or printouts of some kind, which he was studying intently. Harp recognized him from the previous flight: perhaps forty-five and balder than Harp himself, with glasses and a round, vaguely pugnacious face that reminded Harp of Winston Churchill. He was wearing a long-sleeved khaki safari shirt that was faded but well pressed, buttoned right up to his Adam's apple. Harp had pegged him as an academic at first glance, though the charts appeared very businesslike.

"Do you have Ten-D?" Harp asked, squeezing in so that people could pass through the aisle behind him. The man pushed his glasses down to the end of a rather short nose before turning his head in Harp's direction.

"I beg your pardon?"

"I asked if you had Ten-D. I'd actually prefer to sit on the aisle, but I want to make sure it doesn't belong to someone else. I have Ten-F, the window seat."

"I see." The man unbuttoned the flap on his shirt pocket and glanced at his boarding pass. "Ten-D. Ah . . . would you mind switching?"

"No, like I said, the aisle's fine. The plane doesn't look very crowded, anyway."

The man simply nodded and went back to his charts. *You're fucking welcome.* Harp stowed Caroline's typewriter under the seat in front of his own and deposited his raincoat, panama, and shoulder bag in the overhead compartment, next to a fine maroon leather briefcase that no doubt belonged to Mr. 10D. He rummaged in his own bag for the copy of *The White Hotel* he'd been reading on the previous flight, then plucked out his notebook and the

Baktun packet as well. He needed to start keeping his journal right off the top, and there was always more to study.

Dropping the books and packet onto the empty middle seat, he buckled himself in, closed his eyes, and went into a meditation that lasted through the safety instructions, taxi, and takeoff. It was a restless meditation, troubled by bursts of excitement when he thought about where he was going, and by pangs of guilt when he thought about the situation he was leaving behind. He came out of it thinking that he should write a letter to Caroline, something to compensate for his not being there when she returned from Vancouver. But when he reached for his notebook, he found Mr. 10D eyeing the title on the Baktun packet with a certain bemusement.

"Baktun?" the man read aloud. "Does that refer to the Mayan site?"

"You've heard of it?"

"I should think so," the man said dryly. "I'm a member of the staff. I'm going there now."

"So am I," Harp said, extending a hand. "I'm Harper Yates."

The man's hand was blunt and meaty, his grip surprisingly powerful. "Oliver Clubb."

"No kidding," Harp blurted foolishly, unable to match the face in front of him with the image of Clubb he'd created for himself. He'd imagined someone younger and thinner, with a kind of shifty, opportunistic shrewdness. "Oh, of course," he recovered, "you're at Dumbarton Oaks."

One of Clubb's eyebrows, covered with fine, pale hair, arched upward. "And you? I noticed the typewriter: Are you a reporter?"

"Ah, no . . . I'm a freelance writer, a novelist."

"Have you published something?"

"Two novels, so far. The first was called *War College* and was about being in college in the late sixties. The second is a historical novel about the Plains Indians called *Ghost Dance.*"

"Oh yes, I've seen that," Clubb acknowledged. "There was a copy floating around the camp last season. I remember that Katie Smith, our lab director, was quite taken with it. Is she a friend of yours?"

"Never met her. The copy probably belonged to Rick Fisher. He and I go back a long way."

"Indeed," Clubb murmured, his lips pursed with what might have been disapproval. "Are you going to write a novel about Baktun?"

"Eventually," Harp said, hearing an uncertainty in his own voice that annoyed him. "In the meantime, I might write a travel piece to help pay my airfare."

"Oh? Better clear that with Brinton Taylor," Clubb advised with a frown. "He and some of the rest of the staff have agreements with various publications. Just how much do you know about the site?"

"Quite a lot, actually . . . "

"Then you should know that there's not much there for tourists, at least at present."

"True, but that might make it more interesting to the editor of the travel section."

"More exotic, you mean," Clubb sniffed. "What does 'quite a lot' mean? If you *were* going to write a novel about it, where would you start?"

The pale eyebrows formed a double arch of skepticism, reminding Harp of his amateur status and inspiring an uncharacteristic attack of diffidence. But the fact that Clubb clearly didn't expect him to have a good answer also piqued his scholarly pride; he hadn't suffered through all that rigor just to let some officious expert put him down.

"Let's see . . . I'd probably start with the death of the last Shell ruler, Shell Star, in 9.18.10.0.0, right? I'd do his burial and the dedication of Stela Sixteen, just to give the reader a sense of how things were done in true Classic style."

He'd brought the eyebrows down into a squint of reappraisal, which only goaded Harp to go on.

"Then I'd get into the lives of my characters, who would be involved in the struggle for power that apparently ensued between the heirs of Shell Star and the family of the man in Burial Twenty-three, the people you call the Kan Cross People. Gradually, I'd begin to make the reader aware of the troubles that were occurring at the other Classic sites, like the fall of Palenque and the Mexican takeover at Seibal, and the disruption of the lowland trade routes. I'd show how this would've impinged on Baktun, which suddenly wouldn't have had the same clout with the traders in the highlands and on the coast, and thus less wealth for buildings and burials. Which is probably why the Kan Cross People won." Harp paused, meeting Clubb's gaze with a kind of belligerence. "Okay so far?"

"So far. You've obviously done some homework."

Harp opened the packet on the seat between them and pulled out his copy of Clubb's article, which was smudged and dog-eared from use and was highlighted all over with yellow felt marker. He slapped it down on top of the packet and sat back.

"The heart of the novel," Harp went on, "would probably center on all the strange stuff that went on in Group B after the completion of the Tenth Cycle and the dedication of Stela Seventeen by Kan Cross Ahau. You know, like the burial of Stela Nine and Ten, and the resetting of Seven, all the evidence for a possible revitalization movement. Everything must've been up for grabs then, in terms of what they believed."

Clubb glanced up from the margin notes he'd been scanning. "I'd differ with that interpretation. I'd say they were holding on hard to what they had."

"Not if they were trading the jade they looted from the old tombs and caches," Harp argued. "And why, if they were being so Classic, did they pave over their only ball court and not build themselves a new one?"

"You've been reading your friend Richard's work, as well. I personally think he makes a bit too much of the ball court. We may yet find one somewhere else."

Harp couldn't resist a sarcastic smile. "We might find a lot of things. Like a whole cache of Fine Orange pottery, or a Mexican-style stela. That would give the plot a different twist."

"Unlikely," Clubb said, but then dropped the article and waved his blunt fingers in a vague gesture of capitulation. "I obviously underestimated you, Mr. Yates. I had the impression that this was all just a lark to you, something to fill the time between books."

"It started out that way," Harp confessed, "but then rigor set in, and I didn't want to be the only guy who didn't know what was going on."

"How much do you know about Baktun ceramics?"

Harp shrugged. "I read your preliminary report on the sequence, and Helga Kauffmann's article on the incense burners. I stuck mostly to the late phases."

"Would you like to see the analyses of last season's sampling? I can assure you that they're not in anything you've read . . . "

Harp could recognize a peace offering when he heard one, though he would've preferred a simple apology to an invitation to hard thought. This is what he got for being such a brash rookie.

"I surely would," he said with a rigorous nod, and promised himself a drink as soon as the flight attendant came around.

ON THE GROUND in Villahermosa, Harp collected his duffel bag and backpack, presented his passport and visa at Immigration, and joined one of the lines for customs inspection. His hearing hadn't fully returned after the descent, and a litany of newly familiar ceramic terms was playing like a tape loop in his head. *An unslipped temperless flaring-rim tripod plate with hollow mammiform legs, late Rana Phase.* He now knew what Fine Orange pottery was all about, and he'd gotten his only laugh out of Clubb by dubbing it "Mex-Maya Tupperware." While not the most patient of teachers, Clubb had certainly been exhaustive.

As a result, Harp was slow to comprehend what the customs man was up to, with his repetition of the phrase "It's new" in regard to the typewriter, and his stacking of Harp's cassettes into several piles, as if to reveal the significance of their number. The man's English was nearly as rudimentary as Harp's *español,* but Harp caught the word "duty" loud and clear. He was about to attempt a fuller explanation of where he was going and what he was going to do there when he noticed that the man had picked the Santana and Billy Joel tapes off of one pile and was turning them over thoughtfully in his hands.

La mordida, Harp thought, but knew enough not to say it aloud. Instead, he nodded at the tapes and raised his eyebrows inquiringly.

"You like American music, señor?"

"*Sí.* Some very much."

"Well, if you see something here you like," Harp suggested, fanning out a hand in a vague gesture of offering and looking away for a moment. When he looked back, the man's hands were empty and the tapes had disappeared.

"*Bienvenidos, señor.* Enjoy your visit."

Enjoy the music, Harp thought, but he didn't say that aloud, either. Just stuffed the rest of the tapes into his shoulder bag, collected his gear, and went to meet Brother Rick, humming a few bars of "Soul Sacrifice."

"HARPO," Brother Rick said with satisfaction, giving him a power shake and then wrapping him in an embrace that made him feel momentarily frail. Harp was about two inches taller but thirty pounds lighter than Rick, maybe forty pounds now, though Rick had the frame to carry it. He also had a full head of dark brown hair and a matching beard, and by god, he *looked* like an archaeologist in his blue work shirt and faded jeans, with a bandanna around his neck and a battered straw hat in his hand. He turned to introduce the two women who were with him, and Harp blinked in surprise and swallowed the greeting he'd had in mind, since neither was Winnie Gordon, Rick's significant other for the past several years. He'd assumed that she'd be along, since she and Rick had met at Baktun.

"This's Rita Gertner, one of Helga Kauffmann's students at Brandeis," Rick said, introducing a short woman who looked about nineteen. Oversize, dark-framed glasses sat upon a curving, Mayanesque nose above an engagingly guileless grin, and her black hair was as naturally curly as Harp's. Among the gear at her feet was the boom box Rick had predicted.

"Great, I brought some tapes," Harp said as he shook her hand. "You like sixties music?"

"The Beatles . . . ?" Rita said tentatively, turning with Rick as Clubb came up to join the group.

"Ollie," Rick said blandly, shaking his hand. "This is . . . "

"I met Mr. Yates on the plane," Clubb interrupted. "I couldn't fully persuade him to accept my interpretation, but you won't have to teach him the ceramic sequence."

"Thank god for *that,*" Rick laughed. "Oh, this's Rita Gertner, one of Helga's students. And Kaaren Seyerstad. Kaaren's doing a postdoc at Arizona while they work up a line for her. Oliver Clubb . . . Harper Yates."

Harp had been sneaking glances at her, trying not to stare, but now that he could, he saw that she was as gorgeous as he'd suspected. Ash-blond hair in a pageboy, flawless peach-tone skin, eyes the blue of a glacial lake. God, even dimples when she smiled, a smile that felt like a reward for being alive to see it.

"Harp," she said, trying the name out. "Rick told me a lot about you on the drive down."

"Uh-oh," Harp said with mock chagrin. "Did he tell you that he's always been a bad influence on me?"

"And where's Winifred?" Clubb was asking. "I expected that she'd be with you."

"Yeah, well, she decided not to come," Rick said with an elaborate shrug. "She landed a big contract job north of Phoenix."

"And she took it?" Clubb said, incredulous. "Brinton's going to be disappointed. He was counting on her to do the on-site osteology."

Rick shrugged again. "I've done some of that, and so has Kaaren. She did her thesis on Anasazi burials."

That diverted Clubb into questions about where Kaaren had done her thesis (Stanford) and with whom she'd worked. He seemed to enjoy looking at her as much as Harp did. For his part, Harp wondered why Rick hadn't said anything about breaking up with Winnie, if that's what this meant. And if he'd driven all the way down from Tucson with Kaaren, how had he kept his eyes on the road? Harp cast a quizzical glance in Rick's direction but couldn't catch his eye, which seemed fishy.

"Whattaya say we haul outta here and get you checked into the Olmeca?" Rick suggested, once Clubb gave him an opening. "Two of Muldoon's recruits got snowed out in Chicago, so we have another day here, at least. Give us time to check out the museum and La Venta Park."

"I've never cared much for zoos," Clubb said disdainfully, as they gathered their gear and started down the low-ceilinged corridor. "And I've always thought it was a terrible way to display the Olmec sculpture."

"Those big heads, you mean?" Harp asked. "They're here?"

"In the park," Rick said, as he and Kaaren swung open a set of glass doors, letting in a blast of tropical air that made Harp realize that the terminal had been air-conditioned. The air seemed to smell of oil and rotting orange rinds.

"Dr. Kauffmann said I shouldn't miss them," Rita Gertner put in eagerly, "and the museum has some of the Yaxchilán lintels."

"They've got some good stuff," Rick agreed, smiling at her enthusiasm. He was carrying her boom box for her, and Kaaren had relieved Clubb of his briefcase. Harp was loaded down like a pack mule and had begun to sweat inside his raincoat, but he could smell flowers and tortillas now, too, and beyond a line of taxis that were all considerably older than Rusty, he could see neon signs blinking in Spanish. He glanced sideways and saw Rita grinning up at him, sharing the pleasure that must've shown on his face.

"We're *here,* huh?" he suggested, and she bobbed her bushy black head, causing her glasses to slide down her nose. She pushed them back up with a finger, her grin still in place.

"No place else I'd rather be. I've wanted to go on a dig since I was twelve."

"You've got a few years on me," Harp allowed. "I've only wanted it since October."

"It's gonna be awesome!" Rita declared, with an unfettered enthusiasm that made him feel old as they went out into the Villahermosa night.

. . .

THE FOUR OF THEM—Rick, Kaaren, Rita, and Harp—were leaning on the guardrail of the fence that surrounded the pool, staring in awe at the creature that lay sprawled out on a small island in the middle. It was perhaps the most fearsome live thing Harp had ever seen, at least twelve feet long from its blunt snout to the tip of its serrated tail, the scutes on its back standing out like notches cut with an ax. It wasn't moving but had its head raised and its huge jaws agape, revealing a glimpse of pinkish membrane behind the rows of sharp, finger-length teeth.

"*Caimán,*" Rick said matter-of-factly.

"Holy moly," Rita murmured.

"Holy shit," Harp said emphatically. "I thought they were supposed to be scrawny things, poor-man's crocodiles."

"That sucker'd eat you regardless of your income level," Rick said with a kind of relish. As they watched, the translucent film covering the *caimán*'s eye suddenly peeled back, revealing a black, extremely predatory pupil. They all recoiled slightly, and Harp saw Kaaren shiver and move a little closer to Rick. Harp shook his head, his envy muted by resignation and a certain relief at the removal of temptation. He'd learned last night that even though Rick hadn't officially broken up with Winnie, he and Kaaren had been sleeping together since their night in Tampico. For numerous complicated reasons, Rick didn't want anyone else to know, and he'd sworn Harp to secrecy before sending him down to the bar so that he and Kaaren could use the room. Harp was willing and able to keep his mouth shut, though their mutual attraction seemed hard to miss as they led the way down the path, their heads inclined toward each other and their bodies rigid with the effort of not touching.

"This's an *awesome* park," Rita said, lingering behind with Harp as he scribbled a description of the *caimán* in his pocket notebook. He glanced around at the dense tangle of vegetation that lined the path and the trees that formed a nearly solid canopy overhead.

"Seems less like a park than a half-tamed forest," he observed. "But that's what makes it neat."

"Are those notes for a novel or a travel article?" Rita asked, peering around his shoulder because she wasn't nearly tall enough to look over it. Harp tucked the notebook away and started them moving up the path.

"I dunno," he admitted. "Villahermosa's not exactly one'a your prime tourist towns, unless you're an oilman or someone who gets off on boomtown squalor. Most people aren't charmed by the smell of crude oil on the breeze."

"Oh, that's not really so bad; you get used to it. The people are nice, and the Olmec sculpture is *fantastic.*"

"That it is," Harp agreed. "It just oughta be somewhere on the way to a nice, white-sand beach. Once they got it on the trucks to bring it here from La Venta, they shoulda just kept going toward Cancún."

"But you just said this was a neat place!"

"I'm not your average tourist," Harp said mildly, pausing to examine some tiny brocket deer that were grazing inside a wire enclosure. Rita made an exasperated hmphing sound that was already beginning to seem familiar. The sound of a vexed enthusiast. Rita had an abundance of what used to be called "pep," and Harp had never been able to help himself around people like that. Age had only made him a little less cruel in his deflationary tendencies.

"Vex pepuli, vex dei," he murmured to himself, as they followed Rick and Kaaren into one of the glades that held the Olmec sculpture. There, in the center of the sunlit clearing, was another of the massive stone heads, a rounded chunk of basalt that was perhaps eight feet high and as many around. The face was commensurately broad and heavy, with thick, protruding lips, a flat nose, and blankly staring eyes, all surmounted by what looked like a tight-fitting helmet. Harp already had the basic description down, so he didn't bother to take out his notebook. He reminded himself, though, that the Olmec had carved these things around 1500 B.C., after hauling the stones an incredible distance to La Venta. Without trucks.

"So . . . whattaya think now, Harpo?" Rick teased. "Does that look like your basic were-jaguar?"

Earlier, they'd been discussing an article that saw a resemblance between certain Olmec carvings and infants afflicted with Down's syndrome. The author had suggested that the Olmecs might've regarded such infants as were-jaguars, supernatural beings worthy of portrayal in stone. Given the enormous distance in time, this speculation set a new standard for boldness, making Clubb seem cautious by comparison.

"Dig the helmet," Rick pointed out. "Could also be a linebacker, or maybe a motorcycle cop."

"The infant on the relief sculpture back there seemed a more likely candidate," Harp allowed. "This guy just looks . . . *thick.*"

"But we don't even know if they were portraying themselves," Kaaren said, "or the image of some god."

"That's right," Rick agreed, showing some uncommon respect.

"I'm also remembering that Von Daniken used these in *Chariots of the Gods,*" Harp recalled, "claiming they were spacemen."

"He made the same claim about the Chacs at Chichén Itzá and Tlalocs at Teotihuacán," Rick said scornfully. "You wanna get tossed outta camp, just bring up Von Daniken around Brinton Taylor. He goes berserk at the notion that 'alien visitors' taught the Maya everything they knew."

"I can't imagine Brinton Taylor going berserk over anything," Kaaren scoffed, and Rita nodded earnestly in agreement.

"Well, it's not *my* kind of berserk," Rick admitted with a grin. "But he has a certain look that can make you feel like you've just shit in the sherd bag. So don't say I didn't warn you!"

Rick laughed loudly, startling a troop of monkeys in the trees overhead, who startled the people below by moving off with much chattering and crashing of branches. Harp looked up and saw a small simian face, surrounded by a ruff of dark, reddish-brown fur, staring down at them with an expression that could only be described as ferociously peeved.

"Howler monkeys," Rick said. "Wait'll you hear them in the wild."

This one chattered irritably and went off after the others, making a racket worthy of an animal twice its size and shaking loose a small shower of leaves and twigs.

"He thinks he's wild enough," Harp said, laughing as a falling twig bounced off his panama. The only one in the glade not laughing was the Olmec, whose stare remained fixed and unamused after three and a half millennia. Harp noticed a distinct resemblance to Oliver Clubb, and he wondered if Brinton Taylor also had that same, terminally serious gaze.

"Onward, boys and girls," Rick urged. "Gotta get a move on if we wanna see the museum before we pick up Muldoon's boys at five."

"I'm glad they gave us a chance to see this," Kaaren said, drawing nods all around.

"Awesome park," Harp said sincerely, but Rita thought he was mocking her and merely hmphed. He shrugged and followed along, deciding that he was probably one of the terminally vexatious.

THE HOTEL OLMECA BAR was just off the lobby, a windowless room that still had Christmas streamers strung across the ceiling and tinsel hanging from the plastic potted palms. Harp and his companions had the large round table wedged into the corner directly opposite the bar, where a couple of men in work clothes were drinking and shaking dice out of a leather cup. There had originally been seven in their group, but Muldoon's boys—Brad and Eric—had moved away as soon as the discussion had begun to get truly rigorous. They were drinking Tecate at a table closer to the bar's color TV, which was showing *The Love Boat* dubbed in Spanish. Harp's glance caught Doc in the process of uttering a typically laconic one-liner, which came out on the sound track as a torrent of rapid *español.* Brad and Eric cracked up at that, nudging each other and slapping the table in front of them hard enough to make it shake.

Harp brought his attention back to his own table, where the topic was the persistence of the Classic tradition at Baktun—not exactly a table-banger, but gripping enough to those involved. Rick and Oliver Clubb were going at it over the significance of the buried ball court, with Kaaren and Rita throwing in occasional questions of their own. Harp probably should've been taking notes, but the communal bottle of mescal—from which they'd all had a shot to toast their venture—had gravitated to the side of the table where he and Rick were sitting, and they'd been chasing down shots with Bohemia beer. Harp saw drunkenness looming just ahead, but at the moment he'd attained a state of lucid detachment that allowed him to observe the interplay of personalities without losing track of the discussion, an authorial trick.

"If the ball game had truly been a major element in their ritual repertoire," Clubb was saying, "one would expect to find more than one court, and certainly one closer to the Main Plaza."

"Not necessarily," Rick argued. "The West Plaza is contemporaneous with the earliest stratas of the Main Plaza—it's not a late addition. Maybe that was the proper place for the ball court, so they kept it there. Or maybe they had a series of them in different places, and they were all either razed or covered with platforms we haven't trenched yet."

Clubb took a small sip from his iceless gin and tonic and raised an eyebrow at Kaaren, who was sitting to his right, at a discreet distance from Rick. "Or perhaps this was the first ball court they'd ever had, and they decided it wasn't for them."

"You're saying it was *new*?" Rick demanded.

"I'm suggesting it could have been a relatively recent experiment. You haven't given us a date on it yet."

"Right, I've been holding out on you," Rick said sarcastically. "C'mon, Ollie, you know how little I got to see before I had to close it up for the season."

"That hasn't stopped you from assuming it has great significance," Clubb said. "Why shouldn't I have an equal right to assume it has much less?"

"All I assumed was the significance the ball game has within the Classic tradition. We have plenty of evidence for that. That's not the same thing as assuming a late date for the ball court simply because we don't have any date at all."

"Both of your hypotheticals assumed longevity," Clubb pointed out with a shrug, as if it were a distinction without a difference.

"But Dr. Clubb," Rita broke in. "If it was an experiment that failed, wouldn't that undermine your larger argument?"

"I wouldn't think so," Clubb decided, before swiveling his head to look at her. Then he pinned her with his eyes. "What's your reasoning?"

Rita blushed, and for a moment she appeared too intimidated to go on. But then she gathered her courage and plunged ahead. "Well . . . wouldn't that mean the ball game was an import from somewhere else? So even if they rejected it, they were being influenced from the outside."

"Good point," Kaaren murmured, and Rick gave Rita a smile that made her blush deepen. Clubb was a little slow in mustering a comeback, though he tried to carry it off with his usual aplomb.

"That would be a Classic influence, though, wouldn't it?"

Rick took him up on that, but Harp suddenly found it hard to listen. Watching Rita stand up to Clubb had broken the spell of his detachment and made him want to get in there and take a side. He remembered the idea that had come to him this afternoon in the museum, when they were looking at the Yaxchilán sculpture and comparing it with that at Baktun. It was a question, actually, and it seemed so simple and basic he was afraid the answer might be obvious to everyone except him. That was one of the perils of being self-taught: He didn't know what everyone was supposed to know, which made every simple question a potentially embarrassing gaffe.

He found his hand creeping toward his shot glass and pulled it back. *Good god, performance anxiety*, he thought. *You're worried about your credibility as a scholar.* He saw that Rick and Clubb had reached a standoff on the ball-court issue. During the lull that followed, Rick lit one of Harp's cigarettes and poured more mescal for himself, grunting in bemusement when he found Harp's glass still full.

"You've been unusually quiet, Mr. Yates," Clubb noted. "Nothing to add?"

"How'd they do it?" Harp blurted, and felt himself blush at the silence that greeted his apparent non sequitur. It occurred to him that he was drunker than he thought.

"How did *who* do *what*?" Clubb inquired.

"The Baktunis. How'd they keep the foreigners out?" That question hung a while. "I mean, these 'Mexicanized Maya' or whatever you want to call them got in everywhere else, either by trade or by force of arms. They may've taken over completely at Seibal. But you were saying this afternoon," he reminded Clubb, "that the images of warriors and captives that appear on the monuments at Yaxchilán and the other sites never showed up at Baktun. Neither did the fine paste pottery, as far as we know. So . . . if they didn't fight back, and they didn't buy in, what *did* they do?"

"You haven't really proposed a mechanism, Oliver," Kaaren agreed, in a thoughtful tone that was a balm to Harp's ears. He reached for his beer and took a long, satisfying pull.

"Barbed wire?" Rick suggested, but Clubb ignored him, frowning as he weighed his response.

"Perhaps they hired mercenaries, or were more warlike than the monuments indicate," he said finally. "If they still had some role as an intermediary for trade with the coast, that might've provided a certain immunity."

"That ended with the fall of the Shell dynasty," Rick said, jumping back in with renewed aggression. "Yet the Kan Cross People carried on for another forty or fifty years. In a Classical fashion, according to you."

"Perhaps they were trading on their past prestige," Clubb shot back, tight-lipped but clearly flailing.

Rick squinted at him. "Just what do you trade when you do that? Coats of arms and family trees?"

"You're trivializing the concept. They had centuries of religious refinement and ceremonial performance, plus their knowledge of the calendar and celestial events. And they had the capacity to preserve and pass it on by means of the hieroglyphs."

"So they were carrying on a brisk trade in wisdom and esoteric knowledge," Rick said derisively. "Just the sort of thing that doesn't show up in the archaeological record, so we can't check it. And I suppose they took something equally perishable in return. How about fast-food burgers and paperback books?"

Clubb suffered their laughter with a bleak but tolerant smile, then used it as an excuse to push back his chair. "I think we've descended from the trivial to the absurd. I'd prefer to get some rest and be fresh for Palenque tomorrow."

"Me, too," Rita agreed, and Kaaren stood up with her. Rick gave Kaaren a veiled glance and poured more mescal for himself and Harp.

"*Buenas noches.* Breakfast's at seven."

"Are you gonna finish that?" Rita asked, lifting her chin at the bottle, which was still about a third full.

"I guess we'll have to," Rick allowed, "unless you wanna stay and help."

"Not on your life. Harp can have my hangover."

"Thanks a bunch," Harp called after her. "I'll let you know what it was like."

LATER, the two of them were alone in the bar. Even the bartender had split, and the TV sat blank and silent, flanked by souvenir Olmec heads wearing Santa hats. Harp noted this distantly, his perceptions tending to spark and then wink out rather quickly, extinguished by the tidal flow of alcohol beneath his skin. He was feeling detachment in many parts of his body but only fleeting moments of lucidity.

"You bought the dream," Rick was saying, perhaps for the second time.

"What dream?"

"The Amurcan dream, as Lyndon woulda said. You thought it was gonna make you rich 'n' famous."

Harp remembered—they were talking about *Ghost Dance.* "Yeah, well, the advance and all the hoopla got my hopes up. But it was more than that. I toldja about the way this one just about wrote itself, didn't I?"

"You said it was an inspired book," Rick said laconically.

"It *was.* The next piece just kept falling into place. That's why it hurt so much to watch it go under so fast. It wasn't just a commercial failure, it was a denial of magic."

"Bullshit, Harp. Only in *your* head. Not in the heads of the people who read it. I lent it to half the people at Rana Verde last season, and they all got off on it. One of the students even painted a T-shirt to look like the ghost shirt on the cover, and claimed it made him impervious to mosquitoes." Rick laughed drunkenly. "He held out for two days before we caught him scratching."

Harp's smile felt crooked. "The cover was supposed to ward off the bullets of unfriendly critics. Not much we could do when most of them didn't even take a shot at it."

"That sucks," Rick agreed. "But how long you gonna let it fuck you up? The book came out over a year ago."

"And it's already being remaindered."

"So? That just means a whole buncha people will buy it for two ninety-eight and be looking for your next one. They can't take back the advance, can they?"

"Nope. We already spent it on the land in Vermont, anyway. The paperback sale was supposed to pay to build a house on it, only there wasn't any paperback sale."

"So pitch a tent," Rick said unsparingly. "If you'd written it to get rich, it wouldn'a been half as good."

Harp grunted but let it go. How'd they get off on that, anyway? He'd been telling Rick about his midnight forays and had him roaring over the Lawn Animals' Christmas. Then he must've said something that put Rick onto the suck-it-up-and-stop-your-sniveling track, but he couldn't remember what it was. Something about elf theft being an antidote for deep literary depression. He'd thought he was still being funny.

With an uncoordinated flourish, Rick poured what was left of the mescal into their glasses, leaving the worm at the bottom of the bottle. "Last drunk for a while. Might as well make it a good one."

"Now you tell me," Harp muttered. "So what's going on with you and Kaaren? I was expecting to get kicked out of the room again tonight."

"We decided we'd better cool it for a while."

"How come? What's with all the secrecy, anyhow? Does Brinton Taylor have a rule against staff members shacking up?"

Rick took a sip of mescal and made a face as sour as the liquor itself. "Brinton's married to his work, and he expects the same dedication from everyone else. Anything that distracts them from their work is a kind of adultery. He has special disdain for people who get distracted by their emotional lives."

"But it's gotta be *more* of a distraction to cool it."

"You're telling me," Rick said with a certain vehemence. Then he looked down at the table and shook his head. "There's also the matter of Winnie."

"You and Winnie met at Baktun, didn't you?"

"Yeah. We were the big camp romance that season. And Brinton winked at it cause she was his favorite grad student at Chicago and I was his protégé from the Field School. Sorta like the son and daughter he never had."

"A match made in archaeological heaven, so to speak."

"For a while, anyway," Rick said with a shrug. "Then about six, eight months ago, she decided she was fed up with academia and went to work for a private outfit that does contract archaeology. She's already second in command and she loves it, especially the pay and the lack of departmental bullshit. If Brinton knows about that, he probably thinks it's some kind of hobby."

"Does he think she's coming to Baktun?"

"I dunno whether she told him or not. She's been outta town half the time and I was up to my ears in the dissertation, so we haven't been communicating real well. I thought that might change once I finished, but it didn't. So

. . . when Kaaren came into the picture . . . there wasn't much left to feel guilty about, y'know?"

Harp studied the label of the empty bottle, which featured a golden eagle soaring above the brand name. He drained his glass and felt synapses take flight over the rolling grey hills of his brain. "Still sounds like adultery, by Brinton's definition. Does Kaaren know all this?"

"We talked about it. She's not real happy, but she wants to make a good impression on Brinton, too. We'll work it out."

Sure you will, Harp thought, but decided not to take his revenge by saying so aloud. He pointed at the bottle instead. "Are we gonna suffer for this tomorrow?"

"Not if we take some Alka-Seltzer before we crash. Mescal tends to be merciful about hangovers."

"Let's crash, then," Harp suggested, and let out a laugh that was half a belch. "Sure wouldn't mind vexing Rita on this one."

4

FOR THE FIRST hour and a half of the drive to Palenque, Harp kept wondering when the rain forest was going to start. But the view out the window remained a constant panorama of open, rolling grassland that was swampy in the low places and supported only a few, random clumps of trees. The only items worth recording in his notebook were the buzzards circling in the sky and the humpbacked Brahma cattle wading through the fields with white egrets stalking around them like sentinels. He finally decided to snatch another twenty-minute meditation, drawing an I-told-you-so hmph from Rita when he closed his eyes. But he felt no compulsion to explain either transcendental meditation or how it collaborated with Mescal the Merciful. He simply let his mantra soothe his nervous system while listening with one ear to the disquisition Clubb was giving on the controversy surrounding the age of the ruler buried in the Temple of the Inscriptions.

When he opened his eyes again, there were hills rising up on his side of the Land Cruiser: lush, thickly forested hills with trees covering even the highest ridges. He blinked in amazement and reached for his notebook, squinting in an effort to penetrate the shadowed mass of greenery. He saw trees growing around, on top, and out of other trees, their trunks wrapped with thick vines and their branches festooned with bright-green epiphytes trailing bunches of long tendrils. Filling the spaces below and between were thorny shrubs that looked like evergreens, plants with waxy leaves the size of serving platters, deep beds of ivy and spear grass, and bursts of red and pink and yellow flowers that glowed like jewels against the dense background of green. The vegetation was almost frightening in its profligacy, and the odor wafting through the half-open window was raw and powerful, like a freshly turned compost heap.

"The steenking jungle," Harp murmured happily, and Rita clicked her tongue at his belated appreciation.

"We're almost there," she informed him. "I thought you were planning to sleep right through."

"Sleep?" he said uncomprehendingly.

"Don't tell me you weren't."

"How can anyone sleep while Pacal's age remains in dispute? Though frankly, I would tend to trust the glyphs rather than a hasty, late-season peek at the bones. Wouldn't you?"

"I . . . I wouldn't trust you about anything," Rita snapped, and turned to look out the window on the other side.

The road zigzagged up the steep hill, completely shaded by the overhanging canopy of the trees, then emerged into the sunlight glaring off the paved surface of a parking lot. There were only a few other cars in evidence, but Rick made a circuit of the lot before finding a semishaded spot to park. Then he held off a rush to the ruins, putting Brad and Eric to work transferring the gear from the rack on top of the Land Cruiser to its interior and assigning Kaaren, Rita, and Harp the task of making sandwiches for the whole group.

"No concessions here," he explained, as he and Harp pulled out the big ice chest they'd filled in Villahermosa. Harp was amenable to the chore, recalling the salutory effect that breakfast had had on the shakiness and sour stomach with which he'd awakened, the sole punishments meted out by Mescal the Merciful. He peeled and sliced avocados and onions while Kaaren and Rita handled the bread and mustard and packaged meat. Clubb, meanwhile, had his camera out and was polishing his lenses and testing his flash attachment.

"I've been here four times," Clubb said as he tinkered, "and this is the first time it hasn't been pouring rain. The *nortes* tend to blow in at this time of the year."

Harp glanced up and saw a single buzzard hovering against the pure Mayan blue of the sky. "You think you'll need the flash?"

"Most of the glyphs are inside, especially those that still have pigment on them. I'm interested in color coding."

"Right," Harp agreed, feeling he should've known that Clubb wouldn't be taking snaps to show his friends back home. "Where are the clubfoot panels?" he asked Rick, who'd taken upon himself the task of opening Cokes. "Did you read that article about physical deformities in the ruling line?"

"God, you sure do glom on to the weird stuff," Rick said, challenging him with a grin. "Two days after he starts studying, he calls me up. Does he wanna know about the glyphs or the Long Count or how to read an eclipse table? Nooo, he wants to know about hallucinogenic enemas!"

Harp shrugged and grinned at their laughter. "And penis perforators," he added, making Rita blush pink under her baseball cap.

"I read the article," Clubb said. "I thought the evidence of acromegaly was somewhat persuasive, but the alleged clubfoot is more likely a stylized dance pose."

"The Stroll," Harp suggested.

"The Hokey-Pokey, I'd say," Rick insisted, grinning widely when Kaaren broke up laughing.

"What's the Hokey-Pokey?" Rita asked.

"Late Classic Amurcan Party ritual, before your time," Harp said, standing up next to Rick to demonstrate. As they linked arms chorus-line fashion, Harp realized that this kind of clowning was a ritual, too, one that went way back with them. As long as they could make each other laugh, everything was all right.

They were putting their left feet back in when they were interrupted by the arrival of two extra-long red vans that swung around the lot and parked nearby. Each was piloted by a young couple who were obviously driver and guide, and each contained about twenty passengers, American tourists whom Harp judged to be Terminal Late Classic in age, that is, somewhere between fifty-five and seventy-five. They were all wearing oddly shaped red name tags pinned to their blouses and sport shirts, and they spent a long, noisy time getting organized before the guides led them off toward the entrance kiosk.

"Uh-oh, the infamous Red-taggers," Rick said. "Might as well take our time now."

"Who're they?" Kaaren asked.

"A tour group from Illinois, though the people come from all over. I ran into a buncha them here two seasons ago. They fly into Mérida, get bussed out to Uxmal and Chichén Itzá, then take the train to Palenque and Oaxaca before winding it up in Mexico City. It'd be a pretty good tour, except they run them through the ruins in a couple of hours."

"How long do we have?" Rita asked anxiously, glancing up from her lunch meat.

"The rest of the day. And believe me, it'll get better when they're gone. Whatever you do, try not to get hooked into taking their pictures for them."

"Don't be so churlish, Richard," Clubb scolded. "They still pay the full fee, and it takes some volume to keep a place like this even minimally solvent."

"*You* take their pictures, then," Rick told him, and laughed wickedly. "Most of the ladies seemed to have some pigment on them."

"That *is* churlish," Kaaren groaned, and Rick laughed again.

"Like I said: no concessions."

THE TRAIL into the ruins led directly to the Temple of the Inscriptions, which stood atop a nine-tiered pyramid that was built into the tree-shrouded hill behind it. *My first temple,* Harp thought, standing back to take a good, long look at it from below. He knew that it wasn't one of the biggest or most spectacular of the Mayan temples, but its proportions seemed perfect, so that it struck the eye with a force that was satisfying rather than daunting. The central staircase rose up out of the terraced front of the pyramid, widening as it descended, like a runway to the shrine above. Brad and Eric were already halfway up, taking the steps two at a time, and a trio of Red-taggers were almost to the bottom, though still hanging on to each other and leaning backward to keep their balance.

Harp waited until the three Red-taggers were down before he started his climb, finding immediately that the steep, narrow steps had not been conceived with size-eleven feet in mind. Rita had started up with him, but she quickly shot out ahead, showing her temple experience by zigzagging from side to side. *She's Mayan size,* Harp thought ruefully. He knew a similar traverse would make it much easier for him, but he wanted to go straight up, figuring that that was probably how it was properly done. So he adopted a stately, somewhat pigeon-toed pace, climbing on the balls of his feet with his head erect and his body leaning into the incline. He tried to imagine doing this in one of the costumes he'd seen on the lintels and stelae in the museum, with a twenty-pound jade belt around his waist and one of those towering feather headdresses that looked like a drum major's nightmare. It suddenly occurred to him that the spears and staves they often carried were probably good for balance during climbs like this. Otherwise, you'd have to be feeling pretty holy to keep your eyes fixed on the temple and resist the temptation to watch where you were putting your feet.

The strain on his calves and thighs finally forced him to stop and rest about three quarters of the way up. He resisted rather easily the urge to look back, already seeing too much open space out of the corners of his eyes and feeling the first, prickly stirrings of acrophobia. He forced himself to go the rest of the way straight up, though, arriving at the top platform half out of breath. He got himself well away from the edge before turning, pulling off his panama and mopping the sweat from his forehead with his handkerchief.

Then he let himself look, and felt a surge of gratification that made him smile what he knew was an utterly foolish smile. The whole site was spread out before him: ornate, vaguely Oriental constructions of stone and stucco that stood on raised platforms or small hills of their own, surrounded by cleared areas of emerald-green grass. The darker green of the forest, softened by a veil of hanging mist, closed in around the site on three sides, but on the fourth the view opened out over the billowing tops of the trees to the broad green sweep of the savanna below, which extended all the way to the horizon. And over it all a sky of the purest, unsullied blue. An exclamation of sheer delight rose and caught in Harp's throat, and he didn't know how to let it out. A laugh seemed as inadequate as any of the words that came to mind, and he was afraid of letting loose a disrespectful howl.

He was distracted from his reverie by the appearance of Rita, who came out onto the platform wrinkling her nose in disgust.

"Somebody's smoking inside the shrine," she reported with a backward toss of her head. Then she saw the way he was staring out at the site and immediately raised her camera, swiveling from side to side in a vain attempt to frame a shot. "I don't have the lens to do it justice."

"I don't have the words," Harp murmured.

Rita tipped her head back and squinted up at him from under the bill of her baseball cap, the Pentax poking out of her chest like a third breast. "I can't believe it. You sound almost humble."

"It happens," Harp said, shrugging and smiling what he realized was a sheepish smile. He shook himself and popped his hat back onto his head. "You ready to brave the smoke for a look at Pacal's tomb?"

"I'm ready if you are," Rita declared. "But you should look at the glyphs inside the shrine first. They're really beautiful, and I can show you Pacal's birthdate."

"Lead the way," Harp said, turning toward the shrine. "Believe it or not, I'm willing to be shown. . . . "

AFTER CROSSING the small river (barely a trickle in this season) that ran through the site, Harp and Rita came up alongside the man-made hill that supported the Temple of the Sun. All three temples of the Cross Group stood on artificial eminences, facing inward from the western, northern, and eastern sides of what must once have been a common plaza, but was now an uneven, grassy swale. They were small, elegant structures with wide doorways, mansard roofs, and the remains of tall roof combs that had probably once been stuccoed and painted like sacred billboards.

Harp had lagged behind to jot down a description of a bird flying by overhead, which he decided had to be a toucan. Its bright yellow bill was as long as the rest of its body, which it propelled through the air with rapid beats of its short, black wings. When he finally got around to the front of the hill, Rita was almost halfway up, nearly to the restored segment of the staircase. Harp knew that the Temple of the Sun was the only one of the three to have undergone any significant restoration, but a sudden impulse made him turn away and head for the northern eminence that supported the Temple of the Cross.

Caroline, he thought with a mixture of longing and guilt. The few days he'd been away seemed much longer than that, and while he'd gotten off a brief letter, he hadn't truly had her on his mind. He'd been too busy dealing with the web of personalities in which he'd become enmeshed in a startlingly short period of time. He realized that he hadn't really been alone since he landed, a strange and somewhat overwhelming circumstance for someone who ordinarily spent *most* of his time that way. He'd often described himself as a "self-made loner," a reference to the hard weaning from company he'd undergone during his years in Canada, an exile that had begun as a political gesture and had gradually become a vocational choice. It'd been a while since he'd enjoyed the experience of being one of the crew.

He was still climbing the hill, following the narrow path beaten down through the grass and scrub and the humps of ancient, jumbled stone, when Rita let out a shrill whistle to get his attention. She was standing in front of the Sun temple, her palms raised in a quizzical gesture. She pointed to the temple behind her and made an "Okay" sign, then to the Cross temple, making wiping motions with both hands. Harp just smiled and waved back and went on. He wanted to *see* the panel he'd shown Caroline in the library stacks, on his way to seducing her. The memory caused a distinct swelling in his groin and gave him a fresh shot of stamina, propelling him up the hill.

He didn't pause to examine the moss-draped roof comb or the crumbling stucco sculptures on the front of the temple. He went right for the panel on the back wall—and discovered almost immediately that the panel wasn't there. The panels on the interior jambs were in place, the attendant warrior and the smoking shaman facing each other across the open space of the doorway, but the large central panel with the cross and the muan bird was nowhere to be seen. He studied the jamb panels for a while, vaguely wondering if that was a controlled substance the shaman was smoking. He glanced again at the place where the panel should have been.

"Talk about running into a blank wall," he mumbled, and went back out and sat on the edge of the disintegrating platform. He dug a cigarette out of the long-sleeved shirt tied around his waist and lit up, gazing over at the Temple of the Foliated Cross, an even more dilapidated structure on the hill to the east. He wondered if he should regard the vanished panel as a bad omen, a symbol of the true state of affairs between himself and Caroline. What if she went back home to her folks and decided she could do without her elf-stealing, unemployed, erstwhile househusband? Or could do better, like with some slick, unctuous power in the profession? Janet had dumped him with as little advance warning, though she'd claimed he should've seen it coming.

Harp didn't really believe that his marriage was in that kind of trouble, but he felt obligated to entertain the doubt, on the grounds that you couldn't subscribe to only half of the mystical package. If the gods were still sending messages, you had to read them all, taking the bad jokes along with the rare gifts.

Gradually, though, the warmth of the sunlight and the quiet beauty of his surroundings began to make brooding seem ungrateful, if not downright sacrilegious. The Red-taggers had departed shortly after noon, and at the moment the only person in sight was a workman chopping brush on the other side of the grassy "plaza." The man's machete flashed rhythmically in the light, but the intervening distance reduced the sound to a muted chipping that blended in with the calls of birds in the forest. It occurred to Harp that Pacal had probably never had it this good. The temples might've been whole and gloriously painted and the plaza clear and level, but he never would've had it all to himself. *So who am I to bitch?* Harp thought, and decided to accept the omen as a warning and a challenge: Watch out—it could all disappear.

Rita was out in front of the Temple of the Sun, snapping photos of the stucco sculptures that decorated the roof and wall piers. Then she capped the camera and headed in his direction, a short, bandy-legged figure in shorts and hiking boots, a canteen slung over her shoulder and a Boston Red Sox cap pulled down over her curls. She'd told him—in an early conversation, before he'd started vexing her—that she'd wanted to be a shortstop until the age of twelve, at which point she'd come upon a magazine article that featured color pictures of Copán, one of the premier Mayan sites. It was unlike anything she'd ever seen before, and the female archaeologist in one of the photos gave her her new calling. She was so hooked that she'd traded her Sweet Sixteen party for a trip to Copán and Tikal, and she'd turned down Smith and Radcliffe in order to study with Helga Kauffmann at Brandeis.

Harp had remarked at the time that she'd gone straight from childhood to a career, and while she'd given him the whole, long list of her extracurricular activities, she hadn't convinced him that she'd had a real life outside the classroom. There was no mention of parties or dates, and she recalled her advanced placement courses with a fondness usually reserved for the big game or the senior prom.

She climbed the hill with the same single-mindedness, not looking up until she'd reached the end of the path, about fifteen feet from where he sat. While she caught her breath, she lifted up her camera and framed him for a shot. He'd lit another cigarette, and he let it dangle roguishly from his lips, knowing that he looked like Panama Red with his face shadowed and his hair bushing out from under the brim. It was in a way traditional; a lot of the old Mayan hunters had looked like prospecting bandits out of a John Huston film.

Rita snapped the picture and came up to offer him the canteen, waving her free hand at the cigarette.

"Must you?"

"I'm communing with the spirit of the old dude on the jamb panel," Harp said, though he took a last drag and tamped it out in the dirt.

"He's one of the Lords of the Underworld," Rita informed him, peeking inside the temple. "I was trying to warn you. The Cross Panel's in the museum in Mexico City."

Harp made a sound he realized was a hmph. "Carried off by a power in the profession, no doubt."

"What's that supposed to mean?" Rita asked, peering under the brim of his hat. "Are you okay? I was watching you through the telephoto, and you looked sorta sick, or depressed."

"Just testing," Harp said, and gave her a smile. "I'm fine. I think I just needed to be alone for a while. Nothing personal."

"I was inside the temple for ten minutes before I realized you weren't with me," she admitted sheepishly. "I was reading the Initial Series out loud to you."

"Sorry I missed it. You do that real well."

Rita yanked his hat down over his eyes. "There you go again, making fun!"

"Please . . . spare the hat, huh? It's my only protection against a sunburned brain. And I'll try not to make fun of you. You just gotta be a little less *earnest* all the time, because that makes it irresistible."

Rita squinted at him, causing her glasses to ride up her nose. "What's wrong with being earnest?"

"Nothing, when practiced in moderation. In excess, it leaves you defenseless against the inevitable disappointments and betrayals. Whatta you do when you make an earnest effort and still wind up getting screwed?"

Rita seemed to redden slightly. "Try harder."

"What if you try harder and it doesn't help? What if you see that the failure's not your fault, but you're still the one who's failed?"

"That hasn't happened to me."

"No? No one's ever tried to thwart you? Nobody ever told you that maybe you should give up archaeology and go into English or nursing or something more feminine?"

"No, well, maybe once . . . but I didn't listen. Now you sound like a feminist."

"My wife's a feminist," Harp snorted. "I'm just a fellow traveler."

"I think you're totally cynical."

"Is that the opposite of totally naïve?"

"That's what you think I am, don't you?" Rita demanded. "I bet you weren't this cynical when you were my age."

Harp considered it for a moment. "No. But I was getting there. There was this thing called the Vietnam War going on at the time, and it was all anyone needed to become cynical."

"Were you . . . did you go there?" Rita asked, sounding a bit chastened.

"No way I was gonna go there, as long as we were killing people. I went to Canada instead."

"You were a draft dodger?" Rita blurted, eyes wide behind her lenses. Harp gave her a tolerant smile.

"It was an honorable calling, at the time. And technically, I ended up a conscientious objector. But I went to great lengths to make myself objectionable."

"I can believe that," Rita allowed, though she seemed to be in a kind of shock compounded of disbelief and incomprehension. Too stunned to hmph. Harp stood up and resettled his hat.

"Well, now that you know the ugly truth about my patriotism," he suggested mildly, "wanna go check out the Foliated Cross?"

"I don't mean to judge you," Rita said hastily. "I just never met anyone . . . like that."

"We're all over the place," Harp assured her. "You wanna read about it, I've got a copy of my first novel I can lend you. It's called *War College.*"

"Really? You actually wrote about dodging the draft?"

"About how I got there, anyway," Harp laughed. "They can't arrest me for that."

"I'd *love* to read it," Rita said eagerly, and for once Harp felt no urge to deflate her. He simply nodded and gestured for her to lead the way, scooping up the canteen and falling in behind her as she went down the path. They had just reached the bottom when suddenly something started roaring in the forest, a hoarse, bestial roar so loud it seemed to break over them in echoing waves. Harp froze in his tracks, his mind telling him *bears* or *lions* but not believing either.

"What the hell is *that*?" he blurted, in a voice that rose almost to a squeak. The workman across the plaza heard him, Harp noticed, and seemed to be laughing. Rita was most definitely laughing.

"*Choven,*" she said in some foreign tongue, grinning at his bewilderment. "Howler monkeys."

The beasts roared again, sounding like a pack of banshees getting it on inside an echo chamber. Harp shook his head, able to think of only one thing to say.

"Wild . . ."

THE SUN was going down behind the trees, turning the sky a golden blue and casting long, leafy shadows across the parking lot. The white egrets were going by overhead in ragged vees, their long necks tucked back in a curl against their chests. The five who had returned were sitting around the Land Cruiser, sipping Cokes from the ice chest and waiting for Clubb and Kaaren to join them. Rita was inside the vehicle, avidly reading Harp's novel, and Brad and Eric were sprawled out on the grass nearby, arguing languidly about Big Ten basketball. Rick had bummed a cigarette from Harp, and the two of them were sitting with their backs against the front bumper, gazing at the Palace Tower in the distance while they smoked and talked. Harp was feeling whipped, many years beyond nineteen, but he could see that this had just been a detour for Rick, who was getting revved up to hit the road for Rana Verde.

"They were in the palace, last I saw them," Harp reported wearily. "Clubb was giving her a deluxe tutorial in the glyphs, and she seemed to be soaking it up."

"She needs to. The field's nearly as new to her as it is to you."

"She gets a bit more respect from Clubb than I got. They stopped and looked at the clubfoot panels with us, though."

"And? What was the consensus?" Rick asked, smirking through his beard.

"Hokey-Pokey. Though we also had one vote for chronic foot cramps due to a lack of salt in the diet. One of Muldoon's boys took a sports medicine course at Illinois to satisfy his gym requirement."

Rick blew out a cloud of smoke and laughter. "I like the practical application of irrelevant knowledge, I really do. But he should also consider the fact that there's a ball court here, and where you had the ball game, chances are you also had salted peanuts."

"No doubt," Harp agreed. "This probably all belongs in *American Antiquity.*"

"Right! 'The Role of Ball Game Concessions in Lowland Maya Subsistence Patterns.' "

They tossed the idea back and forth for a while, amusing themselves but gradually becoming half-serious about its potential as a satiric monograph. Harp found the strength to start writing some of it down in his notebook, but he almost fell over when Rick sat up with an abruptness that shook the bumper.

"You're *not* gonna believe this. Look!"

Harp followed his gaze and saw a man limping across the grass at a rapid rate, heading at an angle toward the path that led into the ruins. He was Mexican, wearing a blue shirt and black pants that fit him badly and appeared torn, his head and feet bare. Harp was about to ask what was so unbelievable when he suddenly perceived the cause of the man's limp. His right foot was fixed in a rigid curl that made him rise up on his toes before coming down hard on his other foot, lurching sideways to throw the stiff foot forward.

"That's *it,* exactly," Harp said in an awed whisper. "Right off the panels."

"So much for the Hokey-Pokey theory," Rick concluded. "Dude's really trucking along, too."

The man was, in fact, going much faster than Harp could imagine himself moving at the moment, even on two, unclubbed feet. He got to the path just as Clubb and Kaaren came over the rise, but he limped past them without slowing or offering a greeting. Kaaren's head swiveled to watch him pass, her blond hair fanning out beneath the brim of her panama, but Clubb was talking to her and didn't so much as glance sideways.

"Did you see him?" Rita asked from behind them, her voice urgent with excitement. "Did you see him?"

"Sure did," Rick called back. "Pacal's bones may be gone, but his foot's still in the gene pool."

"My mind is blown," Harp said helplessly.

"But after thirteen hundred years?" Rita queried, sounding helpless in her own way.

"Could just be a coincidence," Rick allowed. "But he didn't look like a tourist to me."

"He had Pacal's nose, too," Rita added softly. Harp rubbed his eyes and shook himself, feeling drained and giddy at the same time. Then he looked out at the Palace Tower, silhouetted against the fading sky, and spoke to no one in particular.

"I wonder if they make him pay to get in . . . "

5

New Belvedere

As CAROLINE JERKED the suitcase up and heaved it in ahead of her, the storm door whooshed shut on her back, nudging her through the doorway. She shook rain from her hair and switched on the living room lights, seeing at a glance that everything was as intact and tacky as she'd left it. The tales of suburban squalor with which she'd regaled her family—borrowing freely from Harp's diatribes—really hadn't done it justice. Of course they'd thought she was exaggerating just to shock them.

Leaving the suitcase at the foot of the stairs, she went through the house quickly, flicking on lights and turning the thermostat up to a habitable temperature. The long drive through fog and icy rain from Dulles had left her enervated and edgy, so she made herself a cup of tea and added a liberal dose of brandy. Judy and Willard had collected the mail and piled it in neat stacks on the dining room table, and Caroline stood looking at it wearily, thinking there was much too much for only a week's absence. She didn't want to resume her professional life just yet; one tired drive through the fog and rain was enough.

Then she saw a blue airmail envelope sticking out of a stack and took a chance, letting out a small squeal of delight when she saw the return address of the Hotel Olmeca in Villahermosa, Tabasco, along with a portrait of a stone head that seemed to be wearing a helmet. Then she noticed another blue envelope in a different stack and was rewarded a second time. This one had a typewritten address (on her typewriter), and he'd crossed out the Olmeca return and typed in a P.O. box in Comitán de Domínguez, Chiapas. The postmark was about a week later than the first.

"You get a gold star, Harp," she said aloud, and took the two envelopes and her cup into the living room, where she wrapped an afghan around her legs and sank into the depths of the sofa. The first letter was handwritten on notebook paper, in Harp's distinctive, childish mix of printed and cursive lettering. It was dated the day he'd left, for which she silently gave him another star.

Dear One:

Welcome home! I'm assuming this won't reach you before you leave for Vancouver, but I thought it would be nice to have something waiting for you when you got back. Don't know how long I'll last, since I'm whipped out from a long day of travel, which included meeting and matching wits with Oliver Clubb (of Persistence Theory fame) on the plane. You would've been proud of my display of rigor; I almost had myself convinced that I knew something.

At the moment, I've been exiled to the hotel bar because Rick's upstairs in our room with another member of the crew, a gorgeous blond postdoc named Kaaren who drove down with him from Tucson. For reasons I don't fully understand, Rick has sworn me to secrecy, so a little while ago I had to pretend (to an undergrad crew member named Rita who'd spent some time telling me about her teenage obsession with the Maya) that I really wanted to stay and have another beer by myself rather than crashing for the night. I think she already has me pegged as an alcoholic wastrel.

So how was your visit to the Western Front? I remember that house too well, the lair of Emily and the Grand Dragon, with its slate floors and huge fireplace and soft leather sofas. And the view out the back of the mountains and the Georgia Strait, which Ian always showed off as if he'd built them himself. Did you succumb to the urge to take him up on his let's-happily-pillage-the-environment rap? How about the urge to drink too much? I usually gave in to that, on the theory that it made Emily seem warmer. Does that still work? Did it ever? It was, in any event, a good excuse to drink. Better than the one I have now.

Beginning to fade and still no sign of Rick. Gonna have to sprinkle saltpeter on his huevos rancheros if he keeps this up. Just wanted to say that I love you and I'm sorry I wasn't there to suffer the familial embrace with you. I wish I could be with you now to hear the atrocity stories and groan sympathetically in all the appropriate places. If you wrote them down in a letter, I could sympathize from a distance. It's not the same but it'll have to do, till the real thing comes along.

love,
Harp

Caroline sipped brandied tea and sank deeper into the sofa, feeling the latest in a long line of guilt pangs. She'd been so shitty to him before he left, blaming him for what her parents made her feel. She'd even done it in their preferred mode: the prolonged and pointless guilt trip. She'd seen it all so clearly in Vancouver, in that house, which was just as he'd remembered it. Except now Emily was the one who drank, and Ian the Grand Dragon had lost some fire to the drugs that kept his blood pressure in check. Neither had been able to drive her to drink, and she hadn't returned in need of sympathy.

The second envelope was plastered with stamps, to compensate for the weight of the four sheets inside, which were thick with single-space type. A veritable field report.

Domingo
The Hut of Usher

Dear One:

Here it is, the middle of my fifth day at Baktun, finally a Sunday, the only official day of rest. Boy, can I use it. Brinton Taylor hosted a midday brunch with rum punch and lots of shop talk on a more civilized level than the usual day-to-day. They're probably still at it, smoking the real Havanas Brinton got from his friend the Mexican Minister of the Interior (impressive dude, Brinton, though that'll have to wait for another letter & a better grasp on the man).

As an alternative, Ulysses Cole took a bunch of the young and/or indefatigable off for an afternoon of what he calls "bushwhacking." Needless to say, I fit neither category, and not even a loss of macho could make me pretend. I'm past the outright pain of the first couple mornings after, and last night I stayed awake for a whole hour after supper. I will no doubt survive and may even round into shape eventually. But jeez, this archaeology is fucking *hard* work. Tossing stones and shoveling dirt, humping the wheelbarrow, shaking the screening box, whacking the bush with a machete on the survey crew. The Mexican workmen do most of the really heavy stuff, but when you're part of a crew (and not the supervisor), you tend to take up whatever task is next and nearest, whether it rightfully belongs to you or to, say, Vicente. At least *I* tend to, partly out of instinctive Midwestern work ethic (do your share), and partly because I know that Vicente is watching. Besides, I can't pretend that I'm better than Vicente & company at the "finer" things (reading depths & levels, stringing grids, brush & trowel work) that might be thought to belong to gringos. Some of the students unconsciously observe the racist pecking order and then don't know why no one comes to help them when they get stuck. I get stuck often enough to be properly humble.

But lemme tell you how I came to have a room of my own, a privilege otherwise reserved for the high muckety-mucks like Brinton and Helga

Kauffmann (who isn't here yet but has a guest hut waiting for her). Because Brinton has an unusually large number of fully fledged archaeologists on the staff (eight; most digs have one or two), the camp has an unusual number of buildings, laid out in a horseshoe pattern around a patch of forest that's been thinned out into a kind of park. (And all in the literal shadow of the Temple of Kan Shell, the biggest and best-restored pyramid at the site.) The lab and the dining hall are at the apex, two long, open buildings with overhanging thatched roofs and screened sidewalls, the only places with electric lights. On the south side of the "park" are Brinton's hut, the guest hut that Helga is expected to occupy, and a two-room hut shared by Rick and Oliver Clubb. The common folk are on the north side, in two identical barracklike buildings, the women's & men's dorms in that order, screened off from each other by a small grove of shade trees.

When we rolled in five days ago, I was sent down to the men's lodge along with Brad and Eric, a couple of burly frat boys from Illinois who aren't even anthro majors and who seem to regard the world as their summer camp (but can those suckers *work*). We got there to find that there were only two remaining spaces in which to hang a hammock, and since I was at least ten years older than all the other guys and the only one not still in school, the role of odd man out naturally fell to me. Someone suggested that Ulysses Cole and Emory Muldoon might have room in their hut, which was the next one down. So I moseyed in that direction and found Ulysses at home, storing what looked like canned goods in a trunk in the back corner. The hut was easily large enough for four, though they'd filled some of the extra space with trunks and specimen boxes and a trestle table. There was even an extra hammock hanging on a peg in the far corner.

I've since learned that Ulysses is the camp maniac, a kind of hyperactive legend. He collects butterflies and insects and always has a bunch of makeshift experiments going on—things like tree cropping and fishing and replicating a native garden. He also organizes bushwhacking expeditions and moon watches and relay races up the sides of pyramids (with a beer chugged at every level). His written work has the same sort of eager empiricism, and I always figured him for someone I would like. He's about my height and lanky, with hair and beard redder than yours and a high-cheekboned, hollow-cheeked New England kind of face. He always wears army fatigues and a web belt loaded down with canteen, flashlight, trowel, and godknows what else. Looks like a walking Swiss army knife.

On this occasion, I'd walked in before knocking, and he reacted as if I'd caught him masturbating. He actually backed me out of the cabin while I was trying to introduce myself. The first thing he said to me (without bothering to introduce himself) was: "You're kind of old for student labor, aren't you?" I admitted that I should've been old enough to know better, trying to lighten him up, but then he spotted the typewriter and started sneering at it, asking if it doubled as a chainsaw or something useful. At which point, I told him to forgive my toolish ignorance, but I was looking for a place to sleep, and was there any room here or not? (There was, of course; I could see it.) But he said not, so I said thanks for nothing and started back the way I'd come.

He let me go a ways, then called out and pointed through the trees to a small, dilapidated hut about 25 yards further north. He told me that they'd used it last season and while it might need some fixing, it was probably still sound. Then he grinned and said that the army ants had gone through it recently, so I wouldn't have to worry about vermin in the walls or thatch. He seemed to enjoy telling me that enormously.

But I went to check it out, and the rest, as they say, belongs to the annals of jungle gentrification. The mud plaster had eroded in lots of places and sprouted weeds in others, and the thatch is so brittle it looks like it might disintegrate in the first rain. But nothing really horrible had taken up residence, and there was a dorm bed with decent springs but no mattress, a couple of empty packing crates as tables and storage, and a broom to rout out the spiders. I got a mattress, screens for the window and netting for the door, a folding chair, candles and a flashlight, and a hurricane lamp I have to use sparingly because kerosene is in short supply. Since I'd already stolen a water glass and an ashtray from the Hotel Olmeca, I was all set.

I must admit that it was kind of spooky the first couple nights, with bugs wapping against the screens and critters rustling around in the thatch (made me yearn for a return of the ants), and even larger critters doing their nightly business outside (made me yearn for a more substantial door). But I got used to it, and the noise I hear from the men's lodge makes me glad I'm not there. Somebody has a fetish for Peter Frampton and plays "Baby, I Love Your Way" at least once every night. My hut is on the path to a small cenote nearby (a sinkhole in the limestone, like the quarry we used to swim in in Vermont), and I go down there every morning to wash at a place where some of the water seeps out, checking out the night's tracks and listening to the howler monkeys roar at the rising sun. Saw a pair of scarlet macaws yesterday morning and it buoyed me up all day.

I hear Peter Frampton; why didn't somebody take that guy out bushwhacking and lose him? Did you ever get my last letter? Better save this for me, cause this may be the only writing I can do until I build up some stamina. I miss you and wish I could take you to the cenote and show you the view from the top of Kan Shell's temple. You can see all the way to the Lacantún River and beyond, into Guatemala. Group B is in that direction, but we've been told to keep our distance from the river, lest we be mistaken for guerrillas or smugglers by the Guatemalan army patrols that keep an eye on the border. Apparently they're not real friendly.

The Frampton fanatic appears to be temporarily sated, so I think I'll grab a second meditation while I can. You oughta give it another try yourself—helps lighten the daily sensory overload. Not that I don't love your Way, just the way it is. Write and tell me about it; make me a happy camper with a letter from home.

loveya,
Harp

Caroline sighed, sorry there wasn't more to read, then stuffed the letters back into their envelopes, making a mental note to start a file. How long had it been since they'd corresponded? She'd almost forgotten how good his letters were, the way he had of throwing his voice on the page. God, she had so much to tell him, so much she'd figured out while walking Wreck Beach in the rain, or just sitting at the dinner table, watching her mother finish the wine.

She emptied her cup and struggled up out of the sofa, thinking she'd get started on it right now, since it usually took her a couple tries to get into a letter. But as soon as she reached her feet the fatigue hit her, cushioned by the brandy but still too powerful to resist. No gold stars for her; Harp would have to wait another day for her reply. Her suitcase could wait, too, and she made only a halfhearted attempt to turn out the lights.

But as she staggered up the stairs, the phrase that had come to her so often in Vancouver came to her again. It had to do with elf stealing, and Harp not writing, and how quickly they'd turned that whole disturbing episode into an amusing memory. As if it'd never happened. *Denying the collapse.* She knew she'd copped the phrase from something Harp'd told her about the Maya, but she couldn't remember what, or even if she had it right. Tomorrow, she resolved, tomorrow she'd write and ask him, and tell him what it meant to her. What he meant to her. She took that memory to sleep with her, and went under so fast she never noticed she was alone in the bed.

Baktun

WITH BRINTON GONE to Mexico City to confer with the Pemex brass, Sunday dinner wasn't anything special, and no one hung around afterward to talk. Ulysses led one bunch off to visit Tigrillo, a minor ceremonial center about five kilometers to the east, and Katie Smith's daughter, Lucy, talked her mother and Muldoon and a few others into going for a swim in the cenote. Rick gave Kaaren an inquiring glance, wondering if he dared to propose a quickie in the jungle, but she just laughed and said she was going to wash her hair and write some letters. He said he'd check on her later and she was agreeable, indicating, he thought, that the rejection was neither personal nor permanent. He reminded himself to do some washing of his own, now that yesterday's rain had filled the shower tanks.

He looked around for Harp next and was surprised to find that he'd already left. Rick had distinctly heard him turn down Katie's offer to join the swim club, and he surely wasn't going to go off with Ulysses. Which left writing or sleeping, either of which made him eligible for interruption, to Rick's way of thinking. So, after checking that all the supplies and equipment were secure and the vehicles locked up (Brinton had left him nominally in charge), he grabbed a quart bottle of beer and went down past the women's and men's lodges, turning north on the cenote path, which wound through a grove of corozo palms. Lots of young plants had sprung up in the spaces between the mature trees, which had been stripped of their fronds for thatch, so his eye-level vision was obscured until he came into the clearing where the hut stood.

And there was Harp, in only shorts and sneakers, standing with his back to the path, doing something to the wall of the hut. *Plastering,* Rick realized, as Harp took a trowelful of reddish glop out of the bucket in his other hand and slapped it into a hole in the wall. His awkward, half-frantic motion made it clear that he'd never laid any brick, but most of the glop was sticking, and he was quick to smooth it into place. He already had about half of the wall patched.

Rick grinned and sidled forward, examining the holes Harp'd dug to obtain some of his materials, which consisted of three separate piles of sand, red dirt, and limestone marl. The holes still held water from yesterday's rain, and Harp had used one of them as a basin for his plaster mix. Harp turned just then, and Rick laughed out loud: Harp's arms were dusted white with limestone powder, and his face and torso were liberally smeared with streaks of red. With his hair bushing out limply beneath the bandanna around his forehead, he looked like a hippie in full war paint.

"Half on the wall, half on yourself?" Rick suggested. "You look like a refugee from Woodstock."

"Hey . . . so I'm not neat. But look, this shit actually works!" he exclaimed, waving his trowel at the wall. "I was just tinkering when I started out, but this really does the job."

Rick handed him the bottle and poked at one of the patches with a finger, finding it reasonably firm. "It does, at that." He turned back, gesturing at all the implements and the heaps of materials. "Lot of work just to make plaster, though. Why didn't you just grab a bag of mortar mix from the supply shed?"

Harp grimaced and rubbed his chin with the back of his forearm, adding another streak of red to his half-grown beard. "I tried that. But I misread the Spanish and took the wrong stuff, and then Cole caught me coming out of the shed and gave me so much shit that I just said fuckit."

"You shoulda asked me . . . "

"Yeah, I know, but it was actually more fun this way. I asked Vicente what he'd use to fix a house, and he gave me a whole demonstration: handful of this, handful of that, this much *agua.* All the other guys started kibitzing, giving me their family formulas and giving each other shit. If I understood more Spanish and a little Mayan, I could've written a monograph."

"Jesus, that's a page out of Ulysses's own book," Rick snorted. "The Practical Ethnographer. What is it with you two, anyway? Did you say something to piss him off?"

"Didn't have to. The guy acted like a prick the first time he laid eyes on me. Kicked me outta his hut like he didn't even want me to *see* it. What's he got in all those trunks and boxes?"

"Specimens, mostly. Bugs and bats and all kinds of gruesome things. I guarantee you wouldn't want to see his collection of local leeches."

"That's what he made me feel like," Harp said shortly, handing the bottle back and taking up his trowel. Rick drank and watched him work for a few moments, trying to make sense of the encounter, which didn't sound like Ulysses at all. He was impatient with people who fucked up or couldn't keep up, but usually it took some provocation to make him ornery. And he was usually eager to show off his specimens . . .

"Wait a minute—was this the day we arrived?" Rick asked, and Harp nodded without turning around. "That explains it, then. You caught him filling his bribe box."

That brought Harp around.

"You ever notice that there aren't any vending machines around here? Yeah? Well, Ulysses had me bring down a buncha stuff for him, most of it junk food of one kind or another. The kinda stuff the kids'll start craving once they've been down here for a while."

Harp squinted at him. "But what's he wanna play Candyman for? The kids already follow him like lemmings."

"For a while," Rick allowed. "But if he holds true to form, he'll start losing some of his volunteer bushwhackers soon, and I mean that literally. Every season, we have to organize at least one search for someone who got left behind. He doesn't do it on purpose; he just forgets that other people need to rest occasionally. Even the ones who don't get lost get *tired,* and they start finding other things to do on Sunday afternoon."

"So then he bribes them with cookies?"

Rick laughed. "He gives little parties at night, and makes the expeditions seem more like picnics. He's not an evil guy, Harp. Just a bit driven."

"A bit," Harp scoffed, turning to slap more plaster into place.

"Okay, hate him, then," Rick said with a shrug. "I'm not the camp counselor. How're you getting along with everybody else?"

"Fine. I even got along with Cole when I was out on the strip survey with him."

"You know that we rotate the student workers around for a while, give them a taste of everything and everybody. Then we see who attaches to whom . . . kind of natural selection."

Harp looked up from stirring his bucket and nodded. "Yeah, I've seen it happening. Even Clubb has his acolytes. So far, I've liked working with you and Muldoon the best. But I felt like I talked too much the day I worked with you. Took too much of your attention."

"I felt like I was showing off," Rick admitted. "I wanted you to see all the things I could."

"I'm content to bullshit all day," Harp assured him, reaching for the bottle. "But you're probably not, and it's not fair to the kids. I mean, you've got Eric—*Eric*—actually interested in learning some archaeology."

"Motorhead," Rick said fondly, using Brad's nickname for his friend. In return, Eric always referred to Brad as "this animal here," which had been shortened to This Animal.

"And Rita and that kid named Jim have already attached themselves to Muldoon," Harp went on. "I was doing the same thing to Muldoon that I did with you, but when I caught myself and shut up, they were more than able to fill the silence. So it might be better if I maintained my marginality for a while."

"You've always been good at that," Rick said dryly. "Okay, but don't be shy about plugging into something if it turns you on." He accepted the bottle and took another lukewarm sip, surveying the building in front of him. "Say . . . any chance that this, ah, 'apparent residential dwelling' might be uninhabited for a couple of hours after dark?"

Harp shot him a swift, fierce glance, his face again appearing painted for battle. "The last time, I got stuck sitting in the bar until eleven."

"I won't do that to you, I promise."

"This's a small town, and the bed squeaks. I could get an undeserved reputation."

"A first for you," Rick scoffed. "I'll put the mattress on the floor. C'mon, man, this's important. I'll owe you a big one."

Harp appeared to consider that for a moment, then gave him a smile that was distinctly gloating. "No, you won't. Not if we finish plastering today."

"Oh, man, lemme owe you one," Rick groaned, waving the bottle in denial. "You haven't got enough plaster, anyway."

"I would if I had a horny archaeologist digging for me. That's the deal: If you want to turn this apparent residential dwelling into a House of Carnal Delights, you have to help refurbish it first."

"Goddam, I walked right into this," Rick growled as he reached for a nearby shovel. "Just remember that you could end up on permanent assignment to Ollie Clubb."

"Not while you have a libido," Harp chortled.

MULDOON HAD SOLICITED volunteers at dinner the night before, and since another sultry day was expected, the crew assembled a half hour earlier than usual for breakfast, eating cold cereal in the near darkness. Then Muldoon loaded them up with canteens and tools and knapsacks of supplies, jokingly calling for the next mule until they had everything and could begin the hike to Group B. Half asleep and half buzzed on reheated coffee, Harp took what he was given and plodded along like a proper mule behind Brad and Eric, who carried their burdens with an ease that made them appear weightless. Wet leaves pawed languidly at their sleeves as they moved through a stretch of dense forest, the noise of their passage awakening a few birdcalls and sending unseen creatures slithering off into the undergrowth.

The sky was beginning to lighten when they came out into the open again, at the northern end of the causeway that spanned the deep, thorny ravine separating Group A from Group B. The causeway was in the process of being restored, and some of the Mexicans working on it had already arrived and were squatting in a cluster next to the path, smoking pungent, hand-rolled cigarettes. Rick and Ulysses were supervising that project, which aimed to clear and solidify a path wide enough to permit the passage of motorized vehicles, thus doing away with the need for human mules. They had most of the regular workers at their disposal, which was why Muldoon had been compelled to recruit an extra measure of student labor. He'd warned them all that it was going to be heavy work, but he'd also tantalized them with hints of the possible importance of what they might find, if they could move enough rubble out of the way.

The causeway had a general downward slope, hastening their steps until they were halfway across, when the line slowed and began to close in on itself. Here the path took a sudden plunge down into a jumbled gully, the result of the foundation having been undermined by the seasonal accumulation of water in the ravine. Mosquitoes hummed in the mist that filled the bottom of the gully, and the path up the other side was steep and slippery, chewed up by the feet of those who had gone before. Harp used the shovel he was carrying to lever himself upward, adding his share of grunts and curses to the common chorus.

The rest of the causeway was in fairly good repair, lined on both sides by neat rows of palms that had grown up along the low parapet walls. They passed an unexcavated mound at the end of the causeway and walked through a grove of rain forest giants, huge cedars and mahoganies and ceibas. Because of its relative inaccessibility, Group B hadn't been logged out by the timber company with which Brinton Taylor had an agreement, which meant that only the Main Plaza had been thoroughly cleared, and that most of the Group's dozen or so buildings lay in the twilight shade of the forest for the greater part of the day. At this hour, even the plaza seemed dim and mysterious, the grassy expanse studded with tree stumps like random, minor altars, the ghostly white slabs of stelae standing out against the half-cleared terraces and ruined buildings behind them.

Harp was fully awake now, excited to be here. This was where the first inhabitants of Baktun had settled in the Early Classic, on a long ridge of tableland above the Lacantún River. And where the next wave of settlers, hundreds of years later, had begun their Late Classic resurgence, creating a ceremonial center in the style of the great Petén sites. The Shell dynasty had had their start here before moving north to build the larger and more elaborate complex of Group A, and their last heirs had returned during the Terminal Classic in an apparently unsuccessful attempt to resurrect their family's past glory. On the basis of what he'd learned from Muldoon, Harp no longer considered Group B to be the key locale in Baktun's final drama, but that didn't make him love the place any less. The encroachment of the forest only made it seem more like what a "lost city" was supposed to be, adding rather than detracting from its power. Harp made a mental note to urge Brinton not to invite the loggers in.

The only other time Harp had worked here, Muldoon had been clearing the lower terraces of the North Acropolis, a small hill composed of platform upon platform, with three temples standing upon separate summits, the central one being the highest and largest. The two flanking temples had not been excavated (one had a large ceiba growing up through its fallen roof), and the pyramid platforms on which they stood were still mounds of stump-studded earth. The central temple, Structure B-3, however, had been restored and fitted with a temporary roof, and the multiple platforms supporting it had been cleared back to their limestone façades, revealing the way the pyramid had grown, stage by stage. In the time since Harp had been here, Muldoon had cut a four-foot-wide trench down through the central north-south axis of B-3, almost to the level of the plaza. Within the platform that supported the final temple, he had found an earlier structure, B-3-2nd, dated by the ceramics in the fill to the time of Lord of Shells but containing no burial. Beneath that, he had recently discovered a third temple, B-3-3rd, still largely intact and still bearing traces of red-painted plaster on its walls. Muldoon had tunneled through the sealed doorway into a chamber filled with large, dry-laid chunks of limestone, the very rubble they had come this day to remove.

The tarps covering the trench were quickly laid aside, and Muldoon began to arrange the available troops. He assigned Rita and her friend Jim (who was a little taller but probably not as strong as she was) the task of screening and bagging the loose debris that a grad student named Andrew (one of Clubb's coterie) would collect and bring out in a wheelbarrow. The rest were arranged in a line that extended out of the tunnel and up onto the adjacent terrace. As the stones were removed, they would be passed back from hand to hand and finally piled up on the terrace, out of the way of traffic in the trench. Brad and Eric were the last two in line on ground level; Harp was up on the left-hand terrace with a grad student named Max, a skinny blond kid with a ponytail who was one of Ulysses's most devoted followers. Brad and Eric's job was to toss, heave, or push the stones up onto the terrace, where Harp and Max would collect and stack them as neatly as possible.

After passing out work gloves to everyone, Muldoon looked at Eric, who was six-four and had the shoulders of a tight end, and then up at Harp. He ignored Max, who was as scrawny compared to Harp as Harp was compared to Eric.

"I heard you played basketball," Muldoon said. "Still got good hands?"

"Pretty good," Harp admitted, letting his vanity get the better of his judgment. Muldoon smiled slyly through his beard.

"Get ready for the alley-oop, then. Keep the stones flowing . . . "

Muldoon went back down into the trench, and soon the stones began to flow back out in earnest. They were mostly in the ten- to twenty-pound range, unworked and vaguely oval in shape, like petrified footballs. Brad would cry "hut one!" as he tossed a stone to Eric, who'd catch it and raise it up to his shoulder in shotput fashion, cry "hut two!" and heave it up to Harp. Harp caught a few as he would a ball, gathering it in against his chest before turning to pitch it to Max. But that was too much work and bruised his breastbone besides, so he quickly learned to use the momentum of Eric's toss to his own advantage, scooping up under the stone while it was still in the air and passing it on to Max like a hot potato. Max was even less eager to catch anything heavy, but he was young and nimble, and he became quite adept at deflecting the flying stones just enough to make them land where he wanted on the pile. Once they got their rhythm down, it became a kind of lithic ballet.

Harp hadn't noticed that the sun had risen until he felt its heat boring through the weave of his panama and had to wrap a bandanna around his forehead to keep the sweat out of his eyes. Max stripped down to a tank top, which, with his rooster cut and the turquoise stud in one ear, made him look like your basic undernourished rock star. Big stones were coming out now, too big for anyone to toss, and he and Max would have to stoop to lift them or sometimes simply to roll them toward the pile. *Lift with your legs, not your back,* Harp kept telling himself, though it was getting hard to tell which muscles were doing the work, since they all hurt. *You're thirty-five,* his mind groaned, then added in disbelief, *and you're doing this for free.*

Muldoon finally called a break, telling them to drink a lot of water but not to go far. Harp and Max sprawled out on the rock pile, passing a canteen back and forth and joking about how good even treated water could taste. There'd been a certain wariness between them at the outset (Max had been there the day Ulysses belittled Harp for taking cement rather than mortar mix), but the job had demanded too much cooperation for that to continue, and they'd long since sweated it out of their systems. Harp could've made it rough on Max by insisting that they switch places occasionally, a thought that'd occurred to him several times, and probably had to Max as well. But while the division of labor hadn't been equal, it'd been fair, and it'd kept the stones flowing. That was all they'd really had to prove.

A group had gathered down where Rita and Jim had their screening box, and people were holding small bits of refuse up to the light and talking about them animatedly. Eric had gone to join them, standing on the edge of the group with a diffidence that made him slouch. Brad climbed up the terrace to join Harp and Max, his sleeveless sweatshirt black with sweat and his muscular arms roped with distended veins. He had the swollen, neckless torso of a ferocious iron pumper and the round, freckled face of a mischievous choirboy, a combination that had apparently made him the despair of his high school football coach, who could never get him sufficiently interested in knocking other people around.

"This Animal," Max greeted him affectionately. "You guys were really humping down there."

"Cleared three more feet, the man said." Brad shrugged, his shoulders almost touching his earlobes. "It's cooler down there than it is up here."

Harp handed him the canteen, pointing with his chin at the group around the screeners. "Your buddy's been hooked."

"The Motorhead? Yeah, it's like he found an eight-hundred-horsepower engine nobody'd ever seen before. He usually only gets that way around cars."

"The new Maya Classic sedan," Max suggested, "from Baktun Motors."

Brad let out an easy chuckle. "Yeah, with a trunk full of rocks."

Eric was returning, stretching his long legs only a little to take the stepped terrace in two bounds. He pushed back the brim of his John Deere cap and drank deeply from the canteen Brad handed him.

"So . . . what's in the fill?" Max inquired, and Eric nodded as he swallowed, obviously eager to report.

"Lots of stucco fragments, some with paint still on them. Professor Muldoon thinks it might be from an old roof comb."

"Pottery?"

"All little pieces, like it was redeposited. Unslipped redware and burnished black," Eric quoted from memory, frowning to get it right. "Pom Ek Phase . . . "

"No polychrome?"

"Not so far."

Harp gave Max a curious glance. He didn't know much about the Pom Ek Phase, which was Early Classic, the rather dull, mostly unpainted pottery produced by the first Baktunis. "Could we have an Early Classic temple here?"

Max tossed his head, showing him a flash of turquoise. "It'd be the first. We think their temples were perishable, like wood. Anyway, the platform's definitely Late Classic. They probably had some old fill left over and dumped it in."

"*They?*" Harp repeated. "Who we talking about here? The folks before Lord of Shells?"

"That's who probably built the temple. It was Lord of Shells's people who probably dumped the Pom Ek sherds in, when they were building the platform over it. All this stone we're pulling out probably came from something else they razed. They scavenged all over when they needed fill."

Harp smiled at all the "probablys," but his next question was cut off by Muldoon whistling them back to work. Eric popped up from his crouch, briefly windmilling his arms for balance.

"Maybe we'll know before too long," he suggested hopefully.

"What's the rush?" Brad asked, following him back down into the trench. "Shit's been sitting there for a thousand years already. It sure ain't going anywhere . . . "

. . .

THEY CLEARED another three feet before lunch, breaking once to switch the rock-piling operation to the opposite side of the trench. That gave Harp a chance to strain the muscles on the other side of his body, evening out the pain. Lunch consisted of everything Muldoon had thrown into a pack on his way out of the kitchen that morning: a loaf of bread and a stack of day-old tortillas, canned sardines and pineapple, a jar of olives and a box of raisins, peanut butter and jelly, some overripe finger bananas, and a bag of mandarin oranges. They heckled Muldoon about the weird combinations this produced while polishing off everything he'd brought.

After snoozing in the shade for a while, Harp saw Rita go out into the plaza to take some pictures, and he decided to join her. The sweat had cooled but not dried on his body, leaving his skin clammy and his muscles in danger of stiffening up. He stretched and rolled his shoulders as he strolled out into the sunlight, blinking at the glare off the exposed limestone surfaces around the periphery. Rita was kneeling in front of the half of Stela 7 that was embedded in the plaza floor in front of B-3, in line with the trench. It was the upper half of the monument, Lord of Shells from the waist up, his elaborate headdress intact but most of his face smashed off.

"For scale," Rita said, waving him into the picture. Harp struck a pose with his elbow resting on the rounded top of the stela, which just came up to his shoulder. The slab was about twice as thick as he was and was rough and striated on its back side. It had been reset here during the Terminal Classic, presumably by members of the Shell family after they'd lost power at the center of the site. They'd also built the final temple on top of B-3, making this the locus of their revitalization movement.

"Take your arm down," Rita scolded. "You look like you're hugging him."

"Hey, without him, none of us would be here," Harp said, though he adopted a more respectful stance. "You know where the other half of this wound up, don't you?"

Rita didn't look up from her focusing. "In the fill of the platform that was built over the ball court in the West Plaza of Group A. I was here when you were asking Dr. Muldoon all those questions, remember?"

"Right," Harp agreed with a trace of embarrassment. "So the next question is: Was it broken *there,* and this piece rescued and brought here? Or was it brought here intact, and then the Kan Cross People cracked down and trashed the place? From the way the temple was vandalized, Muldoon thinks the revitalization movement might have been forcibly suppressed."

Rita snapped the picture and stood up, rewinding as she came toward him. "Just like Kent State?"

Harp tipped his hat back and squinted at her. "You've been reading *War College.*"

"I just finished it last night. Actually, I read most of it twice."

"What'd you think?" Harp prompted, when she didn't bubble on with her usual enthusiasm. Rita sighed and tugged on one of the curls that billowed out from under her Red Sox cap.

"I'm still thinking about it. It seemed really real when I was reading it, but I couldn't believe that you guys spent so much time getting stoned and acting crazy. Why didn't you all flunk out?"

"You had to work hard to do that. We did some schoolwork; we just weren't earnest about it."

"*You* were," Rita insisted. "I mean, your character, Jake, was. He just didn't show it to anybody else. It was like you made each other ashamed of doing anything right."

"The war made it seem shameful to just go on with business as usual," Harp said, "and the draft made it seem pointless. But yeah, we screwed around a lot on our own. I wasn't trying to make us into angels."

"You didn't," Rita assured him bluntly. "But you liked yourself more as a devil. You still do."

Harp grinned. "Since this world doesn't exactly seem like heaven . . . "

Rita pointedly ignored the gibe, looking past him to where Muldoon and the others were coming out of the trees.

"Katie Smith wants to read it next. Should I give it to her?"

"Sure. I gave her my copy of *Ghost Dance,* if you're interested in reading that. She's already read it once."

"I know. She's a real fan of yours," Rita said, with an insinuating glance. "She showed it to me and it looked like a completely different kind of book. Even if it is on the same subject."

"How's that?" Harp asked in surprise.

"Well, the Ghost Dance was a revitalization movement that failed, right? The same could be said of the sixties, in your version of it. Though you'd probably say it was forcibly suppressed."

Harp was too taken aback to say anything. Rita laughed and gestured with her camera at the replanted piece of Stela 7.

"Don't you ever write about anything else?" she asked mockingly, and walked off toward the trench, leaving him alone with Lord of Shells, wearing an expression that felt as blank and smashed as the stela's.

"You're getting cynical, Rita," he called after her belatedly, then lowered his voice to a growl only he could hear. "And you're too damn young to know how to vex me . . . "

THE FLOW of stones slowed as the day grew hotter and Muldoon had to stop more frequently to shore up the ceiling. They were reportedly getting close to the rear wall of the chamber, which was a relief to all of them, even Eric. After a pause to let Andrew sweep up and trundle out another wheelbarrow full of debris, work started then stopped again, and word came back down the line that Muldoon had found something. Brad was summoned into the tunnel and came back out to get another pick.

"There's a place in the floor where the plaster's been patched," he reported, then saw the expression on Eric's face and handed him the pick. "Here, you go. But watch your head in there . . . "

Harp and Max forgot their fatigue and hung over the side of the trench, peering into the darkness and listening to the tentative chipping of steel against plaster. Then the sound became a muffled thump, and Harp imagined the point of the pick digging into something soft and marly. That went on for quite some time, interspersed with the rasping of a shovel, before Eric came out and gestured for Andrew to bring the wheelbarrow.

"There's a slab underneath," Eric said to the others. "Professor Muldoon says somebody should go for a couple more crowbars and as many lamps as you can find."

"We're on our way," Harp assured him, as he and Max stood up together. Brad started to accompany them, but Eric caught him by the arm.

"We need This Animal here to help us pry up the slab. It's gonna be a bitch."

"No pain, no gain," Brad murmured happily, as Harp and Max jumped down and went off across the plaza at a trot. They'd slowed to a fast walk by the time they reached the causeway, but they kept that pace all the way back to the camp. As they were leaving, loaded down with a crowbar and two heavy halogen lamps apiece, Harp couldn't resist the urge to pop into the lab and tell everybody what they'd found. He noticed the way Katie Smith started to yell because he'd let the screen door slam, then stopped and smiled when she saw that it was he. Something funny happened in his chest, and he suddenly realized what Rita had been nudging him about. Before Katie could reach him, he made a general announcement of their find, said he had to run, and did so.

"Slow down," Max complained finally, when they were halfway down the forest path. "They won't get it open before we get back."

"Right," Harp muttered, feeling profoundly inattentive. *On my way to becoming an item, and Rita knew it before I did.*

They ran into Rick and Ulysses on the causeway, and this time Harp let Max do the telling. He described it more temperately as a "possible burial," which had a decidedly different ring than the "tomb" Harp had announced to the people in the lab. Rick exchanged a glance with Ulysses and fished in his pocket, coming up with a twenty-peso coin. He rested it on his upturned thumb, showing them the kneeling Mayan ballplayer engraved on the face.

"Appropriate . . . heads or tails?"

"Heads," Ulysses decided, betting on the ballplayer. But the heavy silver disc spun in the air and landed showing the Aztec eagle perched on his cactus, tearing at a serpent with both talon and beak. Ulysses unbuckled his belt with all its dangling accoutrements and handed it to Rick.

"In case Muldoon doesn't have everything he needs," he explained. "Dental picks are in the snap case."

Rick fastened the belt and looped it over his shoulder, and as soon as his hands were free, Harp and Max each gave him a lamp to carry.

"Thanks, guys," Rick said sarcastically.

"Welcome to the pack train," Max laughed, and turned to assume the role of the bell mule, leading them south toward Group B.

AS ERIC had predicted, raising the capstone turned out to be an arduous, painstaking process—in short, a bitch. The basic task of prying a two-hundred-pound slab of limestone out of its beveled niche in the floor was complicated by the tight quarters in the tunnel and by an ardent desire not to jar a lot of debris loose onto whatever lay below. Harp spent most of his time pressed back against the wall in a half-crouch, shining a lamp wherever light was needed, inhaling the plaster dust stirred up by the whisk brooms Rita and Jim were wielding in their effort to keep the floor clean. Brad and Eric were doing most of the grunt work, directed and assisted by Rick and Muldoon, and with all the bodies packed into the low-ceilinged shaft, the air had become damp and rank, reminding Harp of a handball court after a hard match.

They finally got one end of the slab up far enough to jam a stout log under it, which then provided a fulcrum to lever it higher. When they had it up about two feet and securely braced, Muldoon stuck a flashlight and then his head down into the hole underneath.

"It's not deep . . . maybe four feet," he reported, his voice echoing hollowly. "No inscriptions visible on the walls . . . lots of debris on the floor. Something white, looks like bone." Muldoon pulled his head back out, blinking owlishly at the lamps trained on him. "I can see part of a ribcage. Let's get this thing all the way off . . . "

They got it off much the way the Maya probably would have, tugging and heaving it up onto a bed of log rollers, and then slowly rolling it out into the uncovered portion of the trench. As he scuttled out ahead with Max to lay down another log, Harp was startled by the sound of applause. He didn't dare look away until the slab had come to a complete rest, but then he glanced up and saw people sitting along the terraces on both sides of the trench, backlit by a pale orange sky. Katie Smith's twelve-year-old daughter, Lucy, leaned over the edge and flashed him a mouthful of silver braces.

"You look like Casper the Friendly Ghost!"

Harp looked over at Max, who was wearing the same head-to-toe coating of lime dust, and the two of them exchanged an exaggerated shrug that drew more laughter from the onlookers. Rita chose that moment to snap a flash picture of them and the capstone.

"Two ghosts not dancing," she snickered, poking Harp in the ribs as she squeezed by him and went down the tunnel. Max followed her as soon as he could see again, but Harp decided to stay out where the air was fit to breathe. Katie appeared next to her daughter and handed down a canteen, giving him the gap-toothed smile that'd been the impetus for Lucy's braces. He nodded in thanks and drank deeply, then poured some over his head, feeling the sting of the places he'd banged against the ceiling inside.

"Had enough treasure hunting?" Katie suggested, shaking her head at his offer to return the canteen. Harp decided that he liked her smile just the way it was. He liked *her,* and he was too old to let the prospect of a little gossip scare him off.

"I'm one whipped grave robber," he admitted, and sat down on the capstone. Rita's flash was going off behind him at regular intervals as she recorded the original disposition of the tomb.

"You were so excited when you came into the lab," Katie said. "You were like a little kid."

"Exactly," Harp murmured, cringing inwardly at the memory. "A little kid with his first tomb."

There was a commotion behind him, and the people on the terraces craned forward to look. He turned his head as Rick brushed by, followed by Eric, who was cradling a substantial piece of painted pottery in his arms, beaming over it like a proud parent.

"Half a tripod plate," Rick said to Clubb, who'd gotten down into the trench in a hurry. "Placed next to the head of the corpse. We left the other half in place."

Eric had lowered it for Clubb's inspection but wasn't about to let it out of his hands. The plate was worn in places, especially in the center, but elsewhere the colors were still rich, the background a deep red and the band of glyphs along the rim outlined in black on cream. Visible in the center were part of the torso and trailing leg of a figure wearing a water-lily headdress.

"Wow," Harp exclaimed softly, causing Eric to widen his smile.

"Whattaya say, Ollie?" Rick prompted, when Clubb seemed unable to speak. "An heirloom from the Petén . . . probably Middle Classic at the latest."

"Tepeu One," Clubb whispered, nodding to himself. He looked up at Rick with sudden urgency. "Anything else?"

"Two more skeletons, small ones, near the feet of the first. Might be animal bones. Nothing else large enough to bring out today."

The others had in fact begun to file out of the tunnel, and Harp handed the canteen to Muldoon, who accepted it with a grateful nod, drinking and passing it to Brad. Then Muldoon laid a hand on Eric's shoulder, turning him away from Clubb so that the rest of the crew could appreciate the find. Somewhat to Harp's surprise, Clubb surrendered his place and walked out of the trench.

"Savor it," Muldoon advised. "There aren't too many days like this one."

"Don't savor it too long," Katie called down from above. "Ramona's holding dinner for us."

"Dinner!" Brad repeated enthusiastically, but Muldoon made them put the tarps back over the trench first. Then they gathered up their tools and supplies, sharing them out among the spectators, and began the long but triumphant walk back to the camp.

6

THUNDER RUMBLED in the distance, and another gust of moist air came through the screen in front of him, briefly cooling his already damp face. It was so dark out there that they'd had to turn the lights on, and so humid that it seemed it might start raining indoors at any moment. *Okay, Chac,* Harp prayed silently, *come on down.* It was diversion he desired, as much as cooling. Anything to keep him from nodding off into the pile of sherds on the table before him.

"You're daydreaming again, Harp," a mockingly officious voice said behind him, and he swiveled on his high stool to see Lucy standing there, rubbing one index finger over the other in the sign for "shame."

"It's my job," Harp grumbled. "That's what novelists do."

"Not in the lab, they don't," Lucy said primly, pointing past him at the table. "There's your job."

It was a pretty fair imitation of her mother, though Katie had never run that particular number on Harp. She'd be more likely to poke him in the kidneys and whisper something salacious in his ear.

"That's not a job, it's punishment," he said, swiveling back. Lucy pressed in beside him, leaning against his hip, her hands on the raised front edge of the table. It occurred to him, fleetingly, that she made more contact with him than her mother did.

"Oh, *those,*" Lucy said, making a face. "I sorted a whole buncha them. They're boring as shit."

She also liked to swear around him, something Katie didn't tolerate, even though the phrase itself was vintage Katie.

"I bet when you were a baby," he told her, "you thought shit was pretty fascinating stuff. You probably played patty-cake with it."

Lucy whacked him on the leg and backed away in horror. "I did *not!*"

"Most babies do," Harp said mildly. "It's normal. Don't all teenagers want to be normal?"

"Whatta *you* know about normal? That's the grossest thing I ever heard! Agh, I could puke just thinking about it . . . "

"Be my guest," Harp offered, waving a hand toward the table. "It's bound to be more interesting than what's here."

That grossed her out completely, and she whacked him again and went off pretending to gag into her hand. Katie had said that he had a way with the girl, and he supposed that this was proof. You just had to know how to speak their language.

He went back to ignoring the sherds, which were from the fill they'd taken out of Structure B-3-3rd. Early Classic Pom Ek burnished blackware, gouged and incised and occasionally gadrooned, and always well worn from multiple dumpings. Nobody'd wanted it even then. All the good stuff from the tomb was back on Clubb's table, the beautiful tripod plate already glued together and standing on its own. Clubb estimated that it was already over a hundred years old when it was brought here, almost certainly (on stylistic grounds) from Tikal or Uaxactún, just as Clubb had predicted in his account of the origins of the Late Classic Baktunis. This was not the first confirmation of that part of his theory, but it was easily the most dramatic, and it already had him speculating that the migration west from the Petén must've been peaceful and planned, if they'd had time to pack their heirlooms. Rick referred to it as Ollie's Folly II.

The splat of rain on the leaves outside brought Harp out of his reverie, and he stared out through the window screen just in time to get his first good look at Sancho Panza, the camp pig.

At first he thought it was a dog, one of the mangy, half-wild curs that occasionally came scavenging around the camp. It was black and white and about dog size, but it moved with a stiff, rather dainty gait, quite unlike the usual mongrel slink. Once it was closer, trotting across the open Bermuda grass that surrounded Kan Shell's temple, there was no question of its porcine nature. It even stopped for a moment to root at some morsel hidden in the grass.

Harp watched until it disappeared, wondering how it'd stayed out of his sight for the last three weeks. He'd certainly heard enough about it. Apparently, someone (he'd heard different people being blamed) had had the bright idea of having a greased-pig contest at last season's end-of-season party, in addition to the customary soccer game between the staff and the Mexican workers. Unlike the game, however, the contest had been intended solely for the workers, as if their desire to supplement their diet would naturally outweigh any concern for dignity. To his credit, Ulysses had made a fuss and had insisted on entering himself and Rick and some of the students.

Still, no one had been able to catch the pig, who'd run rings around Mexicans and gringos alike before escaping into the forest. Everyone had assumed he'd be food for one of the jaguars or pumas that prowled the forest, but the wily porker had somehow survived the off-season and was still around when the crew returned this year. That'd earned him a unique immunity from the depredations of the workers, who tended to kill any live thing that crossed their path, whether it was edible or not. But they left Sancho Panza alone, perhaps as a demonstration of their comprehension of what the contest had been about.

The staff, for their part, regarded him as a mascot, and it was said that Ramona, the head cook, saved a bucket of scraps for him every day. Someone had even claimed, in Harp's hearing, that the pig sometimes resided in Ulysses and Muldoon's cabin, a notion too outrageous and personally insulting for Harp to entertain. He disliked Cole enough without knowing that he'd been put out for a pig.

There was a grand roll of thunder, the gods announcing themselves, and suddenly the rain was coming down in sheets that seemed to dance across the grass toward him, soundless until it hit the road and then the thatched roof of the lab. The pandemonium overhead made everyone in the long room stop and look up, then around at their companions. Kaaren Seyerstad, who was working on the B-3 bones at one of the center tables, seemed startled when Harp pumped a fist in the air and shouted into the din.

"Wayta go, Chac!"

She gave him what he thought was a tolerant smile as she came over to look out the window. The rain was pounding the earth like a drum, and water was pouring off the thatch in a curtain that blurred everything beyond it.

"I hope they got an early start back," Kaaren said, so quietly he had to strain to hear her. "This'll turn the road to soup."

Brother Rick, with Rita along for company, had driven to Comitán earlier in the day. They were supposed to pick up Brinton Taylor and Helga Kauffmann, along with the mail and supplies.

"The Land Cruiser can go through soup," Harp assured her, but she didn't respond. Up close, she appeared tired and haggard, though of course she wore it well.

"How you doing with the bones?" he asked after a moment, knowing how seriously she took her work, particularly the osteology that had fallen to her with Winnie Gordon's defection. She'd even left an osteology text in Harp's hut one night when she and Rick had used it, making him wonder how much carnal delight they were enjoying.

"I think I finally have them sorted out," Kaaren said, reluctantly turning her gaze away from the rain. "We have an adult male of above-average size, probably in his forties, with frontal deformation of the skull and evidence of arthritis and dental caries. There's also a parrot—possibly a scarlet macaw—the skull and part of the tail of a crocodilian, the jawbones of two different jaguars, and . . . and an infant of undetermined age and sex."

With the rain drumming so close at hand, Harp saw her falter before he actually heard the catch in her voice, the sudden fall in tone that made him want to say he was sorry. He let out a grunt of startled sympathy.

"Somehow, that gives the collection a rather gruesome cast."

"Yes."

"You're assuming that the . . . child . . . was a sacrifice?"

Kaaren seemed to flinch at the term, but managed to bring her voice back up to a level tone. "Given what we know about Mayan mortuary practices, and the fact that this was a man's tomb, it's the most likely assumption. It's what Rick and Oliver and Emory Muldoon all assumed."

"Case closed," Harp suggested.

"Pretty much. You must think I'm being ridiculously sentimental."

"Overly empathetic, maybe," Harp ventured. "If there is such a thing. Wait a minute—were the animals killed for the occasion?"

"I don't think there's any way to tell," she replied, frowning at her own indecision. "The jaguar mandibles appear a good bit older than the rest, but we won't know until they're tested."

"So they might've been heirlooms, too, just like the tripod plate."

"Possibly. What're you suggesting?"

Harp shrugged. "Why assume the child was sacrificed when you don't assume the same thing about the animals? Maybe the kid had some special significance to the ruler, like the only child of his favorite wife. Or one of those were-jaguars the Olmec had. Maybe the bones had been saved to be reburied with him."

He finished out of breath, and Kaaren just stared at him, her features softening into a smile so unguardedly affectionate it made him blush. She compounded his confusion by leaning forward to kiss him on the cheek.

"That's the nicest story anyone's ever made up for me," she said as she pulled away. "Thank you for having such a kind imagination."

"Sure," Harp murmured as she left him and went back to her table. He was still waiting for the glow to wear off when the Land Cruiser came wheeling up to the door at the far end of the lab, and there was a second suspension of activity in the room. Doors slammed and he caught a glimpse of Brinton's snowy hair in the background as Rita came bustling into the room, followed by a gnomelike figure who was shaking out an umbrella. Helga Kauffmann, Harp realized belatedly. On the basis of her reputation, he'd imagined someone tall and austere, the aristocratic grande dame of the Mayanists. The real Helga Kauffmann was shorter than Rita and slightly humpbacked, so that she appeared to be looking out at the world from beneath an overhang. Her straight black hair was cut squarely around a broad, Eastern European face, thick-lipped and heavy-browed, with bright dark eyes behind a pair of industrial-strength glasses. It was a remarkably mobile face, creased rather than wrinkled, and all the creases seemed to vee upward when she smiled in response to Katie Smith's greeting, bobbing her head in a determinedly ingratiating way.

Brinton led the way up the central aisle to Kaaren's station, where he performed the introduction with his customary grace.

"I am so pleased to meet you," Helga said, bobbing and smiling effusively as she shook Kaaren's hand. Without coming fully to rest, she tucked the umbrella under her arm and leaned over the table, which came up to her chest. "And what do we have here?"

Kaaren drew a breath and shot a quick, anxious glance at Brinton. But she had to exhale as she bent to address Helga, and that seemed to activate her voice and get her going. Helga coaxed her on with nods and questions Harp couldn't hear, though they all seemed to roll Kaaren forward rather than bring her up short. Rita and Katie also joined the discussion, both paying a deference to Helga that she deflected onto Kaaren, always giving her the chance to respond first. *Wayta go, Helga,* Harp thought, detecting a glimmer of a smile on Brinton's long, angular face as he leaned in to listen. Brinton also had a talent for drawing people out, but he was so reserved you always wondered later whether you'd impressed him or convinced him you were a complete fool.

Clubb and his coterie of students came up to join the group, prompting further introductions and then a general migration in the direction of Clubb's table. Harp noted that Clubb was giving Helga the kind of glowing attention he customarily paid to Kaaren.

Rick had lingered behind with Katie, who was emptying the contents of the canvas mail sack out onto an unoccupied table. Harp decided he could meet Helga later and went over to see if there was anything from Caroline in this load.

"How was the road?" he asked Rick, who was holding an envelope in a gingerly fashion, as if it were a bill he didn't want to open. Katie had her back to them while she sorted through the rest.

"Piece of cake," Rick said with a shrug. "The last wash was a bit tricky, but we made it. I got the stuff you asked for out in the truck."

"Great. Anything for me?" he asked Katie, trying not to sound too anxious. Without turning around, she lifted a thick manila envelope and examined the seal in the corner opposite the row of stamps.

"MacPherson, Department of Sociology, Mid-Atlantic U," she said as she passed it back over her shoulder. "That your wife?"

"Yep."

"Looks like you're still popular back home," Rick said laconically, as Harp hefted the envelope. The flap came open easily, having been thoroughly stressed in transit, and he pulled out an inch-thick sheaf of printed matter. On top was a Xerox copy of an article on revitalization movements from a recent issue of a sociological journal; the yellow stickie from Caroline said she'd come across it while reading on the plane. This was followed by several articles clipped from newspapers and periodicals, all apparently having to do with current events in Mexico and Guatemala. Next was a piece from a glossy magazine that featured a color photo of Kan Shell's temple on the first page and turned out to be a transcription of a talk Brinton Taylor had given to a conference of engineers in Banff, Alberta. Harp stared at it in wonder, figuring it must've come from Caroline's father, who was the dean of the engineering school in Vancouver.

At the bottom was Caroline's letter, a long one on Mid-Atlantic stationery. Harp's eye was immediately drawn to the title she'd typed in caps at the top of the first page: "DENYING THE COLLAPSE." Intrigued, he scanned the page and saw it was a description of a dinner-table conversation she'd had with her parents and Janet, in which the subject had been he—specifically, his reasons for going off to the jungle. Emily and Janet were apparently the aggressors in the discussion, with Ian weighing in as an unexpected ally.

A sudden feeling of exposure made Harp look around at Rick and Katie, who were absorbed in reading their own mail. Rick let out a muffled snort and stuffed a single sheet back into its envelope. Katie was considerably more demonstrative.

"Oh, shit!" she said in disgust. "The cheap fuck!"

Harp and Rick exchanged a startled glance. Katie had a personal check clenched in one hand.

"Your ex?" Rick guessed aloud, and Katie crumpled the envelope in her other hand and threw it on the floor, breaking her own strict rule about not littering in the lab.

"I had a messenger hand deliver the bank slips," she said through her teeth, "so he could deposit the child support directly. Instead the sonuvabitch sends the check *here.* He knows how long it'll take to send it back for collection."

"Guess I shouldn't bitch, then," Rick decided, after a respectful pause. "At least Winnie sublet the house before she moved out."

"That's the difference between women and men," Katie snapped. "Men never miss a chance to screw you."

They watched in silence as she stalked off toward her office cubicle in the corner, the angry twitch of her hips a parting reproach. Harp glanced at the letter in Rick's hand.

"A belated Dear John?"

"In a manner of speaking. Can't say I didn't see it coming."

"Guess not." Harp decided to save his own mail for later and slid it back into the envelope. "Has Kaaren ever been married?"

"Once, right outta college. Lasted about as long as your first one did."

"Any kids?"

"Not that I know of. Why?"

"Well, I was talking to her before, and she seemed really distressed by the notion that the kid in the B-Three tomb might've been sacrificed for the occasion."

Rick gave him a puzzled frown. "It probably was. I told her that myself."

"Yeah, she said you had," Harp said dryly, and Rick bristled.

"What the hell was I supposed to tell her? That it just crawled in there when nobody was looking and died happily ever after? What'd *you* tell her?"

"I made up a good lie. She didn't believe it, but she was grateful for the effort."

"What're you telling me?" Rick demanded. "That I shouldn't tell her the truth when she asks me a question?"

"Depends on how it's asked. You haven't noticed that dealing with the bones is making her nervous?"

"Of course I have! I know I put her on the spot, making her fill in for Winnie. I've been coaching her at night, for Chrissakes. It's not her strongest area, but she's getting better."

"At the osteology, maybe," Harp allowed. "I'm talking about something that goes deeper. Like to when *she* was a child. Did she ever get abused or molested when she was a kid?"

"Jesus, I dunno! I barely knew her before we left Tucson. You think she tells me that kinda thing for bedtime stories?"

"Look, I'm not trying to browbeat you. I'm just telling you what I picked up from one conversation. A little kind attention right now might go a long way."

When Rick simply stared at him stubbornly, Harp sighed and picked up the packet from Caroline.

"Test it for yourself," he suggested. "I'll stay out of my hut until nine tonight. That should give you time to figure out what to say."

"A good lie?" Rick said sarcastically, as Harp headed back to his station. Harp raised his shoulders in a suspended shrug.

"Better a good lie than a cold truth . . . "

ULYSSES BLEW his whistle and the survey line started forward again, one measured pace at a time, simultaneously cutting paths for themselves and scanning the ground ahead for signs of unusual features. Harp was on the far left end of the line, responsible for the twenty-five meters to his right, between himself and Rita. He kept his heading with a pocket compass and his distance by periodic glances in Rita's direction. The undergrowth in this part of the forest wasn't terribly thick, so he could see her clearly, taking deliberately long strides as she scanned the terrain to her right. The ground was fairly level, too, and they could've been making good time on this section were it not for all the features they were finding. It'd been stop and go all morning, and Harp was finding it tedious and wearing.

"Feature!" Rita shouted, and Harp came to a halt even before Ulysses blew his whistle. He saw Rita take about five steps to her right, gradually rising to the top of what was probably a house mound. Ulysses came toward her from his place at the center of the line, a machete in one hand and the mapping board clamped under the opposite arm. He'd measure and map the feature while Rita investigated the area around it, looking for clues to its function. The other three people in line (Max and Eric were at intervals to Ulysses's right) could only sit and bide their time.

Harp knew better than to sit, since the crawling bugs would find him along with the flying ones. The recent rains had been a fertility bath for the local insect population, which meant long sleeves and work gloves, plus frequent applications of camp-issue bug dope. The vile-smelling compound did keep the flies and mosquitoes at bay, but it felt toxic on his skin and stung like hell if it got into his eyes.

Knowing there wouldn't be time to get into the book he'd brought along, he pulled Caroline's letter out of his rucksack and leaned back against the trunk of a tree. This was his third reading, so he took up where he'd left off at the last feature stop. Back at the dinner table with Caroline and her family.

> Emily, of course, saw it as another example of your talent for freeloading. "He's so clever at finding jobs that carry no risk of remuneration," was the way she put it. Janet was even less tolerant. She remembered Brother Rick as your past partner in crime and concluded that the two of you were going off to the jungle so you could get drunk and eat mushrooms or whatever other illegal substances were available. They made all the usual disdainful gestures, but I could tell neither one of them really cared about what you were doing or why. They were just trying to stir me up, poking me through the bars of my self-restraint. They wanted to make me defensive, knowing that would lead to defiance and the eventual emergence of Crazy Carrie, the girl they love to criticize and coddle. And I could tell they didn't really care about her, either, not even insofar as she might still be me. This was just a game they couldn't help playing, another form of elf theft.

Harp skipped ahead in the letter, looking for her formal definition of the term.

> ELF THEFT: Perverse and antisocial behavior masquerading as legitimate protest, social satire, or the expression of forbidden truths; the sort of malicious mischief practiced by those with a dangerously misplaced sense of moral purpose.

He could smile at it now, though ruefully. The first time he'd read it he'd felt caught dead in the crosshairs, and it'd made him flinch. He flipped back to the dinner table.

> I was briefly tempted to explain the origins of elf theft, which would've allowed me to tell the story of the Lawn Animals' Christmas, which I was dying to do. But they wouldn't have taken it in the proper spirit, and I would only be adding to your reputation as a flake. So instead I started

telling them what the past couple years have been like for us, with me finishing my dissertation and starting a late scramble for a career while you were watching your book go down in flames and your teaching career come to an abrupt end. As I told it, I began to recall things I'd noticed at the time, signs of pain and trouble. Like the fact that I wasn't hearing your typewriter banging away above me when I was in my study. They were very clear to me in retrospect, as if they'd been neatly folded and put away in the memory for some less harried future occasion. Part of each of them was my memory of not responding, of thinking "He'll get over this in his own time" or "I haven't got the energy to deal with this right now." When I realized just how little I'd been there for you, I began to feel lucky that you'd taken to elf stealing rather than running off to have an affair. I would've deserved it if you had.

Ulysses's whistle shrieked and Harp jumped and fumbled the letter back into his rucksack. The line moved ahead without him while he dug out his compass and picked up his machete, and the effort to catch up had him sweating in a hurry. God, he felt like a slug today. He'd thought he'd finally gotten into shape, so that a little humidity and a few thousand extra bugs shouldn't drag him down. He glanced at the compass and couldn't read it immediately because of the sweat in his eyes and the gnats hovering in front of his face. While he was focusing on the dial he tripped over a root and almost went down, flailing with the machete for balance. He recovered and went on, wishing he truly were a freeloading flake, so he could just say fuckit and sit down to rest.

The ground seemed to drop off beneath him, and he suddenly realized he was going downhill. A vague memory of going up made him whip a glance over his shoulder, and he thought he discerned a definite hump behind him.

"Feature!" he yelled, breaking out in a different kind of sweat at the thought that he'd almost missed it. This survey was unscientific enough without missing what was right under his feet. Ulysses blew his whistle and Harp turned back and began hacking at the undergrowth with his machete, trying to clear enough of the hump to get a fix on its contours. It seemed too narrow to be a housemound, too wide and irregular to be the remains of a wall. He dug down through the leaf mold with the point of the machete, turning up dirt and roots and then more dirt. Ulysses had arrived and was doing the same thing at the other end of the hump, with as little success. They each dug in three more places without producing the telltale scrape of metal against stone.

"So where's the feature?" Ulysses demanded.

Harp was soaking wet and too winded to speak. A mosquito bit him on the back of the neck and he just restrained himself from swatting at it with his machete hand.

"Sorry, false alarm," he muttered, looking down at the hump that was just that—a hump in the earth.

"No shit, Sherlock," Ulysses said with a contemptuous snort. "Well, you're still a rookie, no matter how old you are, and everybody gets one wrong call. Just don't let it happen again."

"I won't," Harp said tersely, forcing himself to meet the other man's eyes. Ulysses gave him a nasty grin.

"I won't be so forgiving the second time, so try to keep your eyes open and your imagination under control."

Harp let him get out of earshot before he swore, but there wasn't much force behind it. He just felt tired and stupid, and he knew he'd better save what energy he had to help him make it through the rest of the day. This was truly going to be an exercise in denying the collapse.

HE MADE IT through dinner and was back in his hut, staring blankly at the typewriter, when he realized that what he was feeling wasn't simply fatigue. A wave of dizziness almost made him fall off his chair, and then the chills and aches came on in earnest, followed shortly by violent spasms in his lower parts that sent him running for the doorway. It was the first of many hasty exits in a night that became distinctly hellish, Harp stumbling around in the thornbushes with the flashlight waving wildly as he barfed or grappled with his pants. He wasn't certain, but he thought he'd spewed bile all over a fer-de-lance once, startling the creature too thoroughly to provoke a strike. There was no respite from the misery for what seemed like hours, until he was finally able to keep down a Lomotil tablet, which put a lock on his whimpering sphincter and sent him into a narcoticized sleep.

He had a dim recollection of Rick coming in to check on him, murmuring sympathetically about *la turista* and telling him to sleep it off, advice Harp hardly needed. Thirst and the rising heat in the room woke him later, and he shakily managed a few sips from his canteen, swallowing down a throat sore from retching into a stomach retched tight around emptiness. The water hit bottom like a stone, driving him into a fetal position until the cramps subsided. Then he heard voices and had to look down at himself to be sure he was dressed. He was wearing the same T-shirt and jeans in which he'd sweated and shivered and blundered through the bushes to shit, and they looked and smelled like it. But he was too weak to do anything except lie where he was and let the visitors come. The first voice he was able to recognize belonged to Lucy Smith.

"Oh, *double gross*!"

She'd obviously found the place where he'd puked the first time, a geyser he'd launched from just inside the doorway, on his hands and knees. At the time, he'd been damned proud to've made it that far.

"Don't make him feel worse than he already does," Rita scolded. "Stop holding your nose."

The two of them came into the room on their tiptoes, Rita lugging her boom box and Lucy a brightly striped *bolsa.* Rita went over and lowered the sacking that served Harp as curtains, mercifully dimming the light pouring into the room. Harp managed to raise his head.

"I'm alive," he announced, in a croak that made his throat hurt. "I think."

"We brought you some food," Lucy said, "and some Cokes. Rick sent the Cokes and Ramona made the food."

"It's her special pozole," Rita added.

"Oh god, that corn shit?" Harp groaned.

Lucy let out a chortling laugh. "He's well enough to swear!"

"We'll just leave it here until you feel like eating," Rita said, taking the *bolsa* from Lucy and putting it on the floor next to the bed. "I also thought you might like some music, since there's nobody here to keep you company."

"Bless you," was all Harp could think of to say, but it seemed to please Rita. She put the stereo down next to the *bolsa* and began to demonstrate how it worked.

"I haven't got the strength to turn a dial . . . "

"Want me to put something on for you? I brought Simon and Garfunkel's greatest hits. They're from the sixties, aren't they?"

"Perfect," Harp murmured, exhausted by all this talk.

"It'll play through and then shut itself off," Rita said, "so you won't have to get up unless you want to. We'll come check on you later."

"Eat your corn shit," Lucy advised with a parting giggle, as Harp sank back into sleep to the strains of "Homeward Bound."

THE CEREMONY was being held in the basement of his father's drugstore, in a clearing among the cases of soft drinks and cartons of Kotex. Harp was wearing a loincloth and sandals, beads on his chest, and a tall headwrap of soft cloth. He had to look up at Lord of Shells, who was resplendent in a jade-and-shell pectoral and a headdress of quetzal feathers. Harp felt his heavy-lidded gaze like a weight on his shoulders. The Lord handed him a piece of bone, a femur incised with rows of delicate glyphs and the grotesque faces of supernatural beings. No words were spoken, and Harp knew somehow that the bone was supposed to tell him everything he needed to know. Deciphering it was his responsibility, part of the challenge he was being given. He had to figure out *how* to prove himself worthy, then do it. There was pride and some satisfaction in the Lord's eyes, but there was also an unsparing glint that said *You will be forgotten if you fail.*

Harp nodded that he understood, and Lord of Shells leaned forward, the shells on his chest rattling softly like poker chips, and kissed Harp on the cheek. The people around them—Rick and Caroline and Clubb among them, Helga Kauffmann beaming—began to disperse as the ceremony ended, and there was a muted crash, as if someone had stumbled into the soft drink cases . . .

He woke to the smell of vomit and the sight of a bristly pink pig snout only inches away from his face. The nostrils dilated briefly, revealing a light crust of crud that was the source of the smell, and then the curious brown eyes behind them saw him staring back and went wide with alertness.

"Sancho," Harp muttered, and the pig backed away with quick, skittering steps. A gust of wind billowed the netting over the doorway, revealing the gap that Sancho had used to enter. Harp raised himself up on an elbow, expecting the pig to flee. It was claimed that Sancho never let anyone face him if he could help it; he always found a way to get behind you. At the moment, however, he seemed to be standing his ground, looking right at Harp. Harp allowed himself to be touched by this apparent display of trust, remembering the peculiar affinity he'd had with Rufus, the barn cat who'd adopted him in Vermont. Then he glanced down and saw the overturned *bolsa,* and understood both the crash in his dream and Sancho's boldness.

"So, you'd steal food from a sick man? Some faithful companion *you* are, Sancho Panza."

The pig cocked his head, displaying a deep tear in one ear. A bottle of Coke had rolled out onto the floor, and when Harp found himself reaching for it, he realized for the first time that he was feeling a lot better. Weak as a noodle, but no longer sick. With a concerted effort, he retrieved the bottle, then pulled the *bolsa* closer and found the opener that Rick had thoughtfully provided. The glint of metal in his hand made Sancho shy and angle his hindquarters toward the doorway.

"Just a church key," Harp explained, prying the top off the heavy green bottle. Coke had always been their premier hangover remedy, a combined dose of sugar, caffeine, and liquid, everything the ravaged body craved. Even warm it was soothing, and it went down well enough to make him consider some of the food Rita'd mentioned. The *pozole* he'd had before had tasted like watered-down cornmeal mush, but Ramona's offering was thicker and had a honeyed taste that ended with a bite of chiles, which warmed him up and made him feel his skin. He dipped some up with a tortilla and it tasted even better, so that he had to remind himself to eat slowly. A plaintive grunt from the keenly attentive Sancho made him remember his manners and toss a tortilla to the pig, who scarfed it without hesitation.

He soon found himself looking at the bottom of the bowl and was amazed. His stomach was gurgling loudly but felt okay, and he'd been sitting up for a while without feeling the effort. He could become a fan of Ramona's corn shit. He mopped up the remnants with the last tortilla, made a ball of it, and flipped it toward Sancho, who batted it out of the air with his snout and sucked it up as soon as it hit the floor.

"That's it, *muchacho,*" Harp said, displaying his empty hands. Sancho grunted with what might've been disappointment, or perhaps disbelief. He ambled forward and sniffed at the *bolsa,* which lay on its side and held only the single remaining Coke. He shied slightly when Harp set the bowl down in front of him, then edged forward and swiftly licked it clean, turning it over in the process and licking the outside, too. Then he turned and trotted right out the door, enlarging the gap in the netting with an indifferent toss of his head.

"You're welcome," Harp called after him. "Come back and see me again, real soon."

THE SUN was down and the light was fading rapidly when Katie Smith called out a greeting and pushed through the netting with a *bolsa* in her hand. Harp was lying on the bed, clean and fully dressed, his teeth brushed and his beard trimmed, hands folded on his chest. Katie set down the *bolsa* and squinted at him curiously.

"How's the patient?"

"I felt good enough to get all cleaned up for dinner. Then I didn't have the strength to go."

"It came to you instead. Just rest until I get it set up . . . "

He caught a tantalizing whiff of perfume as she turned away, which also made him notice the way she'd fluffed out her hair, so that it framed her face with feathery curls. She was wearing a sleeveless knit jersey and tight black jeans he'd never seen her wear around the lab. With her usual economy of movement, she put together a couple packing crates for a table, lit some candles for light, and set two places with tableware, napkins, plastic cups, and foil-wrapped plates. When she brought out a corkscrew and a bottle of Mexican wine, Harp figured it was time to sit up.

"What's the occasion?"

Katie was squatting next to his packing-crate desk, looking through the tapes he had piled up inside. She shrugged and gave him a brief over-the-shoulder smile. "I felt like having a civilized meal, and I thought you could use one too."

"Is that why Lucy didn't come along?"

"No, Lucy's eating with Rita in the women's lodge. Rita wasn't in shape to go to dinner either."

"Don't tell me I'm contagious."

Katie swiveled around to look at him. "She's in bad emotional shape. You know Jim Zorn, the boy she's been working with?"

"Yeah. I thought they were an item."

"So did Rita. Rick needed a couple of volunteers to work with Helga Kauffmann, and Rita volunteered the two of them without asking Jim first. He got all huffy about it and made her unvolunteer him, and he did it in front of a bunch of other people. She was crushed."

Katie swiveled back without waiting for his reply, and he watched her fit a tape into the machine and punch the play button. Of course she'd chosen the Keith Jarrett tape. She tilted her head toward the speakers for a moment, smiling to herself, then rose and turned to face him.

"That's nice. Why are you shaking your head like that? It was the only one that looked like dinner music."

"No, it is," Harp agreed, shaking his head to show he hadn't meant to shake his head. "It just has some memories attached to it."

"Oh." Katie sat down on the other side of the table and picked up the wine. Then she clicked her tongue in exasperation and put the bottle down. "Memories of your wife, no doubt."

"You guessed it."

"I always push just the right button, don't I?" she said wryly. Then she shrugged and went to work with the corkscrew. "I still want a civilized meal."

Harp laughed and picked up his cup after she'd poured for both of them.

"To your health. And Rita's," Katie proposed.

"To Rita's. And yours," Harp countered.

They drank and peeled the foil off their plates, inhaling the fragrant steam that rose from the food, which consisted of baked chicken, yellow squash, creamed spinach, and a large dollop of Ramona's *pozole.* They ate in silence for several minutes, listening to Jarrett's piano. Harp finally looked across at her and found her studying him with an intentness that didn't waver when he stared back. Coyness was obviously not one of her faults. He noticed that her brown eyes had golden filaments around the pupils and were set a little too close together, which was perhaps what made her gaze seem so unnervingly frank.

"Thank you for this," he said belatedly. "I'm feeling more civilized already."

"Do I make you nervous, Harp?" Katie asked in a musing tone, ignoring the thank-you. "I didn't think I did, at first. But you've been acting real careful around me lately. Was it something I did, or did you just remember you were married?"

"You do get right to the point," Harp murmured, reaching for his wine.

"It's a flaw in my character. I like to know where I stand with the people I'm attracted to."

"Is this why they call you Takesnoshit Katie?"

She smiled. "Maybe. But you're evading the point."

"Okay," Harp said in resignation. "The truth is, I made myself nervous. Because I wasn't even aware I was flirting with you until Rita teased me about it. I'm not used to having anyone around to flirt with. Especially not someone as attractive as you."

Katie's smile had a triumphant gleam in the candlelight. "So you *are* attracted to me."

Harp laughed. "There's no safe way to respond to that."

"I didn't think you were someone who liked to play it safe."

"That's been my history," Harp admitted. "But I'm trying to learn how."

"Why?"

She was teasing, poking him through the bars, and Harp suddenly remembered his dream, the challenge inscribed on the bones. And an earlier warning sign. He spoke with a seriousness that surprised him almost as much as it did Katie.

"Because I realized it could all disappear."

"Your marriage, you mean," Katie said tentatively. She was staring at him again, as if trying to get a fresh fix on his face. "I didn't think men ever worried about that. Most of them seem to believe they can always go back home if the affair doesn't work out."

"I'm not talking about affairs. I'm talking about losing touch with the person who knows me best. And with myself, as a result."

Katie let out a genuine, full-fledged sigh. "I think you've answered my question. Dammit. After what happened to me, I swore I was never gonna let myself be the other woman. Not unless the marriage was demonstrably shot and both sides knew it."

"At our worst, we were far from that."

"You're lucky, then. And your marriage is safe with me. I won't lure you into infidelity. But you have to promise me in return that you won't act like a nervous husband if I happen to flirt a little."

"I think I can handle that," Harp said and smiled. "Does that mean I'm free to tell you how lovely you look tonight?"

"That's precisely what it means," Katie said, laughing and pouring them both some more wine. "Go ahead, be free. I'm all ears . . . "

LUCY BROUGHT Rita out later, and Harp and Katie did their best to cheer her up with stories of the scornings they'd survived, or for which they'd gotten their revenge. When they ran out of consolation, Harp cranked up the boom box and put on a sixties revival, telling Rita the music was still revitalizing. To prove it he gave a couple brief exhibitions of what Lucy called "spastic dancing," wearing himself out in about two minutes each time.

When Brother Rick came in the Grateful Dead were playing "Turn On Your Lovelight" and Harp was up for the third time and showing some stamina. They all called for Rick to dance and he grinned and broke into a shuffling boogie that Lucy found a little tame.

"A definite geezer!" she declared with gleeful disdain, dancing behind her mother when Rick made a halfhearted grab for her.

The song ended with a shout and the advice to "leave it on," followed by prolonged applause. Harp collapsed onto a chair, too tired to tend the machine when it fell silent. A moment later Rita seemed to notice Rick's presence for the first time and bolted from the room.

"Hey, I'm on your side!" Rick called after her, but she was long gone. "Damn, everybody there was. Fucking kid made a scene over nothing."

"It's late. We'd better go too," Katie said, handing one of the *bolsas* to Lucy and fishing a flashlight out of the other.

"Thanks for the dinner, and the good company," Harp said, obeying Katie's gesture that he remain seated.

"Thanks for the spastic dancing, Harp!" Lucy taunted as she followed Katie toward the door.

"You're welcome. Oh, on your way out, check the spot where I barfed out the door."

"Why should I?" Lucy demanded suspiciously, but then went and did it anyway. "It's all gone! You *mowed* it."

"Not me," Harp said, beaming innocently. "You could call it Lunch on the Lawn with Sancho. He paid me a visit this afternoon."

"He *ate* it? That's the grossest . . . "

She couldn't finish and went off gagging into the night. Katie looked back and rolled her eyes. "A perfect end to a civilized evening. *Buenas noches.*"

"Didn't mean to break up the party," Rick said, once they stopped laughing about Lucy. "I just came out to see if you might be up to some light duty tomorrow. I still need a second helper for Helga."

"What's she doing?"

"She wants to clean the monuments and test some defoliants and preservatives. The equipment's not real heavy, and I guarantee you'll learn a lot. Frankly, you'd be doing me a favor, 'cause I can't get any of the other kids to volunteer. There's too much good stuff being dug at the moment. Brinton and Muldoon are doing another structure in Group B, and I'm starting a partial excavation of the buried ball court in the West Plaza."

"Sounds good," Harp agreed. "But so does a chance to work on the monuments with Helga Kauffmann. Don't these kids know who she is?"

Rick laughed. "Eric the Motorhead said he'd rather dig a new hole than scrub an old stone. Unquote. That seemed to be the majority opinion."

"Sign me up, then," Harp decided. "I should be strong enough by tomorrow, and I owe Rita some tender loving care."

"Speaking of which," Rick said, pointedly sniffing at the air. "You've been getting a little from Katie, too, huh?"

"She brought me dinner."

"Better watchit. Next thing you know you'll *be* dinner," Rick said with a laugh. "Don't get me wrong, I like Katie. But she's displayed some definite man-eating tendencies, checks 'em out and then chucks 'em out. Ulysses was just one of the guys she used up real fast."

Harp grimaced and waved a hand in dismissal. "That displays good taste. Anyway, I don't care about her shady past. I'm not on the make and she knows that."

"Oh well, in *that* case," Rick said mockingly, patting him on the shoulder. "I'm sure Katie just wants to talk about your novels and have a spiritual relationship. Yeah, I'd believe that if I were you."

"You bastard, you're just getting back at me for telling you to be nice to Kaaren," Harp said as Rick walked toward the door. "It worked, too, didn't it?"

Rick stopped halfway and looked back with a grin. "Sure. So did some time alone in this House of Carnal Delight. The one thing leads to the other, y'know? I'm just saying those good lies of yours can be dangerous when you start telling 'em to yourself. *Adiós* . . . "

"Cynic," Harp muttered. Done in by the dancing, he sat limply in the chair, watching moths dive-bomb the candles and wondering if he was on a similar kamikaze course. What a pair: Shady Katie and the Elf Thief. Maybe they could live down the past together. Or maybe not.

He pushed himself up out of the chair, incapable of another clear thought. "Ulysses," he said with a snort, and headed outside to piss.

7

New Belvedere

WHEN THE INTERVIEW was over, Roger Hammet escorted Caroline from the room, a warm hand on the back of her elbow, a polite murmuring of thanks for being so forthcoming. Out in the hall, he briefly dropped the mask of neutrality he'd worn for the last two and a half hours and gave her a congratulatory wink.

"I think that went well," he confided in a voice too low to be heard inside.

"You do?"

"Trust me," he advised, and winked again before returning to the committee.

Caroline went down the hall and up the stairs to her office. She felt vaguely disembodied, not back to herself yet. A kind of schizophrenia had set in halfway through the interview, when she'd realized the questions had become absurd but couldn't stop herself from trying to answer them. No one else seemed to think they were ridiculous, or if they did, they weren't going to intervene. Roger least of all. He seemed to have taken Herod as his model of impartiality.

The envelope from Harp—oversize and reinforced with shirt cardboard to protect the photos he'd sent—was on her desk. It'd arrived as she was leaving the house, so she'd only had time to glance through it and discover it didn't contain a letter. A disappointment then and a disappointment now. The sound of his voice, even off the page, would've done her some good, and she was dying to know what he'd thought of her letter. Instead he'd scrawled a note saying he'd been sick but was making a comeback, and he asked her to pass the enclosed along to his agent if she thought it was publishable. He'd written a factual account of the discovery of a tomb at Baktun, a piece obviously aimed at a lay audience. From her brief scan, Caroline had the impression he'd captured the drama of the find rather well, but then explained it to death at the end, his prose getting stiffer the closer he stuck to the facts.

And no trace of his real voice. Caroline sat down and shook the photos out of the envelope. There were several black-and-white snapshots of the inside of the tomb, bones and pottery sticking out of a pile of debris at the bottom of a hole. The hands and feet of live humans intruded on the margins but no faces were visible. Then there was one of Harp standing in a trench along with a younger guy who resembled Rod Stewart. They looked as if they'd been dipped in flour and then been caught unawares by the photographer. Harp had written GHOSTS NOT DANCING on the back along with a photo credit to Rita Gertner.

Caroline laughed aloud, getting the joke for the first time. She'd been too nervous earlier. There were also three color shots: one of him sitting in front of a ruined temple (TEMPLE OF THE CROSS, PALENQUE), looking like a degenerate outdoorsman; another of him standing next to an oddly truncated monument (STELA 7, LORD OF SHELLS), sporting a new beard that was darker than his hair; and the last of a damaged but still beautiful Mayan plate, a dancing figure against a dark red background. Caroline could see the last two looking good on the front page of the accent or travel sections, and the article would serve once an editor loosened up the prose. She made a note to herself to send it all off to Harp's agent as soon as possible.

She looked at the two color shots of Harp—before and after the beard—and wondered if they represented a deeper transformation. The first Harp looked ready to traffic in elves or any other sort of contraband. The second looked like the guy who'd written the article: someone disciplined enough to sit down at the typewriter after a day's work in the field.

There was a knock on the open door and Roger Hammet came in. He perched on the corner of her desk and gave her a knowing smile.

"Now tell me you were being modest before," he suggested. "You *do* know how well you handled yourself, don't you?"

Caroline pushed her chair back from the desk and swiveled sideways to face him. "You mean because I didn't lose my temper."

He laughed. "Well, that, of course. I meant the fact you didn't get rattled when the questioning got tough."

"If you're talking about Fedderman and Pohl, I wouldn't characterize their questions as 'tough.' 'Inane,' maybe . . . "

Roger cast an involuntary glance at the open door, then ran a hand through his thick black hair, smiling gamely. "Sometimes you have to let the mossbacks rave. They won't be heeded but they must be heard."

"Why?" Caroline asked, annoyed by what that glance implied. "Why do they get to spout nonsense when the rest of us don't?"

"Because they're full professors. You seemed to know that during the interview, thank god. But okay, if you need to vent some anger, go ahead."

For a moment, Caroline was too angry to speak; she wanted to vent him right out of the room. But she got ahold of herself and brought out a steady voice.

"I don't need to vent anything. I just feel I wasted an hour defending my scholarship to people who hadn't read much of it, and who'd misunderstood what they had read. And after that, when they started asking about my age and citizenship and what my husband does, what they were doing was just plain illegal."

"Perhaps," Roger allowed. "Would you have preferred to argue the law with them? This way you got those questions out of the way without antagonizing anyone or letting them think you had something to hide. Now it can't be used against you later."

"Why would . . . oh, never mind. I'm just glad it's over. When will you vote?"

"Probably not for another week or two. We're still waiting for the outside evaluation on one of the other candidates. At this point, though, I think I could safely say you're our top candidate. Please don't quote me on that, however." He was smiling again as he eased himself off the desk. He gestured loosely at the photographs. "What's your husband up to now? Hunting pink flamingos in the wild?"

"He's working at an archaeological site in Mexico," Caroline said, hearing a righteous note in her own voice. "So I have to be my own househusband."

Roger nodded sympathetically, appearing not to recognize the term as his own. "Well, if it gets too lonely, let's have dinner some night. My wife often leaves me to fend for myself, too."

Caroline stopped herself from questioning the ethics of such an offer, since she had better reasons for resisting it. Like her husband and his wife.

"I'll let you know," she said vaguely, pushing back up to her desk.

"It's an open offer," he said in parting. "Keep it in mind if you feel the need for some company. Ciao."

She waited until he was gone, then picked up the picture of the bearded Harp and leaned back in her chair. His pose was upright and solemn, but she thought she could detect a sly curl to his lips. Was this the career for which she'd been ignoring him? Pointless questions from her colleagues and a veiled proposition from the chair of the committee? She looked at Harp, who appeared very whole next to the shorn-off Lord of Shells. She sent him a silent, yearning blessing, wanting him to be well, whatever was happening to her. *The elf thieves are everywhere,* she told him; *your departure from their ranks will not be cause for mourning.*

Baktun

HELGA KAUFFMANN bobbed along in the lead, a gnome in faded khaki, lugging the black satchel that held all the data sheets and specimen bottles. She was breathing audibly but maintained a pace that Harp—loaded down as he was—found quite comfortable. He had Helga's extension umbrella in one hand and an aluminum stepladder in the other, and strapped to his back was a tank of defoliant with spraying gear attached. He was walking about half a ladder's length behind Helga.

As they came out of the forest and into the semicleared area around the West Plaza, Helga switched the satchel to her left hand and pointed at the ground with her right.

"Hole," she said succinctly, and Harp murmured an acknowledgment, though this one was a fresh-dug burrow and would've been hard to miss. Still, if anyone was gonna miss it . . .

He paused next to the hole and looked back over his shoulder, the tank putting a definite strain on his neck. Rita was about twenty yards behind him, an inveterate straggler of late, despite all his efforts to divert her and cheer her up. This wounded-dove routine was getting to be a pain.

"Hole!" he barked, and went on without waiting to see if she'd heard. He caught up with Helga and followed her into the sunlit plaza, looking around to orient himself. To their immediate left was a three-tiered temple pyramid, Structure A-20, the primary temple during the reign of Kan Cross Ahau. To their right, at a distance, was the platform and range structure that had been built over the ball court. Rick and his crew were already at work, digging out the near end of the platform.

Harp had just spotted Rick among the workers when he heard a cry behind him. He turned to see Rita lying on her face, the tank canted forward over her head as if it had fallen on her from the sky.

"Damn, I tried to warn her," he muttered, dropping the ladder and umbrella and struggling out of his harness.

"It was bound to happen," Helga said with a surprising lack of sympathy. She obviously hadn't been fooled by the stiff upper lip Rita had tried to put on around her.

Rita had gotten herself into a sitting position by the time they reached her, and Harp helped her out of her harness and then came around to unlace the boot she had stuck out stiffly in front of her. She grimaced and sucked air through her teeth as he eased the boot off her foot.

"How bad is it?"

"It's just a sprain. I'll be okay," Rita said unconvincingly. Her eyes were hidden by her sunglasses, but her face was pale and she sounded close to tears. Harp glanced up at Helga.

"I could get somebody from Rick's crew to help carry her to the road, and then go for the Land Cruiser."

"I'll be *okay,*" Rita insisted. "It's not broken."

"You're certain of that?" Helga asked her, and Rita swallowed and nodded. "Then help her around to the front of the temple, Mr. Yates, if you can. I will help too."

Harp got Rita up on her good foot, looping an arm around her back and instructing her to grab hold of his belt. Helga let Rita rest her other hand on Helga's humped shoulders, and the three of them hopped and staggered around to the front of the temple, weaving their way around the tree stumps that studded the grassy plaza. Harp finally lowered Rita down with her back against a cracked and eroded pedestal altar. Behind the altar loomed the nearly blank façade of Stela 17, the so-called Baktun Stela for which the site had been named.

Helga knelt down next to Rita and began talking to her in a way that didn't invite an audience, so Harp went back for their gear, bringing Helga's satchel and Rita's rucksack of personal items in the first load. When he returned with the last of it, Rita was sitting with her bootless foot propped up on the rucksack, wearing her Red Sox cap and her regular glasses, which seemed to deepen the shadows around her eyes. Helga was standing beside the altar, and laid out on top of it were an ancient Zippo lighter, a plastic bag filled with greyish lumps, and a blackened incense ladle. Helga had used this paraphernalia once before, the first day they'd gone to work in the Central Plaza. Harp squatted down so Helga wouldn't have to look up at him while she spoke.

"Apparently, Mr. Yates, you already know about what has been troubling Rita."

"Everybody knows," Rita said in a pepless voice, and Harp could only nod in agreement. She and Jim had become even more of an item by ceasing to be an item.

"You should not have kept this from me for so long, either of you," Helga said sternly. "It could have resulted in a more serious injury, and it has certainly resulted in lost time. A good crew must be of one mind in the field." She held up a hand to ward off their apologies. "That is all the scolding I will do. Rita has agreed that she must put this behind her before she falls into a deeper hole, and I have offered to perform a ceremony of cleansing and renewal. Will you join us in this?"

Harp pulled on his beard and looked at Rita. "If I'm invited."

"You are," Helga assured him. "But we must have your wholehearted participation. Without any of your usual irreverent jokes."

Harp was still looking at Rita. "Whatta *you* say?"

"You're not as cynical as you pretend to be," Rita said with a wan smile. "But no teasing me about it later."

"May I fall into a deep, dark hole," Harp vowed. Helga turned and bent over her satchel, which opened out like a salesman's sample case. She straightened up with a piece of olive-green cloth in her hands, though once she'd molded it into shape it was clearly a hat: a soft canvas fedora with a contrasting band and eyelet airholes, a real Banana Republic special. Helga held it out on her upraised palms.

"One of my doctoral students gave me this, but you know I can never stand to wear a hat, not of any kind. So I have my umbrella, and you should have this."

"A new headdress," Harp said approvingly, reaching over to pluck the Red Sox cap off Rita's head. "You gave up on shortstop long ago, young lady."

Rita only had time to fluff out her black curls before Helga—as if fitting a crown—lowered the fedora into place. Helga's eyes widened as she backed away, and she glanced at Harp to see if he shared her reaction.

"Oh, *yeah,*" he murmured. The stylish downward slope of the brim seemed to follow the curve of Rita's nose, giving it grace rather than prominence. And her eyes, shielded from the glare, seemed magnified by the large round lenses of her glasses. The overall effect was of rakish innocence, the young foreign correspondent on her first overseas assignment.

"I had only hoped it might fit," Helga said helplessly.

"You're not gonna believe what that does for you," Harp said. A sudden gifting impulse made him reach up for the small pink and grey feather he'd stuck into the crown of his panama. "Scarlet macaw . . . found it at the cenote yesterday," he explained as he rose and inserted the downy feather into the band of the fedora. It seemed perfect, too.

Helga was beaming and bobbing her head, her hands clasped in front of her, and the blushing face Rita turned up to him already appeared halfway to renewal. He wondered if it could really be this easy but just as quickly banished the thought, knowing better than to sully the magic with doubt. He went over to the altar and held the ladle still while Helga crumbled a ball of sticky grey copal into the bowl.

"*Pom,*" Helga intoned, the Mayan word for the incense used in the ancient ceremonies. She applied the flame of the Zippo and a plume of white smoke curled upward, sweet at first whiff but sharply resinous deeper in the nose.

"*Pom,*" Harp repeated softly, deciding, without his usual irony, that this was a truly Classic moment.

SINCE STELA 17 was over eight feet tall, they'd inspected and sampled the front, back, and sides first, leaving the rounded top of the monument for last. It was late in the afternoon before Harp ascended the ladder for a look, and he found a rich variety of plant life growing in the crevices of the glyphs, which were traps for moisture and airborne debris. He had to stand on the last step before the top of the ladder just to bring his eyes level with the carving, which made the collection of samples rather precarious and difficult. On another day he probably would've found a way to put it off until tomorrow, but the ceremony had left him with an extra measure of equanimity, so he told Helga and Rita he'd give it a shot. If they got it sampled today, they could start right in on the cleaning tomorrow morning and maybe have it cleaned and sprayed by noon.

He was scraping a piece of crusty yellow lichen into a plastic pill bottle when Rick strolled up leading a group that included Kaaren, Max, Eric, and a couple of the other undergraduates. They were eating oranges and drinking from canteens, and after greeting Helga they began to plague Rita with unwanted solicitations. Harp had set up the ladder behind the stela, and it was a testament to their fatigue that no one had yet looked up to see him peering down at them.

"Hey, some folks are still working!" he called out, causing them to jump back from Rita. Rita smiled and lifted up her hands for the pill bottle he tossed down to her. "Number nineteen, top center," he reported. "Yellow dendritic lichen on uncarved surface. Poor adhesion."

Helga jotted that down in her notebook while Rita filled out the label on the pill bottle. Rick looked up at Harp and grinned.

"What else you got up there besides lichens?"

"All kinds of crap. Two kinds of moss, more lichens, some insect larvae, and a lotta slimy black algae." Harp gripped the top edge of the stela with one hand and fished another pill bottle out of his shirt pocket with the other. He made sure he had his balance before he went after some of the algae with a slender spatula.

"What kind of glyphs?" Rick prompted. Harp replied without taking his eyes from his work.

"Baktun glyphs, just like on the sides. The standard version alternating with the head variant. Oh yeah, and in small script here it says . . . lemme see . . . '*hecho en Mexico.*' "

The joke drew enough laughter to discourage Rick from further harassment, and after briefly deferring to Helga—who graciously turned the show back to him—Rick launched into a description of the monument for the benefit of his younger companions.

"Okay . . . this is Stela Seventeen, as far as we know the last stela erected at the site. Certainly the last *dated* monument we've found. It commemorates the completion of Baktun Ten in the Long Count, at about A.D. 830. It's one of the few stelae at the site that wasn't moved from its original position, though at some point it fell or was toppled over backward. Which is why the portrait on this side is almost completely gone. This's a harder limestone than the earlier monuments, but a thousand years of rain will wash away anything. However, you can still see"—Rick had stepped up to the stela and was pointing with his finger—"evidence of what was apparently a single standing figure. We assume this was Kan Cross Ahau, the glyphic name of the ruler given on the back. This"—Rick's arm stretched up high enough to distract Harp—"this dent is probably where the face was."

Home now to a good crop of moss, Harp mused. He popped the cover off the bottle with his thumb and spooned a gruesome-looking dollop of blue-black algae into it. As Rick moved his group to the left side of the monument, Harp had a clear toss to Rita, who made a leaning one-handed grab as the bottle sailed past.

"Still got the hands of a shortstop," Harp commended her. "Number twenty, top right. Blue-black algae growing like filigree in the relief portion of the glyph. Very slimy but quite striking in appearance. Looks like somebody painted in the outline."

" 'A slimy filigree,' " Rick repeated, drawing laughter from his companions. "Apt if unscientific terminology. As he told you earlier, what we have here is the baktun glyph alternating with its head variant in a continuous row. It goes up this side, over the top, and down the other. When Morley made his first reconnaissance of the site back in the twenties, he uncovered this and was so impressed by all the baktun glyphs that he called the site Baktun. The repetition of the period glyph in this fashion is really unusual, wouldn't you say, Helga?"

"Most definitely," Helga agreed. "I have seen nothing like it except on altars. It shows the enormous importance they attached to the completion of Baktun Ten."

"Would you say it's a departure from Classic Mayan style?" Rick asked. Harp was scooping up his last sample but stopped to hear the answer. The Classic nature of Stela 17 was one of the crucial assumptions in Clubb's Persistence Theory.

"A departure from convention, perhaps," Helga allowed. "The glyphs themselves show a certain flamboyance of execution that is typical of the Terminal Classic. So I would say there is decadence but not a departure."

Point to Clubb, Harp thought. He got the sample into its bottle and dropped it into his pocket, gathered up his tools, and climbed down off the stepladder. The ground felt solid and good beneath his feet and he stretched to relieve the aching tension in his limbs.

"What'd you get?" Rick asked. Harp responded by stepping past him and calling it out to Rita and Helga.

"Number twenty-one, top far right. Encrusted grey matter on roughened surface of glyph. Turned to a kind of fluff when scraped. Possibly ash or acid-rain deposit." He smiled and flipped the bottle to Rita. "That's all, folks."

He turned back and listened as Rick read off the Initial Series date inscribed in a double column of glyphs on the back of the stela: ten baktuns, zero katuns, zero tuns, zero months, zero days. In his mind Harp saw it written out—10.0.0.0.0—about as round as a number could get and surely good reason to make a fuss and depart from convention. It wasn't often that all the tumblers came up zero.

Helga interrupted Rick's recitation to point out that the lunar count was off by a day, though she didn't attempt to account for the discrepancy, leaving Harp to wonder if it'd been deliberate or just another example of decadence. Rick went on to point out the kan cross and ahau glyphs at the bottom of the inscription.

"Kan Cross Ahau is the first ruler named after the death of Shell Star in 9.18.10.0.0. A plain stela may've been erected in his honor in 9.19.0.0.0. It was around that time that the ceremonial locus of the site was shifted from the Central Plaza to here." Rick gestured toward the temple pyramid behind them. "Structure A-Twenty was enlarged to about twice its previous size and the range-type structures to the south and east replaced similar but smaller structures. The plaza itself was raised another foot and the platform we've been digging all day was laid down over the ball court."

Harp raised his hand and waved it like an eager schoolboy. "Can we assume from that, Dr. Fisher, that Kan Cross Ahau wasn't a sports fan?"

"I'll defer to Dr. Kauffmann on that one," Rick demurred. Helga shook her head and laughed along with the others.

"I am becoming acquainted with Mr. Yates's sense of humor. He asked me before if I didn't think the ahau glyph looked like a . . . what did you call it?"

"A Mayan Happy Face," Harp supplied with a grin.

"Yes, and then he had to explain to me what that was. I would tell him not to confuse sport with a religious ritual, but that might not be possible for an American male."

"Touché," Harp said, bowing in surrender. The howler monkeys suddenly started roaring in the distance, reminding them of the time and the fading light. With the help of Rick and his crew, they stowed their gear near the ball court, and Harp and Eric took the first shift as bearers for Rita.

"Nice hat," Eric murmured as they started out of the plaza, blushing when Rita smiled at him.

"That's what my friends tell me," Rita said, giving Harp a little squeeze with the arm around his neck. He caught a whiff of copal off her clothes and nodded, feeling renewed for the long march back to camp.

THAT SUNDAY Ramona produced another splendid dinner, the main course her famous Mexican lasagna, which added chorizo, chiles, and corn to the usual ingredients. There was also an array of fresh fruit and sweet rolls, pitchers of lemonade and pineapple juice, and pots of strong black coffee and a bittersweet cocoa that was almost as potent. As Harp poured a splash of rum into his pineapple juice and passed the bottle to Emory Muldoon, he was struck by how different this meal was from the first Sunday dinner he'd attended. Brinton Taylor had run that one like a high academic tea, orchestrating the conversation so that each of the senior staff members got to speak on his or her specialty area. It'd been an interesting and at times animated discussion, but for most of it the majority of the people sitting around the long table were listening in silence.

Today there were eight or ten conversations going at once, due to the fact that the work crews were sitting together as distinct groups. Brinton was still at the head of the table, flanked by Oliver Clubb and Helga Kauffmann, but his conversational reach didn't extend beyond the group immediately around him. Rita was up there next to Helga, though she seemed to be paying more attention to Eric the Motorhead, who'd taken the seat usually reserved for Harp. Harp had come in late and taken a seat with Lucy and Katie at the other end of the table, next to Muldoon's crew.

"You coming down to B this week?" Muldoon asked. "We've got some dirty stones down there, because of all the shade."

"Great," Harp said sarcastically. "I always liked all the trees around B, but I could change my mind."

Muldoon laughed and tugged on his bushy beard. "Probably weren't too many trees left standing in Mayan times, given the demand for firewood and building material."

"Is Brinton gonna have it logged out now that the causeway's fixed?"

Muldoon shrugged. "The agreement he's got with the lumber company stipulates selective cutting, so it shouldn't be too bad. The big trees that shield us from the river won't be touched either."

"Why's that? Oh—because of the Guatemalans?"

"The Guaties used to patrol their side pretty regularly. They may still do it, but we don't get close enough anymore to check."

"My wife sent me some clippings on Guatemala. One of them talked about the 'Guatemalan Solution,' a combination of death squads in the cities and strategic hamlets in the countryside. Is that going on anywhere near here?"

"Probably," Muldoon said, pouring himself more rum. "It is in the highlands, and that's not far south. The Quiché have taken a real beating, from what I've heard."

"Tell him about your run-in with the Guaties," Katie suggested.

Muldoon frowned and hesitated, glancing at Lucy, who was sitting between Harp and Katie. But Lucy was absorbed in a paperback biography of Michael Jackson and appeared to have tuned the adults out. So Muldoon shrugged and told the story.

"It was during the first season. Ulysses and I were doing some semiofficial bushwhacking with a couple of the Mexican workers, cutting our way down to the river. The slope had once been terraced and we were finding structures all over the place, shrines and house mounds and what was probably a monumental staircase along the lines of the one at Yaxchilán. We were so into it that to this day we don't know how the patrol came across the river. All of a sudden they were just *there,* sticking their guns in our faces and pushing us around. Ulysses almost slugged one of 'em before he caught his temper. They all looked about sixteen, except for the guy in charge. He was maybe twenty-five and without question the nastiest sonuvabitch I've ever met face-to-face."

Muldoon paused to drink, his gaze turned inward on the memory. "He had a forty-five automatic, U.S. Army issue, and he kept poking me and Ulysses with it"—Muldoon prodded himself in the sternum—"and calling us spies and communists. He kept saying he was going to 'fuck' us. That was about all the English he knew and he wouldn't listen to us in Spanish. It was real tense until one of his boys broke into Ulysses's pack and found the specimens of moss he'd been collecting, which they thought was funny as hell. They seemed to decide that we were too silly to kill. It occurred to me later that they knew better than to shoot a couple of Americanos with guns they'd gotten from the U.S. government, but at the time I was convinced that bastard with the automatic would do the worst he could think of."

Muldoon's vehemence—or maybe just the profanity—had gotten Lucy to lower her book, and Harp gave him another chance to drink before prompting him to finish. "So they let you go?"

"After beating up on the Mexicans and giving us a lecture on not hiding escaped criminals, which is one of the nicer things he called the Indians he was chasing. Another one was 'animals with clothes.' " Muldoon shook his head in disgust. "Anyway, Brinton reported it to the Mexican government and we had fifty Mexican soldiers camped near B for the rest of the season. They were better mannered but a bit trigger-happy where the wildlife was concerned. Put a significant dent in the monkey population."

"They shot the monkeys?" Lucy cried in disbelief. "What for?"

"For sport, I'm afraid," Muldoon told her. "We weren't sorry when they didn't come back the next season."

"Did you go back to the river while they were here?" Harp asked.

Muldoon let out a rueful laugh. "You can bet they wanted us to—they probably would've carried our gear for us. But Brinton didn't want to risk a border war just to get a better look at the staircase. It's a gap in our knowledge we'll just have to live with."

Ulysses came up then, recruiting bushwhackers. Earlier, Harp recalled, Ulysses had circulated a box of chocolate-covered cherries. So far he had only Jim Zorn in tow.

"I was just telling them about our meeting with the Guatie patrol," Muldoon explained. Ulysses grunted, his eyes flashing scorn.

"I hated the army, but I'd reenlist in a second to fight those fuckers. In a second." He exhaled and shook himself, as if it annoyed him to dwell on it. "Anyway, we're going north instead of south today. We've been cutting the *brecha* in that direction and finding lots of features along the way. Any takers?"

"I'm gonna lay in a hammock and read a book," Muldoon said, pushing himself to his feet.

"I'm going swimming," Lucy announced, and scooted out ahead of Muldoon. Ulysses lingered a moment longer—giving Harp the impression even *he* would've been acceptable—then moved on toward the head of the table with Jim trailing along. Katie slid over into the seat next to Harp.

"So, have you finished a first draft yet? Ready to take a break?"

"First draft of what?"

"Your next novel. Isn't that what you've been sneaking off to write every night after dinner?"

Harp smiled. "Indirectly. I had a lot of catching up to do after being sick. I needed to put my notes in order and write down some of the stuff I've been carrying around in my head."

"Well, you must be done with *that,*" Katie said briskly. "So take some time off and come swimming with us."

Harp stretched, feeling the tight inelasticity of deep fatigue. "Now that you mention it, I guess I have been pushing a bit hard. I almost didn't wake up in time to eat today."

"I rest my case. C'mon, Harp. Lighten up and get real, as Lucy would say."

"Okay, I'll come," Harp said, laughing. "I guess I've earned it."

"So have I," Katie said as she stood up. "You don't know the self-restraint I've exercised."

"Self-restraint?" Harp echoed, rising and walking out of the dining hall with her.

"I came out to your hut on two separate occasions, and both times I turned around and left when I heard the way you were typing."

Harp stared at her in bemusement. "You really did? Jeez, you shoulda come in. I wasn't doing anything that couldn't be interrupted."

Katie shrugged and shook her head. "I didn't know that, and I sure couldn't tell from what I was hearing. I figured it had to be important for you to be working so hard that late. So I let you be."

They'd come to the women's lodge, and Lucy called from inside the long building, telling her mother to hurry up and get her suit on.

"Lighten up, Luce," Katie called over her shoulder, then looked back at Harp. "We'll pick you up on the way to the cenote."

"I'll be ready. And Katie . . . thanks."

"For letting you be?" Katie inquired archly. "I'm not sure that's a compliment, but you're welcome anyway. In return, I expect you *not* to let me be so much."

"You've earned it," Harp told her, tipping his hat with a smile as he turned and headed up the path toward his hut.

New Belvedere

CAROLINE HADN'T gotten back from dinner until after nine, and then she'd gone right into the den, as the Ushers called it, to call the number Virginia Evers had given her. She didn't get off the phone until ten-fifteen, feeling exhilarated but also slightly dazed. There'd been too many surprises today, and she wasn't sure how they balanced out. She poured herself a stiff scotch and went to get the mail, which was all junk except for a letter from Harp.

"Please, a pleasant surprise," she prayed aloud, still worried that she'd been too rough on him in her last letter. She went back into the den, a converted bedroom that had hunting prints on the walls, a rolltop desk missing its rolling top, a grandfather clock that didn't work, and a standing bookcase crammed with *Reader's Digest* condensed books and the last ten years of *National Geographic.* Caroline noted the depth of accumulated dust as she sat in the creaking swivel chair by the desk and slit open the envelope.

He'd mimicked her style by giving his the title "A PERSONAL REVITALIZATION MOVEMENT" and beginning with a formal definition.

> REVITALIZATION MOVEMENT: A deliberate effort by members of a society to construct a more satisfying culture.

"That's simple enough," Caroline murmured wryly. Beyond the definition, however, Harp abandoned all formality and launched into a series of disconnected episodes that ranged from the silly to the sublime, all related with a kind of irrepressible zest. These included tales of puking on poisonous snakes, dreaming of Mayan kings, making friends with the camp pig, dancing spastically with the local teenagers, and burning incense for a girl with a sprained ankle. Each was made to sound like a mini-epiphany in Harp's retelling, and Caroline was laughing too hard to worry about how this added up to a "movement."

The final entry was dated five days ago, which made its arrival today a minor miracle. Harp's voice was suddenly rather cozy:

> Writing this by flash- and candlelight because I used up all the oil for the Coleman and won't get any more until we make a supply run into Comitán tomorrow. That's also how the mail will go out, so I want to wrap this up before it gets any older. Another reason I'm writing this in the Hut of Usher rather than the dining hall (where the oil generator provides light) is that it's safe to get stoned here. Yep, you heard right: Cannabis nirvana has come to Baktun. Actually, it's been here all along, but only today did it come to me, like this:
>
> We've taken our stone-saving operation down to Group B, a journey made much easier by the fact that the causeway's now fixed and we can go by truck and Land Cruiser. On the way back today I was riding with Vicente and some of the other Mexican workers who're currently attached to Emory Muldoon's crew, and Vicente asked me if I'd ever fixed the walls of my casa. I'd never had a chance to thank him for the advice he'd given me on how to make plaster, so I took him and three others back for a look. I thought they'd laugh at the rough but effective job I'd done, but instead they were full of compliments and made a kind of occasion out of it, so I felt obligated to invite them inside and offer them the only things I had to offer: cigarettes and mescal (Rick got me a bottle in Comitán). Also showed off your typewriter, which was a big hit with Carlos Kan Boar, an in-law of some kind of Vicente's who has the sunken eyes, high cheekbones, and long black hair of a Lacandon Indian. Whatever you say or do around him, he mostly just stares at you

with a spooky kind of tolerance, as if you were a Martian. But he really got off on the lift-off key and the automatic memory print-out. He's a skinny guy but has this great loud belly laugh—imagine an Indian Santa who's been on a long-term crash diet. If I understood Vicente's translation into Spanish, he was saying "it eats and spits!"

They seemed to understand when it was time to go (down to three fingers in the bottle?) and they all shook my hand and thanked me as they left. The last one out was Vicente's nephew Arturo, a young, kinda flashy guy who combs his hair in a ducktail, laughs too much, and is always ogling the women. He pointed back into the room and then at me and said "Por usted." For you. I didn't have the slightest idea what he meant but thanked him anyway, which made him laugh and repeat "por usted" as he left. A few minutes later I discovered the brown paper bag that'd been left next to the typewriter. Inside was maybe an ounce and a half of what I've come to think of fondly as Baktun Brown, due to its overcured color. Oh, but it works like gold, especially on a brain that's been dopeless for over a month. I was so buzzed I got lost on the way to dinner and ended up in the Central Plaza, which was rather awesome at sunset, just me and the Shell family being stoned together in our separate ways.

I suffered some paranoia afterward, recalling how adamant Rick'd been about not bringing anything in, but a few discreet inquiries at dinner assured me that this wasn't an uncommon occurrence or a setup for a bust. Seems many of the local villagers do a little cash-cropping in grass and often pass it on to the gringos they trust. The unspoken rule around the camp is never to smoke it on the job or where Brinton Taylor might get a whiff. I shall of course play strictly by the rules.

"Oh god, now he'll never come home," Caroline groaned. She took a sip of scotch and savored it along with the last paragraph.

So now the only thing I miss is you. It may not be apparent from the above, but your letter has had a powerful influence on the shape of my revival. You could say it was the precipitating event, in fact. Then the local microbes provided me with a minicollapse so I could feel I was starting over from scratch. Did it feel like that for you when you got back from Vancouver? Sounds like you laid a lot of the old demons to rest. Hope you got the article and photos I sent. In retrospect, the former seems like the product of an overly straight mind, rigid with earnestness. I'll try not to let that happen again. After all, it's my duty to

save the stones,
Harp

Caroline sat a moment, listening to the echoes of his voice in her head. Then she picked up her pen and tore the top sheet off the yellow pad on which she'd taken notes during the phone call. She decided not to bother with a date and printed the title in caps across the top of the page.

STARTING OVER FROM SCRATCH?

Dear Harp,

That title is very tentative, because I'm still trying to figure out what's going on. Please help. This is what happened today:

12:30 PM. I'd just stopped off in my office to dump my books on my way to lunch. I'm standing at my desk when Sylvia Burdette knocks on the door. You've met her on a number of occasions: tall, grey-hair in a bun, glasses on a chain around her neck, a particularly formidable version of the spinster schoolteachers of my childhood. Those she favors (mostly men) claim to find her delightfully eccentric; those with no place under her stiff wing find her intimidating if not downright vindictive. She's the only tenured woman in the Sociology Dept. and has been for at least ten years.

"I thought you might find this of interest," she says, and hands me the latest issue of the ASA job list. She's circled one of the ads in yellow, an opening at SUNY Albany for a beginning Assistant Professor who can teach both sociology and women's studies. It was amazing—the job description couldn't have fit me better unless it'd asked for a Canadian. I felt a little thrill that vanished as soon as I began to wonder why Sylvia had brought me this. Because Sylvia's on the search committee for the job here, and though she's told several people that she's my supporter, she was absolutely no help during the interview. She probably *thought* she was helping me, but all she really did was legitimize the stupid questions the Old Farts were asking.

So why would she want to alert me to a job elsewhere? Was she warning me that I wasn't going to get the job here? Or was this much less friendly, in fact a nasty way of saying she wished I'd get lost? I didn't have a clue, so I just said thank you, which Sylvia accepted with a smile.

"I had an aunt," she said, "who always used to say that you can never have too many umbrellas."

With that, she left, and left me a wreck for the rest of the afternoon. The head of the committee had told me I was their top candidate, but he'd also thought the interview had gone well, and I thought it was a farce. Now Sylvia was suggesting I needed another umbrella.

I had dinner tonight with Virginia Evers, something we've been doing weekly. She didn't find Sylvia's gesture encouraging, either, and she was angry, because she'd made a strong pitch for me on behalf of Women's Studies. But she gave me the number of a friend of hers at Albany, a sociologist named Alice Prager who's written a study of the women who served in the Vietnam War. I'm sure I raved to you about it at some point, because I referred to it a number of times in my thesis.

So I gave her a call, and we ended up talking for an hour about virtually everything, one of the best conversations I've had with anyone in a long time. She advised CO's during the war and wants to read *War College,* which I promised to send her. She already knew about my work, having heard good things about it from one of the editors at the Cornell Press, where I sent my chapters. So she was very encouraging about my prospects for the job at Albany and urged me to apply. She's not on the search committee herself but said she could make sure I wasn't overlooked.

I hung up feeling I'd been handed a second umbrella, which gave me some comfort. But I was still faced with the concern Sylvia had aroused: When had it started raining *here*? After a year and a half of knocking myself out to impress people, was I back where I started, sending off applications to places I'd never been? Had I somehow skipped the collapse yet still ended up starting over from scratch? I wish I had some of your enthusiasm for the prospect. Instead I feel as if I've been pushed out the door just when I thought I was being invited in.

Caroline dropped the pen and sat back in the creaking chair, unable to continue. She was exhausted and felt a whine coming on, a tone she didn't want to use with Harp. She'd have to read this again later to see if she should even send it to him. In the meantime, she'd have to draft a letter of application, update her résumé and reactivate her file at Vermont, and start contacting people to act as references. She'd have to make a fresh investment of hope and put herself out there for further inspection. She sighed and reached for her drink. Here's to revitalizing my career, she thought. If only it were as simple and straightforward as puking on a poisonous snake.

Baktun

WHEN THEY were done for the day they carried their equipment back through the tall trees, Rita still limping slightly but able to haul her share. A few members of the joint Brinton/Muldoon crew had reached the causeway ahead of them, and they helped Harp load the tanks and ladder onto the bed of the truck. Harp gave Helga a hand climbing into the cab and then went around to the back to boost Rita up onto the truck. He noticed that Jim Zorn was sitting up there, too, and caught a glance from Rita that told him she knew it. So he gave her a big smile and slung his rucksack and a canteen over his shoulder.

"I'm gonna stick around and take some impressions while the light lasts," he explained. "If I'm not back for dinner, send out Sancho Panza."

"Communing with the spirit of Lord of Shells?" Rita teased, and Harp laughed and held up a hand so she could give him five.

"Hold all calls on the psycho-duct," he told her and walked away with a parting wave of his hand, thinking *eat your heart out, Jimbo—see how much fun we think she is?* A little revenge never hurt the process of renewal, he figured, as long as it wasn't obsessive.

He went back down the path toward B's Central Plaza, passing more of the other crew coming the other way, though he didn't waste any explanations on them. As soon as he was alone on the path, he took a sharp right and worked his way through the undergrowth until he was sure he couldn't be seen. He took a piss and waited, and it wasn't long before he heard the truck start up and lumber off in low gear, leaving behind a silence that deepened and then evaporated into the white noise of the forest. Harp started walking again, away from the path and toward the river. After about fifty meters, the undergrowth thinned out and he could see light between the huge hardwoods ahead. He tried to stay behind their trunks as he approached the edge of the ridge, glancing down at himself to be sure he wasn't wearing anything that might stand out against the green. His first view of the Rio Lacantún made him stop and stare: The sun was gilding the trees on both sides and had turned the river a dark copper green, streaked with white where it wound around the rocks in its bed. The forest on the other side appeared to go on forever, undulating over the hilly terrain without leaving a break in the canopy of green.

Guatemala, he thought, and squatted down behind a fallen tree before looking again. But there were no signs of troop movement, no sounds of gunfire to disturb his reverie. He tried to imagine the hillside below him cleared and terraced, long canoes docking at the foot of a monumental staircase. They probably had their fields on the high ground on the other side, with groves of cacao trees in the swampy ravines and stands of fruit and breadnut trees around the thatch-roofed houses of the farmers. If Muldoon was right about the demand for wood, those hills might have looked like a tropical subdivision. And the "lost" city behind him might have been visible for miles.

Sitting with his back against the tree, he dug a joint out of his rucksack and gave himself four measured hits of Baktun Brown, blowing the smoke into the spreading leaves of a nearby bush. When his senses were properly primed, he rose and walked back the way he'd come, sniffing the air and trying to pick individual sounds out of the chorus of birdcall and insect buzz. Getting lost the first time he'd smoked had been an instructive experience, alerting him to how easy it would be to get truly lost, or take a fast tumble off a high platform. It had also awakened him to the fact that he'd been regarding Baktun in only two dimensions—as a workplace and an object of study. He'd been taking notes on everything, piling up analyses and written descriptions, collecting copies of all the various site reports. He'd even roughed out a cast of historical characters and a tentative sequence of major events. But he hadn't taken the time just to wander around, to shut off the recording apparatus in his head and let the senses soak it in. He'd been so busy cataloging the place he'd neglected to inhabit it.

An excess of rigor, he thought as he found the path and took it toward the plaza. The mind kept plowing the same straight furrow until a kind of tunnel vision set in and you no longer thought to gaze up at the sky or try for a glimpse of the things that moved out of the corner of the eye.

He entered the deserted and deeply shadowed plaza and walked across it slowly, focusing his attention on Stela 7, the half-stela of Lord of Shells that his descendants had reset here. The symbol of their revitalization movement, to which Harp had been drawn instinctively. But during a recent reverie he'd realized that what Kan Cross Ahau had been doing in the West Plaza—at roughly the same time—could also be considered a revitalization movement. And the Kan Cross People had apparently come out on top. Did that make the Shell family survivors the underdogs he'd supposed them to be, or possibly something less admirable, like a disgruntled clique of displaced aristocrats? The Shell dynasty had held power for five generations and then had lost it. Perhaps they'd become corrupt and decadent, a burden their people could no longer tolerate. That would make their movement reactionary rather than revitalizing, an attempt to regain lost privilege rather than to create it anew.

In a heretical departure from his dream, Harp imagined himself a follower of Kan Cross Ahau, sent here to deal with the reactionaries in their midst. There'd been fighting and the taking of prisoners; the shrines around the plaza were being desecrated by his warriors. Now he stood in front of Lord of Shells, a stone hammer in his hand, poised for an act of revolutionary vandalism. Perhaps *this* was what he had to do to prove himself worthy. And perhaps he couldn't look upon the stern visage of Lord of Shells, the man who'd brought greatness to Baktun, without feeling an urge to bow. Unlike those who were trying to exploit his memory, Lord of Shells was a man worthy of veneration and respect. But Harp couldn't yield to that urge now, with his men watching him eagerly, the prisoners bound and trembling at their feet. He couldn't show the slightest reluctance to raise his hand against the face of past glory. He had to strike the blow Kan Cross Ahau had ordered and shatter that face forever . . .

He brought the invisible hammer down with a vicious grunt, and he was raising his arm for a second blow when someone suddenly made a loud throat-clearing sound behind him. He jumped higher than he had in years, losing his hat and rucksack and canteen and almost smacking into the stela as he came down. He turned fearfully, expecting Guaties with guns and finding Brother Rick and Brinton Taylor instead.

"What on earth are you doing?" Brinton demanded.

Harp clamped a hand over his heart, which seemed in danger of bursting through his ribs. "Jesus! I thought I was alone."

"Obviously. Do you have some sort of animus against this stela?" Brinton asked, sounding more incredulous than angry.

"No, not in this life," Harp said, blushing at the glance that drew from Brinton. "I was just imagining how it might've been killed."

"I thought writers did their imaginings at a desk. I didn't think they went around acting out the lives of their characters."

Harp darted a glance at Rick, who rolled his eyes in a sympathetic warning and then went blank, as if to say he couldn't intervene. *If you fail you will be forgotten* went through Harp's mind as he picked up his hat and whacked it lightly against his leg before setting it back on his head. His high was long gone, and he reached back for some rigor with a kind of angry desperation.

"I'm sure it looked like conduct unbecoming an archaeologist," he said to Brinton. "But if you really wanna know, I was ridding myself of an unconscious bias."

Out of the corner of his eye, he saw Rick's mouth drop open, then clamp shut before a laugh could escape. Brinton seemed genuinely taken aback, squinting at him quizzically.

"What sort of bias?"

"My bias in favor of the Shell dynasty. I realized I'd been siding with them even after they lost power here. I suppose I picked that up from Clubb's article, or maybe just because they built the best temples and left the most monuments behind. In any case, it occurred to me that maybe they weren't the heroes of the piece after all, especially from the perspective of the Kan Cross People. I was trying to see it from their angle for a change."

"Extraordinary," Brinton murmured. "I must say, you've put an entirely new slant on the old notion of a flight of fancy. I'd always conceived of it as a basically rudderless venture."

Harp smiled. "Flying blind, you mean? Yeah, it's like that, too. But that's part of the fun."

"I'm sure," Brinton said doubtfully. "Well. Richard and I were on our way back to camp, so we'll leave you to your imaginings. But please, Mr. Yates, don't get carried away and fly into anything real. These stones are harder than you are, but they're fragile in their own way."

"Don't I know it," Harp said as Brinton walked away. Rick picked up Harp's canteen and lingered behind to hand it to him. He was still on the verge of cracking up and wouldn't look at Harp directly.

"Now *that* is what I call a good lie," he said, and snorted. "Kill a stela for Kan Cross Ahau."

"A nasty job, but somebody's . . . "

"Never mind," Rick interrupted and started off after Brinton, looking back once to grin and shake his head. Harp watched him disappear up the path, which looked like a black hole in the wall of trees. He drank from the canteen and dug his flashlight out of the rucksack, deciding he was done for the day too. He wasn't ready to start experiencing these places in the dark. He started off, then caught himself and came back to bow before the stela, letting the spirit of Lord of Shells know it hadn't been anything personal.

8

HARP HAD gotten up early to experience the sunrise in the Central Plaza of Group A, so he was already working on his second cup of coffee by the time Rita came into the dining hall. Her limp was barely noticeable, and along with her ritual fedora she was wearing a maroon polo shirt and faded jeans, both of which fit her with an enticing snugness. *Our little girl is growing up,* Harp thought, beckoning to her when she came out with her food. He caught a whiff of sweet-smelling soap as she sat down next to him and removed her hat.

"So it's true," he concluded, giving her a long, sidelong look.

"What is?"

"You're going back to Muldoon's crew. You wouldn't get yourself up this nice to work with me."

"What'd you expect? You know how much I liked working with Muldoon, and Dr. Taylor's down there too."

"So's Jim Zorn. You're more likely to get paired off with him than with Brinton."

"That's his problem. He knew I'd want to come back to Muldoon's crew when I was done with Helga. Let him go dig the ball court if it bothers him to have me around."

"We don't want him," Harp said. "We've got a nice, congenial crew, with

Max and Kaaren and Rick, and a certain tall gentleman recently seen in your company. And me, of course."

"Of course," Rita said with a slight smile. "I appreciate your concern, Harp, but I can handle Jim. I've been doing what you told me—sparkling for everyone but him. It's been working, too; he's been trying to be nicer to me."

"It's called vamping," Harp told her. "And it's best done from a certain distance, with a sympathetic audience. You sure you're ready to deal with him up close and personal, without me for backup?"

Rita laughed. "God, Harp, you're more of a yenta than Helga! How do you know about 'vamping' anyway?"

Harp shrugged. "I had it done to me once. By a girl I'd dumped as stupidly as Jim dumped you. She'd come around and flirt with my friends and look *so* damn good, and so utterly oblivious of me. She had me kicking myself with both feet."

"So what happened?" Rita prompted when Harp paused, his cheeks warming at the memory. "Did you finally crack?"

"Like a well-aged walnut," Harp confessed. "I groveled all over the place and she finally accepted my apology. Then I asked her out and she said she'd think about it and get back to me—in the year 2000. It was 1964 at the time."

Rita let out a whoop of laughter and then clamped a hand over her mouth, though she continued to sputter into her fingers. Harp stood up and pushed in his chair.

"I'm sorry, Harp," Rita managed.

"No, you're not, but that's okay. Just don't use that line unless you wanna totally crush him."

"You know I'm not like that. I'd rather let him make it up to me somehow."

"Good. Then relax and let him do the work. You're looking good enough that you can probably vamp him without even trying."

Rita blushed and waved a hand at him. "You're *blind.*"

"Nope," Harp demurred, and gave her a leering once-over as he turned toward the door. "I'm just a dirty old man . . . "

ACCORDING TO Brother Rick, the West Plaza ball court was a typical Classic Period construction, an I-shaped structure that had a long narrow corridor between high walls as its stem and broad, open end zones as its feet. The parallel walls that formed the corridor were truly massive, twelve feet high and ten feet thick, and each was lined on the inside by a masonry bench that sloped up against it like a ramp. The end zones, in contrast, were surrounded by low walls that seemed intended only to mark their boundaries.

When Kan Cross Ahau seized power at the end of Baktun Ten, he moved the ceremonial center of the site from the Central to the West Plaza, initiating what was thought to be the final phase of construction at Baktun. His builders enlarged the temple pyramid, refurbished the adjacent buildings, and added another thick layer of plaster to the plaza itself. They also went to work on the ball court, though not with renovation in mind. Using the massive range wall of the court as a foundation, they walled off the open ends and filled the corridor to the top with rubble. Then they capped it with a layer of flat stones and another of plaster, and what had once been a ball court had become a long, raised platform. A palace building with three doorways and a vaulted roof was then erected on top of the platform, and a staircase was added on the side facing the plaza.

By the time the archaeologists had their turn, the palace was in an advanced state of collapse but the platform beneath it was still largely intact, completely concealing the presence of the underlying structure. Rick had discovered it by accident at the end of the previous season, while cutting an exploratory trench down through the floor of the ruined palace. The foundation walls provided the first clue, being much thicker than was usual or necessary for such a platform, and when he dug down through the fill and found one of the sloping benches, he knew he had a ball court.

The find had only made it into his dissertation as a late appendix, and he'd returned this season to face the problem of how properly to excavate it. His solution had been to leave the southern half of the platform and palace pretty much as it was, stabilized but not restored, and to remove the northern half entirely, exposing and restoring the ball court underneath. In the time since Harp had last seen it, Rick's crew had removed the tons of debris used to fill the interior of the court and had taken down the wall that had sealed its northern end. The thick range walls were faced with well-cut limestone blocks and had emerged relatively intact, allowing the crew to concentrate their restorative efforts on the sloping benches, which had fared less well beneath the weight of the fill. Seen from above, the ball court looked like a roofless subway tunnel that ran straight into the exposed hearting of the platform.

"Pretty fucking impressive," Harp decided after a long look. "That was a great idea, to only do half. Now you can see both what it was and what it became."

"That's called the structural sequence," Rick said, though he wasn't really quibbling. "I had to fight like hell to get it past Brinton."

"You're kidding! Why?"

"For one thing, it meant destroying half of the palace above. We photographed and mapped it, of course, but it's gone for good. Our permit with the Mexican government gives us the choice of restoring or backfilling our excavations—causing buildings to disappear is not on the list."

They were standing on top of one of the range walls, close to the point where the court dead-ended at the extant portion of the platform. Harp glanced up at the ruined shell of the palace.

"But as you so elegantly put it, the palace was a piece of crap. Classic in style and Postclassic in execution. The buildings in B have held up better."

Rick shrugged. "Still, it's one of the last constructions at the site. Clubb was the one who put up a fuss about preserving it. Brinton was only holding back because he knew he'd have to finesse it with the government. If the palace had been in better shape, I wouldn't have had a prayer."

"Clubb's really into heavy denial where ball courts are concerned," Harp said. "Remember him trying to tell us in Villahermosa that it might be a late experiment?"

"Proven bullshit," Rick said with satisfaction. "The latest sherds in the fill of the range walls are at least fifty years before Kan Cross Ahau's time. It was probably built during the reign of Jaguar Shell, the third in the Shell line."

"And *that*?" Harp asked, pointing down into the court, where a piece of a stela was standing upright against two posts. He'd been down to see it earlier and knew it was the bottom half of Stela 7, Lord of Shells from the waist down.

"We found that buried in the fill of the platform, in line with the central axis of the palace. So we know it was planted there deliberately, and it was stuck down deep, without any cache items nearby. So it appears the Kan Cross People meant to bury him, not honor him."

Harp cocked his head and let out a long breath. "Jesus, they were making a point, weren't they? They didn't just discontinue the game, they buried a bust of the commissioner and paved over the field."

"And built a house for their priests on top of it," Rick added. "That's probably what the palace was."

Rick started them moving along the top of the wall, heading toward the open end of the court. Below them, other members of the crew were doing repair work on the benches or digging test pits in the floor of the court. The floor was still covered by large patches of its original plaster, which had been painted with longitudinal red stripes.

"I'm not sure I like the implications of all this," Harp grumbled as they went down the makeshift steps at the end of the wall. "I mean, shutting down the ball game like that . . . what kinda tight-ass revitalization movement was Kan Cross Ahau running?"

Rick looked at him and laughed. "Jeez, and there you are, out killing stelae for the guy! Maybe there weren't any heroes in this piece, Harpo. Maybe that's the next bias you have to shed."

"Antiheroes, then. There's gotta be somebody to root for."

"The Rah-Rah Theory of Prehistory," Rick suggested mockingly, then glanced at his watch and got serious. "I wanna send you out to Kaaren, who's doing the workup on the end zone. She's got Eric helping her, but they lost Barry, the kid who went home the other day."

"That the kid who picked up the intestinal parasite? What'd he eat that we didn't?"

"I dunno, but that reminds me: We've got his per diem to play with. If you can promise me another month, I can put you on the payroll. Won't make you rich but it might take a bite outta your airfare."

"Hey, *pay*!" Harp said enthusiastically. "The only thing lower than a wage slave is a volunteer. And I've been thinking about how much longer I should stay. Another month seems about right."

"All I need is your Social Security number, then. I already asked Brinton and he didn't have any problem with it. He gave me this funny little smile and said it was always healthy to have a few people around who didn't think like everybody else."

Harp put on a funny little smile of his own. "Always glad to contribute to the collective mental health. Where are Kaaren and the Motorhead?"

Rick pointed through the trees to their right. "They're doing a test pit out back of the outhouse. Since we didn't know about the ball court, we didn't know we were putting the shitter smack in the middle of the end zone."

"You left us plenty of shade, too," Harp observed. "I won't bitch about that."

"Only volunteers get to bitch," Rick said, waving him off. "Go to work, wage slave . . . "

"LOTS OF TRASH," Eric said as he straightened up with another shovelful of dirt. Kaaren put down her clipboard and came around to take hold of the other end of the screening box, and Eric emptied the shovel onto the grey metal mesh. Kaaren and Harp briefly locked eyes and then began to shake the box back and forth and from side to side, draining the dust into the wheelbarrow below and leaving the larger pieces of debris dancing on the screen. In addition to the usual array of pebbles and potsherds, there were splinters of bone and chips of charred wood and numerous long flakes of flint and obsidian. There was also a large black scorpion that staggered around in a circle with its barbed tail cocked until Harp flattened it with his trowel and flicked it out of the box.

"Looks like we've cut into another midden," Kaaren said, picking through the debris with a gloved hand.

"Out here?" Harp asked in surprise. They were about sixty feet out into the end zone, equidistant from the ball court and the temple pyramid, with no smaller structures anywhere nearby.

"They're all over the place. This obviously became a prime dumping ground after they walled up the ball court."

Harp mulled that over while he popped open a paper bag and held it up for the sherds Kaaren was collecting. She rubbed the dirt off a sizable fragment and displayed the familiar red-on-black feather pattern. Late Rana Phase polychrome, probably from the time of Kan Cross Ahau.

"Isn't that unusual?" Harp asked. "Aren't most trash middens near houses?"

Kaaren nodded absently, tossing pebbles out of the box with rapid flicks of the wrist. "It appears that most of it was brought here from elsewhere. They also built a lot of fires, so they might've been burning trash as well."

"This close to the temple?"

Kaaren finished with the pebbles and started bagging flint before she responded. "Well, they could've been ceremonial fires for all we know. None of that material has been analyzed yet either."

"Do you think they also made a ceremony out of dumping their garbage in the end zone?" Harp inquired, giving Kaaren a sarcastic smile when she finally looked at him. She returned it in kind.

"I was warned that you'd rather speculate than work . . . "

" 'Bullshit' was probably the term he used," Harp said, and waved a hand dismissively. "But okay, never mind. Let's not address any of the big questions until all the little details are in. Back to work, wage slaves."

Kaaren laughed but didn't give in to curiosity until they'd shaken their way through several more shovelfuls and Harp had gone to empty the wheelbarrow onto the back-dirt pile. When he returned, she was crouching inside the gridded square of the shallow pit, checking the level attached to the depth line. They'd already taken three of the four quadrants down fifty centimeters to the plaster floor of the end zone, which was cracked and faded but had once been painted a deep, solid red. That was another matter about which Harp had been tempted to speculate earlier, though he'd still been too busy proving he could pull his weight on the crew. The two weeks with Helga and Rita had definitely been light duty, and for the first few hours today he hadn't had any breath to spare on speculation.

"Okay," Kaaren said finally, standing up and brushing off her knees. "You tell *me* what they were doing out here. Was this a ceremonial landfill? How about a campground for pilgrims to the temple?"

"That's a good one," Harp said with an appreciative laugh. He turned to Eric, who was leaning on the shovel. "You see how easy that was? The speculative urge will not die, even under the rigors of a Ph.D."

"We learn to indulge it in moderation," Kaaren said dryly. "Just as I'm indulging you. So what's your theory about the trash?"

"Tell me something else first. Did they do anything to the end zones after they covered up the main court?"

Kaaren shook her head. "You can see for yourself that they didn't pave it over when they repaved the Main Plaza. And while the boundary wall wasn't very substantial to begin with, it appears to have fallen down on its own."

"Okay . . . let's see if this makes sense," Harp proposed. "Kan Cross Ahau decides to make the West Plaza his ceremonial center. So he enlarges the temple and fixes up the other buildings and lays down another coat of plaster on the plaza. And he goes to a lot of trouble to cover up the ball court and turn it into a palace. This was probably all done in conjunction with the dedication of the Baktun Stela, which must've been a big-time event." Harp paused and spread his hands. "So, after doing all that, why would he want to leave this eyesore sitting here? A *red* end zone surrounded by a crummy little wall? And why would he let anybody dump their trash out here?"

"Skip the suspense and get to the sense," Kaaren prompted, smiling at her own rhyme. "You're suggesting he wanted an eyesore here. Why?"

"As a grave marker," Harp said. "He wanted everybody to see his new palace, but he also wanted them to remember what he'd buried underneath it. He wanted to be known as the guy who put an end to the ball game, he was *proud* of it. He sent people to dump trash here as a gesture of contempt."

Kaaren cocked her head, wearing an expression that made her dimples appear skeptical. "You make him sound like a fanatic, an abolitionist of sorts."

"That's it, exactly."

"Like the Ayatollah in Iran," Eric put in, and Harp commended him with a smile.

"Right, a fucking fundamentalist. The kinda guy who wants to take the fun out of everything, including religion."

"*Fun,*" Kaaren scoffed, laughing and shaking her head. "Helga was right. You can't distinguish religion from sport."

"So maybe they dressed up like the gods," Harp argued, "but they still *played* the game, didn't they? With a ball and a court and two teams, somebody winning and somebody losing?"

"They were apparently enacting the journey of the Night Sun through the Underworld. Maybe they had a set script and didn't 'play' at all in the sense you mean."

The possibility brought Harp up short for a moment. "Naw, that doesn't sound right. Where'd you hear that?"

"I just made it up. You see how easy that was?" she said to Eric. "The urge to speculate is both contagious and addictive. The best remedy is to do some real work."

"I can take a hint," Harp said. He picked up the screening box and set it down on top of the wheelbarrow with a bang, grinning when they both jumped. "But you gotta admit, I've given this garbage a whole new significance."

"Is that what novelists usually do?" Kaaren asked, her smile taking the edge off the taunt. Harp leaned back from the rising dust as Eric deposited another shovelful onto the screen.

"Yeah, I guess you could say that," Harp conceded. "But at least we don't sort the garbage into sacks and take it home with us." He laughed and gave the box a shake. "We leave that to the archaeologists . . . "

DINNER WAS just about over when Ulysses Cole rose at the far end of the table and tapped a spoon against a water glass to get everyone's attention. He smiled through his ruddy beard.

"We've all had our heads down in holes, so we were slow to notice that it was time for our annual Full Moon Party. Hope you haven't all bought tickets to the opera, 'cause we're gonna hold it this Saturday night." Ulysses nodded and held up his hands, waiting until the applause died down. "Ramona has assured me that we'll have something as good as last year's goat for the barbecue, which will be followed by music and tribal dancing. The traditional Midnight Moon Watch will be held at the appointed hour in the Central Plaza of Group A; the Reverend Doctor Muldoon will lead the ceremony to the Moon Goddess and all acolytes are welcome. Beer and soft drinks and munchies will be provided, but feel free to bring your own."

He sat down to more cheering, the most unbridled coming from Lucy Smith, who was sitting between Harp and her mother. Katie, for her part, appeared to be remembering something unpleasant.

"I take it you're a party animal," Harp said to Lucy, who was clapping her hands and singing "All Night Long" to herself.

"The biggest!" she proclaimed. Then she made a face and turned to Katie. "Oh god, Mom, Harp's gonna be there. That means there'll be spastic dancing!"

"Not on your life," Harp said huffily. "I'm too old for such undignified behavior."

"That's why you're so good at it!" Lucy cackled, wiggling out of her seat before Harp could make a grab for her. She briefly rested her chin on Katie's shoulder. "Do I have anything clean to wear?"

"If not we'll wash something. Go look. I'll be along in a while; I wanna talk to Harp."

"Teach him how to dance like a normal person," Lucy suggested, displaying her banded teeth in a wickedly glittering smile before dashing off. On Harp's other side, Rick was explaining to Kaaren what Full Moon parties were like; Harp caught the phrase "genuine lunacy," which was high praise coming from Rick. Harp leaned across the empty seat toward Katie. "So, mother of the party animal, you don't seem to share your daughter's enthusiasm."

Katie rolled her eyes toward the ceiling and mimed a remorseful shudder. "Let's take a walk and I'll tell you about it."

Since the moon wasn't yet high enough to penetrate the darkness, they used Harp's flashlight and walked toward his hut. Katie told him that she'd been to three previous Full Moon parties and counted them among the best parties of her life. They'd also produced three of the worst hangovers of her life and a number of incidents that'd become part of camp legend. Harp'd heard about the lewd Moon Goddess impersonation she'd done one year, and about the time she'd passed out inside the shrine atop Kan Shell's temple and had spent the night there because no one knew where she was. He got her to elaborate, anyhow, and despite her protestations of shame, she was soon laughing as hard as he was.

"It really isn't funny," she insisted as Harp led the way into his hut and lit a couple of candles.

"Then why are we laughing?" he inquired, as she moved the mosquito bar aside and sat down on his bed. He straddled the chair across from her and lit a cigarette.

"It's only funny up to a point, and I always end up way beyond that. The last time I ended up in a serious grope session with the Reverend Doctor Muldoon, who's very married to a woman I know and like. We both felt terrible about it later, and it's tainted our professional relationship ever since."

"Sounds like you need a chaperone," Harp said lightly.

"I have something like that in mind, only I was thinking of it as a *date.*"

Harp regarded her warily, his imagination still vibrating with the notion of a serious grope session. "Do people take dates to these things?"

"Not usually," Katie conceded. "And we don't have to make a point of it. But if you'd just let me hang on your arm a bit, it'd save me from being hit on by all the horny archaeologists. And if you'll keep me from getting shit-faced and shameless, I'll do the same for you. Rick's told me stories about what the two of you used to do, and I've seen *him* at these things. You might be grateful for a restraining influence."

"Have I gotten that old?" Harp mused aloud, hedging while he considered the proposition. Given his own tendencies toward excess, it had a certain appeal. And it was probably better to confront temptation than try to avoid it at a Full Moon Party. What gave him pause was the fact that he didn't trust himself any more than he trusted Katie. He might be throwing himself into the arms of temptation.

"Unless you had someone else in mind," Katie prompted, startling him out of his thoughts.

"Like who?"

"You've been working with Kaaren for almost a week. That should be long enough to fall in love with her."

Harp felt himself blushing and laughed. "I gotta admit, for the first couple days I had a kind of crush on her. Felt like a panting idiot until I realized there's something intrinsically sexual about the close quarters and hard physical labor, the intimacy of getting sweaty and dirty together every day. That helped it pass. Besides, Rick's a friend, and I don't cut in on my friends."

"You'd have a better chance with her than Rick," Katie said with offhanded assurance. "He's too much in awe of her, and she's too brittle."

"Brittle as in easily snapped?"

"Brittle as in does not bend easily. Rick's like that himself, as I'm sure you know. Doesn't like to give in if he feels he's being influenced or pressured. She's bound to do both."

Harp gave her an appreciative smile. "You ever think of writing novels?"

"About as often as you think about being lab director," Katie scoffed, though her smile showed her pleasure at the compliment. "So c'mon, gimme a yes or a no. I'm not gonna twist your arm."

He put out his cigarette and squinted at her through the smoke. "Okay, you've got a date. I just hope we don't end up getting shit-faced and shameless with each other."

Katie laughed and rose from the bed, giving herself a languid stretch. Harp got to his feet with awkward haste, kicking over the ashtray in the process. She came right up and laid a hand on his chest, her eyes catching a gleam from the candles.

"We're gonna have a great time, Harp," she promised. "With no hangovers or recriminations later."

"Sure . . . just a couple of wild and crazy guys counting each other's drinks. You're in for a lotta spastic dancing, y'know."

"I love to dance," Katie murmured, coming chest to chest with him, her hands going around his waist to lock over the small of his back. She swayed against him, miraculously soft and absolutely unbrittle, so warm and sweet-smelling it made him shiver. Feathery curls brushed his cheek as she laid her head on his shoulder and they danced slowly in a circle.

"This isn't exactly what I meant," Harp breathed. "But what the hell . . . "

"This is practice," Katie said primly. "To be sure we don't lose control of ourselves on the dance floor. Uh-uh, no dry-humping. This isn't the ninth-grade mixer."

She started laughing and pulled away from him. "I'd better go or Lucy'll come looking for me."

"Why don't you stay and twist my arm . . . or something," Harp said hoarsely, but let her escape to the door. She slipped through the netting, scattering a cloud of moths. "This *is* like the ninth-grade," he said. "Left swollen and hungry on the doorstep."

Katie looked back at him, smiling in the moonlight. "Those were the days, huh? Too young to know what to do, but old enough to yearn for it."

"You mean if we act like adolescents, we may be safe from adultery?"

"It's a theory," Katie said agreeably, turning down the path. "Won't know until we test it. Will we?"

"Arggh," Harp said, an appropriately inarticulate, ninth-grade response.

BRINTON LET everybody off at noon on Saturday, and after lunch Harp stood in line to give himself a proper shower. The cenote always left him smelling slightly algaeish, and he couldn't settle for that after he'd paid one of Ramona's daughters to wash and iron his best shirt and jeans. He would at least *begin* the evening feeling completely civilized.

He was trimming his beard in his hut when Rita came out carrying her boom box and a pack of tapes. She'd been making dance tapes for the party, she explained, and she already had ninety minutes of what she called "modern music," meaning it came from the tapes of the other students. The tapes she had with her had been contributed by some of the older staff members.

"I wrote down some of the titles they told me," Rita said, pulling a sheet of paper out of the pack, "and I figured you could probably tell me what else was good to dance to."

"What is this, the geezer tape? Music of the ancients?"

Rita laughed and began to empty the pack onto the bed. "Well, Muldoon insisted that we put some Frank Sinatra on it."

"That'll be good for a laugh. Whose are these?" Harp asked, picking up a plastic rack that held about twenty tapes.

"Ulysses's. He didn't give me any suggestions, either."

"Holy shit, lookit this: Beatles, Stones, The Doors, Jimi Hendrix. Christ, he's one of *us.* He's even got James Brown in here! You ever hear 'Papa's Got a Brand New Bag'?"

"Can you dance to it?" Rita asked absently. She held out another tape. "Here's the one Katie gave me. She said I should show it to you and see if you fainted."

"Johnny Mathis. Oh god, I'm done for . . . "

"Steady, Harp," Rita said with a grin. "Who's Johnny Mathis?"

"You've been to high school dances. When you got to the point where everybody's just standing still wrapped around each other, what were you listening to?"

Rita blushed. "Phil Collins, maybe, or Lionel Richie."

"Twenty years ago it was Johnny Mathis," Harp told her. "The voice of throbbing romance. You wanna do a little clutch dancing tonight, he's your man." He paused and saw her flush darken. "Speaking of men, you haven't told me how it's been going with Jim. I assume okay, since neither of you has wound up in the infirmary or back at the ball court."

"It's been fine," Rita said blandly. "We're about back to where we were at the beginning, in terms of talking about archaeology and stuff."

"Doesn't exactly sound like the prelude to clutch dancing," Harp suggested. "There's another guy I know who was real disappointed you didn't come to work with us. I had the impression he'd be receptive to a little vamping. Ah! You're lovely when your cheeks are that shade of vermilion."

Rita let out an honest-to-goodness hmph. "Lay off, Harp. He's too tall, and *way* too shy. He'll never have the courage to ask me to dance."

"Ask *him,* then."

"I can't do that! You act like I've been vamping boys all my life! *I'm* shy too."

"I've got just the thing for that," Harp said, holding up the Johnny Mathis tape. He jumped up and went over to get out his own tapes. "But first some rock 'n' roll . . . let's make a tape that'll blow everybody off the floor. Give 'em an excuse later to just stand around and clutch."

AS THEY'D AGREED, Harp picked up Katie at her office in the lab. She was sitting back in front of the window with her feet up on the desk, sipping scotch from a paper cup. She had a beautiful Guatemalan shawl—black with stripes of rose, violet, and bright pink—draped loosely around her shoulders, so he didn't get the full effect until she stood up and struck a pose with her hands on her hips, the shawl bunching up like a collar. She was dressed entirely in black, the top a silky sleeveless number that revealed the tops of her breasts while clinging delectably to the rest of them. She had a choker of shiny jet beads around her neck and had done some tricks with eye shadow and mascara that softened the frankness of her gaze and made it seem frankly seductive.

"Well?" she asked, when Harp continued to hang speechlessly in the doorway, a bottle of mescal dangling in his hand.

"I think it's time to faint," he said, but smiled instead. "You look wonderful." He came into the room, pulling his other hand out from behind his back and extending a fern-wrapped bouquet of forest orchids. "Corsage," he explained. "It comes with Johnny Mathis."

"You've got all the moves, Harp," Katie laughed. She cupped her hands around his and lifted the orchids to her face, drawing a long breath that she released with a delighted smile. "Umm, they're still sweet."

"They won't last long, I'm afraid," Harp said, as she put the bouquet down on her desk and removed the least-wilted flower, a diaphanous blossom that matched the violet in her shawl. She fixed it into her hair above her right ear and gestured toward the rest of the bouquet. "I'll press those in my keepsake album later."

"Much later, I expect. So, are you ready to get this date under way? I notice you're already a drink ahead."

Katie picked up the paper cup and took another swallow. "I needed something to steady my nerves while I waited. You want some?"

"No. To be honest, I smoked a little dope while I was picking orchids."

"Then we're even," Katie concluded.

"Not quite," Harp said, wrapping her in a swift, strong embrace that made her drop her cup in surprise. He pressed himself against her, rolling his shoulders sensuously, then kissed her on the side of the neck and let her go. "There. You got to be the aggressor last time."

"Whoa," Katie murmured breathlessly. "I hope you've got more of whatever you were smoking."

"Sure do," Harp said, bending to pick up her cup and toss it into the wastebasket. Then he tucked the bottle of mescal under one arm and held the other out to her. "The evening awaits, my lady."

Katie hesitated briefly, glancing at her desk, then linked arms with him and craned upward to kiss him on the cheek. "Romance without regret," she said as they headed out. "We just might be old enough to make it work . . . "

THE SUN was gilding the top of Kan Shell's temple and sending shafts of golden light through the tall trees around the camp, though Harp seemed to be the only one who noticed. The rest of the crew was clustered around the firepit where Ulysses was spit-roasting a pig, and their attention seemed equally divided between drinking beer and admiring one another's party clothes. The excited buzz of conversation nearly drowned out the music blaring from Rita's boom box, so Harp couldn't pick out the tune until he and Katie drew abreast of the picnic table on which the machine was set.

"What's that?" Harp blurted in surprise. "Opera?"

Rita and Helga Kauffmann were sitting at the table, Rita in her lucky fedora and Helga wearing a shawl similar to Katie's over a long-sleeved white blouse with lace cuffs and collar and a heavy brooch at her throat. The New and Old World side by side, Harp thought.

"It's *Madama Butterfly,* Mr. Yates," Helga explained. "Oliver Clubb had the tape and didn't think we should be deprived of our opera."

"I sure woulda missed it," Harp declared, then noticed the water beading on the bottle in Rita's hand. "What've you got there? Is that *cold* beer?"

"Very," Rita said with a grin. "Ulysses brought a tub of ice back from Comitán."

"I could learn to like him. Shall we?" Harp said to Katie, who was exchanging compliments with Helga over their shawls. The way Katie came back to his side drew a swift glance from Rita, but Harp ignored it and led Katie deeper into the crowd. He saw other heads turn to mark their passage and he knew they were being itemized, a fact that both amused and annoyed him. Katie was brazening it out, saying hello to everybody, and he briefly got into the act himself, though his mind was on the beer.

And there it was: a galvanized tub filled to the brim with beautiful glistening ice, chunks and cubes mixed together with bright bottle caps sticking up through the slush on top. Brad was happily jamming more bottles down into the ice, but he straightened up with a grin, wiping his hands on his pants legs.

"You the keeper of the beer?" Harp asked.

"Self-appointed. What'll you have?"

"Whatever's coldest."

Brad dug deep and came up with a Dos Equis and a Negra Modelo. He held them both in one meaty fist and opened them with a church key that hung by a string from a plastic wristband embossed with Greek letters.

"You came equipped to party," Harp observed.

"Never leave home without it. We had to have one sooner or later."

Harp clinked his bottle against Katie's and took a long drink, reacquainting his throat with a familiar but long-forsaken delight. He wondered if the Mayan kings had sent runners into the mountains for ice to cool their honey-water beer. He lowered the bottle to find half of it gone and Katie giving him the fisheye.

"I was thirsty."

"I've heard that before. Be good, Harp."

"Depends on what you mean by 'good,' " Harp began, but stopped when Lucy suddenly appeared out of the crowd. She was wearing a blue blouse with a Peter Pan collar and a blue and green tartan plaid skirt, the kind of costume commonly worn by parochial and private school girls. Since Lucy was neither, she no doubt thought it looked "collegiate," the ultimate category of fashion, and Harp was prepared to offer her that compliment. But she went up to Brad without greeting him or Katie.

"Max wants another Tecate, Animal."

"One Tecate, comin' up," Brad said amiably.

"I'm helping Max and Ulysses cook the pig," Lucy said over her shoulder, and Harp and Katie exchanged a smile at the order of the names. With his ear stud and rooster cut, Max was easily at the top of Lucy's crush list.

"Try not to get dirty," Katie advised, picking a piece of leaf off the back of her skirt. Lucy rolled her eyes in exasperation.

"*God.* You don't think I'd go near the *pig,* do you?" Lucy turned abruptly—her gaze flicking over Harp without landing—and went off toward the firepit with the beer in both hands.

"What, not even a taunt?" Harp said. "I must be losing my touch."

Katie sighed. "She asked me this afternoon if it was moral to go on a date with someone who was married. I didn't give her a very good answer."

"She couldn't understand an experiment in mutual restraint?"

"I actually tried, but she knows I like you and she thinks you're a wild man, so it was a hard case to make. I should never have used the word 'date.' It's just too loaded for her right now."

Harp looked over at Lucy, who was standing at a safe distance from the firepit watching Max and Ulysses work. Max was down on his knees, giving the spit a crank while Ulysses swabbed the carcass with barbecue sauce, using a paintbrush and a pail. They were both wearing headbands and a coat of soot and grease that made them look like stokers on a pirate ship. To Harp's experienced eye they also appeared thoroughly stoned.

"This may not be the best place to study morality," he said, putting a comforting arm around Katie's shoulders. Brother Rick came up from behind and slung an arm around both of them, simultaneously gesturing to Brad for another beer.

"Drink up, boys and girls, you're behind!" Rick said exuberantly. He got his beer and turned them away from Brad before going on in a more confidential tone. "Though I'm grateful for the entrance you made. Took a little heat offa us."

"You and Kaaren?" Katie guessed.

Rick gave them a crooked grin. "Yeah, we're out, so to speak. Brinton was looking at me sorta walleyed until he saw you two come strolling up. It was like he'd spotted his first flying saucer."

"Oh, for Chrissakes," Harp muttered. "Hasn't anybody told him that Queen Victoria's dead?"

"You can be the first," Rick suggested, laughing recklessly. "C'mon, we've already got Clubb primed for you. Kaaren's been telling him your theory about Kan Cross Ahau the fundamentalist asshole."

"Terrific. Now I get to be theoretically offensive, too."

"That's certainly the expectation," Rick agreed. "You wanna grab another beer before we go?"

Harp did, but he looked at Katie first. She had the shawl pulled closed in front of her and appeared to be wavering. It occurred to him that she hadn't considered Brinton's reaction before this. Or maybe it was Lucy holding her back.

"If this's getting too sticky," he suggested, "we can call it off."

"What?" Katie asked, snapping out of it with a shake of her head. "No, I was just thinking that I'm real tired of having to answer to everybody. My own conscience oughta be good enough."

"Right," Harp agreed. "And if it isn't, I'm here. The voice of morality in moderation."

Katie laughed and tossed back the shawl, drawing an admiring glance from Rick. Harp crooked his arm and she put her hand on the inside of his elbow and gave him a little squeeze.

"We've got enough beer," he said to Rick. "Lead us to the fray."

Rick looked at them curiously. "What is 'this,' anyway?"

"It's called taking the heat," Katie said defiantly, giving Harp another squeeze. "It's a good way to stay warm."

THEY FEASTED outside under the trees, with candles on the tables and smudge pots on tall poles to keep the mosquitoes at bay. The barbecued pork was easily the best Harp'd ever eaten, and it came accompanied by roasted yams, spinach pie, a tangy cabbage salad, and plenty of Ramona's *fiesta pozole.* Large quantities of cold beer were also consumed, leading to multiple toasts and increasingly boisterous conversation. People all around Harp were getting drunk but he was still fairly sober himself, due less to Katie's restraining influence than to the fact that he'd been doing a lot of talking. Clubb had been primed, all right, but not really by Kaaren. He wouldn't say so directly, but he'd obviously been revising his Persistence Theory and was eager to give his new scenario a trial run. Since Harp posed no professional threat and was locally notorious for his own flights of fancy, he was the ideal foil.

In keeping with the party mood, Harp had tried to be entertaining rather than antagonistic, spinning out his own interpretation and letting Clubb counter it as he would. At one point he simply sat back and smiled across the table at Clubb, admiring the man's narrative audacity. He was now claiming that the burial of the ball court by Kan Cross Ahau and the attempted revitalization of Group B by the Shell family descendants had been complementary efforts, rather than evidence of conflict. The Kan Cross People had taken political control of the site, but perhaps for religious reasons they couldn't assume control of the ball game ritual as well. So Kan Cross Ahau had built a palace over the ball court as a memorial, burying half of Stela 7 in the fill and allowing the Shell descendants to reset the other half in Group B. Far from scorning and suppressing the Shell family, Clubb argued, Kan Cross Ahau had needed their prestige and support, and had encouraged their veneration of Lord of Shells in return for their loyalty to him. Thus, the end zones were indeed grave markers, though ones left standing out of respect.

Once Clubb had laid out his position, Rick, Kaaren, and Katie took over from Harp, going after Clubb on the particulars, like the significance of the garbage dumps in the end zone. Clubb had only his protégé Andrew for support, but he was too shrewd and slippery to need much help. And Harp could almost see him taking mental notes on what he was hearing, gathering material for the next revision. They were writing his monograph for him. Harp mostly just listened himself, injecting a note of levity whenever the discussion threatened to get too heated. He realized he didn't really care who won the debate. It didn't enlarge the picture any to have someone backed into a logical corner or trapped in a contradiction. That just shut off the flow of ideas and possibilities, from which might come the seeds of an even better story.

The topic had been exhausted by the time dessert arrived in the form of banana fritters with ice cream and cane syrup. A bottle of brandy came around with the coffee, and Katie poured a generous but not profligate shot for Harp.

"Nurse that," she told him with a smile. "You've been good so far. Dinner's almost over and we're not drunk yet."

Clubb straightened the polka-dot bow tie he'd put on for the occasion and looked across at Harp. "As always, Mr. Yates, you've instigated a stimulating discussion."

Harp smiled slyly. "Does that mean we'll all get a footnote in your next article?"

Clubb bore their laughter patiently. "It's conceivable. Will *we* all be acknowledged in your next novel?"

"Of course," Harp said without hesitation. "I'll want everybody to share the blame."

Amid the laughter, Kaaren raised her glass and offered a semi-serious toast: "To the truth, wherever and whenever it might be found."

"May it always be stranger than fiction," Harp added. Harp tossed off the rest of his brandy without thinking, enjoying the burn and flush before he realized what he'd done. He turned sheepishly to Katie but discovered she'd done the same thing. She shrugged and put her glass down with an emphatic thump.

"Time to adjourn the symposium. Let's party . . . "

THEY'D ORIGINALLY stepped out to get some air and cool off from dancing, but then they went out into the trees in the middle of the camp to smoke a little of Harp's dope. A strong yet balmy wind was blowing out of the north, bringing in clouds to cover the bright face of the moon and tossing the tops of the trees. It swirled around them on the ground, keeping off the mosquitoes but making it hard to get a joint lit. Katie hadn't smoked in years and seemed to get stoned immediately. By about the third hit she was staring upward, watching the palm fronds thrash against the milk-white sky.

"They look like witches' fingers," she murmured, oblivious of the joint he was holding out to her. He took a last hit of his own and snuffed it out. A minute later she reached back for it.

"Are we done?"

"Witches' fingers?" Harp inquired. "I think you're there."

"I guess I am. Where's that?"

"Here," Harp said with a smile, putting his arms around her and pulling her close. He leaned back against the trunk of a palm and she seemed to melt against him, tucking her head into the hollow of his neck. He hadn't realized that he was getting cold inside his damp clothes until he was suddenly flooded by a warmth that seemed to steam dry the front of his shirt. Katie hugged him and let out a groan that sounded more grateful than passionate, the sound of a weary soul sinking into a soft bed. Harp chuckled and she raised her face from his shoulder.

"You don't know how good it feels just to be held," she told him, making him laugh harder.

"Wanna bet?"

"You don't," she insisted. "You haven't been without it that long. And you know you'll have it when you get back."

"True," Harp admitted. "But it still feels good."

So he continued to hold her, feeling oddly virtuous if not exactly chaste. She'd left her shawl in the dining hall, and the silky fabric of her top had a wonderful slipperiness that set his fingers wandering over the contours of her back, moving from silk to skin with no loss of glide. Katie shivered and arched against him, her hand coming up around the back of his neck, fingers twining around the damp curls and pulling him down for a kiss. He angled his chin, suddenly aware of his beard, but she didn't rush him, pausing to smile before finding his lips. Even then it wasn't a hungry kiss, though as it lingered it became more searching, pulling back and returning at a new angle. Katie's other hand was inside his shirt and one of her breasts was swelling against his palm as his fingers curled and uncurled, his other hand straying down to cup her bottom and lift her gently, pelvis to pelvis. Harp was kissing her bare shoulder, moving the straps aside with his lips, when Katie laughed softly and pulled her head back.

"This's very bad, Harp. We're never gonna make it to Johnny Mathis at this rate."

"A veritable tragedy," Harp said, tilting his head to kiss her again. But Katie braced both hands against his chest and held him off.

"If we keep on kissing, we're done for."

"I was just beginning to remember how."

"That's what I mean."

Harp spread his arms and hung pinned against the palm, feigning crucifixion. But she'd obviously sensed what he'd been feeling, at least at first: the utter strangeness of kissing someone other than Caroline.

"You're right," he admitted. "But you know men have died of unrequited erections."

Katie laughed and thumped him on the chest. "How many times have I heard *that* since the ninth grade? Yet they all survived somehow. You will too. Let's go back and dance it off."

"*Great* idea. You ever see me do the three-legged spastic dance?"

"Pull yourself together," Katie said, grinning mercilessly. "Tuck it in or strap it down. You must've figured that out early on."

Harp growled and turned away, pretending to grapple with a large, unruly animal. "Down boy! Down, I say!"

Katie was still laughing when he caught up with her, and they held hands as they followed the path back to the dining hall. They saw the lights and then heard the beat of the music beneath the roaring of the wind. Harp snorted when he recognized the tune. "Springsteen. 'Everybody's got a hungry heart,' " he sang derisively. "Tell me about it, Boss."

Katie swayed against him, taking hold of his arm with both hands. "Romance without regret," she reminded him. "You're not supposed to go home full."

Harp was contemplating a response when he smelled the cigar and saw Brinton Taylor standing under a tree not far from the dining hall door. Brinton was wearing a blue guayabera that made him look like an aristocratic barber, and when he'd greeted them earlier, he'd given Harp a stare that made him feel like an enemy of good grooming. He seemed to be giving them the same stare as they approached, and Harp resisted instinctively when Katie suddenly steered them off the path toward him.

"Katie . . . Mr. Yates," Brinton said tentatively, appearing as surprised as Harp by Katie's boldness.

"I know we've offended your sense of propriety," Katie said, briskly and without apology. "But I want you to know I'm well aware of how married this man is, and I intend to send him back to his wife with his conscience clear and his scruples intact. But I also intend to enjoy his company while I can, no matter how scandalous it looks."

Brinton appeared thoroughly bemused and had to clear his throat twice before he could reply. "I appreciate your frankness, Katie, but explaining this to me won't stop the rest of the camp from gossiping about you."

"Let 'em," Katie said with a shrug. "The only people who need to understand are my daughter and you."

"I haven't asked you to explain yourself," Brinton said swiftly.

"Nooo," Katie drawled sardonically. "You just look at us like we oughta be spanked. C'mon, Brinton, we're grown people, and we're not doing anything that's gonna cause you grief. I know how much this site means to you. I know how much shit you deal with so the rest of us can do our work in peace.

This is a very special place because of you. You've earned the right to act like the village patriarch, but there are limits, you know?"

Brinton laughed loudly. "Just when I thought I was being flattered!"

"You're being educated. Just because something looks a little out of line doesn't mean it's a threat to camp morale." She gave Harp's arm a demonstrative tug. "This man's good for morale, especially mine. You don't need to waste any frowns on us."

Brinton inclined his snowy head in a gracious surrender. "I stand educated, and chastened." He looked at Harp. "Mr. Yates . . . do you ever engage in any kind of *un*ambiguous behavior? No, forget I asked. No doubt you're good for my broad-mindedness, if not my morale. Enjoy the party. I may see you at the moon watch, if it doesn't rain."

Nodding to both of them, he stuck his unlit cigar into his mouth and walked off in the direction of his hut. Harp leaned back and gave Katie a nod of his own.

"That was quite a speech. Almost had *me* believing in our innocence."

"I meant every word," Katie insisted. "Have we done anything you couldn't tell your wife about?"

"Jesus! Are you kidding?"

"We stopped at one kiss. She wouldn't begrudge me that."

"You aspire to a lewd innocence," Harp decided.

Katie laughed and started them moving toward the dining hall. "Just think of it as ambiguous behavior . . . "

THE ROLLING STONES were wailing from the boom box, into the guitar solo in the middle of the live version of "Sympathy for the Devil," when Harp spun out of the cluster of people with whom he'd been dancing—in true tribal fashion—and found himself face-to-face with Ulysses Cole. Ulysses was still wearing his headband but had put on a loud Hawaiian shirt that was dark with sweat and clung to his lanky body. He danced with a wild enthusiasm that almost made up for his lack of grace, which was complete. Harp felt like Fred Astaire in comparison and was certain that even Lucy Smith would've appreciated the difference.

Perhaps this showed on Harp's face, because Ulysses suddenly bared his teeth and broke into a kind of war dance, Plains Indian style, spreading his elbows and dancing from heel to toe. Memories of dances he'd seen in South Dakota welled up in Harp's mind and he fell into the same gait, rounding on Ulysses, who danced past him backward, going down into a crouch and rising up with his chest puffed out like a prairie chicken. Harp dipped and spun, coming up behind Ulysses's shoulder and touching him lightly on the back with a forearm, realizing as he did it that he was counting coup. Ulysses whirled and brought both his fists up in front of him, shaking them like rattles within inches of Harp's face and grinning fiercely when Harp flinched and turned his cheek.

They separated and Ulysses turned his back on Harp, flailing his arms as the guitar solo rose to its peak. Beyond him, everyone was dancing facing inward, watching the two of them. Then Ulysses whirled back, almost losing his balance but righting himself with a triumphant leer, coming in on the lyrics precisely on cue, shouting along with Mick Jagger, the Devil himself: "Pleased to meet you, hope you guessed my name!"

His arm shot out and his palm unfolded in such a familiar fashion that Harp gave him five without thinking, stinging his fingers and grinning after the fact. Ulysses's grin was almost a snarl, and he wiggled his hips in a parting taunt as he turned back into the crowd, which was whooping and applauding. Harp was breathing hard but managed a haughty shuffle of his own as he danced away.

"What was *that*?" Lucy Smith demanded, bug-eyed with amazement. Harp wasn't sure himself, and he was suddenly too whipped out to respond. Brother Rick stepped in beside him and caught his eye, smiling with the fondness of shared memory.

"Enemies dance," he told Lucy. "Ritualized combat."

Katie came up on Harp's other side and spoke into his ear. "Excess testosterone," she said. "Down, boy."

Harp laughed until he was completely out of breath. "Gotta sit," he gasped, and staggered over and collapsed into a chair by the windows. The dancing went on without him, Derek and the Dominos taking over from the Stones with an ease that was a testament to Rita's taping skill. After a while, he sat up and took the nearest open bottle of beer off the table next to him and drank greedily, certain that he'd sweated out the previous one. The air coming in through the screen behind him was damp and cool and he realized that it was raining, Chac pissing on the moon watch.

The table moved and he glanced over to see Eric sitting back against it, nursing a beer and watching the dancers. Harp followed his gaze and saw Rita dancing with Jim Zorn, who looked as if he'd had a few lessons. He had some nifty disco moves that he'd do on his own and then he'd catch Rita's hand and roll her up against him in a brief jitterbug, spinning her away and catching her again with a speed that left her giddy and laughing. Unfunky, Harp thought, though he knew it was envy speaking.

The next cut was Jimi Hendrix's "Foxey Lady," a song against which Rita had argued strenuously during taping, finding it incomprehensible as dance music. She seemed to get into it easily enough now, though Jim seemed to be straining a bit, the jitterbug rendered utterly inappropriate. Harp suddenly grinned, remembering what that argument had led to. Rita'd gone off to the outhouse in a fit of pique and left him alone with the machine, a decision she would soon regret.

He got up and found a couple of semiclean Dixie cups and poured a little mescal into each from the bottle he'd brought. He sidled up to Eric and handed him a cup, lifting the other in a salute.

"For courage."

Eric looked at him blankly but drank anyway, exuding a nearly palpable aura of hopelessness. Harp leaned back against the table, facing the dancers. "He's a good dancer," he said in a neutral tone. "Real slick."

"Her size, too," Eric said miserably.

"Yeah," Harp agreed, and gave him a moment to hit bottom. "But y'know, he really hurt her feelings not too long ago. He made her feel small in a way you never would."

"Yeah?"

"Yeah. And she likes you."

"She does?"

"Probably enough to stand on her tiptoes if you'll slouch. But you gotta have the courage to cut in."

"Yeah," Eric said, looking hopeless again. Harp laughed and nudged him with a forearm.

"You're gonna have your chance in another minute," he predicted. "Rita's gonna come over here wanting to kill me, and I'm counting on you to restrain her."

"Wait a minute," Eric said, his suspicions aroused. "What're you up to? Whattaya mean, 'restrain' her?"

"Just wrap her up and waltz her off. And when she stops screaming, tell her you think the song is right."

"*What* song?"

"This one," Harp said, gesturing toward the dance floor, where the dancers were tapering off to the last echoes of Hendrix's guitar. There was a pause on the tape of the sort Rita hadn't allowed before this, and Harp saw her frown and look around at the machine. Then an echoing voice let out a long, falling "AHH" amid rising piano chords, and the chorus roared in: "LOVELY RITA, METER MAID, LOVELY RITA, METER MAID . . . "

Rita spun in place, howling in outrage. "Goddam you, Harper Yates!"

Harp stepped out where he could be seen. "It's her birthday, everybody," he announced. "Let's give her a big hand!"

Even those who knew better joined in the applause, gleefully singing along with the Beatles. A few others began to sing "Happy Birthday." Rita came at him with murder in her eyes, her cheeks flaming. "It's not my birthday," she hissed, "and you're the biggest bastard I ever met!"

"My parents might dispute that," Harp said, but let her sock him once on the shoulder, figuring he owed her that much revenge. Then he dodged behind Eric, who was standing like a post.

"I told you not to put that song on!"

Harp peeked out around Eric's shoulder. "You were outvoted while you were out of the room. It's your theme song!"

"Do I look like a meter maid?" Rita demanded furiously. She swung a roundhouse left that missed Harp and thumped Eric in the ribs.

"Now!" Harp urged, poking the big man in the back, and Eric complied by lifting Rita completely off her feet and carrying her back onto the dance floor. She shouted at Harp over his shoulder.

"I'll get you for this!"

"Ingrate," Harp muttered under his breath, then smiled. "You'll like the next song a lot, too."

He watched until Eric set her down, hoping she'd come to her senses and appreciate the way she'd been swept off her feet. When she stayed put, hidden behind Eric, he assumed the big guy had found the wherewithal to confirm her loveliness. Harp turned to retrieve his cup, and when he turned back Jim Zorn was there, angry and standing much too close.

"That was a shitty thing to do!"

"It sure was," Harp agreed. "Almost as shitty as what you did."

"That's none'a your business!"

"It is when you get up in my face like this," Harp told him, straightening up to emphasize his considerable size advantage. At that moment the next song came on, John Lennon's raucous voice asking the perennial question: "WHY DON'T WE DO IT IN THE ROAD?"

Harp grinned at the cheer that went up and was trying to get a glimpse of Rita when Jim came up with his hand from below, popping the cup out of Harp's hand and spraying its contents into his face. Harp blinked and licked mescal off his upper lip; Jim backed off a step, his hands balled into fists. Max and Katie suddenly appeared from two different directions, intervening before Harp could act on the anger that warmed his ears in a delayed reaction. Max got right in between them, corralling Jim with his arms and pushing him backward.

"Chill out, you guys," he pleaded, casting a glance over his shoulder at Harp. Harp held up his palms.

"I'm cool. But you, little man," he said to Jim. "You give new meaning to the term 'dipshit.' "

"Hope your enjoyed your drink," Jim sneered, but let Max herd him away. Katie picked up a napkin and dabbed at Harp's wet face.

"What got into *him*?"

"Damned if I know. He's trying to tell *me* to be nice to Rita."

"That *was* a dirty trick, Harp. The nickname's bound to stick."

"How much can she mind being called 'Lovely'? Besides, I used it to play cupid for her. You don't think Eric woulda carried her off without a little prompting, do you?"

Katie laughed. "Excuse me. Maybe I should call you Mister Romance."

"Pleased to meet you," Harp said with a bow. "Shall we dance? The first Johnny Mathis is coming up and I need to dry my shirt."

"That's what you get for drinking without me," Katie told him, but let him lead her back onto the floor.

. . .

AT ELEVEN o'clock, Emory Muldoon shut off the music and advised all those interested in the moon watch to have a last drink and put on some warmer clothes and their best rain gear. The rain was coming down steadily and the wind had lost all balminess and was beginning to turn the night cold. Muldoon also reminded them to bring something of "true value" as an offering to the Moon Goddess, and he told them to be back in the dining hall by eleven-thirty.

By eleven forty-five only nine had assembled, and it seemed unlikely that any more would appear. Of the camp elders, only Helga Kauffmann had turned out, encased in a heavy rubber slicker with a cowllike hood that made her look like a miniature monk. Her presence didn't temper Ulysses's disgust at the low turnout, which he seemed to take as a personal affront.

"Where's This Animal?" he demanded, and Eric lifted his broad shoulders in a shrug.

"Passed out."

"Goddam short hitter," Ulysses grumbled. He was obviously quite drunk himself, which had made him clumsy and querulous but no less hyperactive. "Where's Fisher?" he asked next, looking at Harp.

Harp shrugged and shook his head, though in fact he possessed rather precise knowledge of Rick's whereabouts. It was the reason he was so wet underneath his raincoat. Driven by the rain, he'd blundered into his hut without seeing the candleglow from outside, and he'd been treated to a brief but breathtaking view of Kaaren's gorgeous ass and the arch of her back as Rick thrust up into her. Harp'd beaten a hasty and apologetic retreat and then had to stand like a penitent in the rain while Rick found his sweatshirt and raincoat and passed them out to him.

He hadn't had a chance to share any of this with Katie because Lucy had made them a threesome and seemed to be doing her best to stay between him and her mother. That's where she was walking when they headed out into the rain at the end of a column that included Ulysses and Muldoon, Helga, Rita and Eric, and Max. As they went up the path toward the central plaza of Group A, Katie glanced back over her shoulder and laughed.

"Look who's behind us."

"Your friend," Lucy said, addressing Harp for the first time. "Sancho the barf-eating pig."

"Why bother to chew if somebody'll do it for you?" Harp said admiringly, and was pleased when Lucy made gagging sounds. That was progress. He'd filled his pockets with provisions in the dining hall, so he dug out a couple of soggy pretzels and tossed one back to Sancho. He offered the other one to Lucy.

"What?" she asked suspiciously.

"For him. A pig can't have too many friends."

"Okay," Lucy said after a moment, sounding almost contrite. She took the pretzel and turned around, brandishing it to get Sancho's attention before she threw. "He caught it in the air! Can pigs see in the dark?"

"Enough to recognize a friend, I guess," Harp said. "How about yourself?"

"What?"

"Can you recognize a friend?"

Lucy pulled back the edge of her hood so he could see the face she was making. "That was sneaky, Harp."

"I'm a master of ambiguous behavior. Besides, I haven't done anything to deserve the cold shoulder from you. Have I?"

"Oh, okay," Lucy conceded, and suddenly grabbed Harp by the back of the raincoat and pulled him over next to Katie, stepping around to the outside. "There, have your fun. I won't even look."

"Lucy," Katie said sharply, but the girl just laughed and dashed off toward the head of the line. They were coming into the plaza, out into a pale, ghostly light that seemed to have been spread over the buildings and monuments with a brush, leaving them coated with a vague phosphorescence. It was hard to appreciate the beauty of it, though, because the rain was blowing horizontally across the open expanse of the plaza, and it seemed to hit Harp in the face no matter which direction he tried to look. They gathered in front of the stela at the foot of Kan Shell's temple, a truncated pyramid that rose in three stages to the shrine at the top.

"Let's go up," Muldoon said, shouting to be heard. "And let's be *real* slow and careful on the stairs. Especially you drunks."

"Right!" Ulysses agreed, and went bounding up the steps, which appeared iced in the moonlight. The rest followed more slowly, Lucy coming back between Harp and Katie and letting each of them take a hand. The stairs weren't as slippery as they looked but they were certainly steep, and everyone was huffing as they crowded into the tiny single room at the top. They were all shivering, too, soaked through from the waist down. Harp pulled out the pint of rum he'd sequestered in his pocket, a weight he'd been feeling against his leg all the way up. He held it out in offering to the Reverend Doctor Muldoon.

"I copped that from the dining hall. If you think it wouldn't dilute our reverence too much . . ."

"Ah, firewater," Muldoon said in a fair imitation of W. C. Fields. "The cold pilgrim's best friend."

He took a healthy slug and passed the bottle around, and no one refused it, not even Helga Kauffmann. She'd thrown back her hood and wiped her glasses and already had some copal burning in her incense ladle. *Pom* and rum, Harp thought as the bottle came back to him. There was just enough left in it for a stiff, warming jolt, which he savored like a true pilgrim. There was a clatter of pig feet on the landing outside and Sancho poked his snout into the room. He backed out again when someone shone a flashlight on him, but came all the way in and stayed when Harp dropped a cookie and a couple of pretzels on the floor.

Muldoon had laid down a towel and put the smoking ladle in the center of it, with an upright flashlight pinning each of the four corners. He stood next to this makeshift altar with his hands clasped over his stomach, wearing a headband that bore a circular badge of prismatic glass, an optical illusion eyeball that opened and closed when he nodded his head.

"Hear us, Ixchel," he intoned, "Moon Mother, Lady Rainbow, consort of Itzamna and Goddess of the Night Sky. Chac has hidden your face from us but we hold your image in our hearts, and we have come to honor you and ask for your guidance and favor." Muldoon made a little bow, drawing a few giggles with his winking third eye. He grinned and spread his hands with a flourish. "Look who has come to you, O Mother. Among us there is a venerated elder, one who has conversed with the ancients in their own tongue and revealed their secrets to us. There are those with doctorates in digging, those who will be doctors if they ever get their dissertations done, and rookies with their first dirt still under their nails. We have several lovely ladies and some ugly bearded men, and a child who becomes a mermaid in the vicinity of the cenote." Muldoon paused and looked around the room. "Oh yes, dear Mother, we also have a novelist and a pig."

Their laughter spooked Sancho out of the room for a moment, but the rain drove him back inside, shaking himself like a dog.

"We ask your blessing on this motley crew," Muldoon went on. "Accept the offerings they have brought and grant them the favor they most wish to have."

Muldoon reached into his pocket and pulled out one of the cigars Brinton Taylor had offered around after dinner. He set it down on the towel and waved copal smoke over it with his hand. Since everyone knew how much Muldoon loved Brinton's Havanas, it was an impressive offering, and several people murmured in approbation. Harp was stricken by a sudden sense of dereliction that made his skin prickle. He'd meant to bring the snakeskin he'd found, but the confusion at the hut had driven it from his mind. He made a surreptitious survey of his pockets, which held two cookies, a pretzel, the empty rum bottle, and a wad of paper napkins. The others were going up one by one to squat and lay something on the towel. Harp realized he hadn't thought about a wish, either. What'd he really want? *Everything* was his first thought, but that seemed a bit broad. Did he want success as a writer or simply the best books he could write? And what did that matter compared to his marriage? Maybe it was some power or character trait he needed, from which all the rest would follow.

Katie nudged him with an elbow and showed him what she planned to offer: the fern-wrapped bouquet of wilted orchids he'd given her at the beginning of the evening. A romantic memento for the Moon Goddess. He nodded approvingly and she gave him a smile that was unambiguously affectionate yet in no way suggestive of more. It was an extraordinarily sweet smile for her.

As she went forward, Harp hastily patted himself down again, this time discovering the cigarette pack in his shirt pocket. Tobacco was an appropriate offering, he thought with relief, then realized he had something he valued much more. Sweet smoke for the Moon Goddess, help her stay high.

When his turn came he crouched in front of the towel, his wet sneakers making squishing sounds. He took a moment to study the other offerings, which looked like a collection of personal fetishes. There was a piece of antler, a monkey skull, some colorful stones and stolen potsherds, several Mexican coins, and a button bearing the dreadlocked visage of Bob Marley. He put a couple of cigarettes next to Muldoon's cigar and then hesitated with the joint in his hand, aware of the others watching, aware that he could be on his way home fast if Brinton ever heard about this. But it was the only thing of value he had to offer, and the risk only made it seem more valuable. The Goddess would just have to see that no one squealed.

He poked the tip of the joint into the burning incense to get it lit, took a couple puffs to keep it going, and set it down carefully in the bowl of the ladle. *Inspire me, Mother,* he prayed as he blew smoke over the other offerings. *Let me be revitalized.* He stood up and nodded rather curtly to Muldoon, who cocked his head in bemusement, blinking and winking like a syncopated sign.

"Fragrant," Muldoon murmured. "Well, there it is, Mother. Enjoy. I'll come back tomorrow and collect what's left, so as not to confuse the archaeological record."

"Amen," Ulysses said emphatically, and everyone began to stir and shiver, remembering their discomfort. Harp saw weary faces in the waving flashlight beams, and he was grateful when Katie threw an arm around his waist and propped him up with a shoulder. They shuffled out onto the landing, into the stinging rain.

"Do you have any more food, Harp?" Lucy asked, and he let her empty his raincoat pocket and feed what was left to Sancho, who then trotted around the corner of the shrine toward whatever path he'd used to get up.

"He's not the most demonstrative friend," Harp said, pleased that she had offered him her hand for the descent.

"I don't care," Lucy said and giggled as they started down. "At least he doesn't ask any sneaky questions."

WHILE KATIE put Lucy to bed, Harp waited in her office in the lab, doing what he could to make himself warm again. He closed the shutters, found a blanket in a cupboard and wrapped it around his wet legs, and helped himself to some of Katie's scotch. He set the flashlight upright on the desk and put his feet up next to it, leaning back in the swivel chair and feeling that he might never move again. The Exhaustion Theory of Fidelity: too beat to be bad. He listened to the rain drumming on the thatch overhead and the muted sounds of music and voices from the dining hall, where those with the stamina were still partying. He hoped that Rita and Eric had somehow defied the laws of physics and learned to execute a proper clutch by now.

"Don't get up," Katie said as she came in, waving her flashlight as she shook back the hood of her raincoat. She sat on the edge of the desk next to his feet and poured some scotch into the cup he'd left out for her. "Lucy was asleep before I left the room. And you look like you could go any minute."

"Go where? I'm already gone. How come you're still on your feet?"

"I'm happy," Katie said, resting a hand on his blanket-wrapped legs. "It's been a wonderful date, Harp."

"It has," he agreed with a smile. "I'm wonderfully exhausted."

"Good. Maybe you won't be angry, then." Katie slid open a drawer in her desk and groped around inside for a moment. Then she stood up and dropped an envelope on his chest. "That was in the mail Ulysses brought back from Comitán today. I think it's from your wife, though I didn't read it. I just saved it for you."

Harp held the envelope up in front of his face, though there was only enough light to see that it was Mid-Atlantic stationery. He looked back at Katie, who was regarding him over the rim of her cup. "Were you afraid I'd crap out on the date?"

"Yeah, or that you'd feel so inhibited you wouldn't be any fun. But it made me feel dishonest to hide it from you, and I almost gave it to you before we went to dinner. God, I wish I had, because I never really got it out of my mind. When we were kissing in the trees, I knew you were thinking about her, but so was I! I felt like I'd left her sitting here at the desk, waiting for me to bring her husband home."

Harp laughed. "Which you have, with scruples more or less intact. Now I understand where your speech to Brinton came from."

"Guilt," Katie said flatly. "Concealing evidence is a crime in my profession. I was also tempted to read it, find out for myself if she deserved your scruples."

Harp mustered the strength to pull his feet off the desk and stand up. He dropped the letter into his raincoat pocket, unwound the blanket from his legs, and came over to where she was sitting.

"I'll overlook your criminal behavior," he told her. "But in return you gotta tell me what you wished for up there."

Katie gave him a shrewd smile. "Why? You figure it had something to do with you?"

"Actually, no, not from the way you smiled. But it was my corsage you used for an offering." He reached out and put his hands on her waist, discovering that she'd changed into a fleecy sweatsuit that felt enviably warm. She gave him a duplicate of the temple smile, affectionate but not hungry.

"I wished for a true romance, someone I truly liked and liked being with. All the time—not just in bed. Sex should be the bonus, not the sole reward. I'd gotten so cynical about men I'd forgotten that. You did have something to do with reminding me," she admitted, leaning forward to kiss him lightly on the lips. "What'd you wish for?"

Harp shrugged. "I didn't know what I was going to wish for until I did it, and then it was undeniable. I asked to be revitalized, sort of a broad version of true romance."

Katie laughed and stood up to embrace him. "May our prayers be answered."

He simply held her against him, his hands around her back inside the raincoat. The inclination to move had left him again, except for an area around his hips. Then his hands began to get interested, too.

"You're not wearing anything under this, are you?" he murmured.

"I didn't think you had the strength to notice," Katie said, backing off slightly in a deliberate enticement of his hands. "Okay, last pawing at the doorstep, a little take-home excitement . . . "

Harp pawed her rather expertly, he thought, taking tactile impressions so vivid he could see the bare flesh behind his eyes. "There's one part of me that still wants to be bad," he boasted as she broke away from him.

"Beat it, Harp," she advised, putting a flashlight into his hand and turning him toward the door.

9

HE'D GONE to sleep to the sound of the rain, and it was still sprinkling when he awoke, what seemed like many hours later. His watch had stopped in the night and the sky was too overcast to tell where the sun was, but as rested as he felt, it had to be at least noon. He was even hungry, and the possibility of missing out on Sunday brunch altogether had him up and dressing in a hurry. He brushed his teeth but decided he could skip meditating, and he left Caroline's letter—still unopened—on top of his typewriter.

He jogged to the dining hall, amazed that all the dancing and climbing the temple stairs hadn't left him stiff in some part of his body. His ankles didn't even crack like they usually did in the morning. When he got to the hall and found only Brad inside, he was keenly disappointed, having worked up a real craving for a whole meal. Then he realized that Brad was cleaning up the remains of the party, not brunch, and a glance at the clock on the wall told him it was—unbelievably—only 9:45. He was *early.* Brad gave him a quizzical stare.

"You gonna help? Or are ya too hungover?"

"Me? Naw, I never did get drunk last night," Harp said with a kind of surprise, and came over to pitch in. "I must be revitalized."

In fact, it was a little scary how good he felt. He hadn't been *that* restrained last night and he certainly never expected such immediate and tangible benefits from his offering and wish. Maybe the Moon Goddess was partial to dope.

When the tables were clear, he and Brad put them end to end and laid out napkins and flatware. It was ten, and they were still the only ones who'd shown. Ramona rewarded them for their labors by heaping their plates with bacon and eggs and *pozole* with salsa, garnished with slices of melon and orange. Ever since Harp'd praised the curative powers of her *pozole,* she'd been giving him a double helping along with a big smile. Today he actually had the appetite for it and dug in with gusto.

"How come you're not hungover?" he asked Brad, who was chowing down with his customary panache. "I heard you passed out."

"I did," Brad said between mouthfuls. "Slept right through the moon watch, I guess. But I woke up for the party afterward. The Motorhead was dancing with that girl, but Rick and Ulysses and Muldoon were hanging out drinking and telling funny stories. They were so bagged, man, I wouldn't expect to see any of them for breakfast."

Helga Kauffmann and Brinton Taylor came in and sat down at the head of the table. Helga beamed at Harp, bobbing her head over her food. "I was telling Brinton about our ceremony, Mr. Yates. I thought that it was right to be respectful but not too solemn. The gods can recognize dilettantes."

"Did the Reverend Doctor Muldoon truly refer to Helga as one who spoke for the ancients?" Brinton inquired.

"*With* the ancients," Harp corrected. "And he didn't claim it was a first-hand conversation."

Helga laughed her throaty, Germanic laugh, her eyes squinted shut behind the thick lenses. Brinton smiled at Harp with a good humor that seemed untainted by suspicion, putting to rest Harp's concern that Helga might've told him too much.

"And how did he describe you, Mr. Yates?" Brinton asked.

"In a category of my own, close to that of camp pig."

Ulysses came shambling in in the middle of this, wincing visibly when the sound of their laughter hit him. He was still wearing the Hawaiian shirt and headband, but they looked soiled and slept-in rather than jaunty, and his eyes appeared to have been tie-dyed a painful shade of reddish pink. He managed the merest of nods in greeting as he went past to the kitchen.

"The walking hangover," Brad murmured admiringly. "That's what I call a *hard* drinker."

"He can have the title," Harp decided. Ulysses returned with a plate of fruit and bread and a pitcher of orange juice, and he proceeded to eat and drink with a grim tenacity that had nothing to do with hunger. It was agonizing to watch and Harp soon stopped, wondering why someone would poison his body and then try to force-feed it. That seemed beyond hard, into the realm of self-hatred.

Brinton was telling Helga about the excavation of the palace in Group B, and Harp listened absently while he ate. He was still amazed to be so alert so early in the day, and it had him contemplating a radical temperamental departure: writing in broad daylight. He seldom wrote anything before about four in the afternoon, and never before noon. He just wasn't awake in the right way. But right now the notion of reading Caroline's letter and responding immediately—in one sitting—had an appeal as stimulating as Ramona's coffee.

When Ulysses abruptly pushed back his chair and stood up, Harp expected to see him run for the door. That food was bound to come back up more easily than it'd gone down. But instead Ulysses looked across the table at him and Brad.

"Anybody wanna do some bushwhacking?"

Harp laughed in disbelief, but Brad looked back at Ulysses and slowly shook his head. "Sorry, man, not the kinda workout I need today. Wanna put some fluids back in before I do a hard sweat."

Ulysses grunted disdainfully and left without waiting for Harp to refuse more formally. Harp had a second cup of coffee and smoked a cigarette, lingering in the hope that Katie would turn up. He wanted to show off his revitalized self, just in case it didn't last. He was too full of energy to wait for long, though, and he soon cleared his dishes and headed back toward his hut.

The rain had stopped but the sky remained a uniform bright grey, with a damp, balmy wind blowing. The wind took him back to the night before, pawing Katie under the palms and feeling restraint melting away in the heat of the moment. The heat rose again and he wondered how he could ever tell Caroline about any of this. Just a little while ago he'd been thinking about describing the date in his letter, but that suddenly seemed like madness. He might proclaim it as a victory for fidelity, but Caroline would more likely see it as the sexual equivalent of elf theft. No way, he told himself, and tried to put the idea out of his mind. But it hung there stubbornly, shaming him for having such cowardly good sense. If he neglected to mention the date now, how was he going to explain it later? And if it was true that nothing had happened, why didn't he think he could make Caroline believe it?

He realized that he'd come to the path to his hut without seeing anything he'd passed, and he stopped to collect himself. He felt half-aroused and slightly dizzy, and he wondered where his previous clarity had gone. This was revitalization run amuck. Then he glanced up at the trees tossing against the sky and understood. The grey wind blew here, too.

He was still standing where he'd stopped when Ulysses came around the corner of the men's lodge. He was wearing his implement belt and carrying an extra canteen and a machete.

"Well?" he demanded brusquely as he came up. "You wanna go or not?"

The voice jolted Harp out of his paralysis, but it still took him a moment to comprehend the request. "Why would you want me along?"

Ulysses shrugged. "Why not? It's another pair of eyes to look, another arm to cut trail. Another mouth, I'm sure."

The insult was offered casually, and Harp was surprised by how much it stung, and by the strength of his own reaction. "I think you'd rather be alone," he snapped, and turned toward his hut.

"Yates," Ulysses said, and the note of pleading in his voice brought Harp up short. "It's rough terrain, even where the *brecha*'s been cut. Easy for somebody alone to get hurt and hard for anybody else to find him if he did."

Harp turned all the way back to face him. "Whatta you expect to find out there?"

"As far as I got the last time, I saw something that looked like earthworks, and a standing structure. It was getting dark and I had to leave, and then I got sent down to the ball court. This's the first chance I've had to go back."

"How far out?"

"Five, six kilometers. There's a number of what I think were shrines, at regular intervals. They're in bad shape, but I turned up some late Rana Phase sherds at one of them."

"Okay, I'll go," Harp said abruptly. "On two conditions: that you don't try to run me into the ground, and that you don't leave me to find my own way back."

Ulysses laughed and then grimaced as if it hurt his head. "Christ, I'm in no shape to run anybody into the ground. And I've never ditched anybody intentionally."

"I don't wanna be the first."

"You won't be. Now c'mon, let's go if we're going."

"Lemme get my stuff," Harp said, motioning for him to follow along to the hut. He didn't know if he'd regret this later, but it was probably better to be following one of Ulysses's whims than any of his own. Rough terrain or not, it might still be the safer path, on a day of grey wind.

IN SPANISH, *brecha* meant an opening or a breakthrough. In the parlance of the site, it referred to any one of the four arrow-straight paths that radiated outward from the center of Group A, oriented with some precision to the cardinal directions. The Pemex geological crew had cut the three that went east, west, and south, but they'd apparently found the terrain to the north too daunting, because they'd never finished the job. It was indeed rough country, thickly forested and torturous in contour, with low, rocky hills alternating with deep ravines and stretches of swampland. Even the Baktunis had not built much in this direction, except for the shrines Ulysses claimed to have found.

Once out of the wind, Harp's clarity and alertness came back and he needed all of it, because for a while Ulysses could only plod along behind him in a hungover squint, often blundering into stumps or thornbushes even after Harp had called out a warning. The *brecha* was marked with wooden stakes at measured intervals, which should have made it easy to follow. But in many places it remained a theoretical construct: a pair of stakes planted on one bank of a ravine or swamp, with a second pair visible on the far bank. To get from one point to the next, they took the real path around, climbing or wading while beating back the brush with machetes. There was plenty of room for error during these detours, which could be extensive and disorienting, but Harp found that he was a pretty good pathfinder if he kept his attention focused on the task. He took pride in not leading them into anything worse than what they were trying to avoid, and in finding his way back to the *brecha* without wasted effort.

After an hour without mishap, he relaxed enough to expand the range of his observations, beginning to see the birds and animals whose sounds he was hearing above the insect drone, and then to notice the butterflies, lizards, and snakes that made no sound at all. Spider monkeys and military macaws glided through the canopy above, and Harp became adept at spotting them against the green, darting swift upward glances between scans of the trail, so as not to miss any of the snakes that slithered across his path. He was also aware of Ulysses's return to consciousness behind him, so when he caught a glimpse of a tawny feline shape off to his right, he made his guess out loud.

"Ocelot?"

"Yep," Ulysses confirmed. "Had something in its mouth, too."

Ulysses soon began to offer unsolicited sightings, quickly proving that he saw far more in the forest than Harp did, and that he knew the names of just about everything he saw. It became clear that he was a compulsive explainer who wanted an audience more than company, but Harp didn't mind learning more about the wildlife, which was much more various and abundant here than around the camp. When they stopped for a rest Harp took a notebook out of his rucksack and scribbled descriptions of all the new species he'd seen, with Ulysses throwing out additional tidbits about their diets and mating habits.

"How do you know all this stuff?" Harp asked, flexing his writing hand as he put the notebook away.

Ulysses shrugged. "I was in agriculture for a while, and then veterinary science, and I ended up a biology major."

"You were probably an Eagle Scout, too."

Ulysses regarded him warily, as if searching for a judgment in the suggestion. Then he turned and took the lead for the first time, speaking without looking back. "You probably weren't."

"Nope," Harp agreed with a laugh, marching after him. "Never could learn my knots."

During the next hour, they made side trips to two of the so-called shrines, which were little more than thigh-high piles of rubble atop platforms that'd sunk back into the forest floor. Ulysses did find some late Rana Phase sherds to keep Harp's interest up, and he pointed out evidence of burning on the interior of one wall, suggesting that it might indicate a termination ritual. Apparently, the Maya often built fires and broke pottery inside temples that were being superseded by newer structures.

"Was the burial of the ball court a termination ritual?" Harp asked.

"Of a sort," Ulysses allowed.

"Was it done with respect or prejudice?"

"Hard to tell. Muldoon would probably say prejudice, because he sees evidence of it in the terminations in B."

"Clubb's now saying it was respect. He has the leftover Shells serving Kan Cross Ahau as Baktun Boosters."

Ulysses let out a derisive laugh. "He would," he said, and walked on without further comment.

The *brecha* came to an end at the far side of a logwood *bajo,* a seasonal swamp that was mostly dry now except for knee-deep puddles left by last night's rain. They picked their way around the soft mudflats and the hummocks of saw-toothed sedge grass, passing gnarled logwood trees that leaned at odd angles due to slippage in the wet season. The path went two feet into the undergrowth on the other side and then stopped, its termination marked by stakes bearing fluorescent plastic tags. Ulysses uncapped his second canteen and drank greedily, his hands shaking. He'd been tiring visibly for the last twenty minutes or so, as if his hangover had caught up with him again.

"Which way now?" Harp asked, sipping more judiciously from his own canteen. Ulysses had sat down in the grass, and it took him a moment to raise his machete and point to the east.

"I went along the edge of the *bajo* about fifty meters and then cut north. I marked the trail with toilet paper but it's probably all washed away. Watch out for snakes—I saw a lotta them the last time. The mosquitoes were bad, too; better put on more bug dope."

Ulysses hadn't shown any concern for snakes or mosquitoes before this, but Harp was willing to be prudent and smeared the vile-smelling lotion on all his exposed skin, even taking off his baseball cap to coat the dome of his head. Ulysses went through the motions with the repellent but he was basically just resting, his face pale behind the red beard. Harp lit a cigarette and looked down at him.

"I hope you feel better than you look, 'cause you look like hell."

Ulysses bared his teeth. "Pleased to meet you." He reached into a pouch on his belt and pulled out a Hershey bar. He broke it in two and stuffed half into his mouth, holding the rest up to Harp. Harp snorted, remembering Rick's reference to Ulysses's "bribe box." But he took the chocolate and ate some, grimacing at the way Ulysses was devouring his portion. Another force-feeding.

"Don't you ever give your body a break?" he asked. "You know, a little rest, a little pleasure, maybe even some comfort?"

"Why should I?"

Harp shrugged. "I dunno . . . 'cause it's the only body you've got? I'm not talking pampering, just a little basic self-regard."

"You've got enough of that for both of us," Ulysses sneered, pushing himself to his feet. Harp stood up to him stubbornly.

"Enough to wonder why you've treated me like shit ever since you first laid eyes on me."

Ulysses gave him a sour smile. "I knew who you were. Your picture was on your book."

"Which book?"

"The one about the draft dodger. Fisher lent it to me."

Harp took a last drag and put out his cigarette. "And?"

"It was pretty good," Ulysses admitted grudgingly. "Took me back to college and the sixties. But then you got all righteous at the end, trying to make it sound like some big moral battle with the government. You couldn't just admit you didn't wanna get your ass shot off."

"Is that why you went? Because you *did*?"

"I went because I wanted to see for myself. I didn't wanna hide out in college and let them send some poor black kid in my place."

Ulysses pulled his machete out of the ground and headed out along the edge of the *bajo,* and Harp went after him. He didn't pursue the argument, though, because he'd gotten an answer to his essential question. He could stand being despised for what he believed, and he wasn't about to convert a vet on the subject of the war. If Ulysses didn't know they were on the same side by now, he never would.

When Ulysses found the entry point he plunged into the forest without apparent regard for snakes, whacking away at the undergrowth with an excess of zeal. Harp gave his arm a rest, content to hang strips of toilet paper at intervals as trail markers. At the rate Ulysses was wasting energy, he'd have to be the leader on the way out, too. Harp was beginning to feel like a paragon of rationality and self-control in comparison; the grey wind seemed to blow around Ulysses in a constant gale.

Twice Harp volunteered to cut trail, but Ulysses pretended not to hear and went on whacking away, occasionally clanging his machete off tree trunks. He walked right under a coiling boa without seeing it and had his head down when Harp caught the first glimpse of the temple. It registered immediately as a temple because it was raised up on a platform and was largely intact, a squat rectangular building with a single doorway and a vaulted roof with half a roof comb still in place. Harp thought he could make out stucco designs on the roof comb and was so excited he couldn't speak. *We discovered this,* he thought, forgiving Ulysses for all his macho compulsions.

"Hey!" he said finally. "Take a look at what we found!"

Ulysses stopped and looked back at him blankly, then swiveled and saw the temple. He stood transfixed for a moment, then started for it on the run, forgetting all need for a path. Harp laughed and ran after him, weaving his way between trees and thornbushes with enthusiastic grace and reaching the foot of the platform at the same time Ulysses did. They both saw the snake slither into the temple above; it was too big to miss and made them pause to get their breath.

"Fer-de-lance?" Harp asked, though he'd seen enough of them to know. Ulysses nodded and went up the grassy slope with care, tapping the ground ahead of him with his machete. They made it to the doorway and peered into a room filled with jumbled stone from the partially collapsed roof. There was another doorway directly opposite this one and no sign of the snake, though chances were good it was somewhere inside. Ulysses stuck his machete point first into the ground, whipped out a notebook and pen, and began to write and draw what was in front of him. Still buoyant with excitement, Harp walked around to the other doorway, a most unusual feature for a Classic Mayan temple. A brilliant black and yellow spider hung in the middle of the web it'd spun across the doorway, and Harp decided there wasn't any point in disturbing it just for another peek. He noted that there were stucco designs—including what looked like half a face—on this side of the roof comb, too, and the undulating contour of the platform indicated a staircase beneath the covering of earth and vegetation.

Looking out with his back to the temple, he saw what Ulysses had described as earthworks: a humped, uneven ridge that rose up about six feet from the forest floor. It didn't look like much as he walked toward it, and when he climbed to the top he found that it didn't drop off on the other side. It sloped down slightly but then leveled off and extended for some distance ahead and to the left and right, supporting a decent grove of corozo palms. Gotta be a geological feature, Harp thought, having passed over several similar ridges on the way here. He walked along the edge of it and stopped to take a piss, turning in a circle and spotting no other discernible features in the immediate vicinity. What the hell was this temple doing way out here with nothing around it?

Ulysses appeared atop the ridge about fifty feet away, his machete sheathed on his belt and his notebook in hand, showing no signs of clumsiness or fatigue.

"Walk to the end and count paces back to the middle," he called to Harp, who obeyed with the sense that Ulysses didn't consider this a geological formation. He walked about fifty feet, until he could see the ridge sloping down ahead. A big chicozapote tree was in his path and he stepped around it, noticing that its roots were buried just as he heard a muted crack, the snapping of wood. He instinctively jumped sideways and when he landed the ground gave way and he plunged downward, hitting bottom with a jolt that briefly knocked the breath out of him. His hat was gone and he was enclosed in a blackness that smelled like rot and seemed to embrace him with a sucking grip. He thrust upward in panic and broke back through the crust of matted vegetation, gasping for air and flailing with his arms like a drowning man. He was sitting at the bottom of a hole he'd made himself in a pile of loose vegetal matter that kept collapsing inward on him as he struggled for a purchase. It reminded him of fall leaf piles he'd played in as a kid, only the stuff on the bottom of this pile was in an advanced state of decomposition and stunk horribly. He felt wetness seeping through his jeans and struggled harder, then gave up when he succeeded only in bringing more garbage down around him. He settled back in the evil-smelling muck, feeling the harder shapes below it on which he'd broken his fall.

He looked up and saw Ulysses crouching on the ridge next to the chicozapote tree, about six feet above him.

"You okay?" Ulysses asked.

"I dunno . . . I think so. More scared than anything else. I thought I was being buried alive. What the fuck is this?"

Ulysses took out his trowel and scraped at the edge of the ridge, exposing layered stones. "This is obviously a wall. You're probably sitting in a moat or a courtyard." He tossed down the trowel. "Poke around a little while I get a line around this tree."

Taking a deep breath, Harp rolled onto his hip and struggled to his knees, very nearly burying himself a second time in an avalanche of decaying leaves. This garbage was full of bugs, too, beetles and centipedes and things he didn't dare look at too closely, but that made him dig harder to clear some space for himself. In the process he found his machete, completely coated with black slime but a much better implement for bailing garbage. If he threw it far enough, the crap didn't fall back in on him. He used the trowel to remove the muck, flinging it like plaster.

"Hey," Ulysses said from above. "I didn't say to do an excavation. The rope's almost ready."

"I'm down to flat paving stones, very smooth," Harp reported. "Now what the fuck is *this*? It's the thing I landed on with my hip, put a fucking dent in me."

"Yates!" Ulysses said more urgently. "Don't move anything."

But a swipe of the trowel had revealed that this was no ordinary hunk of stone, exposing curves and indentations that hadn't been carved by nature. "Holy shit!" Harp said eagerly, dropping the trowel to strip off the remaining slime with his fingers. It moved when he rocked it, so he tensed his stomach muscles and pulled, hugging it against him as he rose slowly to his feet.

"Goddammit, Yates, I told you . . ." Ulysses began, then couldn't find any words when Harp turned and displayed a stone frog with blank round eyes and oval markings incised on its ridged back.

"I give you Rana Verde himself. Sucker's heavy."

"It's probably basalt," Ulysses murmured, staring down at it raptly. "Looks just like the one Brinton had." He blinked and frowned at Harp. "Now put it back exactly where you found it."

Harp laughed. "Shut you up for a minute, though, didn't I? Don't worry, there's a hole in the slime." He lowered the frog back into place, the memory of how he'd found it still vivid in his mind. It settled down with a soft sucking sound, and he patted it on the head before straightening up. He tossed the trowel and his machete up to Ulysses and used the rope he received in return to pull himself up onto the wall. Ulysses handed him a canteen and started laughing.

"Jesus, you are a sight! Smell real good, too."

Harp shrugged off his rucksack, which—like the rest of him—was slathered with greenish-black goo. "I feel like I've been tarred and leafed. My hip hurts like hell, too."

"You couldn't have fallen in a better place. That frog's our permit to excavate here. The temple might've been enough, but this cinches it. Brinton'll be out here himself tomorrow. God!" he exclaimed, as if seized by a sudden realization, and jumped to his feet. He went along the inside edge of the wall, hacking at the crust with his machete and the heel of his boot. In some places it appeared solid, but in others it collapsed as it had beneath Harp. This "ridge" was obviously rotten at its core. Ulysses came back and stood over him, grinning the way he had when he'd played devil the night before. "Do you know what Brinton has always thought his frog was?"

"A lawn animal," Harp suggested, feeling in no mood for guessing games.

"A ball court marker!" Ulysses exclaimed, not even hearing him. "Look at the thickness of this wall, and you said you found paving stones down there. This one was buried, too, only not as well."

"A ball court," Harp muttered. "We found the fucking ball court."

"It'll be a bitch to excavate out here," Ulysses went on, talking to himself. "We'll have to haul everything in on foot . . . probably have to camp out here to save travel time." He looked back down at Harp. "You ready to travel? We should get on back and tell the others. Gonna mess up everybody's work schedule for tomorrow."

"Gonna mess up their theories, too," Harp said as he got to his feet. He hurt in a number of other places besides his hip, and the shock of the fall and near-burial had taken something out of him as well. "I can travel, though I'm not gonna set any land-speed records."

"Me neither," Ulysses said agreeably. "Though this's the best I've felt all day. Nothing like a find to pick you up."

Harp held his machete away from his body as he clambered down the other side of the wall. He remembered how this day had started and felt that its promise had been fulfilled. "It is indeed a grey wind that blows no good," he said aloud, offering his share of the find to the Moon Goddess, the only one who could've inspired him to fall into such a fortuitous hole.

10

Well the danger from the rocks is surely past;
Still I remain tied to the mast;
Could it be that I have found my home at last?
Home at last?

—Walter Becker and Donald Fagen,
"Home at Last"

Mid-Atlantic

A ROTTEN DAY, a rotten mood, the sure knowledge that she had no dinner date and nothing at all to eat at home. Caroline decided to put off pleasure entirely and stayed in her office grading student papers. It was March but so chilly they'd had to turn the heat back on, so steam was bumping sluggishly through the baseboard pipes, providing a bass line to the staccato patter of rain against the window. Half the people she'd spoken to today had expressed concern over the possible effect of this cold snap on the fabled cherry blossoms, which Caroline barely recalled seeing last year.

Just before four, Roger Hammet knocked and stuck his head into the room.

"You going to hear Murray's talk?"

"It completely slipped my mind," Caroline confessed, and felt tempted after the fact. Some fresh, sophisticated ideas might bring her out of her funk. But then she remembered she was going out of town next week. "I better pass, Roger. I'm up to my ears in student papers."

He pushed the door all the way open but remained standing in the doorway. "Well, there's a couple things I need to talk to you about, so I'd better do it now. First of all, why'd you sic Virginia Evers on the head?"

Caroline shook her head in unfeigned surprise. "I don't know what you're talking about."

"She went to Charlie to let him know—again—how strongly Women's

Studies feels about your retention. Charlie told her the department was doing everything it could to retain you. He sent me to tell *you* that he doesn't appreciate being pressured."

"Roger, I didn't sic Virginia on anyone," Caroline insisted. "I didn't have any idea she was going to see Charlie."

"Maybe she'd somehow gotten the impression you were looking elsewhere," Roger suggested. "Lots of people seem to think you're interested in the job that just opened up at SUNY Albany."

"Really," Caroline said, able to guess who one of them might be. Roger waited another few seconds before he realized she wasn't going to elaborate.

"You are, aren't you?" he prompted. "Interested."

"Wouldn't you be in my place?"

"From what I've heard about it, they've been trying to fill that position for two years, and the search keeps falling apart because Sociology wants a scholar and Women's Studies wants a radical feminist. In your place, I don't know if I'd waste the energy when there might be a decision here as early as next week."

"In my place, though, you wouldn't be sure what that decision was going to be," Caroline pointed out. "You might consider it a prudent expenditure of energy."

Braced against the doorframe, Roger gave her a long look. "You know I can't give you any guarantees. I've already told you more about your standing than I should."

"I appreciate that, Roger, I really do. All I'm saying is: If there aren't any guarantees, doesn't it make sense to have as many options as possible?" Caroline smiled and spread her hands. "Isn't that just logical?"

It was so plain to her that she was truly astonished when Roger straightened up with a kind of shudder of exasperation. "You're a woman of little faith, Caroline. I hope that doesn't come back to haunt you."

He closed the door quietly behind him, leaving her alone with the groaning pipes and the rattle of rain on the window. She took a deep breath and was glad he hadn't stayed to hear any of the angry responses that came to her now, one after another. Woman of little faith! Of all the patronizing bullshit . . . how had she ever found the man tolerable, let alone attractive? *In your place.* He couldn't find his way there if she took him by the hand and led him there herself.

She looked back at the stack of student papers and made an effort to put her anger aside. She had to prepare for the lecture and workshop she'd agreed to give at Albany, and because she *could* put herself in her students' place, she wanted to hand their papers back before she left. So she couldn't afford to waste any time being pissed off or petulant. She had to get on with the business at hand, though she suddenly didn't feel like doing any more of it here. She packed up her things, pulled up the hood of her raincoat, and headed for the parking lot, squinting against the windblown rain.

. . .

THIS BETTER BE GOOD, HARP, she thought as she brought in the letter along with the white plastic foam box that contained the *chiles rellenos,* rice, and beans she'd picked up at Tortilla Flats. His last letter hadn't won any stars at all. He'd obviously been drunk or high or both, and he'd turned out a brief, nearly incoherent account of how he and his "former enemy," Ulysses, had discovered a hidden ball court way out in the jungle. They'd supposedly been led there by the Moon Goddess for the purpose of meeting the Green Frog, who lived at the bottom of a garbage pile. He'd also mentioned that he'd been put on the payroll as camp jester and would be coming home in about a month, though she couldn't tell if that was any more serious than what had gone before. He hadn't said a word about her last letter.

His last had been typewritten, though with notably erratic skill. This one was handwritten on notebook paper and he appeared to have made an effort to stay between the lines. Caroline got herself some utensils and a glass of beer and settled down at the dining room table to eat and read.

Darkest Suburbia
Baktun, Chiapas

Dear Caroline:

Greetings from the Gulag, otherwise known as the newly discovered minor center of Rana Verde. Along with four other zealous fools, I've been camping out here for the last three nights in order to save the considerable hike back and forth to the main camp. That way we can get up at dawn and work like dogs until the sun goes down, at which time we crawl into our tents, zip them tight and get under our mosquito bars (a self-supporting frame covered with netting), and don't come out until morning, not even to piss. Believe me, a stinking coffee can in the tent is preferable to exposing a vital organ to the voracious attacks of the local mosquitoes, a/k/a The Lords of the Night.

I'm sharing a tent with a couple of undergrads, one a kid who hates me and won't say a word to me (I helped the Motorhead steal Lovely Rita from him at the Full Moon Party, but that's another story), and another whom we call This Animal, whose idea of intellectual fun is to figure out how many tons of dirt he'd moved that day. So we haven't exactly been rolling in wit around here. At the moment I'm alone in the tent, the others next door playing Trivial Pursuit, except for Ulysses, who's actually out there somewhere, defying everything that goes bite in the night (the snakes like this place, too). I'm lying on my air mattress on the floor, drinking mescal from the bottle and writing this by flashlight surrounded by the homely aroma of moldy canvas, bug dope, and urine-tainted tin. I hadn't figured on this kind of confinement and frankly can't stand it anymore, so I'll go back at the end of the day tomorrow and will henceforth waste the time hiking as the saner people do. We've been busting our butts for over a week but it's all been expended on setting up: Making the trail passable, carting in supplies, doing the preliminary clearing and mapping of the site. We haven't touched the ball court yet, though the exploratory hole I made in the fill has been named Yates Landing. It's still there, with La Rana squatting in the middle of it, a major attraction for all visiting pilgrims. I've been encouraged by several would-be promoters to perform a reenactment of my famous Dive of Discovery, as Brother Rick dubbed it (he even offered me a cut of the concessions).

One thing I have had time to do, while sedating my underemployed brain and waiting for my overstressed muscles to unclench, was to ponder what's been happening to you. I remember Sylvia Burdette. We once gave her a ride home from campus and she spent most of it telling us about how she and her cat communicated telepathically. A weird lady, and definitely a master (mistress?) of ambiguous behavior. I can think of at least 3 interpretations of why she laid the job list on you—a neutral warning, a genuine favor, or first-degree elf theft—but I can't give greater weight to any one of them. Does she know something or doesn't she? Was she trying to help or hurt? Does she know herself? As I said, a masterpiece of ambiguity.

On the other hand, the possibility at Albany sounds like an unequivocal plus. I know how much you dislike the interview process, but you never had an opportunity fall in your lap like this one. You not only fit the job description but you've already spoken to someone there you like, who also likes your work. Isn't there a little magic at work here, perhaps the crafty hand of the Moon Goddess? Be careful how you scoff & quibble; she's probably listening.

So how does it all add up? I found it interesting that unlike the good little sociologist you are, you didn't quantify and tote up the score. So I'll have to put the equation in less scientific terms:

A.) You *thought* you had a bird in hand.
B.) You now *know* you have two in the bush.
Which is better?

I've been trying to adopt a more prudent stance toward my own life choices, but I'd still have to go with B, especially if Sylvia *was* trying to warn you that bird A was getting out of hand. I can understand why you find that possibility hard to accept, since these people have had a chance to get to know you, and you've always believed that sort of knowledge should lead to empathy, and then to compassion. Put bluntly, it should be harder to fuck over someone with whom you can identify, right?

Later: Just broke for about an hour to talk to Ulysses, who paid me a surprise visit. He's not the type for Trivial Pursuit and apparently got tired of being a nocturnal blood donor. With the help of some mescal and a few puffs of Baktun Brown he got looser than I've ever seen him, somewhat along the lines of a tranked Doberman. Apropos of nothing, he resumed a conversation we'd had on our day of discovery (in which he revealed that he'd read *War College* and didn't buy draft dodging as a moral act), telling me about the single combat patrol he'd gone on in Vietnam. He'd been in country for exactly three days when he got sent out, and he was so wired on stories of booby traps and ambushes that he was seeing bugs move at five hundred feet. The only thing that happened the whole day was that one of the guys got spooked by a snake and shot it to pieces. They *all* shot it to pieces, in fact, and he didn't know what they would've done if some human had popped up without warning. He said he used up a year's supply of adrenaline in that one day and understood completely why so many of the combat vets were using drugs. As it was, that was as close as he came to combat, because he got snatched by some AID guys who were experimenting with new strains of rice (Ulysses grew up on a farm and was briefly an Ag major). He said the South Vietnamese assigned to guard the project robbed it blind, and the Vietcong would let them come within a week or two of harvest and then blow up the dikes and flood the crop out. That happened three times before his tour was finally up.

He just told me all this and left. A peace offering, I suppose. He'll probably take it back when I tell him I'm bolting back to civilization. The trivialists have ended their game and Jim came scurrying back and crawled into his mosquito bar, sending silent waves of hate my way. The little twit. If I stayed out here another night, I'd have to feed him to the mosquitoes. Instead I'll go back and grab a shower and a hot meal and some conversation with free souls. And I'll get this off to you on the next run to Comitán. Knowing that my days here are numbered, I volunteered for this slave duty out of a desire to learn all I can about the second ball court before I leave. But there's no wisdom in this kind of suffering. I'll still get paid if I sleep in my own bed, and Rick can fill me in on whatever's found after I'm gone.

So what's the latest? Here's hoping all your birds come home to roost. I'll be there in a few weeks to help scratch out the next life. I love you.

still digging,
Harp

The Aviary Approach to life, Caroline thought, laughing to herself. He sure knew how to squeeze a cliché for all it was worth. And how to speak straight to her heart. It *was* all a matter of empathy, of getting out of yourself long enough to feel it as someone else. There was more than a little magic involved in that, too.

She closed the lid on the remains of her Mexican dinner and carried it out to the kitchen. She thought of Harp "bolting" back to civilization and had to admit he wouldn't find much of it here. She was still camping out, as he'd called it, and she was sick of it too. In the next life, she vowed, they were going to find themselves a place to *live.*

Baktun

ON HIS WAY to the dining hall for breakfast, Harp stopped by Muldoon's cabin and found the older man still getting dressed. Harp separated Ulysses's personal wish list from the other supply sheets, and Muldoon yawned and led the way to the back of the cabin. He unlocked the trunk and began to pull out the usual array of canned peanuts and cookies, chocolate bars, and soft drinks, plus a bottle of dark rum. Since Ulysses no longer had anyone around to bribe, it was quite clear that he was a junk food fanatic in his own right.

"Sorry to keep making you the middleman," Harp said as he loaded the goods into his backpack. "But he'd never trust me with the key to his bribe box."

"I don't mind," Muldoon said. "I just miss the sonuvabitch. He hasn't started wearing feathers or painting his face or anything like that, has he?"

Harp laughed. "Not yet. He smells like the swamp he's been washing in, though, so I try to stay upwind."

"It's crazy. How much can he possibly get done by himself in the time it takes the rest of you to get out there?"

"That's his time for bushwhacking and playing hunches, dropping test pits where he thinks he might find something spectacular. He wants to be sitting on a major find when we arrive someday, just to punish us for crapping out on him."

"Crapping out," Muldoon muttered as he locked up the trunk. "The last two got sick, and he'll wind up with some monster bug if he stays out there too long. He's also drinking too fucking much. Tell him that's the last bottle of rum he's gonna get for a while. Which reminds me . . ."

He went over to a trunk on his side of the cabin and came back with his hand cupped in front of him, holding the cigarettes and the joint Harp had offered to the Moon Goddess. "Forgot to give those back to you," he apologized. "They oughta be extra potent."

"The divine weed," Harp murmured agreeably, dropping them into the pocket of his raincoat. He slung the pack over one shoulder and walked with Muldoon to the door. "When're you guys gonna finish the palace and come help us? We've got a whole ball court to clear."

"You found it, you dig it," Muldoon laughed. "I wouldn't count on getting any of us anytime soon. We're still finding good stuff, and then we're doing a full restoration. It'll be a good counterpoint to the late revivalist architecture around B-Three."

"Old stuff, though," Harp teased. "Wouldn't you rather be unraveling the riddle of Rana Verde?"

"I'll leave the glamour jobs to you and Clubb. Some of us have the old-fashioned belief that the beginning and middle are just as interesting as the end. Maybe more so, since people often don't do their best work when their culture's going to pieces around them."

"You've got a point," Harp admitted as he stepped outside. "I have a natural bias toward the apocalyptic."

"Very American," Muldoon said. "You ever see *Apocalypse Now*?"

"Twice. I think it's a great flick."

"So does Ulysses. He's seen it about six times. Tell him for me that it's time for Kurtz to come out of the jungle."

"I'm just the guy to tell him that," Harp said ruefully. "But I will."

"Think of it this way: It beats having to carry him back in at some later point."

"I hear you," Harp said.

"AH, NEW MULES," Harp said happily, coming up behind Kaaren and Eric while they were eating. He deposited a loaded pack behind each of their chairs. "Nobody goes to Rana Verde empty-handed."

"Mister Logistics," Rick said sarcastically, as Harp slid into the seat he'd vacated between him and Katie Smith. "He didn't use to be such a fucking bully in the morning."

"No," Katie agreed. "He was cute when he was grouchy."

"So my internal clock's running a little fast," Harp said with a shrug. "It comes from being out on the cutting edge. When're you gonna finish with your old ball court and come help us dig ours?"

"With one leap he's out on the cutting edge," Rick said, speaking across him to Katie. "This must be the New Archaeology everybody's talking about."

"I guess if you're on the cutting edge, you never have to take another turn in the lab."

"But he didn't *discover* the lab."

Harp leaned forward to look past Rick at Kaaren and Eric. "You see the kind of envy and rancor that breeds in the backwaters? You're lucky to be escaping. Life is freer out on the frontier."

"Sounds like a speculator's heaven," Kaaren said with a skeptical smile.

"It is," Harp agreed. "For instance, we've already decided *why* they moved the ball court out there. Now we just have to find the evidence."

"Okay, I'll bite," Rick said as Harp sat back next to him.

Harp spread his hands, as if the conclusion were unavoidable. "Same reason the Giants moved to the Meadowlands. More room for parking."

Brinton had a rule against throwing food, so Katie simply pummeled him with the banana in her hand. The others groaned and booed.

"You still wanna go out with these bozos?" Rick said to Kaaren. "It's not too late to find a safe backwater."

Kaaren shrugged. "The end zone's done. And . . . the frontier does have a certain savage appeal."

"Very American," Harp said, commending her. "So that leaves you, Big Guy," he said to Rick. "Why don't you wrap that sucker and come join the ranks of the bozos?"

Rick pushed back his chair and stood up, appearing unamused. "It's a little harder when you don't know beforehand what you want to prove. You'll have to find the parking stubs on your own."

Harp laughed, though he knew he'd overstepped the bounds. Rick had never been any good at finishing things, and the discovery of the second ball court had probably made him even more compulsive about perfecting his own report. When he was gone, Harp leaned toward Katie.

"Oops," he said, and Katie let out a sigh that ended in a laugh.

"At least you know how insufferable you are."

"I have friends who tell me all the time."

"They know how much you enjoy it. They know the reason you're pretending to be obnoxiously proud is because you *are* obnoxiously proud."

Harp nodded in acknowledgment. "I can't help it, I never discovered anything before. What would you recommend? A humbling stint in the lab?"

"We could use some comic relief," Katie admitted. "The only time I see you anymore is when you're asking me for supplies."

"As a matter of fact," Harp said, reaching for the lists in his shirt pocket. Katie slapped his hand with the banana.

"You owe me some lab time, Yates, and I'm gonna get it. No supplies until I have your promise of one day this week."

"I hear the voice of Takesnoshit Katie," Harp said with a grin. "How about Thursday? That'll give Ulysses time to find a substitute mule master, and maybe we'll dig up something worth bringing in by then."

"I consider that a promise," Katie said as they got up and Harp retrieved his backpack. "We'll knock off early and go have a drink by the cenote."

"Sounds civilized," Harp said with a frown. "I could lose my savage appeal."

"It won't be missed," Katie assured him as they walked toward the door. "And say 'please' when you hand me that list . . ."

THE *BRECHA* and its auxiliary trails had been so greatly improved and were now so familiar that Harp could almost walk them without thinking, once daylight had penetrated to the forest floor and burned off the fog that hung over the ravines and swamps. That second dawning took a while, however, and the chill air kept him and his companions moving at a brisk pace for at least a couple kilometers. The dripping gloom of the forest seemed to discourage conversation, making any voice sound loud and presumptuous.

Later, when the four of them had gotten out ahead of the rest of the crew and it was warm enough to strip off a layer of clothing, Harp began to fill Kaaren and Eric in on what they'd actually been doing at Rana Verde. He'd done a lot of this lately, delivering Ulysses's verbal reports to Brinton and carrying messages back and forth. He'd even done some haggling for more workers and had made such a strong case (he'd thought) that he'd felt free to tease Brinton about the ambiguousness of his response.

So the information tripped easily off his tongue and he was quick to anticipate their questions. But Katie had him listening to himself now, and what he heard sounded like the patter of a smug PR man, glib and superficial. Katie had him dead to rights, well on his way to becoming a parody of himself. Humbled, he toned down his presentation, leaving out the canned jokes and not trying to head off the inevitable large question, which Kaaren voiced immediately.

"Unless I missed something, you're saying that you haven't found a sherd of any kind?"

"Not a one," Harp admitted. "The temple was apparently swept clean before abandonment, and we haven't trenched it because Helga's still collecting stucco fragments. She's putting together some fantastic stuff, masks and glyphs and design elements, some of it with the paint still on it. She says the iconography is mostly related to war and sacrifice and the Underworld."

"But no dates," Kaaren suggested.

"No," Harp agreed. "We've got two trenches going at the ball court, one into the range wall and the other across the interior of the court at the northern end line. The fill in the range wall is clean dirt and stone, probably collected locally. Except for the area around Yates Landing and a few other places, the ball court fill is solidly packed organic matter. A bitch to remove, as This Animal here will attest."

"Too many fucking roots," Brad said emphatically, pleased to be consulted.

"There's lots of rotten wood on the bottom, above the slime," Harp went on. "Ulysses thinks they originally filled it with whole trees and dirt. We've found pieces of logwood still decomposing on the bottom."

"But no sherds or artifacts?" Kaaren asked.

"Only La Rana. The slime's eaten up all the original plaster, too. Ulysses has dropped test shafts all over the place but has yet to find anything more exciting than animal bones and scorpion nests."

"Hard to cut much of an edge with that," Kaaren said dryly.

Harp smiled sheepishly. "Frontiers are known for their untapped potential. But now that we have a couple more experienced hands, I'm sure we'll tap into something good."

"Ulysses is sure gonna be glad to see you," Brad said to Eric. "Add a little beef to the crew."

Eric shrugged uncertainly and glanced over his shoulder at Harp. "Ah

. . . I talked to Dr. Kauffmann like you said. She said she could use some help collecting fragments."

"I was gonna offer," Harp said. "But if you want it, it's yours."

"Oh, *man,*" Brad said in disbelief. "Ulysses is gonna have a shitfit if he sees you dinking around with Helga instead'a doing some real work."

"Let him," Harp said. "What Helga's doing *is* the real work, Animal. It may tell us more about the site than anything we dig up."

"That's great," Brad said indifferently. "But we got a lotta dirt to move, and no offense meant, Harp, but the Motorhead can outdig you by a lot."

"What a surprise," Harp said with a laugh. "That just means there'll be plenty left for him to dig once he gets done helping Helga. So go for it, Motorhead. If you're serious about this archaeology business, you should work with the stars while they're still in the firmament, so to speak."

"He's right," Kaaren agreed. "You shouldn't miss the chance to work with Helga. But Harp . . . I was told that Ulysses was the crew chief. That's who usually gives out the work assignments."

"Damn straight," Brad said emphatically.

They'd been following one of the detour trails and had come to a place where stepping-stones had been laid down across a stretch of low marsh. Harp had helped lay them himself, an experience in muck wallowing that made him grimace in recognition. The others had stopped on the bank and were regarding him expectantly.

"First of all," he said to Eric, "Ulysses thinks as highly of Helga as I do, so he'd understand why you'd want to work with her. Secondly, he may be crew chief, but I'm doing all the fucking legwork for him, so he owes me a little authority. I'll tell him it was my decision, okay?"

"Okay," Eric said slowly. "I don't wanna get you in trouble, either. This Animal here's been telling me that Ulysses has been acting a little crazy."

Harp looked at Brad and laughed. "He *started out* a little crazy. At the moment he seems to be on his way to becoming Captain Ahab or Mr. Kurtz. But he's mostly only dangerous to himself."

"Hell, he's been chewing out somebody nearly every day," Brad complained. "He got all over me just because I dumped a load in the wrong place."

"I bet he'd stop if you threatened to kill him," Harp suggested.

Brad gaped at him, then laughed. "*Sure.* That's what you did, right?"

"I didn't have to. But it's what I'd do in *your* place. You don't have to take any off-the-wall shit from him just because he's the crew chief."

"First you take a little authority, and then you recommend threatening the crew chief," Kaaren pointed out. "What's going on out here? You didn't mention any of this over breakfast."

"It's nothing that gets in the way of the work," Harp insisted. "We just have to find a way to coax Ulysses in out of the bush before he gets sick or hurts himself. Muldoon's worried about him too."

" 'Too'?" Kaaren repeated skeptically. "I thought you and Ulysses hated each other."

"We did. We still do at times. But we stopped butting heads when we found this place. That made us undeniable equals."

"Does that mean he'll take your advice?" Kaaren asked.

"Hell, no. We're gonna have to work on him." Harp hitched up his backpack and stepped out onto the first of the stones, looking back over his shoulder. "We're gonna have to make him feel the weight of our collective sanity."

Kaaren laughed and started out after him, followed closely by Brad and Eric. "How do we do that?" she asked.

Harp got to the other bank before he turned to respond. "No more ducking and flinching. When he goes off the wall, we call him on it."

"Call him what?" Eric asked over Kaaren's shoulder, and Harp raised his voice, grinning with sudden inspiration.

"We call him 'Bwana Kurtz' . . ."

THEY STOWED their packs inside the supply tent, left Eric to wait for Helga at the temple, and walked over to the ball court. The outside of the range wall had been cleared down to the original stonework, leaving no question that it was a man-made structure, and a fairly well constructed one, too. The trench into the range wall was still covered with plastic tarps, so they continued on to the northern end and turned into the corridorlike trench that began on the other side of the chicozapote tree. It extended about two thirds of the way across the court and was covered with tarps at its far end, where they'd left off work yesterday.

Ulysses's surprise for today was a new trench along the inside of the range wall, perpendicular to the main trench. Because he had Arturo and Carlos Kan Boar helping him (another surprise), he'd managed to open a corridor into the fill that was six feet wide and about fifteen deep. The garbage-surrounded hole that had been Yates Landing was gone, though the stone frog still marked the spot, squatting on pavement that had been scraped clean of muck. The frog was situated at what appeared to be a juncture between the bench that sloped up against the range wall and a staircase that descended into the court from the top of the wall. The roots of the chicozapote had done a lot of damage to both, so it was hard to tell for sure. Harp quickly scanned the cleared area but saw no sign of sherds or artifacts, either loose or bagged.

Arturo had put up his shovel and lit a cigarette as soon as he saw the newcomers, but Carlos went on shoveling black muck into a wheelbarrow. Ulysses rose from the bench he'd been working on and came over with a trowel in his hand. He'd already sweated through his shirt and his hair and beard were flecked with black; he smelled much worse than the swamp ever did.

"Look who showed up today, *early,*" Ulysses said, gesturing with the trowel. "I guess Brinton finally got the message."

"I guess he did," Harp murmured, seeing him through Kaaren's eyes and realizing it was worse than he'd wanted to believe. Ulysses's face looked gaunt and his gaze was restless to the point of being evasive. Harp spoke bluntly, out of anger at himself. "I thought we were gonna finish the main trench before we started here."

Ulysses shrugged. "Yeah, that was the plan. But when these guys showed up at the crack of dawn . . . "

" . . . you decided to go treasure hunting," Harp finished for him. "So much for the old plan. What's the new one?"

"Ah, why don't you three work on the main trench. You can take that over, can't you, Kaaren?"

"Whatever you say," Kaaren said in a neutral tone. "You're the bwana."

"The what?" Ulysses demanded in surprise.

"The boss, I meant," Kaaren said without cracking a smile.

"Oh. Hey, where's the Motorhead? I thought he was coming, too."

"He has," Harp said, emulating Kaaren's deadpan expression. "He's gonna help Helga at the temple."

"Who told him to help Helga? We can use some muscle here."

"He *wanted* to work with Helga," Harp explained. "So I told him he could."

"*You* did," Ulysses said sarcastically. "How nice of you."

"I thought so, too. Are we not supposed to be nice to anybody under the new plan?"

"What's with you, Yates? You trying to tick me off?"

Harp looked around at Brad and Kaaren, spreading his hands in a helpless gesture. "Did I say something wrong?"

"God!" Ulysses exploded in exasperation. "Get outta here, will ya? I'll come see how you're doing in a while," he said to Kaaren, handing her the workbook. Harp and Brad turned away together, muttering in unison under their breath.

"Yeah, Bwana Kurtz . . . "

"What're they saying?" Ulysses demanded.

"How would I know?" Kaaren said as she also turned away. She couldn't resist a parting shot, though, which she called back over her shoulder. "Give a holler if you find any treasure. We'll be sure to do the same."

KAAREN SPENT a long time studying the workbook while Harp and Brad removed the tarps and started in digging where they'd left off. When she finally came to pitch in, her expression was grim, and her first shovelful sailed over the wheelbarrow.

"This's ridiculous!" she snapped. "All we're doing is moving dirt. We could finish this in half the time if we had everybody here."

"We've been spread pretty thin all along," Harp said.

"That was his choice," Kaaren said through her teeth. "It seems to have become an obsession."

When Ulysses showed up a couple of hours later, Harp was on the highest of the terracelike levels they'd cut into the fill, so he couldn't hear what Kaaren said to him. She let him speak first, and whatever he said was no doubt tactless and critical, since he didn't smile and his gesture was unconsciously dismissive. Kaaren tilted her head back and eyed him for a long moment, forcing him to meet her gaze. Then she began talking in a tone that sounded low and even from above but was also clearly relentless, because she talked for several minutes before Ulysses managed to get in a word. His word merely provoked her to open the workbook and begin ticking things off on her fingers, obviously running through the numbers with him. Ulysses cut her short and said something swift and curt, jabbing a finger in her direction, then turned and stalked off down the trench.

Harp brought a canteen down with him, figuring she might both be thirsty and need some time to compose herself. Confrontation wasn't exactly her natural style, and Ulysses's range these days was from blunt to abusive. He noticed that her hands shook a little as she drank, though otherwise she seemed relatively calm. Brad had also joined them, and he was the first to break the silence.

"What'd he say?"

Kaaren pursed her lips, gazing down the trench in the direction Ulysses had gone. "His opening line was: 'Is that all you've done?' His closer was 'This's your first day here; let me be crew chief for a while before you take over.' "

"What'd you tell him in between?" Harp asked.

"Nothing he didn't already know. He's got ten times the experience I do at this kind of fieldwork, for godsakes, but he's not using it. He's starting to mess up badly."

"Wait a minute," Harp said. "What've I been missing? I mean, I've been giving progress reports to Brinton and he hasn't made any complaints. I've even shown him the operations sheets."

"When was the last time you did that?" Kaaren asked.

"Last week sometime," Harp reckoned.

"No wonder. For the last three days he's taken down most of the data in his personal notebook instead of on the operations sheets."

"I've seen him do that when he was in a hurry," Brad said. "I always figured he copied it down later."

"There are notes to himself to do just that, except he hasn't gotten around to doing it. And why would he be in a hurry?"

"He hops around a lot from job to job," Brad explained, then realized that that wasn't really an explanation. "I dunno, I guess he's afraid he's gonna miss something."

"That's exactly the problem," Kaaren said. "He's been trying to do far too much at once and it's beginning to catch up with him. Brinton probably understood that, even if you didn't, and he sent Arturo and Carlos to help bail him out. So what does Ulysses do? He starts yet another operation!"

"But that's really the first time he's ditched the plan," Harp said. "Prosperity made him greedy."

"Stop covering for him, Harp," Kaaren said impatiently. "You didn't know how right you were when you said we had to call him on it. He's not far wrong yet, but he couldn't pass inspection if Brinton or Rick came out. I think you better tell him to slow down and do it right or he's not going to be crew chief for long."

"*I* have to tell him?" Harp protested.

"He's not going to hear it from me," Kaaren said with a shrug. She gave him back the canteen and picked up a shovel. "You found it together," she told him. "It's yours to lose."

THEY ATE their lunch in what they called the picnic area, a well-shaded spot near the tents that they'd cleared thoroughly and equipped with rough log benches and a firepit. Helga Kauffmann had taken over part of the space for her stucco reconstruction, laying down two large canvas tarps on which she'd drawn—to scale—representations of what remained of the two sides of the temple roof comb. She'd then collected stucco fragments in a systematic fashion, marking each piece with location coordinates in the hope that they might have fallen in a more or less orderly manner. Location had in fact placed several key pieces and color matching had added quite a few more. That left shape as the final and most subtle determinant and made the work truly that of putting together a jigsaw puzzle. The general design was already visible on the tarps: twin jaguar masks surmounted by another mask that was perhaps a long-nosed god, surrounded by a border that contained fish and water lilies and highly stylized reptilians. There was also a vertical row of glyphs on each side of the trapezoidal comb, though these were in the lowest relief and were thus the most difficult to reconstruct.

Eric seemed to be enjoying his apprenticeship with Helga, though he kept unconsciously kneading the back of his neck. Brad had taken to calling him Mayahead, a nickname that seemed destined to replace Motorhead, since it gave Eric such obvious pleasure. Helga was sitting on a foldup leather seat of the sort used by spectators at a golf match, holding half a sandwich in one hand and gesturing with the magnifying glass in the other as she explained the possible meanings of the symbols taking shape on the tarps. As always, her enthusiasm was infectious, and Harp realized with a trace of envy that she was oblivious of what Ulysses was doing with the rest of the site. She'd found *her* focus and her concentration was total and utterly unhurried.

She'd tantalized Harp by referring to identical skull glyphs found on both sides of the roof comb as being "Central Mexican" in style, and she had just begun to answer his follow-up question when Ulysses suddenly strode into the middle of their circle and squatted down in front of Harp.

"Didn't you get the stuff on my list?" he demanded, seemingly unaware that he'd interrupted anything. Harp cast a significant glance over his shoulder at Helga, but Ulysses didn't catch it.

"Yeah, I got it," Harp said. "It's in the blue pack in the supply tent."

"Three cans of orange soda and a can of cashews?"

"Right. Plus a package of cookies, two big Chunky bars, and a bottle of rum."

"*Where?*"

"In the blue pack," Harp repeated impatiently. "That's what Muldoon gave me and that's what I carried here. There's some lab stuff on top but I didn't take it out after we got here. I didn't take anything out."

"*Somebody* did," Ulysses insisted, swiveling on his heels to gaze around the circle of silent faces. "Max? Don't be playing tricks on me, man."

Max exchanged a glance with Harp and shrugged, shaking his shaggy head in denial. "I just dumped my pack in the supply tent. I never went in there again."

"What about the rest of you?" Ulysses asked, peering around at Brad, Eric, Kaaren, and Helga. "Anybody get into the blue pack by mistake? C'mon, I'm not gonna hold a grudge. I just want my stuff."

There was general shrugging and head shaking, except for Helga, who was staring at Ulysses as if seeing him for the first time.

"I opened the blue pack," she said finally. "I needed the lab material to which Mr. Yates referred. The pack was very full but I didn't look to see what else was there."

That left only Arturo and Carlos, who'd chosen to eat by themselves, over near the range wall trench. Ulysses glanced in that direction and then looked back at Harp.

"There's no sign of cookies, chocolate, or rum," he said flatly. "You better not be playing tricks on me either."

"Not me, Captain Queeg," Harp said, bristling at being accused a second time. "That was the last bottle of rum Muldoon was gonna give you, anyway. He thinks you're drinking too much."

"Bullshit," Ulysses snapped, rising in one motion and walking off toward the ball court. A silence followed his departure.

"What has made him so rude?" Helga asked quietly.

"Paranoid, too," Harp said.

"Who's Captain Queeg?" Brad asked. "I never heard that one before."

"*The Caine Mutiny,*" Helga said before Harp could reply. "Humphrey Bogart played him. A mad sea captain. I am afraid the comparison is apt."

"He's been out here by himself for too long," Max put in. "I was trying to tell him that before I got sick."

"Harp's going to try again," Kaaren said pointedly. "Before we leave today. Ulysses can come with us or he can wait to see who Brinton sends out for him tomorrow."

"Yes," Helga agreed. "I would ask Brinton to come himself. Mr. Cole is clearly endangering his own health."

Harp grimaced at the prospect of delivering such an ultimatum. "I'll tell him the campout's over, but lemme have a little bargaining room, something to offer him in return."

"Like what?" Kaaren asked suspiciously.

"Like we let him pretend it was his own idea and not something we forced on him. He tells Brinton he's burned out and needs a couple days off to rest and bring his records up to date. For our part, we don't say anything to make him sound like Bwana Kurtz."

"Brinton will see that for himself," Kaaren predicted.

"Maybe," Harp allowed. "He'd still be more likely to let him rest up and come back as crew chief. If we all complain about him, though, Brinton would have to take him off for good."

Kaaren looked at Helga, who cocked her head for a moment before nodding in agreement. "It is always better to persuade than to punish, yes? We want to tame his enthusiasm, not destroy it."

"Is that okay with everybody else?" Harp asked, drawing nods all around. He wished it felt more okay to him. He wished he could believe Ulysses was persuadable.

"He's all yours, then," Kaaren concluded. "Good luck . . . "

WHEN HE couldn't put it off any longer, Harp took off his work gloves, picked up a canteen, and went off over the top of the fill rather than using the trench. He threaded his way through the palms and came out above the new trench at its far end. Arturo looked up at him and grinned quizzically. Ulysses was writing in his notebook and took a bit longer to recognize Harp's presence.

"Whatta you want?"

"You, Bwana Kurtz," Harp said. "We have to talk."

"I don't have time for your games, Yates."

"The game's over, Ulysses. That's what we have to talk about. You wanna hear it from me or from Brinton?"

Ulysses slapped his notebook shut with a scowl, but then stood looking at the ground, drawing deep breaths. *He knows,* Harp thought, feeling a certain measure of relief. He turned and walked through the palms toward the middle of ball court, hearing the sound of dirt and stones falling as Ulysses climbed up out of the trench. Harp stopped next to the test shaft Ulysses had dug in a failed attempt to find the center court marker that was a common feature of Mayan ball courts. Harp stared down into the crudely cut hole, thinking he saw something squirming around in the blackness before the stench of the slime at the bottom made him back away. Ulysses was leaning against a tree a few feet away, regarding him with a kind of baleful resignation.

"So what's this about Brinton? You gonna rat me out?"

"No, but it wouldn't be hard, would it? Just show him some'a the blank operations sheets, holes and half-dug trenches all over the place . . . you even look like a treasure hunter."

"Yeah, right," Ulysses said wearily, passing a grimy hand across his face. "So who *is* gonna rat me out? Fisher's sweetie, la angel de Charlie?"

That was one of Arturo's less suggestive names for Kaaren, and Harp let it pass in silence. He reached into his shirt pocket for the two cigarettes he'd taken from his raincoat at lunch, offering one to Ulysses. "These were blessed by the Moon Goddess."

"I shoulda brought my peace pipe," Ulysses muttered, but he took one and let Harp hold a match for him.

"Nobody's gonna say anything about you," Harp told him, shaking out the match. "But you've gotta come back in and ask Brinton to give you a rest."

Ulysses straightened up, blowing smoke out his nostrils. "How long a rest?"

"That's up to you. How long before you could come back out here and do it right?"

"You tell me. You're the one who thinks I need a rest."

"*Everybody* thinks so," Harp said. "Muldoon told me this morning to tell 'Kurtz' it's time to come out of the jungle."

"Right, just when I finally get enough workers to cover what I'm trying to do," Ulysses said bitterly, crushing his cigarette underfoot in an unceremonious fashion. "What does everybody think is gonna happen if I take a couple of days off? I don't know how to rest."

"Then start learning. Or were you planning to go up in smoke before you reached forty?"

"Something like that. People been telling me to slow down and take it easy all my life. It doesn't work."

"Hey, nobody expects a total personality change. But whether you wanna admit it or not, fatigue takes its toll, and so does solitary confinement, which is what living out here is like."

"Some of us aren't afraid to go out at night."

"Yeah, but blood loss takes its toll, too. C'mon, man, give it up," Harp urged. "If you keep on going the way you've been, you're gonna fuck up the site and yourself. Brinton'll have to pull you off it completely."

Ulysses made a sound that was half grunt and half growl and stepped past Harp to stare down into the test shaft. He kicked some dirt and stones into the hole and spat after them. "A couple days," he said, turning back to Harp. "Who runs the show while I'm gone?"

"That's up to Brinton, isn't it? Kaaren's the best bet. She's good and she's not interested in taking over permanently."

"Don't leave her alone with Arturo. He's a flake," Ulysses said bluntly.

"I'll tell her, and Brad and Eric," Harp promised. "I'm not gonna be out here myself on Thursday. I can use some time away from it too."

"Sure, all the half days you've been putting in," Ulysses sneered. "You gonna tell me now what you did with my stuff?"

"Jesus! How many times do I have to say it? None of us took your goodies. Got it?"

"I trust Carlos and I don't think Arturo had the opportunity."

"Is there somebody else out here?" Harp asked.

"I'm beginning to wonder . . . "

"God, you *do* need a rest," Harp said with a laugh that ended abruptly when Ulysses's arms shot out and the heels of his hands slammed against Harp's chest, lifting him off the ground and sending him flying backward, flailing for a balance that was gone. He landed hard on his back and bounced, his legs and torso wrenching in opposite directions before he hit down again and skidded to a rest in a patch of thorny weeds. He was still vibrating from the shock of the impact when he looked up and saw Ulysses smiling down at him.

"God, that felt good," Ulysses taunted. "Now you can go brag about how you got me to quit. And the next time you wanna show somebody Yates Landing, you can bring 'em here. *Adiós.*"

Harp groaned and tried to lie absolutely still, though even that hurt. When he found himself rolling onto his side as a prelude to sitting up—a trick he'd learned from a physical therapist—he knew he'd pulled his back out again. No, *he* hadn't done it, he told himself furiously, the anger almost masking the pain. He got onto his hands and knees and had the foresight to put on his hat and sling the canteen over his shoulder before gathering his legs under him to rise. It was a torturous ascent, and even then he only made it up to forty-five degrees. He didn't know why they called it "back spasms" when it felt like a complete muscular lockdown.

Lurching from one palm tree to the next, he propelled himself across the top of the ball court, uncertain how he was going to make the long walk back to camp but knowing he'd have to somehow. No way he was going to go back and explain what happened and ask for help. Let 'em find out from Ulysses. His duty here was fucking *done.*

11

Baktun

KATIE SMITH stood in the doorway of her office and gazed across the lab at Harp, who was working at a low table near the windows, using her swivel chair with a couple of cushions wedged in behind him. He was still sitting with the self-conscious erectness of someone made careful by pain, though he seemed to be growing less rigid by the day. As Katie watched, Lucy came up behind him, tapping him on the right shoulder while sliding around to his left. Harp didn't fall for it and turned his head only slightly to talk to her. Katie knew how the dialogue would go, since it was a routine Lucy ran him through at least twice a day.

"How'dja hurt your back, Harp?"

"Slipped on a log bridge and pulled it out."

"Nobody believes that, Harp."

"It's simple and adequate."

"Everybody thinks Ulysses did it to you."

"Fuck Ulysses."

Katie saw Lucy grin the way she always did at that punch line. Getting that out of him was half the fun. The other half was the exchange of taunts for lies that weren't meant to be believed, a form of banter that made Lucy feel sophisticated. Today Lucy went on past the punch line, drawing what appeared to be increasingly curt replies. The last one made her frown in exasperation and give him a poke in parting. She was still fuming when she came over to Katie.

"What a dork. I'm going down to the cenote."

"What'd you say to him?"

"I asked him if he was gonna stay in the lab for the rest of his time here. 'I just take it one day at a time,' " Lucy mimicked, flattening her voice to capture the undertow of indifference in his. "So then I asked him if he was gonna be boring for the rest of his time here."

"That was cruel, Luce," Katie scolded. "He's been in a lot of pain, more than he lets anyone see."

"Aw, he's okay. I saw him walking around in the Central Plaza last night before dinner, and he wasn't holding his back or anything. Besides, *you* said he was boring."

"I didn't say it so you could repeat it to him. Anyway, what did he say?"

Lucy frowned again. "He didn't even get mad. He just looked at me like I wasn't there and said, 'Why not?' Jeez, when I get like that you tell me I need a kick in the butt."

"I think he's already had one. Put some bug dope on before you go, and be back in time to wash up for dinner."

Lucy went out and it was quiet in the lab, much too quiet on Harp's side of the room. He'd been here a week and hadn't made fun of anything or stirred up a single outrageous debate. The master of ambiguous behavior had become polite and predictable, a model prisoner serving out his time. And all because Ulysses had somehow stabbed him in the back, figuratively if not literally. She could've told him Ulysses hated accepting a favor from anyone and was bound to do something stupid and ungrateful. But Harp wouldn't talk to her about it either. He hadn't tried to put her off with bullshit banter, but he had put her off, saying only "It's done, Katie, better leave it alone."

She glanced across the room and saw him pluck a sherd out of the batch on the table and lean back in the chair to study it. Since he was only supposed to be sorting and counting, Katie guessed he'd come upon an uncommonly beautiful or unusual piece. When she saw him cast a calculating glance to his right—a stiff yet furtive movement—she realized he was thinking about stealing it. That was an urge everyone felt at some point, usually toward the end of a field season, and Katie suspected most people succumbed in some small way. Such mementos often came back later in the mail, along with a conscience-stricken letter of apology.

When Harp paused and then took a long look to his left, Katie knew she'd caught him in the act. At first all she could feel was an incredulous anger. The *nerve* of the man, to think he could come in here and act like a boring dork for the rest of the season, leaving her nothing to remember but swiping a souvenir for himself! Yet along with the anger came a certain satisfaction, a sense that he'd finally given her an opening, something she could use to whip him back into shape.

She started toward him, prepared to deliver a much-needed kick in the butt. If she was going to have him around for the next two weeks, she was damn well going to have the real Harp. But she was brought up short by a ruckus at the back door and turned to see Ulysses, Max, and Brad come tromping in like victorious warriors, dropping gear on the floor and letting the screen door slam shut behind them. Ulysses gave her a huge grin.

"Pay dirt, babe!" he said exultantly, displaying a large piece of pale orange pottery. He flicked a fingernail against it, producing a distinctive metallic ring.

"Fine paste," Katie murmured, recognizing the sound at once. Max held up a bulging paper bag and jiggled it musically.

"And there's lots more where this came from."

"Where's Clubb?" Ulysses demanded, starting up the central aisle without waiting for her reply. He stopped, though, when he spotted Harp near the windows.

"We found it, Yates," he reported, his grin diminished to an awkward half smile. "A whole cache of fine paste pottery. Definitely a foreign import."

"Where?" Harp asked, his face blank.

"Against the inside of the west range wall, just short of midcourt. They smashed a bunch of pots and censers, covered them with limestone marl, and built fires over them. A termination ritual."

Harp stared at him silently for a long moment.

"Well?" Ulysses prompted impatiently.

"Wayta go, Bwana," Harp said, and slowly spun himself around in the chair, turning his back on them. There was a moment of dead silence, Ulysses standing like a stone, nostrils flaring, while Max and Brad exchanged an embarrassed glance. *Oh, Harp,* Katie thought.

"Too bad you missed it!" Ulysses snarled, and continued on toward Clubb's table, the others following in a more subdued fashion. Katie looked at the back of Harp's head and realized she no longer had any desire to kick his butt. He obviously needed much more than that. She turned back toward her office, leaving him to steal the sherd if he wanted—almost hoping he would. At least it would show there was something here he still wanted.

East Hudson, New York

THE LIVING and dining areas of the house were combined in one long, spacious room, which had bay windows at both ends and two ten-foot picture windows in the east wall. Whichever way Caroline turned, she had a view of trees and shrubs covered with yesterday's snow, and beyond them only more trees and a blue sky. Not another house in sight. The light pouring in through the windows seemed to fill every corner of the room, and the patches of pegged pine flooring visible between the Navaho rugs had a warm gleam.

Langdon, the owner, poured himself another glass of homemade raspberry wine while suggesting to Caroline that she and Harp might consider taking out an equity loan on their Vermont land to finance the down payment. Caroline was actually way ahead of him, wondering if she could persuade Harp to sell part of it. Half of the woodlot might do it. There was also all the family money she'd sworn she'd never touch. All she had to do was eat a little crow and swallow a few principles. They could probably buy the house outright.

Then her rising excitement seemed to catch in her throat, shutting off the air. Or maybe she was getting too much, hyperventilating with longing.

"Excuse me—I need to get some air," she said as she rose, startling the Langdons and drawing a concerned glance from Val, the real estate agent. She went out before anyone could ask if she was all right, leaving her hat and gloves behind.

The sun was warm, though, and the snow on the roof was melting fast, dripping noisily from the eaves and rumbling down the drainpipes. It would probably all be gone before it could get dirty. But the unexpected storm had done its work, making her lay over in Albany another night, giving her the chance to see this house. And to want it like she'd never wanted anything in her life. Mrs. Langdon had lent her a pair of rubber boots and they'd slogged through the snow to examine the back of the property. They found droppings under the apple trees where some deer had bedded down during the storm, and they caught a glimpse of one as it fled into the trees that marked the property line. The Langdons' five acres were surrounded by three neighbors who each owned forty acres or more and were not interested in selling out to the local developers. No fences separated the properties, and Mrs. Langdon pointed out several well-cut paths and said she could cross-country ski for miles right out the back door.

Caroline sat in Val's Buick with the door open and her feet on the wet asphalt of the driveway, breathing deeply to restore her composure. She was beginning to feel embarrassed about the way she'd bolted in the middle of the conversation. The Langdons must be wondering if she was a flake, to wax so enthusiastic and then to run for the door. Especially after they'd hit it off so well, making connections that went beyond their mutual appreciation for the house and land. It was almost uncanny. Mrs. Langdon had grown up in Vermont and they'd vacationed there for years. They'd also spent time in Vancouver and Montreal and were moving to New Mexico to be near their eldest daughter, who was an anthropologist studying the Pueblo tribes. They were immediately interested in Harp's last novel, and mention of his current research had Mr. Langdon up and looking for his slides from Chichén Itzá. At that point, Caroline had the definite feeling that the crafty hand of Somebody was at work.

Val finally came out of the house, and the Langdons stood on the stoop and smiled and waved to Caroline. She waved back, feeling the excitement rise again at this apparent gesture of forgiveness. Val stopped to light a cigarette, then rested an elbow on top of the car door and peered in at Caroline.

"You okay? Was it that awful wine?"

Caroline shook her head. "I just got scared. I'm so far out ahead of myself on this, Val. I'm sorry. What did you tell them?"

"What you told me," Val said with a laugh. "That you didn't have the job yet, and didn't own another home, and hadn't even thought much about owning one. I took the liberty of adding that you seemed to be thinking seriously about owning this one. Am I right?"

"Of course. I couldn't hide it. That's what scared me—the impulse was irresistible."

"Why fight it? It's a good buy, and he's only asking for twenty percent down—he came down five percent after you left. He's also willing to offer you a one-year lease on a rent-to-buy basis, so you could either back out or retroactively count the rent as mortgage payments. He wouldn't budge on the interest rate, but ten percent's pretty good these days, and he'll hold the mortgage for ten years before you have to refinance."

Caroline shook her head again, though she couldn't stop herself from figuring what the five percent reduction meant in dollars. "The money may be the least of it. It's more a matter of not believing in the economic system, and not wanting too big a stake in it."

Val snorted with good-natured exasperation, blowing smoke into the air. "I seem to recall having this same conversation with Alice before she bought into her brownstone. As far as I can tell, she's never regretted the decision, and she's still a Marxist, isn't she?"

"More than I am," Caroline admitted. "I know our attitude seems sort of quaint at this point in time, but it's so ingrained in both of us that we never even discussed owning a home."

"Well, I think you should as soon as he gets back from Mexico. Think of it this way, Caroline: If you *do* get the job, would you want to be living somewhere else, knowing you could've had this?"

Val stepped aside to give her another look at the L-shaped house, set back from the road against a windbreak of tall firs and spruces. Harp would love this, if he could ever get over the *idea* of being a homeowner. Caroline stared at it and felt the longing swirl around inside her. "I wouldn't even be here if the snowstorm hadn't shut down the airport yesterday."

"We'd better head in that direction ourselves," Val decided with a glance at her watch. "Oh, Langdon also said if you want to make a five-hundred-dollar deposit, he'd hold the house for you until you know about the job. It's fully refundable if you don't get it or decide not to take it, and would become part of the down payment if you do. It would save them having to show the house to anybody else."

"Let me think about it while we drive."

Val came around the car and got in behind the wheel. "You think about it and I'll time how long it takes to get to the campus exits. I bet it's no more than twenty minutes."

The Langdons' dog, a Labrador/setter mix named Shelley, appeared as they were pulling out and followed them down the driveway. Barking with a kind of abandon, the dog ran along beside them until the Buick hit second gear and pulled away. Caroline gazed out the window at the passing countryside, her emotions in such a tangle she couldn't separate any one out for scrutiny. She wondered if this was what it truly meant to be homesick.

Baktun

WHEN THE tightness in his back wouldn't let him continue at the desk, Harp switched off the Coleman and lit an aromatic candle that discouraged mosquitoes while providing a minimal light. He spread a blanket on the floor and lay down on his back with his knees elevated and his legs extended across the top of his bed. It was a gentle stretch but enough to keep him from locking up if he remembered to do it every couple of hours. The injury itself was pretty much healed, though there were probably weeks of discomfort and caution still to go.

He lit up the joint he'd started earlier and studied the diagram he'd been working on, holding the pad on a slant above his face to catch the candlelight. Then he was past his three-toke limit and didn't give a shit, dropping pad and joint and all pretense of rational thought. His reverie quickly took on an erotic tone, dwelling on a recent dream in which he and Caroline had been frolicking naked on the swing set in the Ushers' backyard. The neighbors were lined up along the fence to watch, but he and Caroline didn't care . . .

Images of the ball game kept slipping in to distract him, so he was only half-aroused when he heard the sound outside—a sharp metallic click that snapped him to and made him fumble hastily with his gym shorts. He had an upside-down view of sandaled feet and bare legs as Katie, Kaaren, and Rita came into the room, holding flashlights upright in front of them like candles. They were wearing bathrobes and had towels wrapped around their heads like turbans, and their faces were solemn and expressionless. They stood over him in a semicircle and turned the flashlights on his face, blinding him.

"Is he dead?"

"Hard to tell these days. Maybe he bored himself into a coma."

"No, he's still smoking. And lookit this: a secret site plan of Rana Verde."

"He steals our ideas but won't talk to us about them."

"He's so *alienated.*"

"He even acts like an alien," Rita said, imitating Lucy's snottiest tone. "Dork from Ork."

The lights went out, leaving him seeing white spots even with his eyes closed. "Ladies," he said dazedly, but Katie's voice cut him off.

"We're not ladies."

"We're the emissaries of the Moon Goddess," Kaaren added.

"We've come to heal you," Rita said.

"You're chiropractors, then?" Harp suggested, unclenching his eyelids for a look. The spots were gone, but they'd snuffed the candle and he could only make out their shapes in the darkness.

"*Now* he makes jokes," Katie said scornfully.

"We heal the spirit," Rita said. "We've come to cure you of your alienation."

Harp let out a mirthless laugh. "It's a chronic condition. I've had it since I turned draft age."

They switched on their flashlights in a simultaneous reproof, blinding him again.

"Your *current* alienation," Kaaren said sternly. "From the good people of this camp."

"From *us,*" Rita and Katie said in unison.

"Oh," Harp murmured. He felt them kneel down on the blanket around him.

"We got the story out of Ulysses," Kaaren went on. "He claims he wasn't trying to hurt you and didn't know he had. We let him know he shouldn't have been pushing you at all, after what you'd done for him."

"Fuck Ulysses."

"It's not that great, really," Katie said casually, taunting him. "Besides, the Moon Goddess doesn't care about him. She doesn't understand why you've let him turn you off to everybody and everything you used to care about. She wonders why you've given him this power over your life."

"He took the power when he knocked me down," Harp argued, knowing he was risking retinal shock but not liking the way this was being turned back on him. "Whether he knew what he was doing or not, the damage was done. And I was the one who was gonna have to live with the pain."

"All by yourself," Kaaren suggested.

"It's my fucking back, isn't it? Sympathy doesn't do much for back spasms."

Instead of blinding him, they fell silent with a clicking of tongues, letting him hear the ugly sound of his own voice. Rancorous and spiteful, and righteous about it. Harp began to sweat, hating the voice but unable to take the words back.

"Cool out, Harp," Katie said gently, trailing her fingers across his forehead in a soothing gesture that made him shiver. "Sisters," she said to the others, "it's clear the bitterness runs deep. He's forgotten what kindness feels like. Let us remind him."

There was just enough light for Harp to see them remove their robes and to realize they were wearing swimming suits underneath. Then three pairs of hands settled on different parts of his body, lightly at first, holding him still when a nervous shudder went through him. Then their fingers began to move over him, kneading and stroking, exploring the contours of flesh and bone with increasing assurance. Katie had his head in both hands, massaging his skull through the bushy curls, working her way down his neck to the taut muscles in his shoulders. Someone else was doing a marvelous job on his left leg, making his hamstring jump in place. They were laughing as they worked him over, sliding hands up under his T-shirt and down into his shorts, one hand giving him an intimate squeeze and then hanging on, as if to measure the result.

"Up," someone said, and they took hold of him and carefully lifted him to his feet, supporting his back but causing the blood to rush through his head like a freight train, throwing off sparks that hung in the air in front of him and glowed. He came out of it to find them pulling off his T-shirt over his head, and the thought that they might strip him completely aroused a reflexive shyness, even in the dark. Instead they closed in around him in a three-way embrace that made the matter of clothing seem utterly irrelevant. He was being touched and kissed and caressed in places he hadn't known were erogenous zones, and though his eyes were open he couldn't tell who was doing what. He made a noise that felt like a laugh but sounded like a sob, and someone kissed him on the nape of his neck, a gesture that touched him so deeply he hyperventilated and went into another rush.

He returned to find the dance slower and more intense, moving to the heavy rhythm of their breathing. A tongue licked his shoulder and bare breasts were being dragged slowly across his back; his hand was trapped between someone's legs and he twirled his wrist against the taut clefted fabric and felt the thighs widen. Someone else seemed to be testing the spring in his erection, pressing it down with a flattened hand. Harp noted this without resisting or pressing back, caught in a state of arousal that was wholly unfocused. He'd forgotten how much pleasure there could be in having a body.

Rita was the first one to break the spell, pulling away and then rising up to kiss him on the cheek.

"You've just been vamped by the Goddess," she told him in a husky voice, scooping up her bathrobe and flashlight on the way out.

Kaaren kissed him full on the lips. "How does your back feel now?"

Harp grunted in surprise. "I forgot all about it."

"See what kindness can do," she said, and went out laughing. Katie was holding him from behind, her arms looped around his waist. He waited until Kaaren was gone before he spoke.

"Tell me what just happened here."

"A revitalization ceremony."

"Yeah, but . . . that last part? Was that planned?"

Katie pressed her face against his collarbone and shook with laughter. "That was totally unrehearsed. How often do we get to grope a guy with impunity? It was a real switch."

"It was Dionysion," Harp insisted.

"Turned me on, too," Katie agreed. She unclasped her hands and slid them inside the waistband of his shorts, giving him an exploratory nudge. "Hmm, still there. What do your scruples say about a little mutual manipulation?"

"They say it wouldn't take much."

"That's all you're gonna get. Anything more would be inappropriate, and your back couldn't take it."

They wiggled out of their remaining clothes and collapsed together onto the blanket, sliding over against the bed. Katie pulled some pillows down and they got comfortable, gradually making contact on all the vital points. By unspoken agreement, they moved their hands very slowly.

"Harp," Katie murmured, between surges of breath. "Were you crying before?"

"Was I?" Harp echoed. He shrugged and nodded at the same time, feeling muscle control slipping away. "If I was, it wasn't from pain . . . "

AS DINNER was winding up, Harp slipped into the empty seat next to Rick and waited for him to finish talking to Oliver Clubb. Rick seemed to be apologizing and was quick to cut it off, rolling his eyes as he turned to Harp.

"I wanna talk to you, too. In private."

"Okay. Just tell me something first. I wanna go back into the field."

Rick flexed his brows in a skeptical frown. "This late? I don't wanna send you home on a stretcher."

"I'll be careful. I thought maybe Helga could use some help with the roof comb reconstruction."

"Jim Zorn's on that. He's still coming back from the bug he picked up camping out with Ulysses. That's the only light duty out there. I've got lots of things you could do around here if you're sick of the lab."

"I wanted to get back to Rana Verde."

Rick shrugged. "Ulysses is in charge of everything else out there, and I don't think he'd make it easy for you. You can ask him . . . "

"Fuck," Harp said, biting off the rest.

Clubb suddenly leaned out around Rick. "I'm going out to Rana Verde tomorrow. To work on the pots that were broken in place. Andrew's going to assist me, but we could always use another pair of hands."

Rick sat back and put on a neutral expression that was a warning to Harp. "Long as you remember to take it easy, it's fine with me."

"Where do I sign up?" Harp said to Clubb.

Clubb smiled archly, a boss's smile. "You begin by telling me what you think the pots mean. You've been absent from the recent debates, and I haven't been getting anything useful out of Cole."

"Maybe he doesn't have anything useful to tell," Rick said.

Harp ignored the second warning, too. He'd been thinking a lot about his past conversations with Ulysses, and if it was his ticket to Rana Verde, he'd be happy to sell the bastard out.

"I can draw it for you," he proposed, and thought he heard a muted groan from Rick as Clubb produced a sketch pad and drafting pencil. Once Harp went to work, it was like slipping the cork from the bottle and letting all his recent unshared ruminations flow out. The diagram he drew had the core area of Baktun at the bottom of the page, with the Lacantún River below it. With heavier strokes, he emphasized the position of the West Plaza, the ceremonial locus of the site during the reign of Kan Cross Ahau. Beginning at a distance from the core, on a direct northerly line from the West Plaza, was the string of small shrines that led out to Rana Verde. The ball court and adjacent temple, with some allowance for the terrain, were also on this axis, with the two doorways of the temple facing north and south.

"I hadn't realized the alignment was so precise," Clubb said, as Harp sat back and let him and Rick crane in over the drawing.

"It's not, actually," Harp admitted. "They don't seem to've been interested in astronomical exactitude or anything like that. But they did seem to want to make it clear they were coming out to meet someone coming from the north."

"Ah," Clubb exclaimed softly. "Intersite competition? There's not much evidence of that at the first ball court, is there, Richard?"

"Not that I've identified so far," Rick allowed. He looked at Harp. "That what you had in mind?"

"Well, we used to joke about how they'd won an expansion franchise and had to build a new ball park out in the boondocks."

"Right," Rick snorted. "More room for parking."

"But more seriously, we thought about what Mayan sites they might've been playing, and the logical possibilities all lay to the east and west. That also didn't explain the need for a court so far from the core. So then we began to wonder if they weren't playing someone less well known to them, someone they didn't want to invite into the ceremonial center of the site." Harp paused and gave Clubb a significant glance. "Foreigners, or what you called non-Classic Maya."

"The Putún Maya?" Rick asked, frowning. "Coming all the way south from Tabasco and Campeche?"

"That's where most of the fine paste pottery comes from, doesn't it?" Harp asked in return. When Rick nodded grudgingly, Harp felt a surge of satisfaction and realized he was getting excited about this all over again. He could see the shape the new narrative was taking, glimpse some of the fictional possibilities it presented. How could he have become alienated from this?

"In your scenario, what was the purpose of these games?" Clubb asked, his brow furrowed intently. "Obviously, it wasn't the encouragement of trade or cultural exchange."

Harp smiled. "Given the deliberate isolation of the court and the shrines connecting it with the center, I'd say it was a kind of ritualized combat with religious overtones. My god's best ballplayers against yours. If we win, you go home and leave us alone."

"Whoa, Harp," Rick cautioned halfheartedly. "I sense a speculative stampede coming on."

Harp's smile widened into a grin. "This means I get to write some great ball game scenes, and Kan Cross Ahau becomes a hero rather than a villain. Instead of the guy who shut down the ball game, he's the guy who used it to keep the barbarians at bay." Harp turned the grin on Clubb. "That's one way to stay Classic in a changing world, right?"

"It's a possibility," Clubb allowed, grimacing at the crudeness of Harp's summation but processing the information nonetheless. He reached for the sketch pad. "May I keep this?"

"Why not?" Harp said breezily. "It's not to scale."

"Hardly," Clubb agreed, with one of his rare laughs. "See you at breakfast."

Rick waited until Clubb had left the dining hall, then looked at Harp and shook his head. "Just remember—you asked for it. Don't come bitching to me later."

"I've heard he's hard to work with," Harp admitted. "If it gets too bad I'll have a back spasm."

"You must've had a brain spasm. Why give him the whole thing? Why not leave him a little to fabricate on his own?"

"Whatever happened to the free exchange of ideas? Besides, you don't want him to get it wrong, do you?"

"Glad you're feeling better," Rick said dryly, and started to get up. Then he had a second thought. "Oh. I had an unexpected visit from Kaaren last night, after the lights were out. What? What're you laughing at?"

"It was a friendly visit, I take it."

"Hell, I woke up already in the saddle. Couldn't keep it quiet, either. Clubb's pissed at me because we woke him up, too."

"But you're not complaining," Harp suggested.

Rick broke into a belated grin. "Hell, no. I just wanna know what you had to do with it. The only thing she said to me was 'We got Harp straightened out, now it's your turn.' What sorta kinky shit you got going on out there?"

"Nothing kinky at all," Harp said, laughing as they went out the door together. "Just the free exchange of kindness . . . "

THEY WERE LATE getting out to Rana Verde the next day, due to Clubb's desire to visit a couple of the intermediary shrines along the way. Upon arrival they paused briefly to pay their respects to Helga Kauffmann, then went straight to the ball court. Harp noticed the new piles of back dirt outside the court and saw that the original exploratory trench into the range wall had been cut all the way through, providing a passageway to the trench inside the wall. With the sun still low in the sky, the trench seemed cool and dark, a roofless tunnel between the range wall and the interior fill. Harp paused to let his eyes adjust, but Clubb went immediately to the line of crushed orange pots that stuck up out of the jumble of broken masonry along the base of the range wall. They were still half buried under a layer of burned material and coarse grey dirt, but when Clubb started taking flash pictures, Harp could see that large segments of some of the vessels were still intact.

"Wow," Harp murmured, genuinely moved by the sight. After all the sherdless dirt he'd sifted out here, this was like finding an unlooted tomb. About ten feet of pots had been exposed, but it looked as if the line continued under the grey-brown mass of fill that had yet to be dug. Kaaren and her crew of Brad and Eric had chosen to widen the trench rather than going forward at this point, digging out a work space around the midcourt deposit. Kaaren came over to greet them and pointed to where the pots ended against the wall of fill.

"We got to that point and ran into some extremely compacted material," she explained. "It's like concrete from the top down. We decided to make some room for ourselves and get the pots out of the way before going to work on the hard stuff."

" 'We'?" Clubb echoed doubtfully. "Where's Cole? Didn't he find this?"

Kaaren smiled a wintry smile. "He did. He's on the other side of the court, cutting a trench like this one along the eastern range wall."

"Looking for a symmetrical deposit," Clubb concluded, quick to recognize an ambitious move.

"Treasure hunting," Harp muttered.

Kaaren laughed and shrugged dismissively. "I've got the operations book now, and they're going to be digging for a long time before they get to midcourt. Let me show you what we've got . . . "

She was still filling them in when Ulysses showed up a little while later, but he gestured politely for her to go on and stood by without interrupting. He looked as if he'd been eating and sleeping regularly, and he'd had his hair cut in Comitán, where he'd spent his two days of R and R. He looked like a new man, though he still wouldn't meet Harp's eye. Harp gave him a chance to do so, to show some sign that he knew what he'd done. But Ulysses kept his eyes averted, hands jammed into the deep pockets of his fatigues, a jiggling leg betraying his impatience with the thoroughness of Kaaren's presentation. *A better crew chief,* Harp decided, *but still a moral pygmy.* Katie had been right: This guy wasn't worthy of the bitterness Harp had been harboring. To enter into an enemies dance with him was to accord him too much respect.

After Ulysses had spoken his piece to Clubb, though, he came over to where Harp was standing.

"Yates . . . the last time you were here, did you take any tools back to camp with you? We're missing a machete and an ax."

It took Harp a moment to believe his ears. Then he let out a snort and smiled with great insincerity.

"No, I didn't. But it's nice of you to ask," he said, and turned away before Ulysses could reply, thinking *dance to that, asshole.*

OVER THE next day and a half, Harp came to understand—in his soul—why people hated to work with Oliver Clubb. The first day Harp was too pumped up to be critical, and too enthralled by the prospect of handling pots that were nearly whole. The task demanded a higher degree of delicacy than he

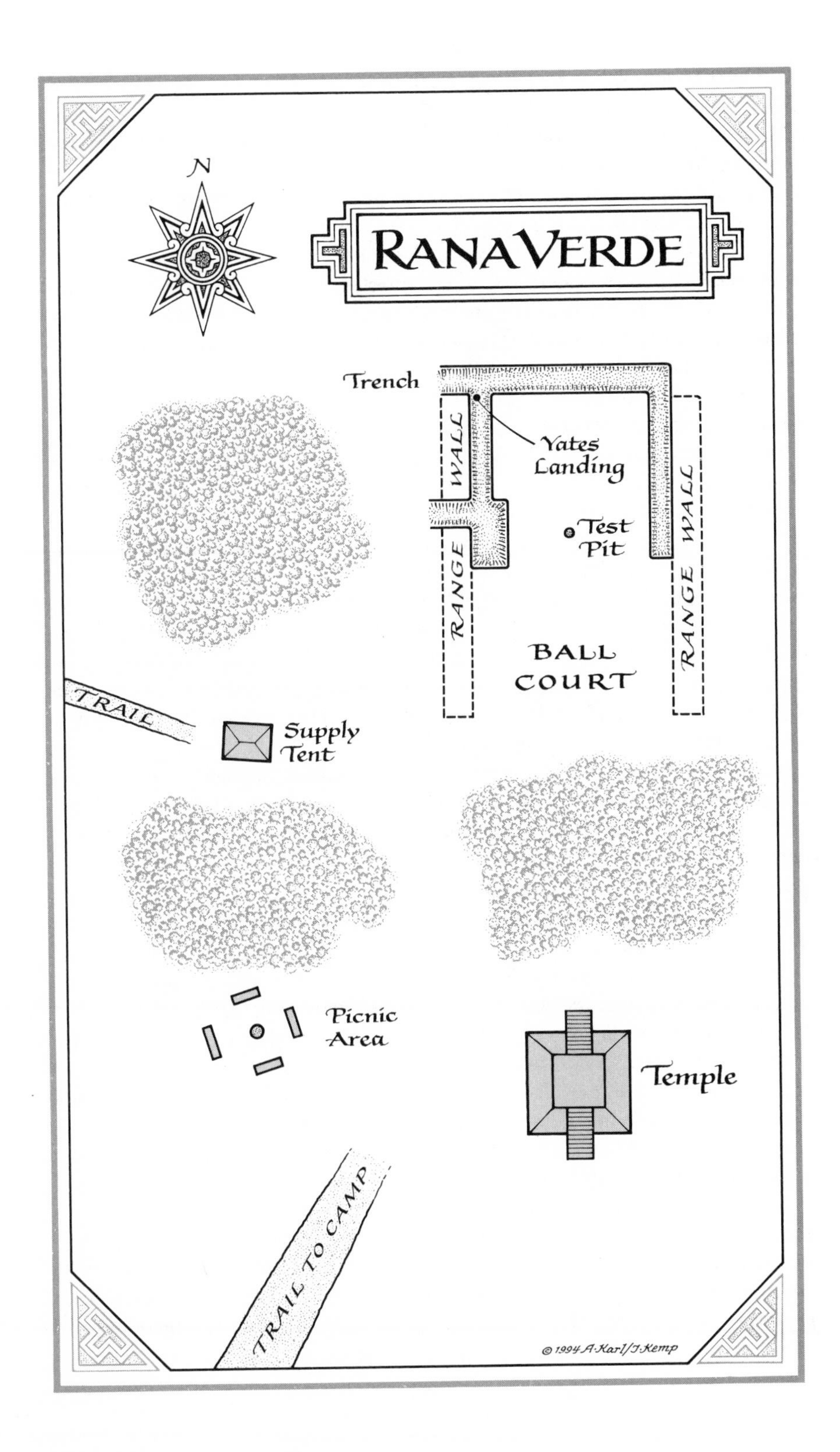
N
RANA VERDE
Trench
Yates
Landing
WALL
RANGE
WALL
RANGE
Test
Pit
BALL
COURT
TRAIL
Supply
Tent
Picnic
Area
Temple
TRAIL TO CAMP
© 1994 A·Karl/J·Kemp

was used to and made him learn some new skills, like how to separate one vessel from another, and how to tell which pieces went with what vessel. Clubb gave him on-the-job training, keeping up a running commentary that amounted to a short course on the qualities of fine paste pottery. Since Harp had everything to learn, he'd soaked it up, unaware of how hard he was working until his body complained about it later.

The second day was harder from the start, the novelty having worn off while the complaints lingered on in his muscles. And the day quickly grew hot and humid, even down in the trench. Since they'd gotten their procedures down yesterday, Harp had expected less talk and more independent work today. He'd even begun to entertain the notion of working up a pot on his own. But Clubb took up where he'd left off, sitting on a pile of stones and issuing instructions to Harp and Andrew, recording the results on the operations sheets and in his notebook. Since there was less to teach, his commentary became more specialized, dwelling on the particular character of these vessels and what it revealed about the people who'd made them.

Harp soaked that up, too, as material for the new and revised interpretation both he and Clubb were formulating. But even as he listened and worked, kneeling in the dust with Andrew while Clubb lectured them from his throne of stones, he felt a growing disbelief that this was happening—that Clubb was actually going to sit there the whole time, talking while they did all the real work, claiming the full privilege of his expertise. He wasn't that old and didn't appear unfit. Didn't it embarrass him to sit there like a potentate and not even get his hands dirty?

By midafternoon, Harp's disbelief was long gone, along with any hope that Clubb might discover a sense of shame. The muscles in Harp's thighs and butt had turned to stone from all the crouching and duckwalking, and despite periodic stretchings his back was painfully stiff. He was sweat-soaked and grimy, and he wasn't learning enough to take his mind off it. Clubb's khakis were limp and there were dark crescents under his arms, but otherwise he appeared as fresh as he had at breakfast. He hadn't slackened the pace of his instructions, either, even though Harp and Andrew were becoming increasingly erratic in their responses. His way of compensating for their fatigue was to stand up and walk back and forth behind them, injecting a note of scorn into any command he had to repeat.

Harp tried several times to catch Andrew's eye, hoping to communicate the mutinous urges stirring in his heart, but the other man had his head down and was plowing ahead like a draft animal, apologizing occasionally for his growing clumsiness. No doubt he was used to this master/slave routine, which had to be less killing in the lab. This foray into the field was an aberration to be endured with the stoicism of a committed protégé. Feeling more than ever like nobody's protégé, Harp responded by deliberately gearing down a notch, making Clubb wait whenever possible and reacting to scornful hints by moving even more slowly. He began to take more frequent stretches, daring Clubb to show any impatience with that.

Clubb just bore down a little harder on Andrew, whose face had taken on an unhealthy flush, his lips a clenched white line against the ruddy pink. Let it go, Harp told himself. They were almost to the end of the exposed pots, but maybe Clubb would find some way to keep them out here for a while. Even if he didn't, there was no point in pissing him off. He wasn't going to let Harp correct him, and nobody else would have sympathy for the attempt. Let it go, Harp repeated internally, making a mantra of it.

But then he looked up from the dustpan he was filling and saw Clubb sitting on his stones, studying his notebook, and beyond him Andrew standing next to the wheelbarrow, his posture sagging and uncertain. Harp perceived Andrew's dilemma immediately. The screening box was piled high with debris and needed to be shaken, but the wheelbarrow beneath it was also quite full. The box was hard enough for one person to handle alone, and with the wheelbarrow full Andrew would have to lift it while he shook it, an impossibility at this point in the day.

Clubb glanced up from his notebook and saw Harp kneeling with the dustpan in his hand. "Andrew," he said sharply, without turning his head. "Yates can use the bucket when you've emptied it."

"What the hell's wrong with you?" Harp burst out. "Can't you see he needs a hand himself?"

Clubb appeared flabbergasted for a moment. "What did you say?"

"I *said,* why don't you help him? He can't handle the box alone with the wheelbarrow that full, and I'm down here on my fucking knees. Would it kill you to get up and give him a hand?"

"You're way out of line, Yates," Clubb said, glowering at him. "Better button it before you get in any deeper."

"I don't think I'm outta line," Harp insisted angrily. "I've worked with just about everybody on the staff, and you're the only one who won't do his share of the small things that keep an operation going. Christ, Helga's got thirty years on you, and *she* pitches in."

Clubb slapped the notebook shut and stood up. "This isn't your operation, Yates, and if you can't stand taking orders from me, you're free to take a hike. I'm not going to put up with insubordination."

Harp put down the dustpan and struggled to his feet, feeling a despair that wouldn't let him quit while he was behind. "You can call it what you like. I think you're running a piss-poor show when we have to do two-man jobs by ourselves just because you don't wanna get your hands dirty."

"I'm sure Brinton will be interested in what you think. I'm not," Clubb said, sitting back down and opening his notebook. He spoke without looking at Harp. "Now get out of here so we can get back to work. Andrew!"

Andrew, who'd been listening in slack-jawed astonishment, came out of his trance with a start. He gave Harp a darting glance, shrugged slightly, and spread his arms to lift the screening box. Twisting his whole body into the effort, he began to shake the box with awkward, fitful motions, his breath squeaking out of his throat. Harp walked past him without pausing to help, picking up his knapsack on his way out of the trench.

He sat down on one of the back-dirt piles outside and smoked a cigarette, letting the adrenaline burn off like waste gas. He realized he'd just gotten himself fired again. And this time he'd been warned, he'd seen it coming, he'd known it was futile before he opened his mouth. But he'd sounded off anyway, pushing himself to the top of another shit list. He wasn't going to have anyplace to work soon.

"You couldn't just let it go," he said in disgust, crushing out his cigarette as he stood up. He didn't know where to go now, so he headed for the supply tent to get some aspirin for his aching body. He was washing the aspirin down with canteen water when Jim Zorn came into the tent and went to the first-aid kit for some medication of his own. The bug he'd caught out here had sent him to the hospital in Comitán, and he'd come back looking pinched and gaunt, his clothes flapping around him. Rumor had it Brinton had tried to get him to go home.

"Still killing the enemy within?" Harp asked, handing him the canteen.

Jim nodded shyly and showed him an impressively large pink capsule. It took him two tries and a great grimace of determination to get it down. Then he lingered, his bony hand on the center pole, looking at Harp and then looking away. Harp sensed what was coming and suddenly felt too old for it.

"Hey," he said abruptly, startling Jim. "Why don't we just skip the apologies and explanations, and declare an end to the feud? I don't need any more enemies, do you?"

"No," Jim said, regarding him rather warily. "You mean it? No hard feelings?"

"A general amnesty and full amnesia. You never had any business hating me in the first place. Rita's the one you have to settle up with."

"Yeah," Jim agreed. "If she'll let me."

"She's got ears," Harp assured him, reaching down for his knapsack. "Just don't ask me what to say to her. I'm the last person who oughta be giving anyone advice today."

"How come?"

Harp realized he wanted to hear how it sounded. How it was going to sound when he had to say it to Brinton. "I got into an argument with Clubb and he kicked me off his crew."

Jim's eyes widened. "What'd you say to him?"

"Too much. Though no more than what everybody who works with him probably wants to say. Only they have the sense not to say it to his face." Harp found himself becoming agitated. It sounded indefensible, and Brinton was not going to be amused. Harp would really have to shut up and take his lumps. He glanced at his watch, saw there were still a couple hours until quitting time, and slipped the knapsack up over his shoulder. "I think I'll take a walk."

"Where?" Jim asked, but Harp held up a hand to him, having spied a familiar blue pack through the slats of an overturned box.

"Great hiding place, Captain Queeg," he murmured, removing the box and opening the pack. A plastic bag filled with miniature Tootsie Rolls was right on top, and Harp helped himself to a generous handful before closing up the pack and putting it back under the box. He gave some of the Tootsie Rolls to Jim, kept a few out for himself, and stuffed the rest into his pocket.

"Reparations," he said as he led the way out of the tent. "If Ulysses asks about them, just say it must've been the Little People."

His nonchalance temporarily restored by the theft, Harp waved jauntily and went off up the nearest path, which led into the forest directly behind the tent. It was a path they'd cut in their early days of bushwhacking out here, and he had a vague recollection that it came out near one of the shrines. It didn't really matter; it was his intention to get lost for a while, before he had to turn himself in to Brinton.

So he walked and chewed Tootsie Rolls, watching out for snakes but otherwise not paying much attention to his surroundings. He decided there was nothing he could say to Brinton, except mea culpa, so he stopped worrying about that rather quickly. What nagged at him was the sense that he'd lapsed back into his old ways, mouthing off to the person in charge and then taking a righteous hike. He'd thought he'd broken out of that, put himself on a new, revitalized track, his elf-thieving days left behind. Maybe that wasn't possible for him. Maybe he was an arrested personality, playing out the draft scenario over and over again, in increasingly petty ways.

He was breathing hard and had run out of candy, so he stopped and fished in his pocket for more. When his fingers came upon something hard and loosely wrapped, he brought that up, too. It was the sherd he'd stolen from the lab, its wrapping the slip of paper on which he'd written the number of the bag to which it belonged. Harp chewed on the candy and held the sherd up to the light. It was about the size of his thumb and similarly curved, probably a fragment from the rim of a bowl or tripod plate. The background slip was reddish orange and painted on it was a single white water lily, outlined in black. The brushwork was exquisite and the colors still glossy, unmarred by chips or scratches. It was from the palace in Group B and was pure Classic Baktun polychrome, produced long before they started playing the fine-pasters out in the boondocks.

The slip of paper reflected his strong ambivalence about stealing it. The sherd had been such an obvious stray—so much finer than anything else in the bag—he'd figured it wouldn't be missed. But after he'd pocketed it, he began to worry that its very uniqueness might've merited a field note someone would follow up later. And they'd find his initials on the tag and no sherd in the bag. He'd almost put it back right then but hedged by writing down the number instead. Then he'd taken the quickest way out of a moral dilemma, forgetting about it completely.

Harp rewrapped the sherd and tucked it into the change pocket of his jeans, so he wouldn't throw it out with the Tootsie Roll wrappers. He started walking again, thinking that the moment of the theft was the point at which he began to backslide. He recalled the conclusion he came to that let him keep it: *I'll be long gone before anyone finds out.* As if he were going into hiding and wouldn't care what anyone thought of him after he was gone. As if he didn't have a stake in Baktun once he was off the premises. Harp shook his head, amazed he could still be so stupid, so careless with his own integrity. How many times did he have to learn to play it straight with the things he cared about?

He was rehearsing what he'd say to Katie when he turned in the sherd, when the path he was on took a sharp turn around a huge ceiba tree and he walked right into a group of people coming the other way. He froze and they scattered into the greenery, permitting only glimpses of black hair, ragged campesino clothing, and startled Indian faces. Then he saw the boy who'd been left behind, crouched a few feet away, staring up at Harp in a way that made him feel like a bearded giant. When no one came back for the boy and he didn't flee, Harp took a couple of Tootsie Rolls out of his pocket and squatted down. He held them up so the boy could see, then tossed one to him. The boy somehow picked it up without taking his eyes off of Harp, who demonstrated how to peel off the wrapper, sensing the boy might need to be told. He couldn't have been more than five, and except for a couple of necklaces, he was completely naked. Harp chewed and smacked his lips to show it was good, but the boy simply stared, the candy clutched in his hand like a talisman.

Then two men stepped out into the path in front of him, and as Harp slowly straightened up he noticed a third appear behind him. They were all short men, their hair falling straight to the shoulders of their filthy tunics, their dark, angular faces utterly Mayan. *Right off the monuments,* Harp thought. He also noticed they were all armed, one with what looked like a homemade musket, the other two with a machete and an ax that were unmistakably camp issue. The barrel of the musket was pointed at his stomach and was as big around as a car's exhaust pipe. Maybe it was an exhaust pipe. Harp carefully held up his open palms.

"*Habla español? Yo soy amigo. Amigo?*"

The man with the musket, who bore a striking resemblance to Lord of Shells, said something unintelligible, though Harp thought he was calling him "*hombre.*"

"*Hombre?*" he repeated. "*Quien . . . ?*"

"*Hambre,*" the man said forcefully, freeing a hand from the gun to point to his mouth with two fingers. Somehow the barrel didn't waver from its target.

"*Comprendo,*" Harp said, and very carefully shrugged off his knapsack. He had half a ham sandwich, an orange, and some cookies left over from lunch, and when he held out the paper sack, the man with the machete took it from him. The only other things in the knapsack were cigarettes and matches, his

Mid-Atlantic sweatshirt, and a notebook and pen. After a brief internal debate, he handed over the cigarettes and sweatshirt, too. That seemed to surprise them in a favorable way, so that the chief lowered his musket to take a look at the red logo on the chest of the sweatshirt. Harp reslung the knapsack and reached into his pocket for the remaining Tootsie Rolls, and this time the chief himself took them from him.

"*Dulce,*" Harp said, and the man nodded as if he understood. Then he looked Harp up and down and asked a question of which Harp caught only a few words, though the import was clearly "What are you doing here?"

"*Las ruinas,*" Harp said, making digging motions with his hands. When that didn't seem to satisfy him, Harp had another thought and dug the stolen sherd out of his change pocket. The man took it from him and grunted, his eyes flicking up at Harp, nodding with undeniable comprehension. Then he was gesturing with the musket in a not unfriendly fashion, telling Harp to go, and Harp realized he couldn't ask for the sherd back.

"*Adiós,*" he murmured, taking a last glance at the boy, who still hadn't moved or unwrapped his Tootsie Roll. He turned and found that the man with the ax had already disappeared, so he started walking back toward Rana Verde. As soon as he was away he felt a rush of relief that let him know his nerves had been standing on their tiptoes the whole time. So much for getting lost for a while. He kept on walking, knowing he had to tell the others what he'd found. Somehow, he didn't think Brinton was going to like any part of this story.

HE TOOK the baseline trench across the court to the new trench Ulysses was digging along the eastern range wall. Ulysses and Max were sitting on a pile of plastic tarps at the juncture of the two trenches, Ulysses writing in a ring binder. When he saw Harp approaching, though, he turned to Max and held out his hand in the classic "pay up" gesture. Max grimaced and gave him a dollar bill, which Ulysses folded neatly and tucked into his shirt pocket before looking up at Harp.

"The answer is no," he said in greeting. "You can't leave Clubb and come work with us."

Harp had only one thing on his mind at the moment and it wasn't his job, so he couldn't come up with a response.

"In fact, I don't want you around, Yates," Ulysses went on. "All you do is cause trouble. First you get all the women on my case, bitching at me about hurting you. And you did such a good job of sucking up to Clubb that you got him accusing me of concealing data. So if you think I'm gonna bail you out now, you can go piss up a rope."

Harp looked away, quelling the urge to plant a fist in the middle of that red beard. It wasn't a strong impulse and he recognized it as a delayed reaction to the fear he'd felt in the forest.

"There's something the crew chief should know," he said to Ulysses. "Is that you?"

Ulysses scowled at him. "What?"

"We've got some new neighbors. Indians."

"Whattaya mean, *Indians*?"

"I mean indigenous people, Mayans without much Spanish blood. They ran when they first saw me, but then a few of them came back. Their leader was a dead ringer for Lord of Shells."

Ulysses sat up a little straighter. "How many people are we talking about?"

"Ten or twelve, maybe more," Harp guessed. "I saw four of them up close, three men and a little boy. The leader had what looked like a homemade rifle and the other two had a machete and an ax that looked like stolen property."

"Did you talk to 'em?" Max asked.

"I tried to. They were hungry, so I gave 'em the food I had, plus some cigarettes and a sweatshirt. They were pretty dirty, and the kid was naked."

"Refugees," Ulysses said abruptly. "Where'd you run into them?"

"On the path that goes south from behind the supply tent. I'd gone maybe a kilometer."

"They weren't Lacandones, like Carlos?" Ulysses asked. When Harp shook his head, he got up and went over to talk to Arturo and Carlos Kan Boar, who were laying down tarps at the end of the new trench. Harp found Max squinting at him.

"What the hell were you doing out there in the middle of the afternoon, anyway?"

Harp had almost forgotten. "I gave Clubb some shit and he told me to take a hike. So I did."

Max grinned and raised a hand to give him a high five, a gesture Harp accepted with a rueful grimace.

"That's worth a buck," Max declared. "What'd he do, make you hunt for a trowel when he had one sitting right next to him?"

"Something like that. I'm not real proud of myself."

Ulysses came back, pulling on his beard and frowning to himself. "Two questions," he said to Harp. "Did they have women with them and were they carrying a lot of stuff? You know, like bags and bundles?"

Harp consulted his still vivid memories. "I'm pretty sure I saw women and at least two other children. I don't know about baggage. The men didn't have anything but their weapons."

"They've probably got a camp somewhere," Ulysses concluded. "You wanna take us out to where you met them?"

Harp considered it for just a moment. "Not really. I suspect they're long gone by now, and I don't think you wanna go hunting for them. That gun looked like it could go off by itself, and he wasn't shy about pointing it at me."

"You didn't tell me they threatened you," Ulysses said sharply.

"They didn't," Harp said with a shrug. "But they let me know that they were armed and I wasn't. They got friendlier after I gave 'em the sweatshirt, but they didn't exactly kiss me good-bye. I'd say, leave some food out and let 'em come to you. They'll know where to find it." Harp lifted his chin to Max and turned to go.

"Where you going?" Ulysses asked.

"Back to camp. I don't have a job here anymore."

He started walking down the end-line trench and was surprised when Ulysses caught up and walked along beside him.

"I suppose you're gonna tell everybody about this," Ulysses said in a low voice.

"I figured I'd tell Brinton first. I have to tell him why Clubb fired me, anyway."

"Ah, look . . . when you tell him, could you not make it sound like these were *hostile* Indians? They were probably more afraid of you than you were of them."

"They weren't afraid of me at all," Harp scoffed. "What're *you* afraid of?"

"I don't want people thinking it's dangerous to be out here. Especially not Brinton."

Harp came to a stop as they drew even with the trench along the western range wall, not far from the original Yates Landing. "I don't need an escort," he said coldly. "I can find my own way off the premises."

"C'mon, Yates, shit. I'm sorry about . . ."

"Bullshit. You're never sorry about anything. It might slow you down and make you think about what you're doing."

"So I'm not sorry," Ulysses said in exasperation. "I'm asking you as a favor, then. Don't get everybody spooked about this."

Harp snorted. "You don't have any favors coming."

"Whatta you want from me, then? You wanna work here, you can."

Harp whirled on him fiercely. "Oh thanks, Bwana! You're just too fucking kind. You think you own the place just 'cause you're the fucking crew chief? You think you're the only one who cares about what happens to it? Think again, asshole. You may write the fucking monograph, but I'll bring this place to life!"

"What are you talking about?" Ulysses asked helplessly, and Harp realized his diatribe had turned scattershot, aiming for Clubb as well. But he didn't care if Ulysses understood him. He shrugged and resettled the empty knapsack on his back.

"I'm talking about moral purpose," he said as he turned away. "About not letting it go . . ."

12

GIVING THE PATCH one last stroke with his trowel, Harp sat back on his haunches and cocked his head, eyeing his work for evenness and a smooth join with the surrounding segments of original plaster. They'd deliberately made the new plaster a different color than the original, so the restored areas could always be told apart, and this made it easier to check his own handiwork. He wondered what the Maya had used for a trowel—a flat piece of bone or wood? Or just a well-callused palm?

It was so quiet in the West Plaza that he could hear parrots squabbling in the trees and Rick humming to himself as he applied cement to the façade of the sectioned platform. The sun had already driven most of the shadows from the ball court and would soon be directly overhead. Almost time to break for lunch. Saturday was usually a short day, but Harp decided he'd go along if Rick wanted to put in a full one. Putting the finishing touches on his ball court was a labor of love for Rick, as well as an escape from writing his preliminary report. It was supposed to be a kind of probation for Harp, but it'd turned out to be an enormous favor, just what he needed to be doing now that his time at Baktun was getting short. He'd been so wrapped up in Rana Verde he'd lost sight of the fact that the West Plaza would be the geographical heart of his fictional world. It was here that Kan Cross Ahau had asserted the power to rule, and Rana Verde only had meaning as an extension of that power. So Harp was grateful for the chance to take some last impressions and expand his stock of notes, and to do it with Rick along for expert commentary.

He wiped off his trowel and stuck it in his back pocket as he stood up. He wondered if a last game had been played here before Kan Cross Ahau covered it up with a platform. Maybe *that* had been the basis for his claim to power, or at least the confirmation of it. His best ballplayers against those of the Shell family, a contest to decide who was most favored by the gods. He might have left the end zones as a reminder of his victory and their loss. Excited by the possibility, Harp headed for the shaded corner where they'd left their knapsacks.

"You ready for lunch?" Rick asked as Harp went past him.

"Just wanna write something down," Harp explained, kneeling to search for the notebook in his pack. Sancho Panza was snoozing within sniffing distance of the food, and he opened an eye but didn't stir as Harp hastily scribbled an outline of his last game idea.

"Whattaya think, Sanch?" Harp asked. "Was it one big game for all the marbles or a best-of-seven series?"

The pig grunted warily and got to his feet as Rick came up to join them. Sancho backed away to a more comfortable distance, then appeared to feel the heat of the sun on his back and ambled off toward the end zone.

"He knows where we eat," Rick concluded as they picked up their knapsacks and canteens and followed him down the court. Harp could feel the hardness of the plaster floor through the soles of his sneakers and was reminded of playground basketball games and the rough shock of taking a spill on asphalt. He glanced at the benches that sloped up against the sidewalls like ramps, suggesting that the game was meant to be played *up* the walls as well as within them. He could easily imagine dashing up the bench to intercept the ball as it ricocheted off the wall, deflecting it with the pads around his knees, hips, or shoulders. What he couldn't imagine was coming down safely after the shot.

"It must've been a rough game," he said to Rick. "The ball was supposedly big and hard, too, right?"

"Solid rubber," Rick acknowledged. "According to the Aztecs, a straight shot to an unprotected part of the body could kill or maim. Why, you thinking of doing a reenactment?"

"Only on paper," Harp conceded with a laugh. "I don't think I have a whole lotta eye-knee coordination."

Sancho was indeed waiting for them near the logs they used as picnic benches, and they'd only just sat down when they heard a vehicle approach and stop on the camp road, which was hidden by the intervening trees. A few minutes later, Katie Smith came down the path toward them, carrying a mesh bag in one hand and a six-pack of beer in the other.

"Beer," Harp and Rick said in unison, in the same reverent tone. They rose with a swiftness that sent Sancho into retreat and met Katie at the remnants of the end-zone boundary wall, relieving her of her burdens and offering their hands to help her over the wall.

"Thought you guys might be lonely down here, with only each other to talk to."

"Harp talks to Sancho, too," Rick reported. "He's always good for an uncritical opinion."

Katie had just returned from the weekly supply run to Comitán, and along with the beer she'd brought green corn tamales and the mail. She pulled three envelopes out of the bag and gave one to Rick and the others to Harp.

"I also got the bus schedule for you, Harp," she added. "And a list of the regularly scheduled flights from Villahermosa. I left them back at the lab."

"Thanks," Harp said absently, staring in bemusement at the letters in his hand. He hadn't really expected to hear from Caroline again before he left, but she'd sent him a rather hefty, three-stamp missive. The second envelope also had the name "MacPherson" typed in the upper left-hand corner, above the return address of the Department of English, University of British Columbia. It had to be Janet, though Harp couldn't remember the last time he'd gotten a letter from her. Their final communications had all been through her lawyer. He looked up and saw Katie studying him with an inquisitive smile.

"Your wife and your ex?" she suggested.

"You got it," Harp said. He gave the letters another glance and dropped them into his knapsack. "Something tells me I shouldn't read them on an empty stomach."

"My mother can wait too," Rick agreed, handing them each an opened bottle of beer. "First things first . . ."

They drank a toast to Katie's thoughtfulness and then shared out the tamales and the contents of their bag lunches, eating and tossing tidbits to Sancho, who was crouched expectantly at the end of the log Harp was sitting on.

"You catch any glimpse of our 'shy neighbors' on your way in or out?" Rick asked, using the term Ulysses had chosen to describe Harp's Indians.

Katie shook her head. "Just some peccaries and the family of spider monkeys that hangs out near the log bridge."

Rick gave Harp a wolfish smile. "Maybe we're gonna have to reconsider the credibility of our only witness. I mean, we know Harp sometimes gets lost on his flights of fancy."

"You see why I find Sancho easier to talk to," Harp said, tossing a piece of tamale to the pig. "Corn shit, Sancho!"

"No," Katie said in a serious tone. "There's corroborating evidence."

"You mean the thefts?" Rick suggested.

"Sort of. Is it theft if things are being left for them on purpose?"

Rick pulled on his beard, mulling over the implications of that. "Who's doing the leaving? Ulysses?"

Katie nodded. "He came to see me before I left this morning. He said he's been leaving food in the supply tent every night and it's been disappearing like clockwork. Night before last, they left him some snakeskins in return." Katie paused for a sip of beer. "He told me all this in confidence. He also gave me a list of supplies he wanted me to buy, off the camp account. Apparently, the crew out there took up a collection."

"Did you buy it for him?" Rick asked.

"I did," Katie admitted. "But I didn't feel right about it, not after Brinton's speech about the perils of contact. The trouble is, he didn't lay down a policy of how we're supposed to act. He just made me worry about what diseases we might be passing on along with the food."

"He's right about that," Rick said forcefully. "These don't sound like people who've had all their shots. But look, as far as laying down a policy, Brinton's in a tough spot. If these folks are refugees from Guatemala, then they're illegals, and he should report them to the Mexican authorities. If he does, they'll send in the troops, and we'll have a bunch of teenagers with automatic weapons hanging around, shooting at anything that moves. If he doesn't report them and the Mexican government finds out we knew they were here—or worse, that we were harboring them—they might be pissed enough to yank our permit."

"What would the Mexicans do with them?" Harp asked. "Send them back to Guatemala?"

"No, they hate the Guaties too much. They'd probably ship them off to one of the refugee camps on the Usumacinta. Brinton visited one with a Red Cross delegation last year and said that the Mexicans were trying, but it was still a horrible place. Not enough food, shelter, or toilets for all the people they had, and no place to work or grow crops. Kids drown in the mud when it rains."

"Brinton should've told us all this in his speech," Katie said. "We're trained to deal with complicated situations."

"Complicated *past* situations," Rick corrected. "C'mon, Katie, anything he says gets fed into the rumor mill and comes out garbled. You know the way he operates; it's always the less said, the better. Especially when he knows Harp's gonna be telling his stories, getting everybody excited about meeting some wild Indians in the woods."

"They *came* to me excited," Harp objected. "I didn't dress it up for them."

"That just proves my point."

"Which is?" Katie demanded. "If we ignore them and pretend they're not there, they'll just go away?"

"I think that was Brinton's hope," Rick said. " 'Course, what Ulysses is doing makes that less likely. Free food is bound to make them more sociable."

"You could stop him," Katie suggested.

Rick gave her a knowing smile. "Right, and make you a snitch and me a scrooge. No, thanks. Besides, Brinton would have to expect something like this to happen. He knows his people, and knowing him, he probably wouldn't mind if we helped out a little before we leave for the season. He just can't have it look like it had his blessing."

"Sounds like 'benign neglect,' " Harp said dryly.

Rick made a face and reached for another beer. "As Brinton said in his speech, we're guests in this country ourselves. We've got no business inviting strangers in for dinner."

There was more irony than conviction in Rick's voice, but Harp and Katie exchanged a glance over his bent head and decided by unspoken consent to let it drop. If the official policy was to have no policy, there was no point in making Rick answer for it. Harp was about to finish off his tamale when he felt Sancho's eyes on him and tossed the last piece to the pig, who gulped it down and came up looking for more.

"Corn shit, Sancho," Harp murmured ruefully. "Better get it while I'm here to hand it out."

HE GOT HIMSELF a glass of mescal before sitting down in the doorway of his hut to read Janet's letter. He slit open the envelope with his trowel, experiencing a moment of déjà vu at the sight of the blue U.B.C. stationery and the tiny pica type Janet preferred. It matched her handwriting, which Harp had always thought was too small and precise to have been produced by a human hand.

Dear Harper:

When Caroline was here in January, she told me you were going off to play archaeologist in Mexico, and I asked for your address without quite knowing why I wanted it. I realized later that I didn't like the idea of her being left alone for too long, and that I was afraid you'd do just that. Obviously, if you're reading this in the jungle, my fear has been justified. So let me say with heightened urgency what I should have said some time ago: *If you care about Caroline's well-being, don't leave her alone so long.* When she has only herself to talk to, she has a tendency to think herself into a corner and then do something drastic to break out of her self-induced bind.

I saw the first signs of this (a certain moodiness and withholding of emotional response) when she was here, and when I spoke to her on the phone yesterday, she seemed even more remote. Getting her to tell me anything about her job situation was like pulling teeth, and though she tried to make light of it by repeating that "everything was up in the air," her evasiveness had a familiar ring. She had a lot of complaints about Mid-Atlantic (some men asked her silly questions at her interview, some tenured woman wasn't as supportive as she'd like), and a lot of starry-eyed enthusiasm about a job she's only just applied for, at a school she wouldn't even name. This "grass is greener" attitude also sounded too familiar. It used to be the warning that things had gotten a bit sticky and she was about to bolt. As you know, she used to do that with regularity, and every time it set her back and cost her enormously. You only saw the tail end of the self-destructive path she was on, but you know how close she came (more than once) to destroying her prospects altogether.

There was a time I despaired of her ever having a useful life, much less a career, so I'm very proud of what she's done for herself. That's why it would be an utter tragedy if she did something stupid now and set herself back again. Her career might never recover and neither might she. You certainly deserve part of the credit for her turnaround, but I suspect you don't know how lucky you've been, too. So while I give you that credit, I also feel compelled to tell you that you're being terribly irresponsible at the moment. Caroline may believe you're being jungle writer-in-residence, but I remember what you and Rick Fisher were like together. You must've smoked enough dope and drunk enough beer by now. Act like a responsible adult for once and get on home where you belong. Don't let Caroline blow the future she's lucky to have.

Sincerely,
Janet

"Oh, man," Harp muttered, dropping the letter onto the grass as if it'd stung him. She doesn't say boo to him for almost ten years, then sends him a guilt trip out of the blue. And she still had the family talent for righteous condescension, doing you a favor by pointing out your flaws.

Still, he hesitated as he reached for Caroline's letter, wondering if the tension of starting over from scratch was getting to her. He'd seen flashes of the old Crazy Carrie during the last job search, but he'd been there to calm her down.

Before he could slit the envelope, though, he saw Max coming up the path toward him. So he put both letters aside and had a sip of mescal while Max strolled up.

"*Por usted,* Señor Harp," Max drawled, underhanding him a paper bag that'd been rolled into a fat cylinder around its contents. "Arturo said we should share the wealth."

"Tell him *muchas gracias.* And same to you. You wanna roll one up?"

"Well . . . maybe in a bit. I gotta favor to ask you. I was wondering if we could stash some stuff out here, just for tonight. It won't take up much room and we'll have it outta here tomorrow."

"Sounds like contraband," Harp said suggestively.

"Naw, it's just some supplies," Max said with an insincere laugh. "We're gonna haul 'em out to Rana Verde tomorrow, and this is on the way. It'll give us a head start on Monday."

"I assume 'us' includes Bwana Kurtz."

"Yeah," Max admitted. "But, hey, you'd be doing me a favor, too."

Harp let him sweat for a moment, then smiled and held up the brown paper cylinder. "You, I owe. Bring it on out. You want me to give you a hand?"

"Naw, we can handle it," Max assured him, turning back down the path. "We won't bother you a bit."

Harp watched him go with a certain exasperation, unable to believe they were really going to try to keep this a secret from him. What was happening to everybody? The discovery of their shy neighbors seemed to have triggered an epidemic of ambiguous behavior.

He took everything inside and sat down on the bed, stuffing some pillows behind his back and opening Caroline's letter without hesitation. The envelope was from Mid-Atlantic, but the onionskin sheets inside were courtesy of the Albany Hilton.

Dearest Harp:

I just returned from a three-day visit to Albany, a day more than I'd planned. As I was having lunch yesterday, only a couple of hours from my scheduled flight, it suddenly started to snow. Big, fat flakes that came floating down like feathers. It was beautiful to look at but very quickly became a full-fledged storm, which messed up the roads and closed down the airport before we could even try to get there. I joked at the time that the sky gods must be sending us a message and got a good laugh, feeling I was stealing your material. Little did I know.

I'd already checked out of the Hilton, so I spent the night with Alice Prager, whom I mentioned in my last letter. She's simply wonderful, Harp, like the friend I've been waiting all my life to meet. We went out walking in the storm and stayed up half the night talking and listening to music. She thinks I was a hit with both factions on the search committee, and she said she was ready to call in all her markers, if need be, to get me the job. Certainly, her presence alone would be a powerful incentive to accept it.

Since I couldn't get a flight out until three the next afternoon, I finally had a chance to get out and see some of the city and the surrounding area. Alice fixed me up with a real estate agent named Valerie Hopkins, who heard a brief history of our past living arrangements and immediately drove me across the Hudson into Rensselaer County, where there's still some farmland and forest. It was sunny and warm but everything was covered with fresh white snow, a marvelous blend of two seasons. Val tried to give me a sense of several different areas and the range of housing prices, even though I'd told her we were more interested in rentals. We only looked at a few houses, and naturally she saved the best for last.

God, I wish I could be saying this to your face, or at least your ear. Then you could hear how amazed I am at myself. I'm sure you will be, too. So take a deep breath and believe that this is really me talking. Harp, I've found a house for us. A place that could be our home.

He stopped reading and took the recommended deep breath, then a couple more, washing them down with a swig of mescal. Was she talking about *buying* a house? He went back to the beginning of the letter to see if he'd missed something. But no, she hadn't been offered the job yet. It was still very much a bird in the bush.

Max and Ulysses came into the room without announcing themselves, pushing through the netting with cardboard boxes in their arms and packs and *bolsas* looped over their shoulders. They set it all down against the opposite wall and went out again, quiet as thieves.

Harp picked up the letter where he'd left off, just as Caroline launched into a detailed description of the house and property, calling on all her literary powers to make him see the beauty of the countryside and feel the ambience of the house. "You're writing poetry, Caroline," he muttered with grudging admiration. She also described her interaction with the Langdons, who sounded like the homeowners she'd been waiting all her life to meet. Caroline used the term "magical" to sum up the experience and wondered tongue-in-cheek if the Moon Goddess was known to cause fortuitous snowstorms.

The next page went directly from the sacred to the profane, into a discussion of mortgage rates and down payments and loan agreements. She did mean *buy.* For an agonizing moment, Harp's eye was snared by the figure of $110,000, and he almost put the letter down. But the fact that Caroline, who hated financial transactions even more than he did, had written it made him continue. She was suggesting they borrow against their land, or perhaps sell some of it to come up with the down payment. She was also talking about using the money that'd been put in trust for her back in her Crazy Carrie days, funds she'd renounced several times over. Harp was too astonished not to read on, though he was relieved when he got to the final paragraph and left all the numbers and dollar signs behind.

I'm not asking you to make up your mind about any of this before you get back, but do give it some serious consideration after the initial shock has worn off. I'm still in shock myself, scared one minute and giddy with anticipation the next. But a couple of things Val Hopkins said to me at the airport have stuck with me. The first was a question: Had I ever thought we were putting our relationship at risk by living in such a basically rootless way? I said no, then looked back on the past year and had to admit she had a point. The second thing she said may be a realtor's cliché for all I know, though she said it with a conviction that seemed personal: "Having a house you love to come home to is a stake in yourselves." I'll leave you with that thought, though I can't wait to see you and tell you everything that got left out of this. Like how easy it was to imagine living in that house, cooking in that kitchen, picking apples off our own trees. God knows we've been camping out long enough. It's time to stop living like refugees.

all my love,
Caroline

Harp glanced up dazedly as Max and Ulysses trooped in with another load. Max must have thought he was giving them the fisheye, because he smiled apologetically and held up a finger as he followed Ulysses out.

"Just one more."

For the first time, Harp took a look at the goods they'd been piling up against the wall. Since most of it was loose or only haphazardly packed, he could tell without leaving the bed that they'd stuck to the staples: coarse cloth sacks of beans, corn, and rice, salt and coffee, onions and dried chiles. He could smell the coffee, along with more pungent aromas he gradually identified as smoked meat and dried fish. The only items he could see that might conceivably be considered luxuries were some tins of cocoa and two mesh bags of oranges and pineapples. This was what real refugees got, if they were lucky enough to stumble on to some generous gringos.

When he finally turned back to Caroline's letter, it seemed to have lost its power to shock him. He could even read the money parts without palpitations of dread, and he noted for the first time that the monthly mortgage payments would actually be less than what they were paying for the Ushers' mausoleum. And some of the things she was describing—the natural beauty, the privacy, the wildlife—were simply beyond price. All they had to risk was some debt, and their pride in being unencumbered and uncommitted to the middle class. In the immediate context, Harp couldn't find much to fear in that, and it occurred to him that there weren't many places in the world where the choice *not* to have a home made any sense at all.

Max and Ulysses brought in their final load and then squatted down with their backs to him, separating the goods into individual loads. Harp put aside the letter and watched. It looked as though they'd need a mule train of four or five people, and he wondered how long it would feed Lord of Shells and his people. If there were in fact only ten or fifteen, it might hold them for a while. But then what? Give them a little more, and then a little more after that? Just string them along until one day you pack up and go home, and they're back to square one? Very American, Harp thought sourly.

Max and Ulysses had the packs and bags lined up against the wall and were huddled in conversation, probably debating what, if anything, they should tell him. Harp was getting tired of this charade, but he kept a straight face when Max turned to ask if there was any way to secure the door when he went out.

"Why, is there food in there?" Harp asked.

"A little," Max allowed, appearing pained.

"In that case, I could pile up some crates in front of the doorway and tack the netting down tight. That'll keep Sancho out, at least."

"Great. We'd appreciate it," Max said with a relieved smile, and he and Ulysses began to sidle out. Harp let them get almost to the door.

"Hey, I almost forgot," he called, digging into his pocket as he rose and crossed the room. He thrust a wad of pesos into Max's hands.

"What's that for?" Max blurted.

"So you can buy 'em some Tootsie Rolls next time," Harp said, and went over to his desk to pick up his glass of mescal. He looked back and saw they hadn't moved.

"Does this mean everybody knows?" Ulysses asked.

"They probably will soon," Harp said with a shrug. "But I was the one who gave you the idea in the first place, remember?"

"We still wanna keep it quiet," Ulysses insisted.

"From Brinton, sure. That doesn't mean you have to treat the rest of us like snitches. Nobody got spooked by my stories. They all wanna help these people as much as you do."

"Thanks for nothing, then," Ulysses muttered, turning abruptly to leave the room.

Max lingered behind, looking at the money in his hand and shaking his head. "Sorry, Harp. I told him we could trust you, but he wouldn't listen." He held up the money. "You really want this to go into the kitty?"

"Sure. Though I'm having some second thoughts about getting these people used to the dole. What happens when we go home?"

"I dunno," Max admitted. "We're worried about that too. But we can't let them starve in the meantime, and we can't let them hunt out all the game. We're supposed to be protecting the wildlife."

"Shit, I hadn't even thought of that. What about helping them grow some crops?"

"That's possible, if we met with them and they wanted to do it. They may be doing it already, for all we know. But we can't let them get into heavy duty slash-and-burn. That violates our permit too."

Harp grunted in frustration. "I guess a handout is the best we can do, then."

Max shrugged and nodded. "They told you they were hungry, right? Maybe if we feed 'em, they'll tell us what we can really do for them." He glanced out at the fading light and tipped his head in the direction of the dining hall. "Speaking of getting fed . . ."

"I gotta Sancho-proof," Harp told him. "This place smells like the market arcade in Comitán."

Max laughed and went out. Harp started moving packing crates over to the doorway, then stopped and sat down on a chair to finish his drink. He glanced at the letter on the bed but didn't reach for it, afraid a third reading might evoke yet another response. He still wasn't sure which of the first two to trust.

Then he realized he didn't have to figure this out by himself. There were people who'd help him if he asked. It shouldn't have come as a revelation, but it did, testifying to the force of his solitary habits.

"I may be on Clubb's shit list, but I'm still on the crew," he said aloud, and tossed off the rest of his drink. Then he folded up both letters and stuffed them into his shirt pocket, figuring he'd try them out on Katie after dinner. She was a bona fide emissary of the Moon Goddess. Maybe she could tell him what to make of a fortuitous snowstorm.

AFTER A very late Saturday night, Harp hadn't planned anything more strenuous for Sunday than a dip in the cenote. But he'd arrived at brunch groggy and half hungover, and before he could find the coffee, Rita had blindsided him with an offer he couldn't refuse. She'd not only asked him in front of Helga Kauffmann, but she'd thrown in a pleading, forlorn look only a complete churl could've ignored.

So instead of floating on his back in the cool green water of the cenote, he found himself trudging along at the rear of a six-person column headed for Rana Verde. It was oppressively hot even in the forest and his clothing was soon soaked through, giving off a fermented odor as he sweated out last night's scotch. The fact that his hands were empty provided small comfort, since he knew they'd be filled with one of Helga's roof-comb tarps on the way back. Andrew would get the other one while the smaller people—Rita, Jim Zorn, and Helga herself—would carry the stucco fragments once they'd all been packed up.

With the temperatures rising day by day and no rain for a couple of weeks, the forest had dried out considerably, its glossy greenness dulled by a fine coat of dust. The dead leaves on the path made a brittle, crunching sound underfoot, and the *bajos* looked like patches of desert, the sinkholes shriveled and fissured with deep cracks. Harp also noticed there were fewer birds and animals in evidence, though he wondered if their shy neighbors had had a hand in that. Ulysses and his volunteer mules had headed out earlier, carrying the supplies that might provide some relief for both refugees and wildlife.

When they stopped for a break, Harp sat down a little apart and waited for Rita to come explain her forlorn look. He figured it had something to do with the way she and Jim had come sneaking into the lab last night, obviously looking for a place to be alone. They'd left immediately when they found Harp and Katie talking in Katie's office, even though Katie had called out to them to make themselves at home.

Rita handed him a canteen and squatted down across from him, cocking one leg out to the side and resting on the opposite knee. She looked tired but gave off an aura of edgy restlessness, as if ready to rebel against the fatigue.

"Thanks for coming, Harp. I know you didn't wanna do this today."

"I was up kinda late last night. Weren't you?"

"Katie came in an hour after I did," Rita said defensively. "I was still awake."

"We had a lot to talk about. Did you and Jim find some privacy elsewhere?"

"We sat in the Land Cruiser," Rita said, then flared up at his smirk. "No jokes, Harp—all we did was talk. Jim said he'd talked to you."

"Yeah, we agreed to bury the hatchet. The time in the hospital seems to have taken all the venom out of him."

Rita nodded earnestly. "He had a dream when he was there in which a priest came to give him the last rites. He *thinks* it was a dream, but he was delirious, so it might've been real. Except for what the priest said. He told Jim he was going to go to Hell for what he'd done to you and me. Jim's not even Catholic, but he believed it in the dream."

Harp laughed. "A powerful sense of guilt. I assume he made up with you, too."

"Oh, yes," Rita said with a fondness that flustered her. She took off her lucky fedora and studied the brim, which was looking a bit scuffed and sweat-stained. She went on in a low voice. "Once we started talking, it was like we'd never stopped being friends. It was even better than it used to be. We just went from one thing to the next without ever worrying about where we were going."

Someone called out that the break was over and Rita was up instantly, as if propelled by the enthusiasm that'd crept back into her voice as she spoke of Jim. Harp rose more slowly, giving her back the canteen as they followed the column out at a discreet distance.

"So where does this leave the Mayahead?" Harp asked.

Rita gave him a sidelong version of her forlorn expression. "I feel terrible about Eric. He's so nice, and so nice to me. But it's hard to talk to him sometimes. He just listens without giving anything back."

"Well, he'll never be glib," Harp admitted. "But there's something to be said for genuine modesty. That's a rare quality these days."

"Oh, I *know,*" Rita moaned, appearing genuinely distressed. They walked along without speaking for a while, scrunching dry leaves underfoot. Jim was the last of the people ahead and kept glancing back over his shoulder as he walked.

"So I suppose you wanna know how to let Eric down gently," Harp suggested finally.

Rita literally jumped in response. "*Yes.*"

"Can't be done," Harp said, and heard her deflate with a windy hmph. But he wasn't teasing. "The only thing you can do is to tell him yourself, as nicely as you can. Don't make him hear about it from someone else."

"But what do I say? It's not like he's done anything wrong or I still don't like him. It's just . . ."

"You like Jim more."

"I can't say that!" Rita protested. "It makes me sound so . . . fickle."

"If you were truly fickle, you wouldn't care what he felt," Harp pointed out. "Or you'd play him off against Jim."

"I'd never be that cruel. But I still feel selfish."

"I can't absolve you of that," Harp told her. "You have a choice and he doesn't. But you wouldn't be doing him any good by pretending. Maybe that's the way you should put it."

Rita was about to respond when they realized they'd closed the gap between themselves and the people ahead, who appeared to have stopped for another break. Then Harp saw Ulysses and Eric in their midst and realized they'd met the secret suppliers coming back. Max and Brad were there, too, all four wearing empty packs on their backs and blank expressions on their faces. Helga seemed to be grilling Ulysses.

"It was a spur-of-the-moment thing," Ulysses insisted. "Just some stuff I suddenly remembered we were gonna need this week. I didn't know anybody else was coming out today."

"But I made an announcement at dinner last night!" Helga cried, craning her head back to look up at him. "Didn't any of you hear me?"

Ulysses dug his hands into his pockets and shrugged. "Sorry. I guess we weren't listening."

Helga glared at him, clearly unpersuaded. "And where are you going now?"

"Back to camp. It's too hot to bushwhack."

"Yes, and too late to help me," Helga snapped. "Go on, then. We can take care of our business without you."

"Sorry," Ulysses murmured, but quickly led his crew down the path. Helga's face hardened as she watched them go. Then she turned and zeroed in on Harp, holding him with her angry eyes while she waved the others onward.

"Let us continue. I want to talk to Mr. Yates."

Even Rita abandoned him without hesitation, casting a wide-eyed glance at Helga as she departed. Harp relieved Helga of her black satchel, which was light and rattled hollowly when he hefted it.

"What can I tell you?" he said carefully, shortening his stride to match hers as they started up the path together.

"Tell me if my suspicions are correct. I know he was not telling me the truth."

"What do you suspect?"

Helga gave him a sidelong, upward glance, scowling at the effort the movement cost her. "You are being coy with me too. That is even less forgivable, because you have seen these people, and you know yourself what it is like to flee your own country."

Harp blinked at her, stung by the accusation even though he couldn't make sense of it. "You lost me somewhere . . ."

"I know from what Rita has told me that you resisted conscription during the Vietnam War. You fled the country, did you not?"

"I went to Canada."

"And how did that affect you?"

"I didn't adjust real well to Canadian society," Harp admitted. "My first marriage broke up after two years."

"Yes," Helga said, investing the word with a certain wistful recognition. "My family left Germany in 1934. We finally settled in Buenos Aires, but there were many stops before that. Many places where we were kept in quarantine for days and then were herded onto a boat for somewhere else. No one would touch anything that belonged to us, except our valuables. They stared at us like we were Gypsies or the carriers of plague. I still have not forgotten the stares."

Harp was silent for several moments, out of respect. "I'm sorry if I sounded coy," he said finally. "But I still don't understand what you think Ulysses is up to."

"Is it not obvious? He is out hunting Indians on his day off! He lied to me because he knew I would disapprove, and I *do*! These people must not be made the objects of idle curiosity. We are not missionaries or cultural anthropologists. We should leave them in peace!"

"Maybe we should help them survive," Harp suggested.

"It does not help them to be hunted."

"Ulysses wasn't hunting them," Harp said bluntly. "He was taking them food."

Helga faltered and broke stride, glancing up at him with a swiftness that must have hurt her neck. "How can he do that? Has he met them?"

"Not yet. He leaves it in the supply tent and they come and take it."

Helga made a humming sound and then fell silent, walking with her chin resting on her chest. Harp looked ahead and saw Rita and Jim walking side by side, their heads together in conversation.

"I cannot decide if this is a good thing," Helga said at last. "Why did he want to hide it from me?"

"He was afraid you'd tell Brinton, and Brinton would feel compelled to stop it. You shouldn't be offended. He tried to hide it from me, too."

Helga gave him a muted smile. "He has not stopped being Captain Queeg altogether. But you are helping him in this?"

"Abetting, anyway," Harp said with a shrug. "The one thing their chief told me clearly was they were hungry, *hambre.* And they were taking from us before we ever thought of giving."

"No, I cannot deny the worthiness of the impulse," Helga confessed, nodding for emphasis. "It is what human beings should feel. Thank you for telling me, Mr. Yates. I assure you I will leave Brinton in peace."

"I suspect that's where he wants to be," Harp said with a rueful laugh. "Don't we all?"

. . .

HELGA'S ROOF-COMB tarps were now a completed puzzle, though it took the eye a moment to appreciate that fact. It was almost like reading a topographical map, with the reassembled stucco fragments standing out like islands against a flat, tarp-grey sea on which the design had been drawn with grease pencil. The border of water symbols and the densely woven background pattern of matting, rope, and feathers had been revealed in remarkable detail, and though the jaguar masks and the faces of the long-nosed gods had been badly battered, some tantalizing traces of fine sculpture remained: the clearly etched whiskers on a piece of muzzle, the arched and leering eye of God K, a curving fang still bearing red paint. The general style was flamboyantly Late Classical, and the once-rich colors (primarily blue, green, yellow, red, and magenta) had been sprinkled with particles of specular hematite that sparkled in the light. There was no longer any question that the two sides of the roof comb presented identical compositions.

Helga let them take a long look, answering their questions while Jim got out the materials they'd use to pack it up. Harp had foolishly forgotten to bring a notebook, but he still asked more questions than anyone else, concentrating on making mental notes. As a reward for his interest, Helga directed his attention to a pair of glyphs that appeared in the middle of the inscriptions on both the north and south sides. One of the pair was the skull glyph Helga had once said was Central Mexican in character. Its companion, which was partially effaced in both versions, looked something like a scalloped shell wrapped by a human hand.

"You see that they are the mirror image of each other," Helga pointed out. "The event glyph precedes the name glyph on the south side and follows it on the north."

"So the skull is a name?" Harp asked intently. "Of an individual or a group?"

"It could be either. The text is deliberately abbreviated and some parts of it are missing on both sides. I can say with some certainty that it's not the emblem glyph of a known site."

"The Skull People, great," Harp murmured appreciatively. "And the event?"

"I know what you are thinking," Helga said with a tolerant smile. "It is most likely a ritual performance of some kind, but it isn't one of the glyphs commonly associated with the ball game. It's similar to the fish-in-hand bloodletting glyph, but I'm fairly certain it's not that. I am hoping to bring up more detail with photography. All I can tell you at present is that on this side the Skull People perform the event, and on that side it is performed for them, or upon them."

"Gotta be the ball game," Harp said with a grin. "Since they were playing against foreign competition, they made up a new glyph."

"Perhaps we'll find they simply altered an old one," Helga countered, dusting off her hands and stepping back from the tarp. "You must be more patient, Mr. Yates. You saw how I jumped to the wrong conclusion earlier. It is always better to let the truth find its way to you, however long it takes."

"What about meeting it halfway?" Harp suggested.

Helga laughed and pointed him to a workplace. "That's done too often. And not only by novelists . . ."

"LOOK," Andrew said tersely. He stood up and took a few quick steps over to the path that led to the supply tent. Harp was finishing up the adjacent quadrant of tarp, just tucking the last plastic bag of fragments into the knapsack, so he was slow to pick up the urgency in Andrew's voice. When he did, he scrambled sideways on his knees and found a narrow sightline through the trees, just in time to see an oddly attired figure look back in this direction and then disappear behind the supply tent.

"There were two of them!" Andrew reported excitedly, coming back to the tarp. "One was wearing some kind of grey cape with a hood. It looked like animal skin!"

"No," Harp said, suddenly realizing what they'd seen. "It was the sweatshirt I gave them."

"Have they gone?" Helga asked.

"They ran when they saw me," Andrew said, stepping back over to the path for another look. "There's no one there now."

"Obviously, they do not wish to be seen," Helga declared. "Let's finish up here and leave them in peace. Come, we're close to the end. Let's not be careless now."

They turned back to the tarps, though every time Harp cast a covert glance toward the supply tent he saw somebody else doing the same thing. Even Rita and Jim had emerged from the trance they'd been in, communing together over the remains of the roof comb. The bagging and packing they'd been doing was exceedingly tedious work, but they'd seemed to find it intoxicating. Harp had crept close once to eavesdrop on what sounded like sweet talk, only to discover they were discussing how to count the coats of paint a particular piece had received.

He'd just stopped peeking and gotten back into the work when he was jerked out of it by Andrew's hoarse exclamation.

"They're back!"

This time they all moved for a look, crowding together again to stare down the same corridor through the trees.

"Is that him with the rifle?" Rita whispered.

Harp nodded, too excited to trust his voice. He hadn't known how much he'd wanted to see Lord of Shells again. The man was standing like a sentry in front of the open flap of the tent while his people went in and came out with their arms full. Harp counted eight different individuals—men, women, and children—though he knew there were more than that involved. There wasn't anything furtive about their movements, but they weren't pausing to celebrate, either. When they were done, Lord of Shells turned and neatly zipped the flap back into place. Then he waited until the man wearing Harp's sweatshirt (with the arms crossed over his chest and tied to his belt) returned hugging a bundle close to his body. The man set the bundle down in front of the tent and disappeared from view. Lord of Shells turned toward the picnic area and stared back at them for a long moment, watching the watchers, then hefted his rifle in one hand and walked away.

"Awesome," Rita murmured, and there was a general exhalation of held breath as they all stood up and moved toward the path. Helga didn't try to stop them, but she made them wait a couple minutes before she led them toward the supply tent. They waited a few more once they arrived, but the forest was quiet and no one returned to greet them. They stood in a semicircle around the bundle, which was wrapped in green leaves and tied shut with a fibrous homemade twine.

"Let us see what they have left us," Helga said finally, nodding to Jim, who had his pocketknife out. Jim knelt and slit the twine, and the rubbery leaves seemed to peel away on their own, revealing a pale green lump dotted with large black spots.

"Another *rana,*" Jim said, moving out of the way.

Then Harp could see it clearly, a replica of the stone frog he'd found in the ball court. Except this one had been painted, and not in ancient times. It looked as if green vegetable dye had been mixed with whitewash, producing a sickly institutional green that reminded Harp of the customs area in the Villahermosa airport. The paint had adhered to the stone with a streaky inconsistency, making the frog look striped in some places and mottled in others. The eyes and the spots and ridges on the back had been painted with a sooty black paint that was already flaking off.

Harp suddenly remembered the woman in New Belvedere telling him "It came like that." He started to laugh but fell silent immediately when Helga whirled on him.

"It is a *gift,* Mr. Yates. They obviously took the trouble to paint it because they thought we would prefer it that way. And they may be watching to see how we receive it."

"Sorry," Harp muttered, hot with embarrassment.

"We must accept this properly. Bring me my bag."

Glad to escape, Harp went back to fetch it. It occurred to him on the way, with another flash of heat, that he might himself be responsible for the painting of the frog. Because of the sherd he'd given to Lord of Shells. If the gringos were looking for painted things, better give 'em what they want. Harp wondered what else they might've found in the forest, out beyond the range of the crew's surveying and bushwhacking efforts. For these folks, after all, bushwhacking was a way of life.

Some of his embarrassment flared when he returned with the satchel, but Helga demonstrated her willingness to forgive by letting him hold the incense ladle while she filled it with copal and lit it with her Zippo. Then she took it from him and waved it over and around the painted frog, offering a brief invocation in what Harp assumed was one of the Mayan dialects. After a moment of silence, she passed the ladle to Jim, who was squatting on her other side.

"Everyone. Give smoke to the gift and say thank-you in whatever way you deem appropriate."

To Harp's surprise, Jim spoke his piece aloud, thanking the frog for returning from the past. Rita added a plea for friendship with the people who'd brought it. Andrew thanked the spirits of the ancestors who had left us this piece of their history.

By the time the ladle got back to Harp it was almost out, and he leaned forward immediately to anoint the frog with the last wisps of resinous smoke. He noticed for the first time that a chunk had been broken off the right haunch, causing the frog to list in that direction. He took a deep breath and tried to think of something eloquent, but instead the words "lawn animal" popped into his mind, and he caught himself before he laughed.

"Forgive my disrespect," he murmured, and let out the breath along with any desire to be clever. "Welcome back."

Helga took the ladle from him and dumped the ashes onto the ground next to the bundle. Then she rose with the ladle and the satchel in her hands and led them up the path in single file, back to finish the job that had brought them here.

13

New Belvedere

A WARM SATURDAY morning in March, and in New Belvedere the cherry trees were in full bloom and the azaleas were just beginning to open. Caroline could smell the fragrance as she opened the doors and windows and prepared herself to clean the House of Usher. She'd done it only once since Harp's departure, and she was supposed to host next Saturday's meeting of her feminist study group. Harp would be coming home soon after that, as well, and she didn't want him to see what an utter flop she'd been as a substitute househusband.

Before she could even get started, though, she ran into the mountain of dirty laundry she'd piled up and decided she'd better deal with it before it mildewed. She'd just crammed the first load into the Ushers' aging Kenmore when the phone rang upstairs. It was the first of three calls in succession, all friends from Mid-Atlantic calling to congratulate her on the job she'd been offered yesterday afternoon. Two said they'd heard from Roger Hammet, one from Virginia Evers. Caroline had been trying not to think about any of this, and her responses sounded flustered and false to her own ear, though none of the well-wishers seemed to notice. They all assumed without asking that she was going to take it, and none were close enough to trust with the news that she was waiting on another job.

The next call caught her in the midst of hauling more laundry down from the second floor. It was a real estate agent, a friend of Roger Hammet's, offering his services to help her locate more permanent housing in the area.

"Not today," Caroline said curtly, then realized she wasn't in a position to be sending arrogant signals. Roger had gotten her a five-to-one vote in the committee and fast approval by the dean, and she didn't know where Albany was in its deliberations. So she apologized to the man and told him to send a card so she could get back to him when she was less busy.

The house was momentarily quiet, but she knew the phone wasn't going to stop, and she didn't think she could take much more of this friendly harassment. The overflowing laundry basket suddenly reminded her of a place that'd been a haven for her in the past, so she carried it out to her car and went back for the rest. Then she went down to the basement, stuffed the first load into the dryer, and cranked the timer up as far as it would go. She'd just collected her purse and car keys when the phone and the doorbell rang simultaneously. She swore at the phone and went to answer the door. It was a deliveryman with a foil-wrapped potted plant for her, a beautiful coleus with multicolored leaves. Not flowers, Caroline noted; another pitch for permanence. The card said it was from Virginia Evers and the Women's Studies' staff.

"You wanna get that?" the deliveryman asked, meaning the phone that was still ringing in the background. "I can wait."

"So can they," Caroline said, reaching for his clipboard. She signed and handed it back. The phone rang on, annoying in its persistence. "You ever hear the expression 'Hell is others'?"

The man made a game attempt at a smile. "Naw. Who said that?"

"Jean-Paul Sartre." Caroline found a dollar in her purse and handed it to him. The ringing suddenly stopped behind her, and she smiled and stepped out onto the stoop, locking the door behind her. The deliveryman preceded her down the walk, casting a curious glance back over his shoulder.

"This like a birthday you don't want or something?"

Caroline laughed but got into her car without lingering, not wanting him to think she was flirting. She buzzed down the window as she rolled past him down the driveway.

"It's exactly like that," she said, and he shrugged and smiled as she backed into the street and made her getaway.

IN THE third mall she tried, Caroline found what she was looking for. It billed itself as a coin laundry and was wedged in between a dry cleaner and a Popeyes Fried Chicken outlet, but it was clean and had the aura of working-class respectability she was seeking, exemplified by the orderly crowding of messages on its bulletin board. Her dissertation had had its origin in a laundromat in Wheeler's Corners, Vermont, and the group of women she'd met there had remained her test for reality as the thesis grew into a broader study of the changing nature of women's social groups. Her working title had been

Laundromat Ladies, which Harp had urged her to use for the book, if she could get a university press to go along.

There didn't seem to be a lot of socializing going on here today, but it was a weekend, and Caroline assumed the regular crew, if there was one, came in during the week. An enormous black woman in a turquoise pantsuit made change for her and sold her some detergent, and Caroline filled three machines, taking nostalgic satisfaction in sliding the coin plunger home. She was leafing through a back issue of *People* magazine when the change lady came over, moving with the cumbersome dignity of an ocean liner, her huge breasts thrust forward like a prow and her hips floating around and behind her. She settled herself with surprising daintiness two chairs away and turned toward Caroline.

"You from outta town, honey? Or'd your washer break down at home?"

The questions were offered casually, but there was a shrewd curiosity lurking in the woman's eyes that made Caroline smile and take a chance. "Are you a sociologist, too?"

The woman laughed, apparently delighted at being caught out. "That what you are? I knew you wasn't the usual clientele. Mosta them bring their own soap."

"I forgot," Caroline admitted. "I did this mostly to get away from the telephone."

"Lord, I know *that,*" the woman said, casting her eyes heavenward. When she lowered them she was smiling, and they quickly got down to the serious business of introducing themselves and making the time pass while the machines whirred and tumbled. The woman's name was Yolanda Suttle, and she was an administrative aide in the hospice unit at the county hospital during the week. Saturdays at the laundromat were her way of putting something aside in case her son, Wesley, did in fact get himself accepted at Georgetown. She was thirty-six and had lost one husband in the Vietnam War and divorced a second, by whom she'd had her daughter, Aretha. As soon as Aretha was older, Yolanda was going back for more night courses toward her degree in public health, so she wouldn't lose the two years of credits she'd already earned.

Caroline had never ceased being amazed at how readily Americans would tell their life stories to total strangers, though Yolanda was one of those Americans who didn't let you feel like a stranger for long. It was clear she didn't put much stock in Harp once she heard he wrote books for a living and had been away in Mexico for almost three months, but she had the highest respect for what Caroline had accomplished in going back late for a doctorate. And she sized up the situation at Mid-Atlantic with a refreshing directness, as if she'd heard it all before.

"Oh yeah . . . when they think it's the only job you ever thought of wanting, they figure you be happy to work like a dog all week and kiss their butts on your day off. But just let 'em hear you're leavin' for something better and all of a sudden they's asking you to lunch and throwing parties for you, want you to remember how much they always loved you. Hunh! I seen it. Had this supervisor one time, old white lady like this one with the umbrellas you're talkin' about. You could please God before you could ever please her, if you was younger than she was. Nobody else was ever supposed to do it as well as her. When I told her I wasn't having any of that, she told me I was uppity. Used that exact word."

Yolanda was helping her fold towels, bundling them up with unconscious efficiency. Even as she fumed over the memory, she glanced around the room, keeping tabs on her customers.

"I hope you were," Caroline said.

"What?"

"Uppity as hell," Caroline said, and Yolanda laughed so hard she had to hang on to the edge of the folding table.

"I sure was," she huffed, wiping tears from her eyes. "All the way out the door. You gonna be fine, Caroline. You still got your sense of humor."

"I've been losing it on occasion," Caroline confessed.

"Well, sure," Yolanda agreed. "You dealing with some big stuff here, your first steady job and all." She lifted a stack of towels and dropped them into an empty basket. "But you got one job in the bag already, right? And the other one lookin' good?"

"I know, I shouldn't be complaining, should I? I just hate waiting for someone else to make up their mind about my life."

Yolanda smiled. "That's cause yours is already made up. You got your heart set on that fine house, and I don't blame you. But if the waitin's getting to you, why don'tcha call up to New York and tell 'em what you got here? You don't have to be uppity about it," she added with a sly smile. "Just let 'em know you in demand."

"I think I will," Caroline decided, and Yolanda laughed as she turned away to make change for another customer. While she was gone, Caroline folded up the last of the laundry and realized it was time to go back and face the house and telephone. She felt ready to do that now, yet she was also reluctant to say good-bye to Yolanda. The sort of instant intimacy they'd achieved was a form of magic too.

"Say," she began when Yolanda returned, but then caught herself. Yolanda rested her fists on her ample hips and raised an eyebrow.

"You're blushing, girl. What was you gonna say?"

"I was going to ask you to have some lunch with me. From next door."

"From Popeyes? It ain't as good as I make, but . . . oh, I see what you saying." Yolanda touched a finger to her lips, regarding Caroline thoughtfully. "It's funny, some folks make you listen for that kinda thing. You can just feel it's there, waitin' to pop outta their mouths. But I never felt that about you, honey. You can offer me fried chicken anytime, long as you get some biscuits and gravy to go with it."

Caroline laughed and grabbed one of the baskets. "Something to drink?"

"Diet Pepsi. Oh, and don't mind them signs sayin' you not supposed to eat in here. That's why we got a office in the back."

"You have a gift, Yolanda, for making things seem easy."

"That ain't what my kids say," Yolanda scoffed, waving her toward the door. "When you come back, you gotta tell me what to say to Wesley about gettin' into college. He thinks he's so smart can't nobody miss it."

"I've thought the same of myself," Caroline admitted with a rueful laugh. Then she hefted the basket and headed out the door, suddenly hungry for lunch.

Baktun

HE WAS standing in a tunnel with some other men, wearing a costume that wouldn't let him turn to see who the men were. Thick leather wrappings encased him from midthigh to just under his armpits, and there were heavy pads around his knees and elbows and a helmet that fit tightly around his head. He felt engulfed in leather and almost lost his balance just trying to look down past his swollen girth to his feet. He was surprised but heartened to see that he had his own sneakers on.

The realization of where he was allowed him to look down the tunnel, and he saw a man in a similar costume framed in a circle of bright light. The man was down on one knee with his padded chest thrust out and his feathered head tilted back, one arm cocked at his side and the other extended in a gesture that seemed more an appeal than an assertion of balance. Harp heard the noise of the crowd, but the man didn't move and the expected ball never appeared.

Then he was jostled and turned and found himself facing Lord of Shells. The original Lord of Shells, tall and imperious, thick lips curling beneath the hooked nose and fierce, hooded eyes. He gestured with his staff, which seemed to spout feathers from its tip, and Harp understood: *Now you will play.* Fear made the costume contract around him, squeezing the air out of his lungs. He didn't know how to play. He could barely move his arms and legs. The ball would crush him.

The ceiling was gone and he realized they were standing in a trench. It was raining, blurring the air around him and giving him sudden hope. He managed to raise his hands and the water sluiced through his splayed fingers. It had to be impossible to play in this. But Lord of Shells shook his head and stared implacably. *You will play.* Then his face was melting and behind it was that of Brinton Taylor, caught in a grotesque howl of derision, white hair glowing in the gathering darkness. *You don't know how,* Harp heard, and was spun, slipping in the mud, the rain closing around him like an impenetrable curtain. He couldn't see, couldn't breathe, and then a skeletal face appeared out of the gloom, a grinning skull that said *come . . .*

Harp came awake with a jerk, bathed in sweat and wrapped in the mosquito netting he'd pulled down around him. He struggled uselessly for a moment before he got control and lay back panting. Then he heard shouting in the distance, a ruckus of voices that seemed to come from the vicinity of the men's and women's lodges. He extricated himself from the netting and sat up, feeling the humid air settle back around him like a shroud. It'd never cooled off last night and he recalled the trouble he'd had getting to sleep. That seemed like a long time ago, days before the dream.

He washed his face, brushed his teeth, and got dressed, feeling he smelled of iodine and algae. The rain in his dream seemed like a taunt, it'd been so long since they'd had water for a proper shower. Yet when he stepped outside and looked up at the sky, squinting at the glare, he saw dark-edged clouds piling up in the west and streaks of white effacing the pale blue overhead. The air was so damp it felt heavy in his lungs, and his T-shirt was already soaked through, adding sweat to his repertoire of lovely aromas.

The ruckus had died out a while ago, and by the time Harp got to the end of the path, there was no one about. The door to the outhouse, however, was hanging by its upper hinge, the hook latch torn off completely. Harp knew from personal experience that the presence of local microbes in their diet could result in urgent and sometimes explosive evacuations. But this looked as if someone had blown himself right through the outhouse door.

He heard the ruckus again before he got to the dining hall, and he walked into an uproar that brought him up short, wondering if their shy neighbors had put in an early-morning appearance. But it soon became clear that Emory Muldoon was at the center of the commotion, and several of the bystanders were only too eager to fill Harp in on what had happened. It seemed that Muldoon had gone to the outhouse for his customary dawn dump and had discovered—or more precisely, been discovered *by*—a six-foot fer-de-lance. Muldoon had already dropped trou and hunkered down when he'd sensed something strange about the shadows overhead and looked up to see the snake dangling from the rafters, its snout about a foot away from his head. Muldoon swore he'd heard the sound the snake's tongue made as it licked the air between them—a "poisonous slurp," he called it—and then he'd simply thrown himself headfirst out the door.

Katie and Lucy Smith had been awaiting their turn outside when Muldoon came flying out, his pants around his ankles and incoherent shrieks coming out of his mouth, and their initial response had been to run, thinking he'd lost his mind. Once he'd calmed down enough to cover himself and explain, they'd received their second scare of the day, seeing the hanging snake and realizing they could easily have gotten there ahead of Muldoon. The three of them had stood by and watched as Ulysses and Max used long poles to pry the fer-de-lance from its perch and drive it off into the forest. Different estimates pegged it at six to eight feet long and as big around as a man's arm.

"My arm or yours?" Harp asked Brad, who was telling him this part of the story.

Brad grinned and flexed his biceps. "Yours, of course. We ain't talking about no python."

"What I wanna know," Ulysses said to Katie, who was sitting next to Muldoon at the end of the table, "is what was scarier: the fer-de-lance or Muldoon with his pants down?"

"I'd have to say Muldoon," Katie decided, setting off a chorus of laughter and cries of "flasher!"

"Which was longer?" Ulysses asked.

Katie pretended to think about it for a moment. "The snake," she said, smiling sweetly at Muldoon. "But only by a little."

Even Muldoon, who looked pale and shaken, cracked up at that, and the laughter went on for several minutes, breaking off just before it became hysterical. As they quieted down, Brinton Taylor stepped in behind Muldoon and signaled for their attention.

"I'm also grateful no one was bitten," Brinton told them. "And I want to warn you all to be extra careful in that area from now on, especially at night. This fellow may have a territorial bent. Use your flashlights and stamp your feet occasionally, and by all means, give him a wide berth if you see him."

Harp nodded along with everyone else, though he was trying to imagine this Brinton howling as he had in the dream. It didn't seem likely he'd ever howled at anything, at least not in this life. It was *your* dream, Harp told himself. Feeling as if he still hadn't left it completely, he got a plate of food and sat down next to Rick and Kaaren.

"It never occurred to me before," Kaaren was saying. "But do we have an antivenom for the fer-de-lance on hand?"

"We do," Rick said. "But we've had it for a while and no one was real sure it would work to begin with. We've had all kinds of close encounters with the suckers in the past, but no one's been bitten yet. If Muldoon had been bitten in the head or neck, he probably would've been done for, anyway."

Kaaren made an exasperated noise and slumped back in her chair. "Just what I wanted to hear."

Rick grinned and nudged her. "Come use our outhouse. I'm tired of flashing Clubb and Helga." He turned the grin onto Harp. "Hey, Harpo, snap out of it! You look half dead. You up for going back to work at Rana Verde?"

"What for?" Harp asked in surprise. He wondered if someone in Helga's crew had leaked word of yesterday's "gift."

" 'What for?' " Rick repeated sarcastically. "Because there's fucking work to be done! Kaaren's run into some super-compacted shit at midcourt. Heavy pick work, though you can pass on that if you want. Whattaya say?"

"I've got arms like snakes, but I'm game," Harp said, perking up a bit at the prospect of witnessing the second discovery of the "gift." Then he had another thought. "Maybe the rain'll soften this shit up for us."

"What rain? It's not gonna rain," Rick scoffed. "It's too late for the *nortes* and too early for the real thing."

"Those clouds to the west look like the real thing to me."

"Naw, we always get teased like that for about a month before the rainy season starts. You'll see, it'll all blow off by this afternoon. Just make us sweat a lot first."

"It's gonna rain," Harp insisted.

"Ten bucks says it won't," Rick said, offering his hand.

Harp shrugged and shook on it. "You're giving your money away."

"Have you been communing with the spirit of Chac?" Kaaren inquired, leaning forward to smile at him.

"Not exactly . . . I just know it's gonna rain."

"Weird with a beard," Rick declared, shaking his head. "No heavy pick for you today, Snakearms. In fact, no sharp instruments at all."

"No rain checks, either," Harp told him. "Be prepared to pay your bets."

THEY HEARD a roll of thunder in the distance just as they were leaving camp, and when Rick glanced back, Harp couldn't resist a smug gesture toward the raincoat tied around his waist. He hadn't figured out the rest of his dream yet, but the sensation of being rained on was still so vivid it had taken on the power of a premonition. The forest had a dreamlike quality of its own, the dusty vegetation wreathed with a wispy white fog that collected in patches where the ground was low. The air was thick with a moisture that streamed down Harp's face and plastered his wilted curls against the back of his neck, yet the dry leaves crunched underfoot with an incongruously desiccated sound. The rumble of thunder was becoming both louder and more frequent, and every so often the leaves overhead would begin to thrash as the tops of the trees were tossed by winds unfelt on the ground. After they'd groped their way through a fog patch so dense it had them bumping into each other, Rick gave Harp a walleyed glance.

"Maybe I should just pay up now and call it a day."

"No way!" Harp said swiftly. "The game must go on!"

"What game? Oh, never mind . . . I can see you're off on one'a your flights of fancy. Snakearms the Storm King . . ."

They went on with the sky growing darker and more boisterous and the air approaching the saturation point. When they finally arrived at Rana Verde, it felt like an anticlimax, and they all stopped for a moment, as if waiting for the rain to drive them back home again.

But then they saw the group in front of the supply tent. Ulysses had been walking ahead with Max, and Arturo and Carlos Kan Boar had apparently been waiting at the site. They were all standing around the painted frog, which was exactly where it'd been left, resting lopsidedly on a bed of wilted green leaves with a small heap of greyish-white ash spread out on the ground next to it. Harp gaped along with the others, though he hung back a bit so he wouldn't have to put on a full show of amazement.

The discussion of how the frog had gotten there was remarkably similar to what had occurred yesterday, though the ash was taken as evidence of a ceremony performed by the Indians themselves. Ulysses also pronounced it a gift, though it didn't occur to him to stage a ceremony of acceptance.

"Why do you suppose they'd leave us a gift?" Rick asked with studied innocence, raising his eyebrows at Ulysses. "To pay us back for the Tootsie Rolls and Harp's sweatshirt?"

Ulysses shrugged. "Maybe . . . who knows?"

"They even painted it for us," Rick persisted. "What've we done for them?"

While Ulysses was fumbling for a response, Arturo suddenly stepped forward, taking off his broad-brimmed hat and speaking to Rick in rapid Spanish. Harp couldn't catch any of it at first, though he'd never seen Arturo so exercised, urgent to the point of being argumentative. As Rick listened and tried to reason with him, Harp gradually understood that Arturo wanted to go tell his uncle Vicente about the gift. He was insisting on it, in fact, repeating something about his "*trabajo,*" his work. Rick kept shaking his head and making reassuring gestures, but Arturo wasn't buying it. Finally Rick gestured toward the threatening sky and made some kind of deal with him, apparently persuading him to wait until later. Arturo didn't look happy, but he and Carlos turned and walked off toward the ball court. Rick let them get out of earshot before he turned to Ulysses.

"I guess you didn't figure in how *they* were going to react. Maybe you can convince him we're not trying to hire these people to replace them. It'll be good practice for convincing Vicente."

"Shit," Ulysses said, and went off with Max in tow.

"What's going on?" Eric asked.

"They know you guys have been leaving stuff for the Indians," Rick told him. "He said it was *their* job to find things for us, and they weren't about to work just for food. I got him to wait until the lunch break or the rain, whichever comes first. But then the shit'll really hit the fan. Vicente'll go straight to Brinton." Rick waved his hands in frustration, then looked down at the frog. "And what the fuck do we do with *this*? They didn't just remove it from its context, they had to deface it, too!"

"Uh-uh, it's a gift," Harp chided. "If we treat it with respect, maybe they'll show us where they found it."

"Great. Vicente'd be real happy to have them do that."

"It's not like we can return it," Harp pointed out. "Maybe if we move it out from under the trees, the rain'll wash it clean."

"Just leave it where it is," Rick said, giving him a sour look. "Let's go do some work before *we* get washed away."

He went off toward the ball court, holding on to his hat in the gusting wind.

Kaaren, Brad, and Eric followed him one by one, casting parting glances at the frog. Left behind, Harp stooped and dipped his fingers into the grey ash.

"You're still welcome," he murmured, touching the frog lightly on the head before going after the others. He didn't try to catch them, approaching the ball court with a deliberation that defied the impending storm. As soon as he entered the narrow corridor cut through the range wall, the wind stopped plucking at his clothes and he no longer had to squint against flying debris. He untied the raincoat from around his waist and put it on, then wiped his face with a bandanna and resettled the baseball cap on his head. Stretching his arms out to the sides, he looked down at his sneakers and laughed. Then he moved swiftly down the corridor, turning right into the wider interior trench, where he was again aware of the wind and the roiling sky overhead.

He saw at once that no one was pretending to work. Brad and Eric were over near the range wall, moving stones to weigh down the tarps that covered their equipment and the last few feet of terminated pots. Rick and Kaaren were standing next to the remaining section of "super-compacted shit," which jutted out into the cleared area of the ball court like a peninsula of the range wall. Even at a distance, Harp could see that it was remarkably smooth on the outside, without the granulated surface and crumbling edges of a normal section of exposed fill. A few fat raindrops splatted down around him as he went up to join them.

"It's a conglomerate of stones, gravel, a heavy clay soil, and lime plaster," Kaaren was explaining, shouting to be heard above the rising din of wind and thunder. "It was apparently laid wet and tamped down, and it's laced with hundreds of sherds, fine paste and Baktun polychrome and who knows what else. We didn't want to start digging seriously until we had somebody to help with screening and bagging."

Oblivious of the pandemonium overhead, Rick studied the way the section sloped downward at its far end. "Looks almost mold-made. They musta done this last, after filling in the rest of the court. They left a hole and packed it in."

"Looks like it," Kaaren agreed, smiling even as she raised a hand against a sudden swirl of dust. "Theory, Harp?"

He stared at her blankly, pulled out of the swirl of his own thoughts. He'd been trying to imagine the court completely cleared, a game in progress. "About this?" he said lamely. "Shit, I dunno. Maybe they were trying to make sure nobody ever played here again."

"Isn't that obvious?" Kaaren said with a quizzical frown. "C'mon, Harp. They buried the whole court, but did a super-compacted job right here. Why?"

There was a sizzling flash and a crash of thunder so close and forceful it seemed to make the ground shake.

"This's crazy!" Rick shouted. "Let's get the fuck outta here!"

Kaaren shook her head and grabbed Rick by the shirtsleeve, leading him forward to the place where the section met the range wall. She pointed to a spot about three feet above the floor, where a small vertical crevice had been chipped out of the joining. Rick leaned over the tarp-covered pots at the base of the wall and peered into the crack. Brad and Eric had come up to join them, and Harp noticed they were both grinning in anticipation. Rick didn't disappoint them with his response.

"Damn! That's a fucking *toe*!" He glanced back over his shoulder in open-mouthed astonishment. "You've got a wall panel here."

"Lemme see," Harp said. But before Rick could get out of the way, the rain started coming down, hitting the plastic tarp like buckshot. Rick and the others ran for it, and by the time Harp got the hood of his raincoat up over his cap, everything in front of him was a wet blur. He turned in a circle, seeing walls of earth all around him, earth he'd have to move with his mind before the game could be played. But hell, he could do that easily after having seen Rick's ball court. And this wall panel might give him portraits of the players, put faces on the Skull People. With that kind of material to work with, what could he possibly have to fear?

He was suddenly aware of the rain whipping against his legs and lurched into motion. A stone the size of an apple lay in his path, and he approached it with a hop, planting his left foot and swinging his right leg back soccer style.

"Play ball!" he shouted into the blowing rain and caught the stone cleanly with his instep, sending it rocketing down the trench. He slid in the mud on the follow-through and almost went down, but he was up again in an instant and ran whooping out of the ball court.

HE GOT to the supply tent only moments before Ulysses and his crew came crowding in, dripping and panting. Arturo and Carlos exchanged a few words with Rick and left again almost immediately, pulling their hats down low and heading out into the rain, which was coming down in thick sheets.

"I take it you didn't have any luck," Rick said to Ulysses.

"It's not just the threat to their jobs," Ulysses said with a grimace. "He reminded me it's been a long time since we visited his village, which means a long time since we brought *them* any gifts."

"He's right." Rick turned and gazed out at the downpour. "Well, this doesn't look like it's gonna stop anytime soon, and the trenches'll be too muddy to work, anyway. Might as well wait till it lets up a bit and then head on back."

"I'm already soaked," Ulysses said with a shrug. "Might as well go face the music."

"We were in on this, too," Kaaren reminded him. "Don't hog all the blame."

Ulysses smiled crookedly and nodded. Max went out with him, yelping at the force of the rain. A few moments later, Eric stood up, ducking when the top of his head brushed the sagging canvas.

"If we're done for the day," he said to Rick, "I'm going too."

"Oh, man," Brad moaned. "Be cool, will ya? You can't even see out there."

"I know the way," Eric said in a tone that clearly implied he didn't care if he could see, and pushed out through the flaps. Brad got to his feet with a groan of reluctance, grabbing on to the centerpole and making the whole tent shake.

"Hell's bells, I don't wanna get soaked just 'cause he's feeling crazy. I think Lovely Rita gave him the kiss-off last night."

Gathering his courage, Brad tucked his head down and went past Rick into the rain. They'd only turned to watch him go when he stuck his head back into the tent.

"The frog's getting clean, anyway," he reported and disappeared for good, leaving the three of them laughing. Rick came over and sat down next to Kaaren, leaning back to give her a long look.

"So . . . you're sitting on a major find and you don't tell anybody about it, not even me. You afraid of claim jumpers?"

Kaaren laughed but nodded. "You know what Ulysses is like. As for you two, I wanted to be sure you were coming to work and not just to grab the glory."

"I'd rather grab glory than work, any day," Harp admitted. "How long will it take us to dig out the panel?"

"That depends on the weather and how hard we work. And how hard that stuff really is. Maybe three or four days, maybe a week."

"That's all I've got left."

"You shouldn't have prayed for rain, then," Rick said.

"I didn't ask for it," Harp said. "I just knew it was gonna come. I got rained on in a dream."

"Don't tell that to Brinton. I've almost got him convinced he can trust you for another week."

A wet gust of wind blew the flaps open and billowed out the sides of the tent, making them all grab for their hats. "Is this what it's like during the rainy season?" Harp asked, raising his voice to be heard.

Rick nodded. "From what I've seen. We've never been around during the heaviest months."

"Guess I'd better check it out, then," Harp decided, gathering his legs under him. "You two probably want to be alone, anyway."

"Here?" Kaaren inquired dryly. "When the neighbors might drop in at any moment?"

"They're shy," Harp assured her with a grin as he stood up. "They'll probably think it's a gringo ceremony of greeting."

"Don't get lost out there," Rick cautioned. "You might have to detour around the *bajos*. Oh . . . here." He pulled a wadded bill from his pocket and tossed it to Harp.

"I love a good loser," Harp said, stuffing the money into his jeans and pulling his hood back up. Then he walked out of the tent, stepped around the frog—which was indeed bleeding its colors onto the ground—and went up the path with the rain beating down on his head.

IT WAS still raining when Harp finally got back to his hut. He found Sancho Panza cowering in the corner and water dripping from a half dozen leaks in the roof. He'd heard Sancho was afraid of thunder so he spoke soothingly to the pig while moving his furniture out of harm's way and putting water glasses under the worst of the leaks.

He stripped off his raincoat and tugged on the wet laces of his sneakers, feeling as if he'd put in a full day. The trip back had taken him an hour longer than usual and it'd been a nerve-racking experience. Everything looked different in the rain, with the foliage sagging down over familiar landmarks and the *bajos* two feet deep and rising. And there were snakes all over the place, and frogs that would come flying up out of the grass and make him think of snakes. There was one remarkable moment, on a fairly straight stretch of trail, when the frogs were springing up ahead of him for as far as he could see, like outriders announcing his coming. The charm of that scene had lasted about fifteen minutes, until a snake that bore a striking resemblance to a water moccasin swam past him as he was wading across the next *bajo.* That's when he'd stopped gathering mental impressions and started concentrating on getting back alive.

He put on his swimming suit and picked up a tube of Prell as he headed for the doorway. "Shower time!" he called to Sancho, who showed his customary disdain for personal hygiene and didn't budge.

Harp lathered up thoroughly and then stood with his eyes closed and his face tipped to the sky, letting the rain wash him clean. He heard a chuckle and opened his eyes to see Katie Smith approaching, an umbrella held over her head.

"I may look ridiculous," Harp said, "but I'm clean."

Katie shook her head and pointed past him, and he turned to see Sancho lying in the doorway of the hut with his snout stuck out through the netting.

"A boy and his pig," Katie said. Then she seemed to remember why she'd come and frowned.

"Something wrong?" Harp asked, picking up the Prell and leading the way to the hut. When Sancho saw them coming, he chose the better part of valor and bolted out into the rain.

"I was talking to Brinton in the lab when Ulysses came in to tell him about the painted frog. That was about two minutes before Vicente showed up to complain."

"Tell me," Harp urged as he began to towel off. Katie dodged a drip from the ceiling and sat on the bed.

"Basically, Ulysses offered himself up as a scapegoat, and that's how Brinton used him. Brinton told Vicente that he hadn't known this was happening and didn't approve of it, and he promised to put a stop to it. Just to show he meant business, he told Ulysses he was off the Rana Verde crew until further notice."

"Right there? In front of Vicente?"

"In front of Arturo and Carlos, too. He also brought up the possibility of shutting down Rana Verde for the remainder of the season."

"He *wouldn't,*" Harp protested, swiveling halfway around in the middle of taking off his swimming suit.

Katie held up a hand to shield her face. "Please, no more dangling serpents." When Harp turned back around, she went on. "You should've seen Ulysses's face when Brinton mentioned a shutdown. It was close to Muldoon's expression coming out of the outhouse. But he didn't try to fight it. I think he figured Brinton was putting on a show for Vicente, who was putting on a show of his own for Arturo and Carlos. There was something false and blustery about all the outrage."

Harp pulled on a pair of jeans and turned around. "Did Vicente complain about us giving gifts to strangers?"

"Not really. But see, Ulysses told Brinton they'd only been leaving a little food in the supply tent. He neglected to mention the load they took out there yesterday. I guess Vicente didn't know about that, either, because he didn't challenge Brinton's claim that it wasn't much."

Harp put on a T-shirt and sat down next to her to put on his socks and boots. "Did Brinton say anything to give the show away? I mean, after Vicente was gone?"

"No, and that's what really bothers me," Katie complained. "I was ready to jump in and admit my complicity, but he never gave me a chance. He just turned and walked out without another word to anybody."

"Maybe it's not a show. Maybe he's not winking the way Rick said he would."

"Then he's going to have a mutiny on his hands," Katie predicted, with a notable lack of enthusiasm.

Harp grunted and picked his wet jeans up off the floor. He removed the belt and began to go through the pockets, immediately coming upon the wadded-up ten-dollar bill. "That's the ten bucks Rick bet me it wouldn't rain today," he said wryly, spreading it open on his knee. He reached into the change pocket and came up with a sodden slip of paper that began to pill and come apart in his hand. The ink marks on it had bled into an illegible blur. "Oh, shit," he said succinctly.

"What's that?" Katie asked.

Harp rolled it between his fingers and flicked it at the wall, where it stuck like a spitball. Then he let out a guilty sigh. "That *was* the bag number of a sherd I stole from the lab."

He felt Katie staring at him and looked down at his boots, which appeared large and clumsy. When she finally spoke, it was in a musing tone that surprised him. "So you took it after all. Good for you."

"What? Are you telling me you knew?"

"I know everything that goes on in the lab," Katie said with a mysterious smile. "Remember that the next time you feel the urge for a souvenir. Now tell me about the sherd. Even without the bag number, we can probably place it on the basis of date and style."

"It was a complete anomaly, a perfect water lily in a bag of utilitarian ware."

"All the better. Lemme have a look at it; I might know where it really belongs."

"Ah." Harp looked away for a moment. "That's another problem."

"You lost it."

"Not exactly. I gave it to Lord of Shells. You know, the chief of the people I met in the forest," Harp added when she looked at him blankly. "I was trying to show him what we were digging for out there. He assumed it was a gift."

"Like the Tootsie Rolls," Katie said and started to laugh.

Harp blushed and shrugged. "What can I say? These things happen."

"Only to you," Katie insisted, shaking with laughter. "God, talk about confusing the archaeological record! No wonder you never told anybody that part of the story."

"I didn't think it would win me any points at the time," Harp admitted. "I must say, you're taking it better than I expected."

Katie took several deep breaths, holding her side. "I didn't think anything could make me laugh today. First the snake, then the storm, then this. I feel like everything's going haywire."

"Let's go to lunch," Harp suggested, pocketing the ten dollars and helping her to her feet. "Maybe Brinton's settled down and remembered how to wink."

Katie picked up her umbrella and shook it as they headed for the door. "If not, we'll have to teach him how."

LUNCH WAS a less-than-jolly affair, with Brinton and Ulysses eating at opposite ends of the table and neither saying a word to anyone about Rana Verde. Ulysses's silence was aggrieved and sullen while Brinton's seemed briskly oblivious, as if he'd resolved something for himself. The other people around the table felt compelled to avoid the subject as well, though there was an undercurrent of unslaked curiosity that expressed itself in roving glances and whispered asides. Everyone had heard something about what had happened, but there hadn't been time to put it all together and run it through the rumor mill. Brinton's refusal to offer an official explanation seemed ominous to Harp, an attempt to starve the mill and bypass camp opinion. It seemed to indicate that this wasn't a show, and that Brinton really intended to hang Ulysses out to dry.

During coffee, Brinton left his place and went around the table, announcing that there would be a senior staff meeting in fifteen minutes, and that everyone else could use the rest of the day as they saw fit. "Don't squander your energy," he advised. "We'll undoubtedly have a lot of digging out to do tomorrow."

The students didn't waste any time heading for the door, and Harp figured the rumor mill would be going full blast in a matter of minutes, a squandering of energy Brinton himself had made inevitable. Harp thought he'd go back to his hut and write down his impressions of the storm, and he'd just turned to say so to Katie when Brinton came up behind them.

"You might as well stay too, Mr. Yates," he said in a rather sardonic tone. "You started this, after all."

Brinton resumed his circuit of the table, leaving Harp staring after him in bemusement. "Jesus," Harp murmured to Katie. "You think he really believes that?"

"I couldn't tell," Katie confessed.

Lucy leaned forward to look at Harp. "You saw 'em first," she pointed out. "And you're still the only one who did."

"Yeah?" Harp said, glancing across the table at Brinton, who was talking to Emory Muldoon. "That's what he thinks."

"Whattaya mean?" Lucy demanded swiftly, smelling a secret.

"Go ask Lovely Rita," Harp suggested. "She was at Rana Verde yesterday."

"Did she see 'em too?"

"Go ask her. Do it privately, or she might not wanna tell you."

"Don't get wet again!" Katie called after her, but Lucy was already rounding the end of the table and didn't look back. Katie raised an eyebrow at Harp. "I hope you didn't make that up just to tease her. She wants to see some Indians in the worst way."

"She'll probably get her chance," Harp said as he stood up. "Because they're out there, whether Brinton likes it or not. It's not something I had to make up."

"But you saw them again yesterday?"

"We all did. I woulda told you, but Helga decided we should keep it to ourselves."

Katie whistled in amazement and stood up with him. "Even Helga. That's why this's gotten so out of hand. Everybody's keeping secrets from everybody else."

"That may be about to end," Harp said with a grim smile. "Let's go join the peanut gallery, the show's about to begin . . ."

THEY ASSEMBLED in the reading area at the end of the dining hall, where a motley collection of furniture was clustered around the bookshelves that held the camp library. Brinton sat in a fan-backed wicker chair with Helga Kauffmann and Oliver Clubb in armchairs to his right and Ulysses and Muldoon on the tattered loveseat to his left. Harp, Katie, Rick, and Kaaren were squeezed together on the long sofa that faced Brinton and the windows behind him. Brinton hiked up his pant leg and crossed an ankle on the opposite knee, appearing completely at ease, unaffected by the tension Harp could feel running through the group like a low current.

"You know I'm not much of a believer in staff meetings," Brinton began with a small smile. "But a number of you requested this, and I can understand the reasons for your concern. I've asked Mr. Yates to join us because he's still the only witness to the existence of our uninvited guests. And because I believe his impulsive generosity upon first encounter has set a precedent that seems to have governed the behavior of several others. Despite my warnings, a pattern of enticement was established that culminated today in a near-revolt of our salaried workers. I want to make clear to you—as I did to Vicente—that this mode of behavior has come to an end and will not be revived."

Brinton paused, apparently to let his audience assimilate the message, since the steely certainty of his tone didn't invite argument or protest. They all listened to the patter of rain on the thatched roof for a few moments before he turned to his right. "Helga, you were one of those who requested this meeting. Perhaps you'd like to begin."

"I would prefer to hear from those more directly involved," Helga demurred. Brinton nodded and spread his hands open to the rest of the group, recognizing Kaaren when she raised a finger.

"Is it true that Ulysses has been removed as the crew chief at Rana Verde?"

"It is," Brinton acknowledged. "He knew what I would think of his attempts to lure these people out of hiding, and he should have anticipated how the workers would react. He was both willful and careless, a wholly irresponsible combination in a crew chief."

"He didn't do this on his own, though," Kaaren said. "We discussed it as a crew, and we were unanimous in our decision to help. If what he did is a crime, then we're all guilty of it."

"Do you feel, then, that you should share his punishment?" Brinton inquired. "Because in that case I'd be forced to close Rana Verde down for the remainder of the season. It's a possibility I'm contemplating anyhow."

Brinton's steely tone had taken on a decidedly condescending edge, as if he were speaking to a naughty child, and Kaaren pursed her lips, her cheeks coloring. "That would be a very bad decision at this point," she said tersely.

"I have to agree with that," Rick put in, polite but troubled. "We'd be leaving it wide open for looters just as we're about to find out what's there."

"I recognize the drawbacks," Brinton assured him. "But we might be leaving ourselves open to even greater problems if we continue our involvement with these refugees." He looked back at Kaaren. "And if what I'm hearing from you is representative of the feelings of the rest of the crew, I don't know how I could trust you to stay *un*involved."

Katie put up her hand with a force that startled him, so that she was already speaking before he managed a nod. "I'm also guilty of trying to help these people. I had some qualms about it, but I'd listened very carefully to your speech and I never heard you say—*clearly*—that we weren't allowed to leave food for them. To make that a crime after the fact and punish people for it . . . well, to call that a 'bad' decision is being too generous. To put it bluntly, Brinton, it's unfair and it stinks."

For the first time, Brinton appeared ruffled, and when he had no immediate reply, Clubb jumped to his defense.

"Perhaps you listened *too* carefully, Katie," Clubb suggested. "The import of his words was certainly clear to me. We were to avoid contact with these people, not seek it out."

Ulysses finally flared to life on the other side of the circle, waving a hand in disgust. "We didn't seek out anything. All we did was leave them food. We didn't stick around to watch them eat. Yates is still the only one who's seen them."

"That is no longer the case," Helga Kauffmann said, quietly but with a firmness that arrested the conversation. She looked right at Brinton. "All of us who were at Rana Verde yesterday afternoon saw them. We watched them take what had been left for them and leave the frog in return, a clear exchange of gifts."

"You *saw* them?" Brinton repeated incredulously. "You saw them and you didn't feel you should tell me?"

"We saw nothing to be gained in telling anyone," Helga said. "We made contact only with our eyes. But it is foolish to think it will stop there. These people need the help we can offer them, and I expect they will come to us again. Rather than wishing they would go away, we should be preparing ourselves to talk with them."

"Right on," Harp said under his breath, adding to the general murmur of approval. Brinton closed his eyes for a moment, pinching the bridge of his nose between thumb and forefinger.

"Do you know what you're suggesting? What the consequences might be?"

"I've thought of little else since yesterday afternoon," Helga told him. "I could foresee great complications for our work here. But I also considered what the consequences might be for them if we refused to help." She paused as if to allow him to consider as well. "They could starve or, more likely, perish slowly from malnutrition and disease. I compared that with what we might suffer, and the comparison was too plainly absurd. If you thought for an instant that our work was endangering the lives of the crew, I know you would shut down without hesitation. Are the lives of these people worth any less than our own? Would you let them die simply to avoid the risk of complicating our work?"

"For heaven's sake, Helga!" Clubb protested. "We don't know anything about these people. We certainly don't know they're going to starve to death if we don't help them."

"We know they're hungry," Helga replied.

"So are thousands of others in both Mexico and Guatemala," Clubb shot back. "Are we responsible for them, too? Or just for the ones who happen to wander onto our site?"

"Those are questions you must ask yourself," Helga advised. "I would certainly think we are responsible for those who come to us for help, when it is in our power to provide it." She looked back at Brinton. "That is another consequence you must consider: What will we think of ourselves if we turn our backs on them now? What kind of people does that make *us*?"

Brinton rubbed his chin, squinting at her ruefully. Then he looked around at the rest of the group. "Is this how the rest of you feel as well? Emory? You haven't spoken yet."

Muldoon nodded with a measure of reluctance, the way he did when a line of speculation was running too far beyond the evidence. "Well, I'm not sure how much we can actually help these people, since we're not permanent residents and we don't have any influence with the Guatie government. But I didn't see any harm in supplementing their diet for a while, and I didn't expect it to cause such a fuss. I think Arturo went off half-cocked, and then Vicente got upset because he had to hear it from his boys rather than from you. That's a loss of face for him. But really, Brinton, what was he gonna do? We employ half the village; it's not like he can walk out and find other jobs for them. And he's not gonna go complain to Immigration. He doesn't want the *federales* nosing around any more than we do."

Brinton was holding himself very erect, and the stiffness came through in his voice. "You're saying I overreacted."

"Well . . . yeah, I'm afraid so," Muldoon admitted. "But I think I could square it with Vicente without too much trouble, if you'd like. He knows it's in everybody's interest to resolve this locally."

Brinton exhaled audibly but didn't otherwise respond to Muldoon's offer. Instead he turned his gaze on Rick. "Richard?"

Rick spread his hands in a plaintive shrug, as if bowing to the facts. "In retrospect, this seems inevitable. But at the time, I figured you had good reason not to lay down any strict rules. Maybe the problem would resolve itself. And you've always given us plenty of room to exercise our own judgment, so I assumed you were giving it to us here. Obviously, a lot of people felt they should help. I don't think anyone did it with the intention of embarrassing you or jeopardizing the project."

"So you also knew this was going on," Brinton concluded.

Rick seemed taken aback and could only stare at him for a moment. "Well . . . yeah," he admitted, looking pained.

"So much for the exercise of judgment," Brinton said curtly. He seemed to jerk his eyes away from Rick, then let them settle on Harp. "Mr. Yates? You're not staff, but you're seldom without an opinion."

It was the kind of thing Brinton said to him all the time, though usually with a smile. Now there was no smile to take the edge off the implicit scorn, and it stung. He felt himself flush, which only made him angrier.

"No, I'm not staff," he agreed. "And I'm probably the last person whose judgment you'd trust. But since you asked, I'd like to second what Helga, Rick, and Katie said. You've obviously hired a bunch of generous, good-hearted people, people who aren't afraid to do what they think is right."

"No matter what *I* think?" Brinton interrupted.

"We didn't know what you thought," Harp told him. "But even if we did, we'd still have to decide for ourselves. Isn't that what Nuremberg was all about?"

"Nuremberg!" Brinton exploded, coming to his feet with an abruptness that sent the wicker chair over backward. "Now I'm certain the inmates have taken over the asylum! Run it yourselves, then. Exercise your superior collective judgment."

"Brinton, please!" Helga cried, but he'd already stepped around her chair and was out the door before anyone could move to stop him. Clubb stood up a moment later, his brow bunched like a fist.

"That was disgraceful," he seethed. "Disloyal and disrespectful. You should all be ashamed of yourselves."

Ulysses growled something that sounded like "eat shit" as Clubb stalked out of the dining hall, but everyone else was too stunned by Brinton's departure to react. Had he howled as he had in Harp's dream, he could hardly have shocked them more.

"Well," Muldoon began, but couldn't complete the thought.

"This is all my fault," Helga said, bobbing her head in remorse. "I should never have surprised him like that. I should have spoken to him last night, in private."

"No," Katie disagreed. "He should've called this meeting a week ago. He always likes to play everything so goddam close to the vest. Only this time he wasn't holding any of the right cards."

"He's never been afraid to admit a mistake before," Muldoon said, finally finding some words for his astonishment. "I thought we were helping him set it right."

With a twitch of restlessness, Ulysses got up and went around behind the loveseat. "So whatta we do now? Go ask him to forgive us? Or try to run things ourselves?"

He was looking at Rick, who slid off the sofa and went to stand in front of Brinton's overturned chair. Rick's face was red and a vein pulsed in his right temple; Harp recognized his grimly determined expression as the one Rick wore whenever someone had let him down or violated his sense of how to act. Harp had done both at various times in the past and he knew there'd be no equivocation now, no surrender to disappointment.

"I think we take him at his word until he tells us otherwise," Rick said to Ulysses. Then he pointed a finger at Muldoon. "The first thing we have to do is get Vicente back on board. You think you can do that?"

"Sure," Muldoon said. "We just have to be straight with him and let him know what we're up to."

Rick nodded. "How about we put him on the Rana Verde crew for a while? So he's there if a meeting occurs."

"Good idea," Muldoon agreed. "He speaks a bunch of Mayan dialects, which could help a lot."

"Yeah, we gotta do a little better than Tootsie Roll diplomacy," Rick said sardonically, permitting himself a brief smile. "I thought maybe you'd like to join the crew too, Helga. You know more Mayan than anyone else on the staff."

"Except perhaps for Brinton," Helga said sadly. "But yes, I'd like to be there."

"Good. What else?" Rick asked, then caught the squinty-eyed look Ulysses was giving him. "Shit, I thought that went without saying: You're back on as crew chief. But hey, let's go out there to do some work, and let them come to us, okay?"

"Okay by me," Ulysses said. Rick looked around at the others, drawing a nod of agreement from each of them. Then he nodded himself and exhaled forcefully, as if some hard and thankless duty had been fulfilled.

"So that's it," he said, bringing the meeting to a close. "It's in our hands now. Let's handle it with care."

14

The poets down here don't write nothin' at all, they just stand back and let it all be.

—Bruce Springsteen, "Jungleland"

Baktun

DECIDING IT was time to create his own lull in the work, Harp straightened up from the screening box. Or at least he tried to. His back had begun to lock down in protest of the steady intensity of his labors, and he had to brace himself with both hands to come fully erect. He looked over at the grid, his eyes smarting from sweat and the fumes of bug dope rising from his clothes. Rick was down on one knee, checking the level attached to the grid line. Eric was inside the square of white string, pecking gingerly with the heavy pick, while Brad stood outside leaning on a shovel. Harp did a little visual reckoning, noting that the grid was still a couple feet above the floor of the trench. Behind it—between them and the wall panel—was another four feet of super-compacted shit, terraced up to a height of perhaps ten feet.

Kaaren finally realized he wasn't helping and looked up from the box. "What's wrong?"

"Just my back. It's asking what it did to deserve this."

Kaaren laughed and nodded, taking off her work gloves and beating them together. "We might be overdoing it a bit," she agreed. "Nothing like the threat of a shutdown to renew your sense of urgency. But you were looking sort of wistful there for a moment."

"Was I? I was just realizing it's Thursday, and look where we are. Even if we keep working like lunatics, I'm probably not gonna be around to see the wall panel."

"When're you leaving—Monday? I hear you're driving to Villahermosa with Ollie Clubb."

"Andrew's going too," Harp told her. "We're splitting the cost of a rental car three ways. I can just guess how we'll split the driving."

"Heads up!" Brad interrupted, coming toward them with a clump of compacted dirt the size of a basketball balanced on the end of his shovel. He dumped it into the screening box with a flip of his wrists, and the taut screen creaked and sagged under its weight.

"Don't make it too easy for us, Animal," Harp said as he reached into the wheelbarrow for the handpick.

"Sorry," Brad said absently, already turning away. "I can get more in the shovel if I don't break it up."

Harp buried the end of the pick in the clump and rocked back and forth until the mass of dirt and clay split and crumbled into several large pieces. Kaaren began to chop at them with her trowel, producing a metallic ring whenever she struck a fine paste sherd.

"If you *do* get to see the panel," she said, "you'll just have Clubb pumping you for details all the way to the airport. I assume he's going back to rush the latest version of Ollie's Folly into print."

"I dunno; he said something about a deadline for a grant. I was frankly surprised he asked me after the run-in we had."

"Pocketbook amnesia," Kaaren suggested wryly. "You know, it occurred to me after the staff meeting that he might've been perfectly happy to see us shut down for the season. Then no one could undercut his interpretation for at least another year."

Harp cracked a big lump with the blunt end of the pick and looked across the box at her. "I'm not sure he's *that* big an asshole. Has anyone told him yet about the pots Ulysses found yesterday?"

"I don't think he's asked. He's still treating us like traitors to the cause."

By unspoken agreement, they put down their tools and shook the box between them, Harp tightening his stomach muscles against the twinges in his back, his face averted from the rising dust. As usual, the screen was left littered with stuff: pebbles, sherds, bits of white plaster and yellowed bone, shiny flakes of obsidian and gnarled strands of ancient root. Yesterday they'd found some pieces of red shell and a fragment of a jade ear flare, lending weight to Helga Kauffmann's suspicion that all the trash from around the temple had been dumped into this special fill.

"Oh, look at this," Kaaren said suddenly, plucking something off the screen. Harp craned forward over the box to see the piece she held out on her gloved palm. It was a shiny, translucent black, shaped like a cursive letter V with a short, jagged stem at the apex. "Looks like a piece of an obsidian eccentric. You've seen those, haven't you? Some of them look like branches from a volcanic tree."

"Burial goods," Harp said, nodding. "Helga's right. She thinks they may even have dug up the dedicatory caches from the temple."

"I wish she were still here," Kaaren murmured, pulling the piece back for a closer look. "She could probably tell us what kind of obsidian this is."

Helga had been summoned to the eastern range-wall trench yesterday afternoon. Actually, they'd all gone over to see the first of what appeared to be another row of terminated pots. The arrangement was identical to what'd been done on this side of the ball court, only these pots were late Baktun polychrome rather than foreign fine paste. Helga had stayed to begin digging them out, and the rest of the crew had gone back to work with renewed lunacy, high on the excitement of the find.

"You think there's a wall panel on the other side, too?" he asked Kaaren, who was carefully tucking the obsidian into a plastic bag.

"I wouldn't be surprised. They've been consistently symmetrical in most other ways." She gave him a teasing smile. "We'll send you pictures of both of them."

"That's assuming some of you survive. I mean, I think it's great that we've recaptured our frontier spirit, but this's like being prospectors during the Gold Rush, with the claim jumpers closing in."

Kaaren laughed. "Don't forget the Indians."

"I probably won't get to see *them,* either," Harp grumbled.

"C'mon, admit it, this's what it's all about. Working hard and making big finds. You know you're damned lucky to spend your last week back out on the cutting edge."

Harp shrugged and smiled. "You've got a point. Not that my back is persuaded."

"You're gonna miss this once you're back in the civilized world."

"I'll console myself with air conditioning and cold beer. Think of a clean bathroom with a flush toilet, a hot shower, and no snakes. Think of clean sheets . . ."

"You'll miss it," Kaaren insisted, holding out a paper bag to him. "Fine paste."

Harp checked the sherds in his hand and dropped them all in. "Yeah, I'll miss it," he confessed. "I'll miss the people most of all."

Kaaren opened her mouth, then closed it with a sad frown. "I was going to say you could always come back next season. But I'm not sure any of us will be invited back."

"Naw, c'mon," Harp coaxed. "Brinton can't stay mad forever, and he can't fire the whole staff. You'll all make up sooner or later."

"Rick's not so sure of that. He feels like the leader of a coup."

"Brinton'll be grateful to him for keeping the place going. Wait and see. I can't, of course, but I don't think he's gonna forgive me real soon, after the Nuremberg crack."

"He was looking for a reason to stomp out."

"Right, and he knew who would give him a good one," Harp said with a rueful laugh. "It's probably just as well. I'll be in the middle of a novel by next season and won't wanna leave it."

"Well, we should give you some kind of send-off, since you're going to miss the end-of-season party. Hmm, maybe you should have a termination party."

"Yeah . . . *yeah,*" Harp said with fast-growing enthusiasm. "We could get a little crazy, break some pots and deface some monuments, maybe bury my hut. The works."

"Speaking of work," Kaaren prompted with a smile. Harp nodded and got down to picking through the debris in the box. He decided he could rest his back on the plane. In the meantime, there was no telling what might turn up, out here on the cutting edge.

Washington, D.C.

SINCE SHE HAD no classes on Thursday, Caroline usually spent the day doing research at the Library of Congress. On this Thursday, however, she drove past Capitol Hill and went instead to the East Wing of the National Gallery, where there was a Kandinsky exhibit. Then she wandered across the Mall to the Freer Gallery and walked through an exhibition of Buddhist temple art, gazing at the elaborate mandalas and serenely smiling Buddhas without bothering to read any of the explanatory material. On the way back to her car, she paused frequently to enjoy the views of the Capitol building and the Washington Monument. It was a mild, blustery day, with puffy white clouds scudding by overhead and pink cherry blossoms floating through the air like confetti. Something was blooming or budding just about everywhere she looked, and she let herself stare like a tourist.

She had lunch at the American Café in Georgetown and then spent two hours in Conran's department store, pricing home furnishings with the Langdon house specifically in mind. It was another kind of research, but the time went by too swiftly and pleasurably for her to think of it in those terms. She found she was able to empty the rooms as she'd seen them and then decorate them to her own taste, an exercise of the imagination she hadn't known was among her skills.

Finally she drove to the National Zoo and wandered around with deliberate aimlessness, ignoring the signs and letting herself be surprised by whatever was in the next cage. The orangutans and gibbons kept her entertained for a solid half hour, and she was lucky enough to see one of the famous pandas execute a series of somersaults while simultaneously munching on bamboo leaves. But then she found herself staring in at a sleek black feline that suddenly stopped its pacing and fixed her with a baleful yellow gaze that made her feel like nothing more than live meat.

Caroline shivered and stepped back, taking a peek at the plaque on the guardrail. It identified the creature as a black jaguar, and the map of its remaining habitat included that part of Mexico where Harp was currently residing. The jaguar stared at her for another moment, then bared its teeth in a soundless snarl and resumed its restless circuit of the cage. It was heavy-bodied but moved silently on large, tufted paws, and as it passed through a shaft of sunlight, Caroline could see the spots beneath the black. *The Night-Sun Jaguar,* she thought, remembering how casually Harp had once tossed that out to her, showing off his knowledge of Mayan cosmology. She shivered again, thinking of him running into the real thing out in the jungle, without any bars to separate author from what he'd only thought of as a symbol.

After that, she couldn't get Harp out of her mind and had to accept that the spell had been broken. She'd intended to treat herself to a celebratory dinner at Mrs. Simpson's, a restaurant only a few blocks from the zoo, but she didn't think she could stand to have only the waiter to talk to. She'd used up her quotient of wordless self-indulgence and needed to *tell* someone and get some verbal reward.

So she popped a Joni Mitchell tape into the deck and headed back to New Belvedere, picking up some Chinese food on the way. She was only halfway through the crispy duck when she realized whom she should call. She also realized she might change her mind if she thought about it for too long, so she wrapped up the duck, got herself another glass of wine, and dialed her sister's office number at the University of British Columbia. It was about 4 P.M. Pacific Time, and she knew Janet often worked in her office until dinnertime.

"Carrie?" Janet asked, performing the verbal equivalent of a double take. "Are you okay?"

"Never better," Caroline assured her. "I called to share some good news, if you've got a minute."

"Of course I do, if you really want to talk. You weren't very responsive the last time I called you. You didn't answer my letter, either."

"I'm sorry, Janet, truly I am. I was trying to deal with a whole lot of uncertainty at that point, and I just wasn't ready to talk about it."

"And now you are? That must mean you've already accepted a job."

"Not yet. I've been offered two, actually, but the one I want didn't come through until this morning."

"I suppose I should be flattered to hear the very same day," Janet said sardonically. "Dare I ask the name of the school?"

Caroline held the receiver away from her face and pretended to throttle it. She took a long sip of wine before coming back on the line. "SUNY Albany," she said in a flat voice. "And as a matter of fact, you're the first person I've called. I was thinking I owed it to you, since you were the one who took the call for so many of my major fuckups. This makes me wonder if you didn't prefer it that way."

"If you believe that, we should end this conversation right now. And never have another one."

"Help me not believe it," Caroline proposed. "Don't put me through this bullshit, acting hurt because I didn't consult with you earlier. Talk to me like a sister. We used to talk that way, you know, even when we'd been out of touch for a long time. When did we stop doing that?"

Now it was Janet's turn to be silent, and Caroline began to regret the choice she'd made. It wouldn't spoil everything if Janet hung up, but it would be a definite blot on the magic. Instead, Janet sighed audibly. "It was after you went back to the States with Harp. That's when we stopped."

"You remember?" Caroline blurted in surprise. She hadn't expected an exact date. "Do you know why?"

There was another sigh. "At the time, I was certain you were making another huge mistake and would be back in six months, heartbroken and all messed up. It seemed absolutely inconceivable that the two of you would straighten each other out and make a go of it."

"I remember you tried to talk me out of it," Caroline said. "But not real hard."

"Would you have listened?" Janet asked, with an exasperation that made the question rhetorical. "Besides, as you probably *don't* remember, at that same time I had just begun my battle for tenure here, which was making Howard act very strangely, or so I thought at the time. I didn't find out the real reason until later. In any case, I didn't have much sympathy to spare for anyone else's problems."

"Did you try to tell me any of this?" Caroline asked lamely.

"Are you kidding? You're running off with my ex-husband, and I'm going to tell you about the problems I'm having with the man I left him for? I could just see Harp smirking at that. I could see both of you smirking at the very notion of tenure, telling me not to get uptight over something so worthless. You may not remember how scornful you could be about academia—about anything that smacked of respectability—but I do."

"No, that I do remember," Caroline admitted. "It held me up for a long time when I was trying to decide if I should go to graduate school. Then I tried to make up the time by becoming a blind careerist. When Harp started acting weird, I didn't even notice it."

"Well, with Harp, it would always be hard to tell," Janet said, then softened the statement with a laugh. "Is he back from the jungle yet?"

"Next week."

Janet laughed again, with more irony. "I wrote to him, too, and told him to get back home and stop you from making a mess of your career. It sounds as if you've done quite well without him."

"I guess I have, though I've missed him terribly. He doesn't know it yet, but I've put a deposit down on a house in upstate New York."

There was a humming silence on the line, followed by the sound of Janet clearing her throat. "Excuse me, but am I still talking to my sister? The girl who always used to say that all property is theft?"

"Yes, okay, I deserve that. All I can say is that I finally found a piece I want to steal for myself. For me and Harp. I don't know if I'm selling out or just growing up, but I was suddenly seized by a great need for a home we could call our own."

"I won't ask how you plan to pay for it," Janet said dryly. "Not just yet, anyway. First I want to hear about the jobs."

Caroline let out a breath and laughed. "Back to where we started out. It took us a while, didn't it?"

"Not as long as it's taken us to talk about why we stopped talking. Now I'm glad Harp didn't listen to me. If he were there, you wouldn't have needed to call me."

"Maybe not," Caroline allowed. "That won't stop me in the future, though."

"I'll hold you to that," Janet said. There was the sound of creaking springs, as if she were settling back in her chair. "Now then, Sister Carrie, start wherever you want and be prepared for questions. I want the whole story of how my wild and crazy sister has finally brought herself to the brink of respectability."

"That's a lot to tell," Caroline said, laughing as she pulled up a chair for herself. "I think it begins the day we moved into the House of Usher, and found out what it's like to be truly homesick . . ."

Baktun

HARP HAD COAXED a Valium out of Katie the night before, and the drug had rubberized his limbs, quelled his incipient back spasms, and sent him off into a dreamless sleep. He woke at first light with the feeling that someone was in the room with him. He blinked his eyes open but saw nothing moving outside the gauzy scrim of the mosquito bar. The doorway was a blank grey rectangle blurred by the dark netting. Raising his head to look made him dizzy, but when he lay down he couldn't find his way back into sleep. His mind was already at work: reckoning whether they'd get down to the top of the wall panel today; remembering he'd promised Katie he'd take Lucy out to Rana Verde with him; wondering if he should try to call Caroline when he went into Comitán on Saturday.

He finally gave up, got dressed, and went out into the fog-ridden dawn. Stamping his feet to frighten snakes, he walked into camp and found no one up. A light was on in the kitchen of the dining hall, but the long dining room was dark. So he walked over to the Main Plaza of Group A and climbed to the top of Kan Shell's temple. He sat down next to the doorway of the shrine, feeling spacy and out of breath. Below him the roofless shells of the surrounding buildings and the tops of the monuments jutted up out of the mist that still covered the plaza floor. The absence of color made him realize the sky was overcast, the clouds formless and a solid oatmeal grey. Harp felt suddenly oppressed and wondered what he was doing up here. He didn't need to see this view again, and in his present condition he didn't look forward to the descent.

Then the wind began to blow in his face, softly at first, but then with enough force to ruffle the limp curls that bushed out from under his baseball cap. He opened his mouth and the air rushed in, filling him with a strange, uneasy buoyancy, as if he were trying to sit still on the surface of a moving trampoline. He felt nauseous and broke out in a sweat, hunching over to keep from being sick. He was in the process of swearing off Valium forever when he realized what this was. A grey wind. Maybe the *greyest* wind.

He grabbed the edge of the doorjamb and struggled to his feet, hanging on to the shrine out of fear he might be blown off the platform. Yet when he was able to turn and look out from the doorway, he found the wind wasn't all that powerful. It was his own lack of substance that made him fearful. He felt empty and weightless, a vaporous being. He could see the tops of the trees, a dark, undifferentiated mass waving in his direction, and what he experienced was no longer the mere movement of air but the pulsing of the entire sky. Dense, weblike patterns began to emerge from the grey, so vast they seemed to swallow his gaze. Before they could swallow him, as well, he closed his eyes and turned his head away, his back to the wind.

He stood leaning against the doorjamb for a long time, feeling something he had no ready name for. Chastened and humbled didn't seem to approach it. Utterly inconsequential was closer. He remembered his angry boast that he was going to bring this place back to life. As if it required resuscitation by someone like him. What did he know? What did any of them know? They drew stories out of the mute stones, out of the fragments buried where the wind couldn't touch them. But they didn't know what animated the wind, what colored the air and hummed in the blood of the people who'd lived here. They would never know any of that. Yet it was here; he could feel it. This place had been abandoned only by its humans.

The wind kept blowing, and he felt none of the euphoria that usually attended his epiphanies. Nor was he tempted to go into the shrine and perform some half-bogus ritual of recognition. If it was the presence of the gods he was feeling, he couldn't pretend to know how to approach them. Collecting what was left of his wits, he crawled out the doorway and went down the stairs on the seat of his pants, one step at a time.

WHEN HE'D MADE the deal with Katie—essentially trading the pain in his back for the pain in her butt—Harp had figured he'd probably come to regret it. Lucy had been her most obnoxious self ever since Katie had told her she was thinking of moving to another job. And Lucy knew Harp had been encouraging Katie in that direction. Given the excesses of heat and mosquitoes and the continued absence of Indians, he hadn't expected her to stick around for more than an hour or two.

Yet here they were, past the midmorning break, and Lucy had not only stuck but had found a useful role for herself. Decked out in mirrored sunglasses, a baseball cap on backward, and a pair of gardening gloves Helga Kauffmann had lent her, she was their designated clod buster, a regular hellion with a handpick. They had the wheelbarrow and screening box on top of the range wall, a short shovel's throw from the grid that was taking down the last section of midcourt fill. Taking a two-handed tennis grip on the pick, Lucy would whale away at whatever Brad or Eric tossed up, reducing it to screenable rubble with an enthusiasm that had yet to flag.

She was also picking up Harp's slack and disguising the fact that he was totally out of sync with the rest of the crew. They were about a foot and a half below the top of the range wall, digging in a controlled fury of anticipation, expecting to uncover the top of the wall panel at any moment. Harp stood above them in a state of benevolent detachment, exposed to the gusting wind and the bright blankness of the sky, his hands often busy but his spirit disengaged. It wasn't every day he had a religious experience before breakfast, and it made this feverish cataloging of dead matter seem decidedly mundane and beside the point. Everybody recognized that the ancient Maya were a deeply religious people, and then they turned back to sifting the material evidence and reconstructing the buildings and checking the calendrical calculations. All that secular stuff, verifiable but untouched by awe. And there was often more than a whiff of condescension in their attitude toward the priests, a tendency to see them as the self-serving manipulators of a naïve and superstitious populace, rather than those who could open their faces to the sky and drink in the wind, standing between the gods and those below.

"Earth to Harp," Lucy taunted, snapping him out of it. He saw that Rick had removed the screening box and was waiting for him to roll the brimming wheelbarrow away.

"You're in the traces," Rick said. "Unless your back can't take it?"

"My back's fine," Harp said truthfully, though he remembered to bend his knees and dig in with his legs as he took hold of the rubber-gripped handles and set the wheelbarrow in motion. "I'm just a spaceman today."

"You sure are," Lucy said, tagging along as he trundled the wheelbarrow along the top of the range wall. They were dumping their back dirt out on the unexcavated portion of the ball court, and the bumpiness of the path made the wheelbarrow lurch and wobble, exposing the tenuousness of his snake-armed control. "Whoa!" Lucy exclaimed. "Are you on drugs or something?"

Harp smiled, reckless but imperturbable. He'd spilled a bit but hadn't lost a whole load yet, and what if he did? Would the gods love him any less for his ineptitude?

"Something!" he shouted suddenly, using the momentum imparted by a downward slope in the path to kick into a run, the wheelbarrow veering wildly from side to side but finally hitting the pile straight on, flipping itself over in an automatic unload. Lucy ran up laughing and he gave her a high five and impulsively swept her up in a hug. She squealed but hung on tight as he whirled her around once and set her down on her feet. They paused to catch their breath, giggling at the astonished looks they were getting from the rest of the crew.

"You're crazy!" Lucy gasped.

"I'm gonna miss you, too," Harp said, surprising both of them by giving the teasing statement a resonant edge of sincerity.

"Really?"

"Really." He squinted at her wryly. "At least I'll miss the Lucy I'm talking to right now. Not the one who's been such a pain in the ass lately."

He bent to right the wheelbarrow and turn it around.

"Did my mother tell you to talk to me?" Lucy asked warily.

"Nope. She just wanted some relief from the bitching." Harp got the wheelbarrow rolling with Lucy walking beside him. "But look at the way you fit yourself in out here. What makes you think you can't do that somewhere else?"

"I won't *know* anybody somewhere else!"

"Not at first, but you'll make new friends. That can be exciting, and it's something your mother needs to do right now. She's been in Pittsburgh a long time and it's gotten kind of stale for her."

"She just wants to meet new men," Lucy said disdainfully.

Harp gave her a sidelong glance. "You aren't gonna begrudge her that, are ya? You're gonna be going out on dates yourself in a few years. You want her sitting home alone with nothing better to do than worry about whether you get home on time? The happier she is with herself, the more she's gonna let you do."

"But what if the new place doesn't make her happy? Then we would've moved for nothing."

"Sometimes that's the chance you gotta take," Harp said. "All I'm saying, Luce, is why fight it? Go with the flow. It's not the last time you're gonna move in your life, so you might as well start getting good at it."

They turned back onto the range wall. Ahead, Rick and Kaaren were crouched on the edge of the wall, looking down at Brad and Eric, who were squatting inside the grid. Another find, Harp thought absently. He gave Lucy an expectant glance.

"Go with the flow?" she repeated scornfully, as if he'd laid a nursery rhyme on her. "Did you just make that up?"

Harp laughed and brought the wheelbarrow to a halt in its previous spot. "Hardly. It's a motto some of us used to live by. It means don't get in your own way. Be open to new experiences."

Rick suddenly stood up and turned to them. "Hey, take a look at this. Looks like a cache."

Kaaren had gotten down into the grid and was working with a dental pick and a soft brush around the circular orange rim of a buried pot. Sticking up inside the rim was what looked like the tip of a deer antler. Dead matter, Harp thought, but knew better than to say it aloud. Kaaren sat back on her heels and looked up at Rick.

"Maybe we should get Helga over to help with this."

Rick shrugged. "We could, but we'd just lose more time waiting. Might as well do it ourselves. We can't take it down any further without getting that out." He turned to Harp. "Might not get to the wall panel today, after all."

"I'll probably survive," Harp said. He realized Lucy wasn't beside him and turned to see her standing on the other side of the wheelbarrow, staring in the direction of the supply tent. Staring at the people who had gathered in front of the tent. Harp reached back and tapped Rick on the shoulder. "Take a look at *this.* I think the wall panel—and everything else—can wait."

THE TWO GROUPS met in front of the supply tent, Ulysses coming to a halt about five feet away from the man Harp called Lord of Shells. The latter held his musket pointed toward the ground, and he and the people behind him had obviously dressed up for the occasion, supplementing their ragged everyday clothes with brightly colored belts and shawls and sprays of feathers. Lord of Shells himself was wearing a conical hat covered with blue and green feathers, a stiff white vest with flower patterns in fluorescent pink and green, a wide red sash around his waist, and a bunch of necklaces around his neck, some strung with glass beads and others bearing religious medals, including a small silver crucifix. On his left wrist was an enormous gold-plated watch that looked fake even at a distance. Harp squinted at the slick shine given off by the vest and saw it'd been laminated in clear plastic.

Ulysses appeared drab and dirty in comparison, though Lord of Shells seemed fascinated by the elaborate implement belt around his waist and the skull-and-roses logo on his T-shirt. Ulysses said hello in Spanish and then introduced Vicente, who addressed the man in tentative Mayan, apparently trying out various dialects until he found one that worked. Then he gave a short speech that sounded welcoming, gesturing to himself and his companions in an obvious explanation of who they were. The only word Harp understood was "*norteamericanos.*"

"It is a variant of the local Chol," Helga Kauffmann explained to those around her, keeping her voice low. She cocked her head to listen as Lord of Shells responded. When he went on at some length, she began to translate in snatches. "His name is Manik . . . they come from a village called Yaxna, Blue House . . . across the river in Guatemala. They were driven out of their homes by the army. Umm, something about guns . . . they were supposed to be soldiers but no one gave them any guns? They are good Catholics, not communists."

The man named Manik repeated the last statement a second time, and Vicente nodded respectfully before turning to speak in Spanish to Ulysses and Rick. Harp used the interlude to take a head count. There were the other two men he'd seen in the forest, including the one now wearing his sweatshirt like a cape; a frail old man whose long grey hair hung loose over his stooped shoulders; six women of various ages, from teenage to elderly; and five children, one an infant peeping out of the shawl slung over his mother's back. Harp had never felt more like an intruder from another world, and it made him think of the Skull People meeting the Baktunis for the first time. He glanced down at Lucy, who was standing very erect, hugging Helga's incense ladle against her chest. She'd pushed her sunglasses up onto the top of her head and was studying the other people so intently she didn't notice him at all. If she felt like an intruder, she clearly wasn't going to let it get in the way of the experience.

"Did you catch all of that?" Ulysses said to Helga when Vicente had finished. Helga nodded and turned to Lucy, getting her to hold the ladle out so she could light it with her Zippo. Then the two of them stepped forward, the smoking ladle shaking slightly in Lucy's hands. Helga greeted Manik in Mayan, lapsing into Spanish only to describe herself, with typical modesty, as "*la maestra* Helga Kauffmann." Manik listened with an astonishment he couldn't conceal, his eyes darting from Helga to the ladle and back again. He bowed and turned as if to summon someone from his group, but the old man was already coming forward. Harp had barely given him a glance earlier, taking his sleepy, incurious expression as a sign of either ill health or senility. Now his eyes were wide and alert, and with his hooked nose and sunken, nearly toothless mouth, he bore a striking resemblance to the smoking shaman Harp had seen on the Palenque wall panel.

The man stopped and made a kind of a bow to Helga, examining her and then Lucy for what seemed like several minutes. Then he reached into the pouch suspended from his spotted black belt and sprinkled something into the ladle, causing it to flare up with a greenish light that very nearly startled Lucy into dropping the whole works. But she held on gamely until he extended his arms and gently lifted the ladle from her hands. All of the people behind him lowered their heads and Harp did likewise, though he kept an eye cocked to watch as the old man turned to the east and presented the ladle with a vigorous flourish, chanting in a high, scratchy voice. Then he presented it to the other three directions, and to the earth underfoot and the sky overhead, the smoke swirling around him and vanishing on the wind. Harp felt dizzy and reminded himself to breathe, coughing when he caught a strong whiff of copal.

When he was done the old man looked down at Lucy, who somehow had the presence of mind to hold out her hands for the ladle, which he gave her with what seemed a nod of approval. Then he crossed his arms on his chest and spoke to Helga in Mayan. She listened and murmured a reply before translating aloud.

"He is Ch'ul Balam, Holy Jaguar. He is their . . . shaman, we would call it. He says it is safe now to mingle and talk."

Ch'ul Balam said something to Manik, who nodded and then looked at Ulysses and smiled for the first time. That let everyone relax, and the two groups broke their ceremonial ranks and converged with shy smiles. Lucy returned the ladle to Helga and went to greet the couple of children around her own age, taking off her glasses and cap and shaking out her hair. The women clustered around Kaaren, marveling at her blondness and darting timorous glances at Brad and Eric, who finally squatted down so as not to seem so imposing. Harp was watching all this like a spectator when he found himself face-to-face with the man wearing his sweatshirt.

The man had stuck some macaw feathers into the peak of the hood that surrounded his round face, making him look a bit like a Mayan Robin Hood. The sleeves of the sweatshirt wrapped around under his arms and across the chest of an embroidered guayabera, and the tasseled ends of his striped belt hung almost to his knees. He was wearing sandals with automobile-tire soles and was holding his machete down along the side of his leg.

"*Me llamo* Harper," Harp said with a smile, jerking a thumb at his own chest.

"Mo'," the man said with a similar gesture and a smile that made him look about seventeen. He ignored Harp's attempt at a handshake and held out his left wrist, displaying a watch with a blank black face. He tucked the machete under the other arm and pressed the side of the watch, which flashed a time of 3:15 P.M., some four hours ahead of Harp's old Timex.

"Digital," Harp said admiringly, and Mo' grinned and nodded, accepting the term as a compliment.

Helga and Ch'ul Balam had taken seats on the ground, facing each other across the cold ladle, and Helga looked up and interrupted the tentative conversations around her. "Someone should go for Brinton, if he will come."

There was a general exchange of reluctant glances, and then Harp found both Rick and Ulysses looking at him.

"Aw, c'mon, you guys . . ."

"You did it the first time," Ulysses pointed out.

"And you're outta here next week, anyway," Rick added.

"Shit," Harp said, turning back to Mo', who was regarding him quizzically. How to explain this? Harp had a better idea and tried it out on Helga. "What if Mo' here came with me? Brinton might find it a little harder to turn me down."

Helga spoke to Ch'ul Balam, who asked several questions and took his time thinking it over. Then he stood up and spoke to Mo', apparently explaining the task, and Mo' nodded in compliance. Ch'ul Balam slowly turned his gaze on Harp, looking him up and down before seeking out his eyes and staring into them. Harp stared back, trying not to seem too bold but not too shifty, either, wondering if the old man had the power to look into the soul of a foreigner. There was certainly nothing shy about his gaze, which was as unwavering as a searchlight. The way Lord of Shells looked at me, Harp thought, and suddenly felt young and impertinent. He gave in with a bow, but as he lowered his gaze, he saw the hand curled at the man's chest, two gnarled fingers holding an amulet strung on one of the necklaces around his neck. Harp focused on it with extraordinary clarity, seeing the delicate black strokes that outlined the water lily and even the tiny hole they'd drilled through the sherd to string it. He straightened up in surprise, blinking at Ch'ul Balam, who gave him a toothless smile and spoke a few words to Helga.

"You may go," Helga told him. "Are you all right?"

"I'm fine," Harp said, though he was still a little dazed by the abrupt shift of focus. He had the impression Ch'ul Balam was laughing at him, though not in an unkindly way.

"Do your best to persuade him, Mr. Yates," Helga added. "Tell him that I feel this is extremely important."

"Will do," Harp promised, and started to lead Mo' off through the crowd. Ulysses stopped him to ask if he had any cigarettes, and Harp gave him what was left in his pack, keeping a few out for himself and Mo'.

"Where you going, Harp?" Lucy asked, as he and Mo' went past her and her new friends, one of whom was wearing the mirrored glasses.

"We're going to get Brinton. Will you be okay until I get back?"

"Are you kidding?"

"That's what I thought," Harp said and waved good-bye over his shoulder.

"Go with the flow, Harpo!" she called after him, and he smiled and kept walking.

THEY'D JUST PASSED the ancillary path to Harp's hut, sticking to the most direct route to camp, when Mo' decided to tell him the story of his recent trip back to Yaxna.

"Harpo, *narrador,*" he said solemnly, using the term Harp had come up with when "*novelista*" hadn't rung any bells.

"Mo', *campesino,*" Harp said with equal respect, nodding when Mo' pointed to his ear and then made scribbling motions. You can bet he'd listen and write it down later, though listening was only one part of how they communicated. The rest involved interpreting simple signs and paying close attention to the acting out of events, a rather rigorous version of charades. Mo' was both enormously curious and endlessly inventive, and he'd made Harp work hard, forcing him to focus all his attention on what was in front of him. Harp's neck was stiff from all the sidelong watching and he could've used another meditation to clear his mind out, but he had to admit that Mo' was a walking antidote for the dissociative effects of the grey wind.

Now Mo' was walking with his chest puffed out, demonstrating the pride he'd felt in being asked to go back to his village alone. Apparently Manik—his brother-in-law and a man he revered—had entrusted him with this task. Then Mo' ducked down into a near crouch in a pantomime of stealth, and Harp slowed with him. Shading his eyes with the flat of his hand, Mo' peered around like a spy as he crept up on Yaxna. Their crops had been burned and all their animals killed, their throats slit, an act Mo' pantomimed with his own machete, grimacing and shaking his hooded head in a way that was both angry and sorrowful. Harp clicked his tongue in sympathy, the way Mo' had earlier when he'd learned Harp had no children.

Their houses were still intact, Mo' went on, shaping buildings in the air. He framed a doorway and went through it, making scattering motions with his free hand and chopping at imaginary objects with his machete, imitating the sounds of breakage.

"Trashed," Harp concluded, unable to think of a Spanish equivalent but finding the sound of the word in line with those Mo' was making. Mo' nodded in approval and continued. There were no "*militares*" in sight when he arrived and he hung around for two days, finally going to visit his home village of San Pedro, where he'd lived before he'd married Manik's sister. At this point, he stopped walking and portrayed a person listening in a sneaky fashion, crouched with an ear to the wall. Then he flapped his fingers to indicate the person talking, and summed it up in one word: "*Judas.*"

The soft *j* threw Harp for a moment, making him think of Jews, who had come up earlier when Harp had confessed he wasn't a Catholic.

"*Apostol de Cristo,*" Mo' prompted.

"Ah, Judas!" Harp cried, nodding in comprehension. "*Sí. Malo hombre. Muy malo.*"

"*Los militares . . . los kaibiles,*" Mo' said, pointing his machete like a gun and then pointing a finger at himself. He'd obviously been betrayed and discovered, and he broke into a slow-motion enactment of his flight, ducking and dodging and going "schew! schew!" in imitation of the bullets flying past. Harp trotted to keep up, feeling like a large target in comparison. They'd apparently hunted him for two days, more than once going right past the place he was hiding. Mo' was hungry and thirsty and had to swim across the river at a dangerous place, but he'd finally made his escape. He indicated his relief by blowing out a breath and patting his heart.

Harp could only mimic the gesture, finding the few words that came to mind inadequate. It was a helluva story, and he was touched that Mo' trusted him enough to tell it. He was searching for a way to convey that as he came up beside the smaller man, who'd stopped at the place where you could first see the site from the trail.

"Baktun," Harp said, guessing that he was staring at Kan Shell's temple, which dominated the view.

"*Kaibiles,*" Mo' hissed and dove into the undergrowth. Harp didn't know what he was talking about but followed suit, getting up on his knees and peering out through the foliage. At first he saw only the unrestored back of the pyramid and the empty expanse of grass around it. But then his eyes caught the movement of the figures marching in single file along the base of the pyramid: four of them, all carrying weapons and wearing camouflage fatigues that made them blend into the background and red caps that made them stand out against it.

"*Militares de Guatemala?*" Harp whispered.

"*Sí,*" Mo' confirmed in a barely audible murmur.

Harp squinted and watched them disappear into the trees that surrounded the camp. He remembered Muldoon's story of meeting the Guatie patrol and shuddered, taking slow breaths to calm the beating of his heart. Then he turned back to Mo' and discovered that Mo' had disappeared as well, vanished without a word or a rustle of movement to mark his departure. Harp experienced such an intense pang of abandonment that he lurched to his feet and ran after him, staying off the path until he was safely around the bend. But Mo' was long gone and Harp knew he'd never catch him, not when Mo' was literally running for his life. Let him sound the alarm, Harp thought, and suddenly felt weak with relief, realizing how lucky they'd been in seeing the soldiers before they'd been seen themselves. He'd almost been an unwitting Judas, blithely leading Mo' into the hands of his enemies.

He'd continued walking back toward Rana Verde, but when he found himself at the juncture with the path to his hut, he stopped to consider what he should do. Prudence told him to keep on walking, put as much distance as he could between himself and the guys with the guns. But the nervous excitement in his gut told him he might have the opportunity to do some good, now that he was here and still undiscovered by the Guaties. Maybe he could scope out the situation without being seen, go for help if it was needed. Or at least know what to tell the Rana Verde crew.

He took a step toward the side path but stopped again, aware of the wind stirring the canopy of leaves overhead. This was not a time to be trusting heroic impulses. But then he looked down the path and had a sudden image of the inside of his empty hut, Caroline's typewriter sitting out on the packing crate, his notebooks stacked neatly atop the pile of manuscript pages he'd already accumulated. *Trashed* came back to him unbidden, and he jerked into motion and headed for his hut, moving like a man with a purpose.

There was no one in sight when he reached the end of the path, but it still required an effort of will to step into the open and walk the twenty feet to the doorway. And even though he felt as if he had a bull's-eye painted on his chest, he tried to adopt a casual gait. If accosted, he was going to play dumb, just a carefree gringo off on a walk in the woods. He slipped through the netting and found everything as he'd imagined it, still untouched. Using a blanket from the bed, he made up a large bundle that contained the typewriter, all his notebooks and papers, and the bag of Baktun Brown. He dropped the Keith Jarrett tape in as an afterthought and lugged the whole load over to the doorway. Still no one in sight, though he could hear a distant murmur of voices from the camp. Hugging the bundle to his chest, he bulled through the netting and made a lumbering dash for the trees. His fear of snakes took over from his fear of discovery as he waded into the undergrowth, but he didn't stop until he felt well concealed. Then he hid the bundle under a dense, thorny bush and crept back out of the forest.

Back in the hut, he sat and smoked a cigarette and considered his options a second time. The brief foray into the foliage had dampened his enthusiasm for trying to sneak around unseen. He definitely lacked his Indian companion's deftness, and it might be the best way to get himself shot. Sitting here until they found him didn't seem like a great idea either. Prudence was now contending with the plain desire to see what was going on, and Harp gave the nod to curiosity by telling himself the Guaties weren't after *him.* They might be bold enough to cross the border in pursuit of refugees, but they'd have to be crazy to attack an unarmed American on Mexican soil.

Deciding he needed to flesh out his alibi, he dug out a clipboard and a copy of a survey map Rick had given him. There was a cenote on it and he could pretend he'd been exploring the one nearby. He stuck a couple of pens and the rest of the cigarettes in his shirt pocket, picked up the clipboard and his machete, and went to make his entrance, hoping his belief in his own safety wouldn't be his final delusion.

There were two soldiers near the outhouse, one standing with his back to the path and the other just coming out through the broken door, fastening his belt with his weapon slung over his shoulder. The latter was the first to see Harp, who stopped and acted dumbfounded as they came toward him with their rifles leveled at his midsection. They had canteens, cartridge belts, and sheathed machetes attached to their waists, and they looked a lot tougher than the teenaged Mexican soldiers he'd seen on the streets of Comitán. Their faces were smudged with bootblack and the red caps were actually berets that bore a couple of small insignia patches, one of which read KAIBIL. They started shouting commands at him in Spanish, and after a moment's hesitation, Harp decided to play completely dumb.

"What's going on?" he asked. "You speak English?"

"No," one of them said, tapping Harp's wrist with the barrel of his gun in a clear command to drop the machete. Harp did, noticing a larger blue patch on the man's upper sleeve that featured an upright sword that was either flaming or bloody. They got behind him and herded him around the outhouse, prodding him in the back with their guns. Brinton and the rest of the camp crew were standing in a group near the women's lodge, surrounded by a loose cordon of soldiers. Harp switched the clipboard from one hand to the other as he was brought up, trying to signal his alibi. Before he got too close, he was confronted by a somewhat older man who was wearing dark sunglasses and hadn't smudged his face like the others. That and the tiny gold bar on his red beret told Harp he was the boss. He had something in his hands that looked like a fat electric pencil sharpener with a short barrel and a wire stock.

"*Dónde están los otros?*" he demanded.

"What? *No comprendo . . .*"

"Where are the others?"

Harp spread his hands in a gesture of bewilderment. "What others?" He brandished the clipboard, hoping Brinton would see. "I was out alone, checking the map."

The man suddenly thrust himself forward, trying to get up in Harp's face and startle the truth out of him. But the protruding fold in his beret collided with the bill of Harp's baseball cap and they both blinked, so the question didn't quite come out with the intimidating force the man had intended. "Where are the rebels?"

"The who?" Harp said, genuinely surprised by the term. "I don't know what you're talking about, or even who you are. What the hell's a *kaibil,* anyhow?"

The man stiffened and thrust Harp away, thumping him in the chest with the stubby weapon. "You don't need to know," he snapped. "Go over there."

He gave Harp a shove in the direction of the group, though away from where Brinton was standing. He went to Brinton himself and began to harangue him in Spanish, apparently quizzing him on where *he* thought Harp had been. Brinton stared back at him stonily and replied with a grudging succinctness that allowed Harp to understand most of what he said. Which was, essentially, that Harp wasn't a staff member and did whatever he wanted, which was why Brinton had forgotten he was out exploring. The commander spat on the ground and called him a liar, but Brinton simply looked past him and didn't reply.

Harp scanned the faces of the captives as he joined their ranks, exchanging brief glances with Rita and Muldoon and a few others. They all seemed tired and apprehensive, but no one was bruised or bleeding, even among the Mexican workers. He took a place between Muldoon and Katie, briefly brushing Katie's hand with his own and wishing he could somehow tell her that Lucy was safe. But the commander was too close and the soldiers around them were facing inward, watching them with a vigilance meant to be intimidating. So he ignored Katie's sidelong glance and kept his face blank, trying to look like a man who held no secrets.

The commander concluded his tirade by telling Brinton loudly, in English, that they'd all stand here until the others returned or someone told the truth. He knew they'd been helping the rebels, he declared, and he wasn't going to leave until they gave them up. Then he turned away and went to sit in the shade, taking a canteen from one of his men and drinking ostentatiously.

Harp glanced over at Brinton, who was several paces to the left and slightly out in front of the group. Everyone else had gone into a slouch at the commander's departure, but Brinton stood like one of the monuments, his gaze fixed somewhere in the middle distance. He seemed as oblivious of the people behind him as of the guards in front, making Harp wonder if he was leading by example or simply expressing his continued alienation from the crew. Maybe he was feeling vindicated, blaming this on their "enticement" of the Indians and their rejection of his authority. At least he hadn't rolled over and sent the Guaties out to Rana Verde. Harp had to give him that, especially after Harp had almost blown the whole show himself.

But then thoughts of Brinton lost out to a growing awareness of the dryness in his mouth and the spreading ache in his back and legs. Time had begun to move with agonizing slowness, marked only by the frequent rotation of the guards. He realized he'd seen this movie before. *The Bridge on the River Kwai.* He let the whistling refrain from the film march through his head for a while as a distraction. Katie was sagging against him, and he wondered how long it would be before someone dropped. Christ, they should all just sit down and dare the Guaties to do something about it, some real resistance. The guards had begun to relax their vigilance out of boredom, and he began to consider a whispered suggestion to Katie and Muldoon. The only things saving them from heat exhaustion were the overcast sky and the persistent wind. Harp opened his mouth to suck some in, wishing it would come up with the awesome force he'd felt that morning, and blow these bastards back to Guatemala. The Baktunis must've felt the same way about the Skull People, and no doubt their priests had called on every god they knew to drive the intruders off. Perhaps they'd built the ball court as a last attempt to funnel the force flowing outward from the sacred center of the city.

Suddenly guns started going off, exploding his reverie and making everyone jump and knock into one another as they came down. Harp recovered to see Sancho Panza come streaking around the corner of the outhouse and go into a desperate, four-legged skid when he saw the crowd of people blocking his path. The two guards in front of Harp simultaneously raised their rifles and drew a bead on the scrambling pig, and before he even knew he was moving Harp had thrown the clipboard and was standing between them, waving his arms and shouting "NO!" They both shot and missed as Sancho righted himself and raced for the forest, shots kicking up dust all around him. The commander opened up with his sawed-off machine gun, cutting a path through the dirt and grass that intersected Sancho's line of flight with deadly accuracy, hitting the pig in the hindquarters and flipping him over. Sancho let out a piteous squeal but was up and moving again in an instant, disappearing into the trees with several of the soldiers in pursuit.

Harp saw that much before he was knocked off his feet, kicked from one side and struck with a gun butt from the other. He went down on all fours, his ears ringing and one shoulder numbed by the blow. An acrid odor filled his nostrils and something hot and round was pressed against the side of his neck, a gun barrel that burned him like a branding iron and made him cry out and jerk sideways.

Then Katie stepped in and pushed the gun aside with her leg, shouting angrily at the soldiers. "Leave him alone! Now!"

One of the soldiers tried to shove her back but she fought him off and held her ground as Harp struggled to his feet in a disjointed attempt to help. Muldoon pulled him upright and braced him just as the commander closed in, his weapon raised like a club. But then Brinton was in the way, bringing the man up short in surprise.

"That's enough!" Brinton snapped, his voice crackling with anger. "You'll stop this right now or answer for it later, you hear me?"

Even though he'd spoken in English, everyone stopped for a moment and the only sound was hard breathing. Then Brinton went on in Spanish, his tone low but clearly threatening, advancing on the commander as he spoke and backing him up. He seemed to be running through a list of names that all had important-sounding titles attached. When he was through he didn't wait for the man's reply, but simply turned and walked out through the cordon of guards, who shifted uncertainly but let him pass. He went right to a spot under the trees where a number of canteens had been left in a pile, scooped up as many as he could carry, and brought them back to the group. The commander had retired to his place in the shade, where he was conferring with several of his subordinates. The guards had also backed off and lowered their weapons.

"What did you say to him?" Oliver Clubb asked, handing one of the canteens back to Brinton.

"Only what I should have said earlier," Brinton said. He took a long drink and gave the canteen to Muldoon, then addressed the whole group. "I apologize for letting this go on so long. But it should soon be over, so please, everyone, sit down and rest."

Harp let himself sink to the ground, trying to favor his bruised left shoulder and in the process rubbing his shirt collar against the burn on his neck, reigniting the pain. He pulled the collar away and then hung on to it, resisting the urge to cover the burn with his hand and put out the flame. Katie wrapped an arm around his back and he leaned against her gratefully, his eyes tearing faster than he could blink.

"Thank you," he murmured.

"You're an idiot," Katie said in a husky voice.

Brinton squatted down in front of them. "Are you all right, Yates?"

Harp dabbed at his eyes with his shirtsleeve, grimacing at what the movement did to his shoulder. "I dunno. Probably."

"That was a damn fool thing to do," Brinton said abruptly. "How do I tell your wife you were killed defending a pig? Why'd you come back here anyway?"

Harp glanced past him, making doubly sure the guards were all out of earshot. "Our shy neighbors finally came to introduce themselves. I was coming back with one of them—to get you—when we saw the soldiers."

Brinton straightened up and took his own look around, while the people behind him leaned in to hear. "What happened to your companion?" Brinton asked.

"His name was Mo'. He went back to Rana Verde so fast I didn't see him leave."

Brinton let out a breath and nodded. "So the rest of them know not to come waltzing in the way you did."

"They should."

"But you didn't," Katie snorted. "You had to come catch the show."

"Something like that," Harp said sheepishly.

Just then they heard a scream from the forest, a high, piercing screech that set off a flurry of gunshots and then a commotion of shouts and men crashing through the undergrowth. The people around Harp whirled and got to their feet, but he simply hunched over and pounded a fist against the earth.

"Shit! They got him anyway."

"No," Muldoon said. "That was a man, not a pig."

"Yes," Katie agreed in a shuddery voice, helping Harp slide around on his butt so he could see. The commander and his men had come out of the shade and were staring in the same direction. Finally a pair of soldiers lurched out of the foliage, bearing a third man between them, his arms looped over their shoulders and one leg held up off the ground. He'd lost his red beret, and he bared his teeth in a grimace of pain before letting his head loll back. More men came out behind them, their arms filled with extra weapons and gear. One of them was carrying a machete in one hand and holding up a thick, dark rope with the other, displaying it like a trophy.

"I've seen that before," Katie said, squeezing Harp so hard she hurt his shoulder.

"I'll be damned," Muldoon murmured.

"The fer-de-lance!" Harp heard someone hiss, and finally recognized the rope for what it was. Brinton came over and looked down at Katie.

"The antivenom's still in the medicine chest, isn't it?"

"I just checked it," Katie reported with a nod. "It's in the blue vacuum pack."

"Good. Emory," Brinton said to Muldoon. "Would you go ahead and get it out? We'll let their medic administer it."

"Right," Muldoon said, and went off toward the lab. A knot of soldiers, led by the commander and bearing the bitten man in their midst, was coming this way, and Brinton surveyed them for a moment before turning to Clubb.

"Oliver, take someone with you and check out the dining hall and the huts. Come tell me if anything's been stolen. Meanwhile, I'll begin negotiating the terms of their departure . . ."

He went out to intercept the commander, steering the group of soldiers past the people on the ground. Harp couldn't catch another glimpse of the victim, but the faces he could see appeared pale beneath the camouflage smudges, the eyes glassy with ill-concealed dread.

"Snake-bitten, every one of them," Harp said to Katie. "I don't think it'll be a tough negotiation."

"Let's go put something on that burn, then," Katie suggested, helping him to his feet. His legs felt unexpectedly weak and he had to hang on to her arm for support. He saw Rita looking up at him, her eyes wide and moist behind her lenses.

"That was a brave thing you did, Harp. You tried to save him."

"A brave damn fool," Harp said ruefully. "But hey, they didn't get him. Thanks to the fer-de-lance."

"We can start looking as soon as the soldiers clear out," Katie said. "We'll find him."

"Believe it," Harp agreed as Katie led him off. "Baktun looks after its own," he added, lifting his face to the wind and speaking to no one in particular.

15

New Belvedere

THEIR TOPIC for discussion was to have been Mary Daly's book, *Beyond God the Father.* But even before the last of the five women had arrived and they'd all gotten drinks and settled in the Ushers' living room, it was clear they would first have to talk about Caroline's choice. They all knew she'd put off a decision on the Mid-Atlantic offer until after she could talk to Harp, and since Virginia Evers knew about the Albany offer, Caroline felt compelled to tell the rest of them as well. They pressed her for details, assuming that the choice remained to be made, and that as her friends and colleagues, they should help her make it. Three of them were her close friends, and as a group they'd established a certain intimacy, so Caroline didn't have the heart to challenge either assumption.

As a result, she was drawn into a lengthy, point-by-point comparison of the two jobs and the two schools, a "weighing of the pros and cons," as Virginia put it. She and the others kept assuring Caroline that they weren't trying to back her into a corner, but at the same time they forced her to hold up the Albany end of the comparison by herself. She quickly found herself sounding defensive, because there were a whole lot of things about which she hadn't bothered to inquire. She hadn't needed to because they simply didn't stack up against the things that were really pulling her north. Somehow she hadn't been able to get around to any of those, and the direction of the conversation only seemed to be taking her farther away. She was afraid the Langdon house would sound like a lame excuse by the time she found a way to bring it up.

Just before they broke for dinner, the emphasis shifted from the nature of the jobs to the more subtle question of where she was wanted and needed the most—that is, where she could do the most good as both a feminist and a female academic. It was the old "the personal is political" argument, to which Caroline generally subscribed, though in this case she felt the truly personal had yet to enter the conversation. That left her at an utter disadvantage, and she began to feel flustered and depressed, suffering the first twinges of a frustration headache.

It was a relief, then, when the phone rang and she could tell them to start eating while she went to take it. She escaped to the den, closing the door most of the way behind her. As she settled into the creaking swivel chair and lifted the receiver, she prayed this wasn't somebody else trying to sell her something.

"One moment please," a heavily accented female voice said, then seemed to speak to someone in another room. "I have your party, señor."

"*Muchas gracias,*" said a voice she would've recognized in any language.

"Harp? Are you there?"

"Carrie. God, I can't tell you how good it is to hear your voice."

"*Where* are you?"

"The Posada San Antonio, in Comitán."

"When're you coming home?"

"That's what I called to tell you," Harp said with a laugh. "I'm leaving from here on Monday with a couple of other guys, and if all goes according to plan, I'll get to Washington Thursday morning. You got something to write with?"

"Hold on." Caroline pulled three pencils out of the soup can on the desk before she found one with a point. She took down the itinerary he laid out for her, which involved a night flight from Villahermosa and a long layover in Miami before his connection to Washington National. "I'll be there to meet you," she promised. "Even though you'll probably be half dead."

"That beats being all dead," Harp said, with what she took for grim humor. "So tell me what I'm coming home to. Did the Albany job come through?"

Caroline cast an involuntary glance over her shoulder and lowered her voice. "Both jobs came through. Did you get my letter about the house?"

"Sure did. By the time I got over being blown away, it was too late to write back."

"So what do you think?"

"Is there any other choice, now that you have the job?"

"No rhetorical questions, Harp. Tell me straight out."

"Take the job and let's buy the house," Harp said in one breath. "Is that straight enough?"

"You really mean it?"

"That's a rhetorical question," he pointed out. "*Yes,* I mean it. Some of the stuff I've seen here," he began, then caught himself, as if wary of being overheard. "I've got lots to tell you when I get there. Let's just say the notion of having a place that's *ours* has taken on a whole new meaning for me. Refugees are supposed to be looking for a refuge, right?"

"Even if we have to go into debt to do it?"

"Somehow, that doesn't seem like one of life's great terrors. Nobody dies for their debts anymore, not in our part of the world." He paused, again giving her the sense he was watching his words. "Are you just playing devil's advocate, or have you had some second thoughts?"

"No," Caroline decided without much hesitation. "I haven't. I've been holding off on an official decision until I could talk to you."

"Well, what more can I say? Oh, yeah: I'm willing to mortgage the land in Vermont, or sell it, or whatever it takes. Does that help?"

"I really didn't mean to push you on that . . ."

"You didn't. But when I thought about it, it seemed the appropriate thing to do. Use the profit from the old magic to fund the new."

Caroline sighed deeply, feeling the tension loosen its hold on her head and neck. "I love you for saying things like that. It makes it so much easier for me."

"What's making it hard?"

"Well . . . at the moment, my feminist study group is having dinner in the living room. They've been doing their best to convince me I belong at Mid-Atlantic."

"Of course. Which makes it rather hard to tell them you're leaving."

"Right. So hard I let them believe I hadn't made up my mind yet."

"Well, now you can tell 'em you talked to your husband and he made it up for you. That's a good excuse for a feminist, isn't it?"

"Thanks a lot."

Harp laughed. "Okay, scratch that. Have you tried telling them the truth? I mean the whole truth, including how you found out about the job, and the snowstorm, and the house . . . ?"

"No, I haven't," Caroline admitted. "I guess I was afraid they'd think I was being smug and self-indulgent, gloating about my good luck."

"You didn't sound that way in your letters. You made it sound right and inevitable. They won't hold your luck against you if they're really your friends. In fact, they'll probably feel less bad about your leaving if they know you were lured away by something wonderful."

"I think you may be right," Caroline agreed. "And I *do* thank you for that."

"Thank the Moon Goddess," Harp suggested. "Or whoever puts snakes in the grass. God, it's weird to be talking about this from here."

"I thought you were doing fine."

"You always bring out my best. But I better sign off so we can get back to camp. Brother Rick's throwing a termination party for me tonight, and my hut's a wreck. Literally. But that's another story . . ."

He trailed off with a bitterness that made her feel he was speaking in code, but she decided not to press him for a translation. "I can't wait to hear them all," she said instead. "I love you, Harp. Have a safe trip home."

"I love you, too. *Adiós* from your *narrador.*"

"What's a *narrador*?"

"Storyteller. Tell 'em a good one."

Caroline sat staring at the bright yellow spines of the *National Geographic*s for a moment, aware of the buzz of conversation from the other room but still hearing Harp's voice. She realized he'd given her a great pitch for openness and honesty while being secretive himself, and she wondered who he'd thought was listening, and what he hadn't wanted to say aloud. He'd certainly seen something more daunting than a mortgage or a roomful of disappointed feminists. As she pushed herself up out of the creaking chair, she decided she'd start over and give them the full story, and not skimp on the magic. Maybe the good-byes would be a little easier, if she could tell it well enough.

Baktun

"WE WERE victims of our own consistency," Rick said, downshifting as the Land Cruiser lumbered down into the last wash before the homestretch back to camp. They were going to make it in time for lunch, thanks to some ebulliently aggressive driving on Rick's part. He was still telling Harp about the long, heart-to-heart conversation he'd had with Brinton last night. "See, most of the core staff have been here for at least four of the five seasons, and as time went on there was less and less anybody needed to be told. Plus there was all the stuff Brinton did essentially on his own, like getting funding and permits and cutting deals with Pemex and the logging companies. He said he came to feel he was alone at the wheel, which was fine as long as things were going according to routine. When the Indians showed up, his impulse was to steer around them, and he wasn't prepared to have the rest of us pull the other way. 'I froze at the wheel,' " Rick quoted, glancing at Harp to be sure he caught the significance of the admission. "That's how he said it to me: 'I froze at the wheel.' "

"Captain, my captain," Harp murmured, distracted by the pain in his left shoulder, which had been throbbing steadily for the last ten miles. It made it hard for him to be as impressed by Brinton's sudden thaw as Rick was. It had come a little late to do him or Sancho any good.

Katie was coming out of the lab as they rolled by, and she met them when they came to a stop next to the dining hall. She opened the rear door so Oliver

Clubb and Andrew, who'd been riding in back, could climb out past the party supplies piled up in the middle. As Harp got out he heard Clubb ask if anyone had been out to Rana Verde today.

"Lucy and Helga went out after breakfast," Katie reported. "But there was no sign of the Yaxnas."

"Helga must've been disappointed," Clubb said. "She felt this man Ch'ul Balam would've been a valuable informant."

"She's more upset about what's going to happen to him now," Katie said, but Clubb just nodded and followed Andrew into the dining hall.

"Any sign of Sancho?" Harp asked halfheartedly, knowing she would've said so first thing if they'd found him.

Katie shook her head. "No, and we had fifteen people out looking for most of the morning."

Rick came around from the rear of the vehicle with a carton of perishable items in his arms. "If you can get the other one, we can unload the rest of the stuff after lunch."

"I'll get it," Katie said, holding up a hand to Harp. "You don't look so hot."

"Sorry, man," Rick said. "I wouldn't've asked you to help load in Comitán if I'd known you were hurting."

"I wasn't, then, and it was for *my* party. I just need some aspirin."

He held the door and let them precede him into the dining hall. He was struck immediately by how different the room sounded today, filled with the concerted hum of multiple serious conversations. There was some laughter but none of the usual banter, the friendly exchange of insults across the table. Brinton had given everyone the day off and had encouraged them to talk about what had happened and what they should do next. Tomorrow's Sunday brunch was to be an open discussion of those very subjects, a sign perhaps that Brinton really did want some company at the helm.

They took the supplies to the kitchen, got plates of food, and found three seats together at the end of the table, with Rick facing Harp and Katie across the corner. As soon as he sat down, Harp dug a couple of aspirin out of his shirt pocket and swallowed them down with water.

"Put some food in there with them," Katie chided.

"Yes, Mother," Harp said mockingly. "Some chilies, maybe?"

Katie colored slightly but didn't smile. "Did you get through to your wife?"

"I did. I also made plane reservations and put my share down on the rental car."

"And got provisions for the party," Rick put in.

Katie gave him a doubtful glance. "We can probably use one, but I don't know if anybody'll be in the mood if we don't find Sancho."

Rick shrugged. "I hate to be a pessimist, but if we haven't found him by now . . . I gotta figure he's hunkered down someplace to let himself heal, or he just kept running until he ran out of blood."

"Don't even think it," Katie said, wincing.

"He was half wild to begin with," Rick pointed out. "Why would he come back here after he'd been shot at?"

"Because he's half tame, too," Ulysses interjected, setting a clipboard down on the corner of the table. "And he can tell the difference between us and the Guaties. I'm setting up crews for a four-quarter survey," he said, then took a moment to look Harp over, glancing at the bandage on his neck and the stiff way he was sitting. "I was gonna ask if you wanted to sign up, but you don't look up to it."

"He's not," Katie said for him.

"What about you?" Ulysses said to Rick.

"Maybe later. I gotta unload the supplies and help Harp clean up his hut."

"I heard the Guaties got it," Ulysses said, shaking his head in disgust. "Bastards." He looked at Katie. "You still a believer?" When Katie nodded, he tore a sheet off the clipboard and handed it over to her. "There's your crew and the sector to cover. Think you can handle that?"

Katie studied the sheet before responding. "Probably. You really think he might've gone this far?"

"Who knows? We're working out from the places we checked this morning. We'll go back over them again on our way in."

"God, I hope we find him soon," Katie murmured.

"We will," Ulysses assured her. He straightened up and surprised Harp by briefly resting a hand on Harp's good shoulder. "Take it easy, man. You already did your share."

Harp gazed after him in astonishment, his cheeks warming as the message sank in. "What the fuck was that?"

"Sounded like a compliment," Rick said.

"From Ulysses? He doesn't know how."

"The Manik effect," Rick suggested, exchanging a glance with Katie.

"The chief," she agreed, turning to Harp. "You went to sleep so early last night you missed everybody's stories. Manik obviously made a huge impression on Ulysses. That was all he could talk about."

"It was real interesting, the way that went," Rick said, with a kind of professional appreciation. "Vicente and I were sitting there too, but Manik addressed almost all his remarks to Ulysses. He picked up that Ulysses was the chief, and I guess he figured that's who he should talk to. Chief to chief, so to speak. And he assumed that Ulysses had the same kind of relationship with his people that Manik had with his own, which was sort of like being everybody's uncle, or maybe their godfather." Rick laughed. "For instance, he asked Ulysses to get him a new rifle, and the reason he gave was that he wanted to give his old one to Mo'."

"How is that a reason?" Harp asked.

"Well, he said Mo' had performed a dangerous task for him and had shown real courage in carrying it out. Therefore, Mo' needed to be rewarded in an appropriate fashion, and the rifle filled the bill because Mo' had learned enough about courage that he wouldn't consider the gun a substitute for it. Manik might've been playing it up a bit for our benefit, but that was the way he talked about all his people. He knew them all well enough to make a clear distinction between what they wanted and what would be good for them."

"An impressive dude, in other words," Harp concluded. "So what was his effect on Ulysses?"

"I think he made him feel like a lousy chief," Rick said with a laugh. "Especially when he talked about you. See, he talked about you the same way he did about Mo'—sorta like an impetuous younger brother who's not mature yet but who's on the right track."

"An apt description," Katie said, and they both laughed at Harp, making him blush.

"Anyway," Rick went on, "Manik wanted Ulysses to know that you'd acted well that time you met in the forest. He thought you were kinda foolhardy to stick around when you were unarmed and outnumbered, but you knew how to be friendly and generous to strangers, and you made them feel it was safe to meet with us. Manik figured Ulysses would want to reward you for that, so he really talked you up. You shoulda seen Ulysses squirm!"

"I love it," Harp said. "Thank you, Lord of Shells."

Their laughter drew a disapproving glance from Helga Kauffmann, so they toned it down for a while and concentrated on their food. Rick's high spirits, though, were irrepressible, and he was soon casting disdainful glances of his own around the room.

"What I don't understand," he said, "is why everybody's treating this like a tragedy. I think we were lucky as hell, the way this worked out. The Guaties went one way and the Indians went the other, and the Guaties never knew they were here. That's about the best we coulda asked for."

Harp nodded in partial agreement. "If Mo' and I had come walking out of the forest about five minutes earlier . . . Christ, I don't even want to contemplate it."

"Exactly. And because of the snake, they left without trashing anything except Harp's hut. I mean, what if they'd done that to the lab? Contemplate that."

"I'd rather not," Katie admitted. "But you're forgetting two things. One, the Indians are still out there somewhere, running for their lives. And two, Sancho's still missing. Some of us don't consider either one a cause for celebration." She pushed back her chair and picked up the sheet Ulysses had given her. "I'm gonna round up my crew. For the sake of your party, you'd better pray we find him. And don't let Harp work too hard."

Rick watched her go, then grimaced and sighed at the same time, producing a dying motorboat sound. "Am I wrong, or just not sentimental enough? I don't wanna lose Sancho either, but if he's our only casualty, I have to feel we got off light."

"You didn't see him get shot."

"Well . . . no. That must not'a been pretty. But you saw it, and you seem to be handling it okay."

Harp snorted. "I'm still in shock. But I'd be out there searching if I could swing a machete. Sancho was one of us."

"Okay, I know when I'm out of step with popular opinion," Rick conceded. "We're gonna have to think about how to do this party, depending on the prevailing mood at party time."

"First we have to face the mess," Harp reminded him. "I haven't been looking forward to that."

"C'mon," Rick prompted, pushing himself to his feet. "I'll do all the hard stuff, just like Mother Katie said. What's with her, anyway? She's treating *you* like a casualty."

"I almost was," Harp said with a lopsided shrug, and followed him out of the dining hall.

HARP HADN'T discovered the trashing until after dinner last night, after Rick and Katie had helped him retrieve his bundle from its hiding place. It was the final shock, and all he'd been able to do was shine a flashlight on the devastation and then retreat to the men's lodge, where he'd spent the night. He returned carrying brooms and a stack of paper bags, with Rick lugging the bundle for him. They set everything down outside, and when Harp hesitated, Rick went in first and held the netting aside for him.

"Good thing you got your other stuff out," Rick said. "Cause they really did a number on what you left."

Harp tried to take it in slowly. The floor was strewn from corner to corner with the debris of what had once been his furniture and possessions. They'd stomped his packing-crate tables into kindling and bent the folding chair out of shape, torn up all his books, and scattered clothing over everything. His mosquito bar and bedding had been slashed and thrown aside, and the exposed mattress had suffered multiple stab wounds in a pattern clearly meant to be fatal to any sleeper.

"Christ, they killed my bed."

"Yeah. Ah, Brinton told me to have you make a list of everything that was stolen or destroyed."

Harp stared at him in disbelief. "What, he's gonna demand restitution from the Guaties?"

"He just might. We also have insurance of our own. Is there something I can write on in your bundle?"

"Take one'a the notebooks with a pen stuck in the binder," Harp said wearily. But he forced himself to walk around the room, picking up clothing and taking an inventory of what was missing. His Coleman lamp, canteen, cassette tapes, boots, and one pair of jeans were gone. They'd left him the jeans with the torn knee but had ripped up his only good shirt and done a dance on his panama, reducing it to a pile of straw. Harp sat down on the edge of the gutted bed while Rick stood and wrote it all down.

"We'll get you another mattress and bedding and everything," Rick promised.

"Look at what they did to the books," Harp said, poking at the debris with the toe of his sneaker. "They must've torn them apart with their bare hands."

"Either of your books in there?" Rick asked quietly.

Harp had a very bad moment before his memory asserted itself. "No. No, Rita and Katie have them." He bent over and picked up a scrap that bore the glyphic head of a creature called Xul, a piece from the Morley text. "Shit, they finished off Morley before I ever got around to reading him."

"Buy another one when you get home," Rick advised. "C'mon, Harp, don't go back into shock on me. You'll feel better once we get this cleaned up."

Harp nodded reluctantly. "What do we do with the trash?"

"We bag it," Rick said, and then his eyes lit up with an inspiration he didn't bother to reveal. "And we start a burn pile . . ."

An hour later, they had the makings of a good bonfire built up on the spot where Harp had once mixed plaster. The only things left in the room were the bed and Harp's traveling bags, into which he'd stuffed his remaining clothes. Rick brought in the typewriter and the bundle of notebooks just to make it seem less barren. Then he went off to unload the morning's supplies, promising to return later with everything they'd need for the party. Harp took some more aspirin, lay down on the perforated mattress, and fell fast asleep.

He had a dream in which he and Caroline and Mo' were walking through an open meadow, eating apples and discussing housing costs, then another in which he woke up and found Sancho sitting next to the bed, wearing a porcine smile. When he actually did wake up, Sancho wasn't in evidence but Rick was sitting a short distance away on a used but sound mattress. Folding chairs were leaning up against the wall behind him, and he'd brought out all the cartons of food and liquor and the cases of beer they'd bought in Comitán. He'd even borrowed some oil lamps and Rita's boom box.

"God, how long have I been out?" Harp wondered aloud.

"Not so long. I brought it all out with the Land Cruiser, only knocked over a couple of palm trees on the way. You were sure out, though, didn't hear a thing."

Harp finally noticed what Rick was doing. He was sitting cross-legged with the notebook open in his lap, rolling joints out of Harp's bag of Baktun Brown. One was dangling loosely from his lips like a thin white tongue.

"Hey, just help yourself," Harp said sarcastically.

"Hey, you can't take it with you, right?"

Harp had a sudden thought. "Did they find Sancho? Is that what this means?"

Rick shook his head. "Not that I heard, and I surely woulda heard if they had. No . . . I'm afraid it ain't gonna be that easy. But I've come up with some ideas about the termination rites."

Harp slowly swung his legs off the bed and sat up. "You're dead set on having this party, aren't you? Pun intended."

"We need it." Rick lit the joint and handed it up to him. "Everybody's too wound up to think clearly."

"How do you propose to unwind them?" Harp asked. He took a drag and passed the joint back. "This won't do it, as long as Sancho and the Indians are missing in action."

"I know. But since we can't do anything about that, they'll have to settle for the next best thing: a chance to terminate their regrets."

Harp grunted in appreciation. "A ceremony. Maybe a ceremonial burning?"

Rick nodded and reached into his shirt pocket. He pulled out a handful of brass shell casings and rolled them out onto the floor in front of him. "A chance to burn off all the bad memories."

"Tell me more," Harp said, and helped himself to more smoke.

THE TWO of them worked the table at dinner, inviting people one by one rather than making a general announcement. It was of necessity a soft sell, since they were playing to a uniformly somber crowd. There was talk of resuming the search for Sancho tomorrow, but it was clear that many people had given up hope. Harp and Rick tried to avoid mentioning his name as they gave their pitch, stressing the beneficial aspects of the ceremony to those who seemed most distraught and the cold beer and tequila to those who showed an inclination to drown their despair. Rita and Helga Kauffmann were two of the former, and they were visibly affected by Harp's description of the ritual, which had been expanded to include all the regrets, misgivings, and bad memories that had accumulated over the course of the season. They both said they'd be there. Brinton Taylor, who'd listened impassively along with them, politely declined the invitation. But he asked Harp to come to his cabin in about a half hour, after coffee. "There's something I'd like to discuss with you," was the way he put it, and then he left the table before Harp could ask him what that something might be.

The last time Harp had been inside Brinton's cabin was the day he'd been fired by Clubb and then met Manik and company in the forest. Brinton hadn't liked anything he was hearing and had given Harp a sharp taste of jungle frost, making him feel his breathing privileges might be revoked at any moment. The only things Harp remembered about the cabin itself were its enviably tight screens and an overwhelming sense of clutter. Several file cabinets and a couple of worktables had been crammed into the room, and every available surface was piled high with maps, files, and reports, with boxes and bags of artifacts stowed away underneath.

That was still very much the case, though Brinton had cleared some space to write on the table he used as a desk. He was pecking away on a manual typewriter, apparently transcribing whatever was on the stack of handwritten pages to his left. There were several such stacks lined up in that direction. He motioned Harp to the chair across from him and picked up the bottle of cognac that stood next to the softly hissing lamp.

"Will you join me, Mr. Yates?"

Harp nodded politely, taking the offer as a sign this was to be a friendlier visit. Brinton poured for both of them, then removed his rimless reading glasses and sat back in his chair, cradling his drinking glass in both hands.

"You're going home in a couple of days, I understand. Back to the suburbs of Washington?"

"For a while," Harp allowed. "We'll be moving this summer to upstate New York."

"Would you be able to run some errands for me in the capital?"

"I suppose . . . what'd you have in mind?"

"I'd like you to deliver a letter to the Guatemalan embassy. Two letters, actually. And possibly—depending on what we decide tomorrow—I'd like you to deliver a third letter to a friend of mine who works for the Associated Press."

"You're thinking of going public about this?" Harp asked, unable to mask his surprise.

Brinton gave him a patient smile. "Uncharacteristic of me, I admit. I blew the whistle the last time the Guatemalans made trouble for us, and I'd avoid doing it again if I could. But I've discussed our options with a number of people, and I've begun to discern a forming consensus. And I fully expect that after Helga has her say tomorrow, everyone will be persuaded that we cannot remain silent. Which means I'll go into Comitán on Monday to report the incident to the Mexican authorities."

Brinton paused to swirl the brandy in his glass and take a small sip. He seemed extraordinarily sanguine about the prospect, more than simply reconciled to it.

"Then what happens?" Harp asked.

"The Mexican government will probably have the army sweep the border and station some troops here. They'll protest the border violation at the United Nations and to the Guatemalan government directly. The Guatemalans will deny everything pending their own investigation, after which they'll deny it again. Our embassy in Guatemala City will no doubt support the denial, as will the administration in Washington. I wouldn't be surprised if they found some way to blame it on us."

Harp was a bit taken aback by the blunt cynicism of the assessment, and he could see that Brinton enjoyed having that effect on him. "So what do you hope to accomplish with these letters?"

"The first two are versions of what is essentially a personal protest. It won't mean anything to the generals in charge, of course. But there are still some people in the embassy who care about the respect of the scientific community, and I want them to know they've lost mine. The letter to my friend at the AP, plus another I may ask Oliver Clubb to deliver to the senior senator from Maryland, would be my way of going public, as you put it. Whether I send them depends on how we choose to deal with the Indian question."

"Which is what, exactly?" Harp asked warily. There was a challenging glint in Brinton's eye.

"Whether we limit our protest to what was done to us, or expand it to include what is being done to them."

"To the Yaxnas? But that would mean letting the Mexicans know they were here," Harp said, leaning forward in his chair. "They'd round them up as illegals!"

"They would certainly want to," Brinton agreed. "But we have to consider whether that isn't inevitable. Use that fabled imagination of yours, Mr. Yates," he suggested with a thin smile. "It's fortunate they got away this time without being seen, but how long can they keep on running? There simply aren't vast tracts of unclaimed land available for them to get lost in. They're unlikely to find a safe place to settle on this side of the border, and quite likely to run into people less friendly than ourselves. So the question is: Do we use this opportunity to publicize their plight, in the hope they might get better treatment when they *are* rounded up?"

Harp frowned and shook his head. "That's a self-fulfilling prophecy—you say it's inevitable, then make sure it is. These people trusted us. We can't turn them in just because we think it *might* do them some good!"

"First of all, we don't know where they are, so we can hardly turn them in. Secondly, if we're silent now, we'll be in a poor position to speak for them later. We will have done them *no* good. Is that the way you would repay their trust?"

Harp didn't know what to say to that, so he sat back and took a drink. Brinton had spoken with a force that belied his previous nonchalance, and he acknowledged this with a self-deprecating nod.

"I must confess that the logic I've been following is largely Helga's. And I must also admit that it gives me pleasure to turn the tables on you. I was about to remind you of the lessons of Nuremberg."

"I guess I've got that coming," Harp allowed.

"No, you were absolutely right. Authority must always be questioned when lives are at stake. I knew that even as I let myself believe you were calling me a Nazi." Brinton studied Harp's face for a moment and then startled him with a laugh. "I would apologize, Mr. Yates, but that seems rather pointless now, don't you think? The important thing is to make the best use of what we know. In that regard, we will have need of your talents, if we do decide to go public. There would be many letters to write."

"You think we can get anyone to listen? Enough to make a difference for the Yaxnas?"

Brinton lifted a shoulder toward his chin in the briefest of shrugs. "That remains to be seen. Helga thinks so, and she can be very persuasive, as you'll see." He abruptly set down his glass. "But I'm keeping you from your party. All I need to know now is whether you're willing to take the letters to the embassy for me. I don't want to entrust them to the mails, and Oliver begged off when I asked him. I think he hopes to work in the Petén in the future."

Harp found himself reaching for the bandage on his neck and completed the gesture so Brinton would see. "I think I can do that for you. As long as I don't have to be nice to anyone."

"You won't have to go any farther than the gate," Brinton assured him. "By the way, I will be making a specific complaint about the way you were treated in both letters."

Harp smiled ruefully. "Will I be identified as the Damn Fool?"

"Only between ourselves," Brinton said, returning the smile in kind. "No, in fact, I'm referring to you as 'a well-known American author who was trying to protect the camp livestock.' I'm also complaining about the way your hut was vandalized."

Brinton nodded and moved his chair back in front of the typewriter, and Harp took the cue and stood up. He drained his glass and set it back down on the table.

"Thanks for the brandy. Would you be insulted if I congratulated you on a remarkable comeback?"

Brinton gave him a swift glance, his eyes narrowed with some of the old suspicion. Then he seemed to catch himself and deliberately lower his guard, shaking his head with a laugh. "On the contrary, Mr. Yates. That reminds me," he added, and handed up a sealed, letter-size envelope that was completely blank on its face. "Put that on the fire for me, would you?"

Harp accepted the envelope with a bemused smile, weighing it on his palm and reckoning it contained at least two sheets, a fair measure of what Brinton had gone through to get back.

"It would be an honor," Harp said, and went to get the party under way.

TWO HOURS later, he and Rick were standing together in the doorway of the hut, surveying the assembled guests. A few were still writing out their regrets on the clipboards Rick had provided; others were talking in low voices or staring silently into space, lost in their own thoughts. Helga Kauffmann was actually talking to herself, apparently rehearsing her lines for tomorrow's conclave. Brad was the only one with a drink in his hand, and he was sipping it absently, daunted by his lack of company.

"Animal," Rick asked, "where's Ulysses and the Mayahead?"

"I think they went out lookin' again," Brad said, in a tone that suggested he didn't quite believe it himself.

"Great," Rick grumbled. "They can share the last vial of antivenom."

Rita had looked up at the reference to Eric, given Harp a doleful glance, and gone back to what she was writing. Jim was sitting next to her on the bed, trying to be attentive but not intrusive, a trick that made him look as if he were sitting on the edge of a precipice. Others in the room seemed equally preoccupied, or just plain exhausted. Harp avoided looking at Lucy Smith, whose dejection was so palpable it seemed to lower the air pressure around her. Just being near her and Katie had made him feel that what they were about to do amounted to dancing on Sancho's grave.

"It ain't gonna work," he whispered to Rick. "Maybe we oughta just burn the offerings and let 'em go to bed."

"Don't crap out on me now," Rick growled. As the Reverend Doctor Fishface, he'd decked himself out in a beaded headband and a gaudy Hawaiian shirt that featured coyotes and cacti instead of flamingos and palm trees. Harp was wearing his cleanest remaining T-shirt, which bore the clear print of a Guatie boot on its back.

"You got your stuff?" Rick asked, and Harp held up the paper bag that contained their props. Rick brandished his own offering, two handwritten sheets he'd folded into paper airplanes. "Let's do it, then."

With some effort, Rick got them all up and led them out of the hut, into the pale light of a yellow half-moon. They formed a loose circle around the burn pile, and Rick clasped his hands in front of him, the airplanes sticking out like white darts, and began his spiel in the unctuous tones of a country preacher.

"Dear friends, we are gathered here in the sight of the gods to mark the departure of Brother Harpo, who has lived and sometimes worked with us for lo these many months. We are here to terminate his presence in our midst. For this purpose, he has asked us to offer up the memories our hearts find hard to carry. Are you ready to begin the offering, Brother Harpo?"

"I am, Reverend Doctor Fishface," Harp replied, opening his bag of props. He stepped up to the burn pile, displaying a plastic squirt bottle of insect repellent. "An end to smelling like something the bugs wouldn't touch," he intoned, squirting an arcing stream onto the pile. That drew some smiles and a few laughs that sounded surprised and helpless. Encouraged, he went on to offer a splash of treated canteen water, a piece of a broken shovel handle, and a handful of back dirt. "An end to wheelbarrows overflowing with *that.*"

They were all smiling now, even Helga and Lucy, and Harp began to believe Rick's contention that they all really wanted to let go and laugh. He pulled half a roll of the coarse camp toilet paper out of the bag and placed it on the pile. "An end to sandpaper regularity."

There was almost general laughter, and Lucy broke out in hysterical giggles when she caught the joke. Taking this as his cue, Rick stepped up next to Harp and held open a hand filled with gleaming brass shell casings.

"An end to uninvited critics of our work," he said with a droll smile, tipping his hand and letting the shell casings clatter onto the pile. The smiles around them vanished abruptly, as if the sound had clicked a switch. Rick's own smile sagged and he shot a glance at Harp, who could only shrug. *We bombed in Baktun* went through his mind in the uneasy silence.

Then heads began to turn, and he saw two flashlights coming up the path from camp. The people attached to them gradually became visible in the moonlight as Ulysses and Eric. They were walking with their heads hanging and their shoulders slumped, a twin portrait of fatigue and disappointment. It occurred to Harp that they'd found Sancho's dead body, and he was surprised by a sudden ache in his throat, a sense of desolation that made him want to sit down. The party's over, he thought, and was angry at himself for thinking it.

But as Ulysses and Eric approached the edge of the circle, they suddenly stopped, clapped hats onto their heads, and began to dance forward, shaking their flashlights and the paper bags they held in their hands. Chanting rhythmically, they snaked through an opening in the circle and danced their way around the pile. Lucy was the first one to comprehend their chant, and she shouted out over them.

"You *found* him?"

"We found him," Ulysses and Eric chanted once more, then broke out in big grins. "He's gonna be okay, too," Ulysses added, and the circle collapsed in around them, grabbing at their sleeves and shouting questions. They just laughed and nodded, and there was a general hugging and slapping of palms.

"How'd you find him?" Rick asked when the tumult subsided.

Ulysses held the flashlight under his bearded chin, making his face appear maniacal beneath the stiff brim of the pith helmet he was wearing. "The final inspiration of Bwana Kurtz: The eyes of brutes shine best in the dark. We just caught a glimmer on our last pass through the area."

"*Where*'d you find him?"

Ulysses lowered the flashlight with a flourish. "Not fifty meters from where he was shot, gone to ground under a pile of thorny crap."

"He couldn't run," Eric put in, "but he didn't make it easy for us to dig him out. We gave him food and water and he *still* tried to bite us."

"I had to knock him out with the chloroform from my bug kit before I could sew him up," Ulysses said. "The bullet just took a chunk out of his ass and kept going. I don't think he even bled much. He's sleeping it off in my hut."

"All regrets about Sancho are hereby canceled," Rick said, speaking to the sky. Then he invited Eric and Ulysses to join the circle and brought the ceremony back to order. "Shall we go on with the offering, Brother Harpo?"

Harp took a deep breath, feeling positively refreshed. "It's time to give our bad memories to the fire," he said, reaching into the bag for the single folded sheet on which he'd written in block letters ULYSSES and SANCHO. He placed it on the pile with a feeling of being ahead of the game, luckier than he deserved to be. The others stepped forward around him, adding packets or rolled tubes of paper to the pile along with small personal objects that filtered down into the loose heap without being seen. Helga Kauffmann sprinkled copal over her offering, and Rick let his airmail offerings spiral down from shoulder height. After they'd all stepped back, Harp removed the last item from the bag and held it out over the pile.

"Brinton asked me to add this to the fire," he explained, setting the blank white envelope on top of the pile. "An end to the divisions in our ranks."

There were murmurs of "amen" as Harp stepped back, and he saw Helga and Emory Muldoon regarding him with open astonishment. Rick raised his arms and let them drop, emitting an exaggerated sigh.

"Dear friends, I don't have to tell you this has been one helluva season. It's been *real* different. We don't usually find ball courts out in the middle of nowhere. We don't usually engage in Tootsie Roll diplomacy with the local refugees, or conduct target practice for the Guatemalan army. In four seasons before this, we hadn't had a single case of snakebite." Rick paused and drew more murmurs. He put a hand to his beard. "It makes a Reverend Doctor wonder: What'd we do to deserve this? Did we do something to get the gods all stirred up? Did we fail to show the proper respect? Or perhaps, did we simply allow some unruly spirit into our midst?"

Rick turned and stared at Harp, waggling his eyebrows in an insinuating manner, and the murmurs swelled to an enthusiastic chorus. Rick crossed his arms on his chest and grinned triumphantly. "I rest my case. We could look for political or economic or even supernatural reasons for all this weird shit happening. But why work so hard? One good scapegoat is worth a thousand explanations, and he'd be the first one to tell us to jump to that conclusion. So I say, let's blame it all on Harpo! He's *never* innocent, and he always seems to be around when the trouble starts!"

The circle cheered lustily, laughing and chanting "Har-po, Har-po!" Skewered in place, Harp could only grin like an idiot, feeling the heat rise off the top of his head. Rick had to hold up a hand for quiet.

"So, dear friends, now we must terminate the Season of Brother Harpo. He came to us filled with the spirit of reckless inquiry and rash speculation, always willing to look beyond the facts and meet the truth halfway. He has proven beyond all doubt that a little knowledge is a dangerous thing, and he's set new standards for ambiguous behavior and theoretical outrageousness." Rick glanced at Harp and smiled slyly. "Which is not to say it hasn't been fun. It's certain to be a lot quieter when he's gone. We'll have to work instead of listening to him theorize, and we'll have to dig our own holes instead of waiting for him to fall into one. Our interpretations will no doubt suffer from a reassertion of rigor and scientific restraint. Most of all, we'll have to keep ourselves entertained." Rick reached into his pocket and pulled out Helga's old Zippo, flipping back the cover with his thumb. "An end, then, to the Season of Brother Harpo. Let us remember without regret."

With that, Rick flicked the lighter into flame and crouched to set the pile ablaze. It went up so quickly they all had to jump back, and then Harp felt hands patting him on the back and shoulders, and Katie came up and kissed him on the cheek. Eyes blurring, he threw back his head and watched the sparks shoot upward and vanish into the stream of smoke that rose against the moonlit sky.

DURING A brief lull in the talk, Rick leaned in between Ulysses and Kaaren and handed a fresh bottle of beer down to Harp on the bed. Harp nodded in gratitude, surprised to find he was thirsty. The bottle at his feet had been empty for a long time, but he hadn't wanted to leave his place next to Helga, at the heart of the debate.

"Anybody else want another?" Rick asked, when some of the others in the group looked up at him. "You know, if you keep on like this, you aren't gonna have anything to talk about tomorrow."

Helga started to disagree, then caught herself and glanced around the room, noting the smaller but similarly intense conversations that had spun off from this one. "Oh, my. You must forgive me, both of you," she said, including Harp with a nod. "I have turned your party into a colloquium, and I have monopolized that."

Harp and the rest of the group protested vigorously, but Helga just smiled and gestured for them to get up and move around. "I insist. I must leave you, anyway, and get some rest. I can do that, now that I know I won't be a lonely voice tomorrow."

"I'm still not convinced, Helga," Ulysses said as he stood up. "But I'll sleep on it."

"We all should," Helga agreed. "But you're young, have your fun first."

"I'll walk you out," Harp said, helping her up as the others pushed back their chairs and headed for the bar. He heard the volume of the boom box rise a couple notches behind him as he held the netting aside and followed Helga out. It was dark, the moon almost down, but she fished a flashlight out of her handbag and switched it on.

"Thank you for telling me about your conversation with Brinton. As you must have gathered, he was not nearly so forthcoming with me. I couldn't tell if I'd persuaded him of anything."

"I think he's learning how to let himself be persuaded," Harp suggested. "It's obvious he was picking things up from one person and trying them out on the next. I just got to him last."

"You're not completely persuaded yourself, are you? About the need to speak out forcefully."

"In principle, I probably am. But I remember Mo' telling me about the Judas in his home village who betrayed him to the Guaties. I'd feel like one myself if we spoke out and only made it worse for them."

"That is why we cannot do it halfheartedly, if we do it," Helga declared, then shook herself, making the flashlight waver. "I am back on my soapbox already. Tomorrow we will all decide together. Oh, but there is one thing I wish you would do, Mr. Yates. In anticipation of future need."

"What's that?"

"Write down everything you remember about yesterday. And everything you've heard from the others. Not just the facts, but impressions and feelings . . . the personal details that might make it more appealing for a popular audience. Like what you talked about with Mo', for instance."

"Michael Yackson," Harp recalled with a fond smile.

"Who?"

"Michael *J*ackson? The pop singer? When Mo' asked me where I lived, I told him Neuva York, figuring that might be more recognizable than Maryland. His next question was: 'Do you know Michael Yackson?' He also wanted to know what a 'thriller' was, which was a little hard to explain."

"Please, do not try with me," Helga demurred. "But that is exactly the sort of thing I mean. I have already begun an account of my meeting with Ch'ul Balam, and I would be happy to share it with you in return."

"I'd like to see that. What was his reaction when Mo' came back without me? I hope he didn't think I'd deliberately led him into trouble."

Helga had been fumbling in her handbag, and she finally came up with a folded sheaf of paper, which she handed to him. "My office address is on that, and my mail is always forwarded to me. It's a copy of the bibliography for my graduate course on the hieroglyphs. My parting gift to you."

"Now I've got *no* excuse for not getting it right," Harp said with a laugh. "Thank you, Helga."

"But to answer your question," she went on. "Both Ch'ul Balam and Manik took the news of the soldiers very calmly, though they did not linger over their farewells. We were more shocked than they were, and I think they could tell. And Ch'ul Balam trusted you before he sent you off with Mo', because of the sherd you gave Manik. The water lily has some special significance for him, about which he was rather vague. But he held it up for me and told me quite directly that it could not have come to him from an evil man."

Harp cleared his throat. "I hope you won't ask me how I came to have it."

"That is between you and your conscience," Helga assured him. "I won't say good-bye now, since I'll see you at brunch tomorrow. I am looking forward to that now."

Harp took a pull on his beer and watched her go down the path, a hunched silhouette against a bobbing circle of light. He'd just turned back to the hut when Katie came out, took him by the arm, and led him away again. "You can't go in yet. They're not through signing your gift."

"Helga gave me this," Harp said, showing her the bibliography as they walked over to the remains of the ceremonial fire. "Everything I never wanted to know about the glyphs."

"You'll like this one, too. Kaaren and I thought it up."

Harp smiled at her perky tone. "What're you drinking? You sound like you're a couple up on me."

"Rum and Coke," Katie said, taking a sip from her paper cup. "And yes,

I'm feeling quite good, thank you. I'm sure you'll catch up once Rick starts proposing toasts."

"I'm glad you're feeling good," Harp told her, laughing. "I'm real glad they found Sancho in time to save both him and the party."

Katie looked down at the dim red glow of the coals that lay beneath a feathery white crust of ash. "It was a double relief for me," she said quietly. "Because once I could accept that Sancho was all right, I had to accept that you were, too." She glanced up at him. "Every time I looked at that bandage on your neck, I saw that soldier sticking his gun there. And pulling the trigger, and you falling dead. I saw that all happen and I couldn't move."

"But you *did* move," Harp pointed out. "You saved my damn fool ass." He transferred Helga's gift to his beer hand so he could put an arm around her. "I hope you gave that memory to the fire."

"I did," Katie said, leaning against him. "And I'm glad I saved your damn fool ass. And that you're so grateful."

Harp gave her a sidelong glance and saw she was smiling again. *Way* ahead of him. "Uh-oh. How grateful am I supposed to be?"

"Enough so you won't disappear on Monday and I'll never hear from you again."

"You know I write letters, and I figured I'd write to you if you wrote back."

"I will. But I was taking that much for granted. What about phone calls?"

"Sure, why not?"

"I'm not going to hang up if Caroline answers," Katie warned.

"I wouldn't expect you to."

"What about visits? I told you I have a sister in western Massachusetts. And Lucy wants to see your new house."

"You're welcome any time. We'd love to have you."

Katie was pointedly silent. "*We?* What I'm trying to get at here, Harp, is whether you're going to tell Caroline the truth about me. About *us.*"

Harp removed his arm from around her and stepped back to take a drink. "You think I should, I take it."

"Of course. Half the story would sound worse than the whole thing, and would arouse a lot more suspicion. I think she'll find it hilarious, once she gets over wanting to kill you."

Harp snorted. "That's encouraging! Suppose I tell her the truth and somehow survive. What's that do for you?"

"It lets her know I'm not a threat—I'm not gonna make a play for you behind her back. And it means you and I can be the kind of friends I want us to be. I wanna be able to talk the way we're talking now, even if we have to do it long-distance." She put a hand on his arm and shook him gently. "This romance business is gonna be rough, Harp. I'd feel a whole lot better if I knew you were there for me. You're the only person I know who can be honest with me and make me laugh at the same time."

"I don't have many friends like that either," Harp confessed. "They get harder to make as you get older."

"So don't miss your chance," Katie urged. "I'd be there for you, too, whenever being a lonely writer starts bending you out of shape. I could be a revitalizing influence, give you a verbal vamping over the phone."

Harp laughed softly. "Now you're talking *obscene* phone calls."

"Whatever it takes. That's what I'm talking about. Are you in?"

"Yeah, I'm in. Even a damn fool couldn't turn down an offer like that. Do we shake on it, or is a blood oath required?"

"This'll do," Katie said, raising her cup and touching it against the neck of his bottle. "To a classic friendship."

"May it never collapse," Harp said, and they drank to it.

SPRINGSTEEN'S "E Street Shuffle" was playing for the third consecutive time, providing the musical background for what they called the Sancho Shuffle, an interactive dance that involved rubbing haunches, bumping booties, and squealing like a butt-shot pig. Max and Ulysses had invented it and given lessons during the second go-round, and by now everyone was out on the floor, bumping and squealing and carrying on.

After several complaints from bumpees, Harp danced over to his bed and removed the trowel from his back pocket. It was his very own Marshalltown (the brand preferred by archaeologists), and everyone present had scratched his or her initials on the triangular metal face. Harp dropped it onto the bed alongside the other gifts he'd received and turned back to the dance, only to be sandwiched by Rita and Jim and given a double bump that goosed him off the ground.

"Doin' the San-cho Shuffull!" they sang gleefully, dodging when he tried to bump them back. The song ended to applause and laughter and cries of "Again!" and they all stood panting and gulping down drinks while Max went to rewind the tape. Rita sidled up to Harp and pointed to the copy of *Ghost Dance* she'd left on the bed.

"I brought your book, even though I haven't finished it yet. Jim wants to read it too."

"Lovely Rita," Harp drawled, raising an eyebrow at Jim. "Is she always this subtle?"

"Sometimes she drops a broad hint," Jim said. He laughed when Rita hmphed and stuck her tongue out at him.

"I'll sign it for you later," Harp said, bending so she could thank him with a hug. "If it'd been here when the Guaties came through, it would already be gone."

"I'm really enjoying it," Rita assured him. "I don't think about who the author is at all."

"I'll take that as a compliment," Harp decided. The music started up again and Rick boogied by and stuck a lit joint in Harp's mouth.

"Feed your head," Rick cackled and disappeared into the gyrating crowd. Harp took a couple quick hits to fortify himself and offered the joint to Rita and Jim, who turned it down with prim shakes of the head.

"I guess it's every pig for himself," Harp said, and flung himself into the middle of what had become a butt-swinging free-for-all. He bounced off Muldoon and recovered in time to sing the refrain along with everyone else and rub haunches with Kaaren.

"You're beautiful when I'm drunk," he said with great sincerity, and Kaaren laughed and gave him a bump that rattled his teeth and made him feel his sore shoulder again. He tried to practice defensive dancing after that, hoping to get through the song in one piece, but the heavy hitters had taken over the center of the floor and were disinclined to spare someone of his size and gender. He was bounced around like a pinball until Brad finally laid a hip check on him that sent him reeling toward the doorway. He caught his balance but let his momentum carry him on out, throwing up an arm to ward off the netting. He heard the crash of a collapsing chair behind him but didn't go back to investigate.

The joint was still clasped in his fingers, and he lit it up again after he'd gone to the edge of the forest to take a leak. The tape had been allowed to play on and other people were coming out to cool off and get some air. Harp saw Ulysses come out and stop to let his eyes adjust to the darkness, pushing the pith helmet back on his head with one hand. He had a liquor bottle in the other hand and he raised it to his lips while he surveyed the area in front of him.

Harp figured Ulysses was looking for him. He'd felt the man angling in on him on a couple of other occasions, but he'd managed to avoid him both times. He still didn't think he wanted to hear what Ulysses had to say, not even out of gratitude for the rescue of Sancho. But then Ulysses spotted him in the glow of the joint and came right over, the bottle swinging in his hand.

"Good party, man," he said with a smile, offering Harp the bottle. Harp gave him the joint and tipped the bottle back, recognizing it as tequila before the fire kicked back up his throat and scorched the taste away. Ulysses sucked hard on the joint, lighting up his face, then blew out a cloud of smoke and tried to give it back.

"Keep it," Harp said, and handed him the bottle as well. "I'm about as high as I wanna be right now."

"Good," Ulysses said, helping himself to another drink and a second toke. Then he exhaled and got serious. "Look . . . I wanted to talk to you, see if I could settle up with you before you leave."

"Why?"

"Because I treated you like shit when you were trying to do me a favor."

"You got that right," Harp said unsparingly.

"I wasn't trying to hurt you, man, you gotta believe that. I didn't even know I had until much later."

"Which didn't stop you from continuing to treat me like shit."

"Yeah. I mean no, it didn't." Ulysses glanced at the joint in his hand and seemed disappointed to find it'd gone out. "Look, I'm not trying to make excuses for what I did. All I cared about was finding everything there was to find before something happened to shut me down. That's the way I've always operated, and it's taken me this long to see that I was wrong. You're not the only one I treated like shit."

"What a surprise."

Ulysses waited for him to go on, then made an exasperated noise and thumped the bottle against his own chest. "You're not gonna make this easy for me, are ya?"

"Why should I?"

"'Cause you're the guy who always used to tell me I needed to slow down and give myself a break. How 'bout giving me one yourself? I wanna terminate Bwana Kurtz."

"You shoulda given him to the fire."

"I had enough to burn. Besides, I didn't make him up—you did. It wouldn't mean anything if I tried to do it by myself."

Somehow the plea slipped past Harp's guard and hit him in a soft spot, eliciting an appreciative grunt. He realized he hadn't given all of his grudge to the fire either, though he'd meant to. He held out his hand and after a moment Ulysses understood and gave him the bottle. He took a big swig and let the tequila burn off the last of his resistance, telling himself he shouldn't stand in the way of what Manik had started.

"So . . . where'd you get that stupid hat?" he asked, handing the bottle back.

"Muldoon. His brother-in-law gave it to him and he's never had the nerve to wear it."

"So he won't mind if we stomp it to pieces?"

Ulysses blew out a long breath and smiled with relief. "He'll figure it's for a good cause. I brought my Doors tape along, too, if you wanna do it to music."

"Something suitably sinister," Harp agreed with a nod. "Let's let the crowd thin out and get drunker."

"I'll be ready when you are," Ulysses said. He took a healthy slug from the bottle and belched. "And Yates . . . thanks. Is there something I can do for you? Like maybe an early copy of the report on Rana Verde?"

"Yeah, I could use that," Harp said, then had another thought. "Hey, when you write it up, are you gonna have one of those introductory prose pieces describing the site and how you found it?"

"That's pretty standard," Ulysses said, then caught Harp's drift. "Oh. You want me to write the story of Yates Landing?"

"Why not? You can take credit for finding the place, but you didn't do that by yourself, either."

Ulysses considered it for a moment and started laughing, sounding genuinely amused. "That's fair. Brinton has the final say on what gets published, though, and he might make me take it out. But I'll put it in the first finished draft and send you a copy."

"Good enough," Harp said. He stepped to the side and gestured toward the hut, indicating the party in progress. But Ulysses stopped him by holding out a hand, thumb cocked for a power shake.

"This shoulda happened at the beginning," Harp said ruefully.

Ulysses shrugged. "Isn't that what comes around again after the end?"

"Eventually," Harp allowed. Then he snorted and clasped the hand, forming a single large fist they shook back and forth between their bodies. "Pleased to meet you . . ."

KATIE HAD let Lucy stay up to witness the termination of Bwana Kurtz, a decision she regretted, since it took her a while afterward to get Lucy calmed down enough to sleep. By then, most of the other women had returned to the women's lodge, and the voices outside told her the party had broken up. As Katie went back up the path she met Rick and Kaaren coming the other way, carrying the empty washtub between them. Kaaren was lighting their way with one of the borrowed lanterns, and Rick had a folding chair clamped under his other arm.

"Harp didn't want to quit," Kaaren reported. "But nobody else wanted to be hungover tomorrow."

"Speak for yourself," Rick grumbled good-naturedly. "I was willing to make the sacrifice."

"I'll see if I can get him tucked in," Katie said.

"Terminate the brute!" Rick called after her, laughing as he lurched off with Kaaren in the other direction.

Katie switched off her flashlight as she approached the hut, following the candle glow up to the doorway. The last time she'd seen Harp he'd been high as a kite, chanting with Ulysses while the two of them did a wildly aggressive do-si-do on top of the Bwana Kurtz hat. She wasn't sure she had the energy left to deal with him if he was still in that state.

But when she peeked in through the netting he was sitting on the bed with his arms wrapped around his stomach, rocking forward over his splayed knees. The room had been cleaned up and was barren except for his pile of belongings and some cartons filled with trash and empty bottles.

"Harp?" she called softly as she pulled the netting aside and stepped in. "Are you okay?"

He looked up at her with a stricken expression that didn't go away even when he smiled, and Katie went to him quickly, glancing around for a handy receptacle. "Are you gonna be sick?"

He shook his head in mute denial, then seemed to realize what his posture was communicating and straightened up, though it cost him an effort.

"Is it your back?" Katie demanded. "Or your shoulder?"

Harp shook his head again and let out a shuddery breath. "I'm too drunk to feel anything like that. It's just . . . loneliness. I don't want it to end."

Katie put her hands on his shoulders and bent to kiss him on top of the head. "Bless your alienated heart." She pushed his gift trowel and the notebook in which he'd been recording addresses to one side and sat down next to him. "You really got to like being part of the crew, didn't you?"

"It's a lot easier than sitting alone at my desk," he said in a husky voice. "It just hit me that I was going back to that, and all of a sudden I didn't know if I was ready. It just seemed overwhelming."

Katie put an arm around his shoulders and felt him trembling. "What're you afraid of, Harp?"

"I dunno . . . backsliding, I guess. Getting hung up again, like I was before I came here."

"Won't happen," Katie said without hesitation. "Look at all the material you've gathered, and you've been figuring out the plot all the way along. If you get stuck you can just call one of us."

"Yeah, I could," Harp said, though he still sounded doubtful.

"Caroline'll be there for you, too," Katie reminded him. "Anyway, maybe it's good to be afraid of it, like getting butterflies before the big game. It gives you a certain edge."

"The cutting edge," Harp said, turning his head to give her a sardonic smile. Katie leaned forward and kissed him on the lips, holding it long enough to feel his arms go around her and the warmth rise up between them. Then she gently pushed him away, scooping up her flashlight as she got to her feet.

"Good night, Brother Harpo. I think you're gonna be fine."

"Party's over, huh?"

"Party's over," Katie agreed, blowing him a kiss from the doorway. "Get some sleep. Tomorrow we get to face the future."

Then Harp was alone again. But before the wistful ache could well up in his gut again, he forced himself to rise and prepare for bed, taking a leak out the doorway and brushing his teeth with canteen water. He mixed himself an Alka-Seltzer and drank it down while he snuffed out the extra candles and undressed in the light of the one still burning next to the bed. Getting the new mosquito bar set up seemed to open the floodgates of fatigue, so that when he was done all he could do was sit on the edge of the bed and let it wash over him in great, enervating waves.

Once he could move, he undertook the final task of stowing his gifts under the bed so he wouldn't step on them if he got up in the night. There was the trowel and Helga's bibliography, a whole handful of feathers donated by a number of people, and a rubbing of one of the baktun glyphs from Stela 17, which Rita and Jim had made for him. The last thing to come to hand was his notebook. He'd chosen the one labeled NOVEL IDEAS #2 because there were still plenty of blank pages in it. Bending to the candle, he opened it near the front and squinted at the entry at the top of the page:

> KAN CROSS AHAU: In process of usurping power, he plays final game in old ball court against Shell family team. He plays *himself*? Though allowed a surrogate, he puts life on the line against a trained professional (a ringer brought in from outside?). His way of claiming divine sanction for his rule, despite his lack of royal blood.

The pressure in his forehead brought Harp back to himself, his face still locked in a squint even though his eyes had given up trying to read. At some point his mind had left the page and traveled off on its own, finding its way to a ball court he knew from both dream and memory. Katie didn't know how right she was. He had all the material he needed, a rich supply of fuel for the imagination. He put the notebook with the other gifts and pulled his legs up onto the bed.

"You will play," he told himself, and blew out the last candle.

Epilogue

May in New Belvedere, and Caroline had the air-conditioning on as she packed books in the downstairs bedroom she'd used as a study. She was dusting them off and trying to pack them away in some kind of order, but the part of her mind not on autopilot had flown the coop and was already decorating the room she'd chosen for her study in their new home. They were driving up to New York tomorrow, with the signing arranged for the next day. They were taking both cars, loaded up with books, winter clothes, and other nonessentials, which the Langdons had said they could store in the attic until they took possession in June. They planned to leave Rusty there and come back down in her car, giving the Langdons time to vacate and Caroline a chance to turn in her final grades and wind up her affairs at Mid-Atlantic. There was still a lot to do in that regard, but she wished she could just have it over with and be in the house, doing all the things that needed to be done to make it her own. She hadn't looked forward to anything with such unalloyed eagerness in a long time.

The exhaust vent for the air conditioner was on this side of the house, so she didn't know Harp had returned until he was standing in the doorway grinning at her. She'd expected to see his hands filled with boxes and rolls of tape, but instead they were hidden behind his back, holding something he wasn't letting her see. The beard and grin together made him look like a beatific imp.

"You'll never guess what I bought."

"Not what you went out for, apparently. I'm on my last roll of tape."

"Oh, that's all out in the car. I wanted you to see this first," he said, though he kept whatever he was holding behind him. "See, right next to the U-Haul place was an abandoned gas station, and this guy was selling stuff out of his car, you know, like ponchos and cheap Mexican rugs and tie-dyed T-shirts. But he also had some stuff that was classic Americana: Mount Rushmore lamps, screaming eagle statuettes, velvet Elvises, blacklight posters of Snoopy on the Cross . . ."

"You didn't," Caroline groaned. "Not Elvis."

"No, much better than that. *Much* better. Behold: Rana of the North." With a proud flourish, he displayed a large plastic frog, perhaps two feet long but so light he could hold it in one hand. It was a lurid emerald green with black stripes down the back, bulging red eyes, and a wide-lipped yellow smile.

It was a bad Disney imitation, the utter vacancy of the smile giving it a kind of imbecilic charm. Caroline started to laugh but then caught herself.

"You *paid* for it, right? This is not a relapse."

"Five-fifty, cash money. The man recommended gravel rather than sand for weight, since it's less likely to leak out around the plug. I know just the place for it. You remember the spot in the windbreak where Langdon said he had to take out a fir that got struck by lightning?"

"I remember a big stump, but not the story."

"Maybe he only told it to me," Harp said with a shrug. "Anyway, what could be more perfect? A spot already sanctified by the sky gods, with a ready-made platform altar and plenty of room for offerings . . ."

"Perfect for what?"

Harp cocked his head and held out the frog, as if it were self-evident. "The Shrine of La Rana of the North, of course. We gotta have a place to pay our respects to the local deities."

"And you think the Frog God is one of them?"

"The particular image doesn't matter," Harp said breezily. "I'm not into worshiping idols. It's the respect that counts, the recognition of the powers that be. Though I *do* have a personal attachment to frogs, and they're greatly favored by the rain gods."

"I never in my life thought I'd be married to a man with a personal attachment to frogs," Caroline confessed and leaned forward to kiss him, craning over La Rana to do so.

"You can touch him. It's good luck."

"For five-fifty, it might be carcinogenic," Caroline scoffed. "But I guess no one'll see it unless we take them back there ourselves. I'll leave the explanations to you."

"No sweat," Harp said, stroking the frog's bulbous head. "You're gonna be surprised by how little will be necessary. The world's full of people yearning for ritual and superstition. You'll be sorry you didn't ask for a cut of the offering take."

"For now I'll settle for another roll of packing tape," Caroline said, turning him toward the living room. "You might want to look at the mail, which came while you were out. Who do you know at the University of Illinois? Is Katie Smith sending you love letters already?"

"C'mon, you weren't gonna razz me about that anymore," Harp reminded her. He set La Rana down on top of the hi-fi and pulled the manila envelope out of the stack of mail. It was addressed to B. Harper Yates and had been fortified with sheets of shirt cardboard and a handprinted warning: PHOTOGRAPHS: DO NOT BEND.

"Illinois has to be Ulysses or Muldoon," he murmured as he tore open the flap and pulled out several sheets of paper wrapped around a pair of photographs. "Oh wow, farfuckingout! Lookit this, Carrie. It's the wall panels from the ball court!"

"I see . . . but they're so *different.* From each other, I mean. How come there're *three* people in this one?"

But Harp was still marveling at the crisp clarity of the photos, and at the fact that both panels had come through intact. There were a few details still obscured by patches of clinging conglomerate, and the pressure of centuries had caused some surface cracking, though nothing had buckled or fallen off. Most amazingly, there were no signs of deliberate damage. The faces of the figures hadn't been hammered flat during the termination ritual.

"Harp? Are these from the same ball court?"

"What? Oh yeah, they faced each other from opposite ends of the midcourt line."

"But they don't even look like they're from the same time period. Look how stiff and rectilinear the three figures are on this one—like mannequins. But the man on the other one is completely naturalistic. Look at the way the feathers flow in the same direction he's leaning."

Harp nodded, his gaze fixed on the photos. "Uh-hunh. Same time period, different cultures. These guys are definitely Central Mexican in character, while the other guy just might be Kan Cross Ahau himself."

"What's he wearing? Looks like shoulder pads and an inner tube."

"Ballplayer's outfit," Harp said with a laugh. He flipped the photo over but found only Rita's name and address, along with a brief note to the effect that she also had shots of the excavation and the terminated pots. "Guess I'll have to read the text," he decided and took everything over to the couch. Caroline sank down next to him, tape and packing forgotten for the moment.

"God, this's exciting," she exclaimed softly. "I'm glad you didn't discover everything without me."

One of the sheets was a piece of hotel stationery from the Posada San Antonio in Comitán, and Harp smiled when he saw it was a kind of group note with a series of entries in different handwriting and a rainbow of different-colored inks. The first was from Katie Smith and explained the circumstances of their being in Comitán, which Harp dutifully summarized for Caroline.

"They apparently pushed the limits of the rainy season a bit too far and got hit with some heavy downpours as they were trying to wrap up and get out. Their final escape is described as reminiscent of the evacuation of Dunkirk, using the truck and the Land Cruiser instead of boats. It took them the whole day just to get to Comitán, so they decided to hole up there for the night."

He briefly scanned the rest of the page, noting that Rick's entry began at the bottom and ran over onto the back. Brinton and Helga were both mentioned, as was Deputy Ambassador Bellesario, one of the people to whom Harp had delivered a letter at the Guatemalan embassy. Harp wanted to see if there was anything new on him, but Caroline was plucking at his sleeve, demanding more information on the wall panels. So he picked up the other sheets, which were the product of a word processor with a dot-matrix printer low on ink. He laughed as he read the title on the first page, then grunted when Caroline poked him in the ribs.

"Aloud, please," she commanded, and he complied with a nod.

Minutes of the First & Last Comitán Ball Court Symposium

PLACE: Posada San Antonio, Comitán (the bar)

PARTICIPANTS: The Mayahead, This Animal, Lovely Rita, Jungle Jim Zorn, The Reverend Doctors Fishface, Smith, Seyerstad, Muldoon, Cole

PHOTOS: Courtesy of Lovely Rita

PURPOSE: The symposium was convened by Fishface, Smith, and Seyerstad for the purpose of updating Brother Harpo on the Rana Verde excavation. They felt this was the only way to prevent him from making up something totally outrageous on his own. Out of a twisted sense of justice, Cole was made recording secretary by a vote of 8–1.

Introduction: A heroic effort by the Rana Verde Crew in the last month and a half of the season resulted in the removal of the tons of super-compacted shit that concealed the carved panels inset in the east and west sidewalls of the court. Concealed within the conglomerate itself were numerous interesting caches and stray artifacts that will not be described here. An inventory & preliminary analysis can be obtained from Katie Smith if you write like you promised and beg hard. We're here to talk about the panels themselves, so listen up, douchebag (so said Fishface to unanimous agreement).

The West Panel: The Skull People, in triplicate. The style of portraiture is reminiscent of the Terminal Classic sculpture at both Seibal and Chichén Itzá; i.e., the so-called Toltec or Mex-Maya thought to originate in the Chontalpa area of Tabasco. Multiple figures standing in profile and ranked order are common at Chichén, as are the curved sticks they hold, which were probably used to deflect darts thrown from spear throwers (don't ask us how it was done—you're the novelist). The fact that all three figures share the same costume and facial features makes us think they represent groups rather than individuals. The fact that they're ranked by height (descending from back to front) makes us think they might represent segmentary lineages, with the tallest representing the "parent" lineage back in the Chontalpa, and the next two representing distinct but affiliated groups of colonists trying to establish themselves somewhere in the Baktun area. There's evidence of this in the Guatemalan highlands and the Pasión River region, including the Terminal Classic takeover at Seibal. Do some homework, Harpo (Lovely Rita said to unanimous agreement). Helga also found some verification in the glyphs but still had a lot to decipher when she left. Kaaren pointed out that the stone for this panel probably came from the same local source as the

West Panel and appears to have been carved by the same hand or hands. Which means the Skulls must've brought a sample of their iconography (on bark paper?—it's not on the Fine Orange pots) and had the Baktunis put it down in stone for them. That's one piece of evidence for the theory that this venture was more cooperative than adversarial. On the other hand (said Muldoon), what does it mean that Kan Cross Ahau shows himself dressed for the ball game and they show up dressed for war?

The East Panel: Yep, this is Kan Cross Ahau, identified three separate times in the glyphs, twice as the ruler of Baktun. The inaugural date of his reign is included in the glyphs along with the names of his antecedents, some cryptic information about the Moon & Venus, and (Helga thinks) a list of religious rituals for which he's responsible. The participants split down the middle on the question of whether his appearance in the costume meant he actually played the game himself, or whether he was also representing his group (i.e., Baktun). An attempt to disqualify him on the grounds of age led to further inconclusive arguments about dating the ball court, and the bartender asked us to quiet down or leave. Katie settled it by pointing out that given a choice, you would undoubtedly opt to make him the Ballplayer King, so why argue? Bets were then offered that you'd *already* made him that, but there were no takers. The sculpture is of course Late Classic in style, showing traces of Terminal flamboyance and a resemblance to the late stelae at nearby Chinkultic, especially in terms of the ball-game paraphernalia.

Conclusions: An informal poll at this point revealed 7 of 9 participants considered themselves more than 50% drunk. This Animal bought tequilas for Rita & Jim to help them catch up, and the Reverend Doctor Muldoon waxed eloquent on the subject of normative drinking behavior among archaeologists. Another round was ordered and we rushed to reach a rough consensus before we all passed out. This is what we came up with:

The ball game seems to have played an important role in Kan Cross Ahau's assumption of power, and he made the destruction/construction of ball courts a conspicuous symbol of that power. In a time of shrinking resources and increasing outside pressures, it was probably a lot cheaper (not to mention safer) than fighting wars and taking captives. So when faced with some organized interlopers trying to settle in the neighborhood—folks who might have less to lose if it came to a fight—he invited them over for a game as a shrewd alternative to attacking them or letting them get too close. It may have been the best common cultural ground they had, and he kept his edge as the dominant ruler by making a big ritual show of it. The Skulls must've been snowed out of their minds by the temple with the double roof comb and their own portrait on the ball court wall. There's no sign of who won or whether the loser suffered—no trophy heads and necks spouting blood like at Chichén—and from the way the court was terminated winning may not have mattered. Helga called it an "extraordinary display of mutual respect." Equivalent & symmetrical ceremonies & caches, and no signs that anything was messed with afterward. We wondered if they even filled it in together. The fact that the panels were buried without being ritually "killed" is also noteworthy. It may mean that all the parties involved were still alive themselves at the end, or maybe that the spirits of the place were so good they decided it was better to cap them than release them. That was Kan Cross Ahau's style, after all, and we're beginning to think he might've been responsible for moving and hiding the other monuments prior to abandonment of the site.

Our final conclusion: This seems to have been an experiment in diplomacy that worked. If the Skulls were the barbarians at the gates and the purpose was to keep them there, then the game did the trick. Baktun was never trashed or taken over like Seibal. On the other hand, the Baktunis apparently missed their chance to tie into the network of trade and cultural exchange that dominated the Postclassic. Maybe that was never an option for them, or maybe they were snobs because they had nothing left to trade but prestige (we found some valuable items in the ball-court caches but most looked recycled). With the coastal trade represented by the Shell family also out of the picture, they must've languished for a while in splendid isolation before packing it in.

All of this remains to be verified, of course, but no one expects *you* to wait. We do expect you to come up with a version of events that isn't a total insult to our intelligence. Bend the facts too far and we'll send This Animal to bend you. Got it?

Yates: Took a while to work up my notes after I got back. You owe us $55 for drinks. Ask me for the preliminary report in a couple of months and I'll send it to you. Time to terminate this brute.

Ulysses

"This's going to be a *great* novel, Harp," Caroline said when he'd finished. She'd been holding the photos while he read, and she passed him the one of Kan Cross Ahau. "The Ballplayer King, and you even have a picture of him in uniform. I think he looks a little like Omar Sharif."

"Brando with a Mayan nose," Harp said, only half-facetiously, since the unbridled boldness of the face invited the comparison. He sank deeper into the sofa and regarded the pages in his lap with gratitude and wonder. "This's truly a gift. Ulysses put in some work to make it so coherent."

"I bet he enjoyed it. Is there anything in there about the Indians?"

"Oh yeah," Harp said and retrieved the page with all the handwritten notes. He found Rick's entry and read it aloud.

Harpo:

Greetings & salutations. I gather Helga's been in touch with you since she went back, so you probably know that blowing the whistle didn't bring in the troops or cause much else to happen, at least that we could see. For some unknown reason, the Guaties and Mexicans are acting like good neighbors these days, so the expected uproar didn't occur. Perhaps for that same reason, Bellesario at the embassy responded to Brinton's letter with surprising speed and concern. He wrote back and Brinton spoke to him by phone from here, and he seemed intent on making up for the violation of our space. He also seems to believe he can make the Army listen. Helga's taken over the negotiations with him and is supposedly angling for a safe conduct pass back to their village for the Yaxnas, plus a promise of no further harassment. You may know more about that than I do. Even if she gets it, there's still the problem of how to let them know. And would they trust it? Should they? Needless to say, they didn't come back to talk it over with us.

Thanks for sending the AP story and your article on the B-3 tomb. Brinton was disappointed the former was so short & didn't appear until p.16. He liked yours and was surprised you could write with so much "discipline." Hope you made some bucks off it. That's about it for now. Send me your new address when you have it. It was a treat to have you here, amigo.

Brother Rick

"You knew all that, didn't you?" Caroline said. "You just spoke to Helga."

"Last week. She's working hard on Bellesario. She wants the safe conduct posted in all the villages near Yaxna, so they'll hear about it if they send someone back to check. She also wants reparations for what was destroyed. I sent her my account of what happened that day, and she wants to show parts of it to Bellesario as a threat—get something done or we'll publish this for all the world to see. I told her she could."

"You haven't shown it to the man at the Associated Press?"

"Cosgrove? No, though he said he wanted to see it when I was done. But it's much too long, and where would it end up? Page thirty-four?"

"Your agent could probably place it with a magazine," Caroline suggested. "It makes up in drama what it lacks in discipline."

"Right," Harp said dryly. "Helga actually wants to try it out on the U.N. high commissioner for refugee affairs if she doesn't get her way with Bellesario. I said okay to that, too."

"Not a lot of bucks to be had there, either."

Harp stared at her in disbelief. "Carrie . . ."

But she was laughing. "Just an integrity check, Harp. I wanted to see if your success with the Sunday supplement had turned you into a mercenary writer."

"Even a mortgage won't do that," Harp growled.

"Good." Still laughing, Caroline dropped the second photo in his lap and pushed herself up out of the grips of the sofa. "Okay, back to work. We still have to pack the books out of my office today."

Harp refilled the envelope and put it on the end table before following her out to the car. "You know, as much as I like the overall interpretation, there's one conclusion I'd dispute," he said as he caught up with her.

"What's that?"

"I think it mattered who won."

Caroline stopped with her hand on Rusty's door handle and looked back at him with a skeptical smile. "To the Maya? Or to a certain author who also happens to be a former ballplayer?"

"You saw the pictures—tell me Kan Cross Ahau looks like a man who doesn't care if he wins or loses. And even if the losers weren't beheaded, that doesn't mean it wasn't better to be a winner. They were playing for the gods, after all, and it's usually assumed the gods are keeping score."

"I think you'd like to believe that yourself," Caroline suggested. "If you could."

"It beats feeling inconsequential," Harp admitted. "I'm just afraid that all we ever get are brief glimpses. Never enough to know for sure."

"That means you have to keep paying attention," Caroline said. She put a hand on the roof of the car and leaned forward to kiss him on the lips. "Maybe that's the way it works."

"Maybe it is." Harp said with a rueful shrug. Then he shook himself, motioned her out of the way, and pulled open the car door. "So let's get on with it. We've got one site to abandon and another one to found."

Caroline looked back at the House of Usher. "If *ever* a place was in need of termination . . ."

"We'll break some dishes before we leave," Harp promised as he handed her a fresh roll of tape. "They'll never be missed."

About the Author

DANIEL PETERS was born in 1948 in Milwaukee, Wisconsin, and was educated at Yale University. He has lived in Vancouver, rural New Hampshire, Maryland, and upstate New York, and currently lives in Tucson, Arizona, with his wife, the feminist writer Annette Kolodny. He is the author of the pre-Columbian trilogy *The Luck of Huemac* (about the Aztecs), *Tikal* (about the Mayans), and *The Incas.*

About the Type

This book was set in Times Roman, designed by Stanley Morison specifically for *The Times* of London. The typeface was introduced in the newspaper in 1932. Times Roman has had its greatest success in the United States as a book and commercial typeface, rather than one used in newspapers.